Dear Mike —

May the pages of
this tale warm
your heart…

And may only
Good news come
to your Doorstep!

Best Wishes + Thanks!

Bad News on the Doorstep

inspired by a true story

By

Joseph Rocco Cervasio

authorHOUSE

1663 LIBERTY DRIVE, SUITE 200
BLOOMINGTON, INDIANA 47403
(800) 839-8640
www.authorhouse.com

First published by AuthorHouse 05/03/04

ISBN: 1-4184-0721-6 (e)
ISBN: 1-4184-0720-8 (sc)
ISBN: 1-4184-0719-4 (dj)

Library of Congress Control Number: 2004105281

Printed in the United States of America
Bloomington, Indiana

This book is printed on acid-free paper.

This book is dedicated to my wife, Maria, for her loyalty; to my daughter, Tina, for her resilience; and to my daughter, Corrine, for her honesty.

It has also been written in memory of three people: My mother, Marietta, our devoted and passionate coach; Dad, the "Rocky" of our household, that handsome ex-Marine who was our biggest fan; and Frankie D'Angelo, my first hero—he had the heart of a lion and the spirit of a saint. The Lord took him home too soon. But, we thank God for what He achieved in Frank's life. He truly was "…of the Angel".

ACKNOWLEDGEMENTS

Someone once said, "Easy is the task that is shared by many." While *Bad News on the Doorstep* never became an "easy" project, its crafting surely was a wonderful journey for me, because of all the people who made their unique contributions. To each of them I am forever grateful. I can assure all readers that this book is really the story of each of these gracious and generous individuals whom I sincerely consider collaborators in this work.

My older daughter, **Tina,** always found time from her busy career as a sports broadcaster to lead the research effort and the final proofreading. My daughter, **Corrine,** would never cease to get my attention from wherever she'd be calling from across the country as a health care executive: "Dad, you're not really thinking about keeping that in the book, are you?" And my wife, **Maria,** would always require my feet being planted firmly on the ground, focusing on maintaining balance in our lives. She totally disagrees with fellow Jersey resident, Mary Higgins Clark, who reminds all writers of the following credo of a fifteenth century monk: "The book is finished, let the writer play." Not in my house! When I assured my better half that *Bad News on the Doorstep* was finally completed, she did not hesitate to announce, "Now you can finally clean the garage."

In addition to my immediate family, closest friends, and relatives, my first-time readers of the original manuscript will forever be the forces in my life that sacrificed personal time to help a fellow pilgrim with a story. Their loving support and gentle criticism will be the essential reasons for any positive reception this book may receive: **Danny** and **Joey Vitiello,** as well as their mother, **Dolores,** read the pages as they came out of their Printing Techniques copy machines. When I return to Nutley after long business trips, I never feel at home until I visit them for their ever-present warm reception. And little sister **Linda Pizzi's** encouraging note was the fuel I needed early on to keep me going. **Mike Geltrude** played in the Mud Bowl as the last single-wing quarterback in Nutley High School history. **Uncle Jimmy** and **Aunt Dot Taylor** brought the fifties alive with youthful enthusiasm. **Genevieve Tolve** lovingly introduced me up front and personal to my hero, her brother Frank. My cousin **Nicholas D'Orsi's** regular calls from Columbus, Ohio further convinced me we had to leave some stories behind for our children. **Donna Zarra,** my beloved sister, did not have to say a word; her emotional response signaled we had to complete the project. **Joanne Cocchiola Oliver,** my wife's dear friend and our energetic Commissioner in town, made me proud to be a small part of telling a tale about our neighborhoods. **Sam Stellatella,** the immortal #30 in Nutley's Hall of Fame list of football greats, daily reminded me the book could not be a fiction; he remembered too much of it actually happening. My brother **Alan** took the time from a busy schedule as the Vice President of Global Sales Strategy and Talent Relationship Management for Marriott Vacation Club International to tell his wife and children that Uncle Joe was involved in something of value. **Danny Riordan** relived the Mud Bowl with me and assured he'll never forget it and his Belleville teammates. His brother **John's** advice from an illustrious career in publishing was invaluable. **Pastor Anthony Ventola** convinced me from a Higher Source that I was in God's will. My sister-in-law **Beverly Corino** quietly gave me the sincere feedback I needed, and her princely son, my nephew **Anthony,** helped me eliminate the less worthy as only a young attorney could. **Judge Frank Zinna,** my childhood friend, teammate, and counsel did what he always does; he loved me for the effort. **Michael Lamberti** quickly informed the readers of *The Belleville Times* that a book was forthcoming. **Ed Marinaro** urged a screenplay, and **Joe Marra** told me the book made his cousin **Joe Pesci** laugh. And **Dr. Michael Kormanicki,** my partner in our leadership design and delivery effort at Marriott, not only became my biggest cheerleader, but he also proved to be the only other person I could ever imagine who would have done what Frank did in the Mud Bowl.

There are those who store the stories of the times and places in question deep in their hearts. **Jimmy Intintola,** my cousin from Fifth Street and Bloomfield Avenue, knew Uncle Pete and enough other tales to fill five books. My cousins **Bob and Judy Davenport**, he, the retired Chief of Police in Wildwood, NJ, and she, the older daughter of **Aunt Margaret Luglio**, lovingly detailed the history of that great Jersey Shore town. **Marty DeRose** emotionally spoke of the music business in our great state and the stars with which he shared the stage. **Ronnie Paglia** made the harmonizing group sounds of the fifties come alive. Thank God **Jimmy Harvey** made it back from Viet Nam, and that he put Rocky in his "Wall of Fame". **Dr. Mike DelTufo** and his nephew **Anthony Landolfi** detailed an unbelievable "quarter to five" story. Principal **Joe Zarra** keeps the tradition alive at Nutley High. **Don Capetta** introduced me to the world of "backstage Johnnies". And **Ruth D'Angelo,** her children **Frank Jr., Mark, David,** and **Erica,** as well as the rest of Frank's family, have honored him with their grace, humility, and cooperation on this book project.

A wise person once said, "A man is a success, when you feel better about yourself, after having been with him." **Pete Noyes,** the Director of Football Operations at Cornell University, is that man in my life, particularly with his urging me to write and his publishing of my articles at that great University.

Be careful what you pray for? Well, thank God that I once asked the Lord to put me on "the Potter's wheel". Yes, I met **Kenny Potter** in Boca Raton, Florida in 2003, and when he began to edit *Bad News on the Doorstep,* I knew my prayer had been answered. "Ouch!" was all I could say. Thank you my good Australian friend, even though you still don't know the difference between a "supersod" (sopressetta) and The Super Bowl!

At 5 AM on the morning of February 13, 2003 I frantically entered my office at Bluegreen Corporation headquarters in Boca. The evening before, my computer and many personal items had been stolen from my rented car. The only backup I had for the book was a couple of floppies still in my suit pocket! **Barbara Rodino** and her staff of **Allan Cohara** and **Joshua Chesner** were there at that dark morning hour to calm my nerves, get me another computer, and quickly backup nearly a decade of written work. Angels were at my side!

In the end, this book would never have been written without the musical inspiration of **Frank Sinatra,** the poetry of **Don McLean,** the **doo wop** of the fifties, and the resilience of **Dion DiMucci.** Here in Newark, Belleville, and Nutley, the examples of **Frankie Valli and The 4 Seasons, Joe Pesci,** and **Connie Francis** have kept so many of us focused on our own destinies. And where would we be without the faithful daily news of *The Newark Star Ledger?*

As I close, I cannot forget what my good friend **Gary Greenip** told me a long time ago: "When you look back, merely glance, and never stare." That was his grandmother's suggestion when a young Gary was looking out his bedroom window one lonely night, shortly after loosing both his parents in a tragic automobile accident. Indeed, let us glance back on the good times of days gone by, forgetting the bad news, and remembering only the best. But never stare; we have too many opportunities before us this day!

TABLE OF CONTENTS

CHAPTER 1 1

    "MAY THE SYMPHONY BEGIN"

CHAPTER 2 19

    "PREGAME WITH UNCLE PETE"

CHAPTER 3 33

    "VINNIE'S VICTORY VOYAGE"

CHAPTER 4 41

    "THE MUD BOWL"

CHAPTER 5 67

    "… FOR OLD TIME'S SAKE."

CHAPTER 6 71

    "POST GAME PLANS"

CHAPTER 7 93

    "VISITORS AT THE VICTORY DANCE"

CHAPTER 8 99

    "MEET YOU AT THE MANGER"

CHAPTER 9 123

    "BROKEN WINDOWS AND BREAKING NEWS

CHAPTER 10 143

    "FROM BASKETBALL TO BACKSTAGE JOHNNIES"

CHAPTER 11 155

"AUNT BELLA TO THE RESCUE"

CHAPTER 12 163

"BELLEVILLE CORNFIELDS"

CHAPTER 13 175

"ROAD TRIP… UNAUTHORIZED"

CHAPTER 14 197

" APRIL FOOL'S DAY"

CHAPTER 15 203

"BELLBOYS IN BROOKLYN"

CHAPTER 16 223

"ROLL CALL"

CHAPTER 17 235

"… A QUARTER TO FIVE"

CHAPTER 18 249

"AND THE WINNER IS …"

CHAPTER 19 253

"ONE SUMMER NIGHT"

CHAPTER 20 263

"DAS BOOT"

CHAPTER 21 275

"WILDWOOD DAYS"

CHAPTER 22 293

"MAMA"

CHAPTER 23 307

"FAR ABOVE…"

CHAPTER 24 325

"HEY, MA, GREENIE'S ON THE PHONE."

CHAPTER 25 339

"BUONA NATALE"

CHAPTER 26 359

"THANKSGIVING EVE, 1971"

CHAPTER 27 377

"THE REST OF THE STORY"

CHAPTER 1

"MAY THE SYMPHONY BEGIN"

In the late fifties some people did not know what a day off was like, let alone a week's vacation. Marietta Bonaducci had just completed her fifty-second straight week of the graveyard shift at the Tungsol electronics factory on Bloomfield Avenue in Bloomfield, New Jersey. Her brother-in-law, Nick Durso, was dropping her off at home for the last time that year. She and Nick's wife, Mary, had been working together for years to ensure their sons would be the Bonaducci family's first grandchildren to go to college.

It was 7:15 AM as Nick glanced at his dozing passenger in the rear view mirror of his pampered, aging brown Packard that he affectionately referred to as Norma, like Norma Desmond, the famous, but fading actress in the film "Sunset Boulevard". Even daily waxing could not delay his Norma's subtle deterioration.

As she did every morning that week, Marietta had fallen asleep on the back seat. Meanwhile, up front next to her husband, Mary, even without her morning coffee, was chatty as ever. "Marietta, time to wake up. You're home at 711 Belmont Avenue, and ya gotta make breakfast for Rocky and the kids. Last time this year, honey. Day off tomorrow." Then with a chuckle she added, "And don't forget the 'andibast' (antipasto) for tonight." She paused, "Marietta's 'andibast', ...no New Year's Eve at Mamma's could be without it."

Mary loved her brother's wife. Humble most of the time, Marietta was feisty and brash when she had to be, and Mary knew her brother needed that rare balance in a wife to keep him on the straight and narrow.

Marietta blushed, "Oh Mary, an andibast's an andibast."

"Honey, but nobody puts as much into it as you do."

Nick interrupted, "Mary, stata sitta, please. (Shut up.) Marietta worked all night. Let her get out and continue her nap inside before the kids and Rocky get up. And let's get <u>you</u> home to do everything <u>you</u> gotta do today." He was always impatient with his wife who was more Gracie Allen than Gracie Allen herself. As Marietta thanked Nick for the ride, he reminded her, "Next week it's Rocky's turn, Madiett. I'm gettin' Norma serviced."

Walking down the driveway in her leather sole shoes was tedious for Marietta. Fallen snow had been melting and then freezing all week. Discount priced snow boots were still awaiting her purchase at Vicarisi's variety department store on Bloomfield Avenue in her old neighborhood of the North Ward of Newark. Chilled, she hugged her leftover "lunch" in its brown paper bag as she tip toed over the ice spots. The yellow Gulden's mustard, covering her "boloney" (bologna) sandwich on white "American bread" that was seeping its way beyond the cold cut and smearing itself against day-old wax paper, would not deter her younger son, Jo-Jo, from feasting on this for breakfast later.

The crunching of the ice beneath her feet sent a chill up Marietta's spine. The biting wind wrestling with the frozen branches high above the Bonaducci backyard forced Marietta to pause. The branches were bending and waving like hundreds of malnourished arms. She stared upwards at the tops of the trees for some message on why she had halted while shivering. She took a deep breath of below freezing air and woke up her mind, made sluggish from those less than pure fumes in Nick's exhaust scented back seat. However, no mystical revelation came.

Reaching for the loose doorknob, Marietta pushed into the unlocked house through the backyard door and flipped on the red furnace switch. By the time her family arose, she wanted to be sure that steam heat would already be seeping through the pipes of the upstairs' oft-painted silver radiators. Then she tossed her wrinkled black raincoat onto the pantry counter, gracefully kicked her wet shoes down the cellar stairs, and put on new satin backless slippers that were a Christmas gift funded by the savings account of her seven year old daughter, Donna.

After her initial ritual of coffee making, this devoted mother of three shuffled to the TV room opposite the center hall stairs. Still wearing her royal blue factory uniform, complete with her pack of Luckies snugly lodged up her left arm sleeve,

2

she headed towards another holiday surprise. This one was from her rotund, adoring, generous, but mischievous older brother, Pete Frassa. Few other middle-class homes in Belleville could boast of such a supple, plush black leather recliner. Every chance she had that holiday week, weary Marietta snuck off to the comfort of that La-Z-Boy. Her husband, Rocky, was convinced that his "Dennis the Menace" brother-in-law had not done his shopping as claimed at the Two Guys' Department Store across the Passaic River in Kearny. Rather, street-smart Rocky felt it was from the back of an "abandoned" truck out of the Carolinas that a bunch of the Bloomfield Avenue "boys" helped Pete select that special Christmas gift for Marietta. Newark had a few empty lots that served well as the home furniture department for those who did such holiday season discount hunting.

Although religious and prudish, Marietta had been too overwhelmed to ask Pete many questions. Compromise was too delectable an alternative. On this December 31 in 1958, she sank into her newly designated throne and began as she did each morning of her adult life...praying for her family, while simultaneously fighting a haunting oppression which always devilishly attempted to minimize her blessings.

The cluttered, but reassuring refuge of home on Belmont Avenue in Belleville, New Jersey was silent on this New Year's Eve morning. The previous day's *Newark Star Ledger* sports page was spread all over the kitchen table, causing Marietta to fail to notice the torn packing skin discarded from a midnight assault by her sons on the imported "supersod" (sopressetta) she'd specifically hidden for her antipasto. Exhausted from the factory and the thought of housework still to be done, Marietta glanced into her living room through the center hallway. She was grateful that at least her plastic covered furniture still appeared clean, neat, and new. Then she experienced a profound peace in the lively, rhythmic perking of her first pot of Medalia D'Oro Caffe. Classical sounds had taken life that would slowly grow in complexity, as moments would follow one another later that day. However, they couldn't stop her from falling into a rare early morning nap that would only last seven minutes.

The brewing coffee had served as the prelude to a blue-collar symphony. A gloriously unique tapestry of tones, which only a few like the inhabitants of 711 Belmont Avenue would ever experience and cherish, had commenced during her sleep. Before the coffee-perking cadence would cease, the high-pitch whistles of the radiators would join with the staccato banging of the steam pipes, signaling that there was still oil in the tank. These motley disturbances to peace and quiet would gradually envelope the very "lived-in" spot-built expanded bungalow home, announcing that another cold winter morning was being birthed in New Jersey. As all radiators upstairs began to collaborate, the slumbering inhabitants began to awaken. Marietta was in the inner sanctum of her retreat, temporarily escaping from the day that would be placed before her.

Now in her mid-thirties, Marietta had endured four difficult pregnancies that brought her three healthy children. She was rapidly losing her acutely chiseled youth. Her bony hands, delicately dainty with often manicured and painted nails, were her strongest link to that pure and innocent beauty that had smitten her football hero husband during the spring before Pearl Harbor. Curly auburn hair still framed her once tight, pure complexioned face that was now getting puffy with age from being a veteran of the debilitating midnight to 7 AM graveyard shift. Her wasp-like waist had vanished due to motherhood at eighteen and pregnancies every four years. Her last, not going full term, cost her and Rocky a girl who would have been three in 1958. A noble, aquiline nose accentuated high cheekbones, and soft hazel eyes clung to days gone by when her long eyelashes seemed to gently dress her innocent glances. She had once been a petite, shy beauty, destined to be a successful executive secretary in New York City. Today she was a thirty-five year old mother and wife with worries for all of her family members.

Aroused by the coffee's aroma, Jo-Jo, the Bonaducci's thirteen year old son, was the first to stir. Then his taste buds awoke as well. His mother's brief reprieve in Uncle Pete's chair had ended moments before. Garlic and onions were frying in oil in preparation for their union with the best fresh tomato sauce that Marietta could buy from Charlie Bucchino's Italian Deli in the Silver Lake section of Belleville, where she did her holiday food shopping; God forbid she shopped at the Acme up the street in Bloomfield where all of the "Amedigans" (Americans, non-Italians) would find their excuses for Christmas and New Years morsels!

Without even seemingly opening his eyes, … stocky, curly haired, and muscular, Jo-Jo reached over to clumsily place the arm of the 45 record player onto the very worn disc. He flipped the "on" button, and The Dell Vikings once again burst into their hit, "Come Go With Me". Now the orgy of sound and smell was taking on an eclectic flavor that was purely Bonaducci. Indeed, Joseph Bonaducci had planted his mark on this early morning New Year's Eve concert, with the rock 'n' roll hit that he and his diminutive, but mature girl friend, Rosemarie Masino, claimed to be "their song". Little did Jo-Jo know that his mother's just completed daily prayer ritual not only included a special request for her straight A-student son to continue his love for music, but that on this last day of 1958, she petitioned her Creator that her second son not call Rosemarie as soon as he came downstairs, like he did every other day.

"Jo-Jo, shut it off. I can't sleep," scolded his seventeen year old brother, Frank, from the bottom bunk.

Lean and statuesque, with thick, wavy black hair and blue eyes that attracted all types of females at Belleville High since he became a local football hero, Frank knew that he would never return to his dreams that morning once his little brother began his daylong spinning of hit records. On the other hand, while acting disturbed, Frank cherished the morning ritual with its sight, sound, and scent show. Although looking forward to college next year, he knew very well he soon would long for this unique morning experience that was natural to his family at 711 Belmont Ave.

Frank had shared the same bedroom since Jo-Jo was out of a crib. Their football banners, from just about all of Essex County's perennial high school powers, were the fruits of a laborious collection process in which they had both collaborated: Barringer, East Orange, Belleville, Nutley, Irvington, Montclair, West Orange, Orange, Bloomfield, Kearny, South Side, West Side, Central, East Side, Weequahic, Seton Hall, and St. Benedicts. They hung gloriously from the warped, faded white molding bordering their tiny room's ceiling. Miniature football and baseball trophies were scattered about, gathering as much dust as the felt flags. (Marietta was often too tired to clean more than once every two weeks.) Pocket knives, rosary beads, football and baseball cards, Catholic missellettes, spare pocket change, Frank's infrequently worn Confirmation ring, broken model cars, ticket stubs from Jo-Jo's first Barringer-East Orange Thanksgiving football game in '51, a straw hat from one of Aunt Bella's Cuban vacations, a Marine combat belt featuring compass, a pouch stuffed with Japanese cigarettes, and the bayonet used by their dad to kill the enemy in hand-to-hand range, *Sport* magazines, Twain's *Tom Sawyer,* Stevenson's *Treasure Island,* three week old *Newark Star Ledger* sports pages, dirty socks, Frank's infamous motor cycle boots, soiled dungarees, and the newest and most cherished morsel of future memorabilia to join in the menagerie of items strangling any sense of order and neatness in the teenage boys' domain—the game program from the already legendary sudden-death Giant-Colt contest only a few days previous, the surprise gift of Uncle Pete, by way of some of the boys from Bloomfield Avenue who picked up some bet winnings in the form of a couple of fifty yard line seats at Yankee Stadium. Of course, two obligatory crucifixes hung on opposite walls, one for each boy.

Frank clasped his hands behind his neck and smiled as his eyes surveyed the jungle-like sleeping quarters. Wherever he would eventually go to college, the environment of his childhood bedroom could never be duplicated.

"Jo-Jo, enough now," was Frank's weak final command.

"Come on, Frankie. It beats listenin' to these crazy ol' radiators." Jo-Jo was reasoning and pleading at the same time. With his tired swollen eyes still refusing to open wide, Jo-Jo was holding his breath that Frank would not insist.

The Bonaducci brothers were distinctively and individually unique, Jo-Jo very much the smaller, yet thicker of the two, having more of his mother's genes than his dad's. His hair was more brown than black, and as he matured, its kinkiness relaxed into tight, but softer curls. His square jaw and protruding chin gave his profile an almost Scandinavian look. Dark, deeply inset eyes seemed to portray a brooding nature. But, he had a naiveté about life and an ever-hopeful attitude that would not leave him as a teenager. While he'd never be as tall and lean as his dad and brother, his powerful frame and low center of gravity would serve him well in his football career as a runner, and later as a quarterback.

Frank was all his father, tall and naturally sculptured. Black hairy arms and legs kept coeds buzzing when they packed Belleville High School gym to watch him on the basketball court for the Bellboys. His powerful thighs accentuated his slight waist. On the other hand, his long, thin nose resembled more of his mother. His eyes featured lashes that women would fight for.

Suddenly, the precocious, adorable daughter of the family, Donna, chimed in from her private, totally pink bedroom adjoining the bathroom. "Jo-Jo, I want to hear 'Donna', … my favorite!"

Other than the Dell Viking's hit, Ritchie Valens' song had become a family anthem. Frank often publicly thanked God that holiday week that Donna's new record player, one of Uncle Pete's other "hot" Christmas gifts, was already broken.

Having clearly dictated her special musical request, Donna next focused on gleefully anticipating her family's continuation of Christmas season festivities with her parents, brothers, aunts, uncles, cousins, and neighbors. Tonight would celebrate New Year's at the home of Grandpa Joe and Mamie Bonaducci on Oraton Parkway in East Orange. There would be everything to eat and drink, and stories to be told, but no smelts, baccala, nor gifts as they had had on Christmas Eve. Even as young as she was, Donna already understood and appreciated the family love and priceless traditions she was experiencing as 1958 came to an end. She would record her experiences and observations in her new personal journal, one of that year's gifts from her parents. And, she would keep it into her adult life.

After two boys, Marietta and Rocky were overjoyed at being blessed with a girl. However, Donna's straight black hair could not be traced to anyone on either side of the family. Marietta would cut it pageboy style, perfectly framing her chubby cheeks, slight chin and round brown eyes. She was a cuddly bunny to all who loved her. Named Donata, after her Grandma Bonaducci, Rocky's sisters never hesitated in spoiling her with gifts and attention, …especially Aunt Bella Bruno.

Meanwhile, Donna's handsome ex-Marine of a father was slowly opening his eyes to the new day, glad that he was home in Belleville and not in an insect-infested South Pacific jungle. He smiled for only his Creator to see, thankful once again for the unmerited favor bestowed upon him. His hairy body shifted itself to the side of the bed, ably buoyed by his massive forearms; his left arm noticeably unique with its fleshy, hairless underside, scarred by a Japanese sniper's bullet on Eniwetok in 1944. The only other visible sign of Rocky's hand-to-hand combat experiences in World War II was his balding head, the thick black locks of his youth left on the sands of Tarawa, Eniwetok, and other miniscule atolls from where so many fellow Marines never came back.

Rocco Bonaducci, who was never known to raise his voice or hand to anyone in his family, always repeated the same message: "Do as I say, not as I did." He would look for any excuse to have a party to celebrate his family, and life in general. It was always his belief that his survival in World War II was a pure miracle from God. During his time overseas, his five sisters, his mother, and his pregnant wife were praying women, and for some reason the Almighty spared this macho, mustached Newark, New Jersey street kid. But just as reliable a father, husband, friend, and Marine that he was, after his feet hit the linoleum floor everyday since his return to peacetime America, a Lucky Strike would be as predictably hanging from his lip. It was as if his first puff signaled that the enemy was elsewhere, and that safety was at hand. After all, it was only when totally secure in the jungles that the Marine officers in charge would allow their platoons of leathernecks to light up.

Unlike his wife, the years had not yet taken their toll on Rocky's appearance. His eyes were lively, bright, and well known in the family for their razor sharp focus on people and circumstances he considered important. Because his job at Jergens, the national lotion and perfume factory, was physical, he had not put on a pound since his Marine days. His face was angular and lean, with a constant smile accentuated by his pencil thin mustache that had been with him since he shoved off from San Diego to defend his country. Never concerned about diet, he sported broad shoulders, a narrow waist, and a chiseled stomach. His powerful thighs still buldged as they did when he was a teenager playing both ways at right end for the Big Blue of Barringer High. While he had played his last college and pro football game eleven years earlier, his lean six foot, one inch frame appeared more prepared for an opposing linebacker now than even the youthful bodies of his two teenage sons. His backaches were simply the lingering effect of his five-days a week compounding job at the factory, and his leg soreness was due to shrapnel still trying to free itself from his body.

Hearing his dad preparing for his morning shave, Jo-Jo finally fully opened his eyes, now tearing from his allergy to the family dog, Blackie. A mutt who was as affectionate as his purchaser, the big-hearted Uncle Pete, Blackie spent more time running around the neighborhood than any house pet should. His dander was spoiling Jo-Jo's efforts to look handsome for Rosemarie. In spite of his eyes' early morning irritation, Jo-Jo sailed off the top bunk bed, breaking Frank's feeble block to slow him up, and instantly appeared behind Rocky who was already leaning at the sink and staring into the cracked mirror.

The morning lesson on life was about to begin. The younger Bonaducci son, who was more expressive and amiable than serene, yet sometimes high-strung Frank, used every chance he had to orchestrate dialogue with his dad. Subjects would vary from what it was like to have killed the enemy in the islands, to Rocky's historic game-winning extra point against traditional rival East Orange on Thanksgiving Day in 1940 when he was a high school senior. Other times Rocky would relate to Jo-Jo the same story about the street fight in which he saved Uncle Pete from some gangsters looking for "numbers" money on Fifth Street and Bloomfield Avenue in the North Ward. They weren't the familiar neighborhood wiseguys who, … recognizing Rocky as his brother-in-law, former football star, and Marine, … would have left Pete alone.

It seemed as if Rocky paused for a puff on his cigarette with every stroke of his Schick injector razor. The aromatic Old Spice shaving cream emitted a sweet scent that invisibly mixed with the contrasting acrid and harsh odor of the lit cigarette. Splashing on his Mennen after-shave after the trimming of his pencil-thin mustache, he affectionately slapped Jo-Jo on both cheeks with the evergreen lotion.

With the early morning symphony of sensory enhancing experiences now at its climax, it seemed like just another morning at the cozy, yet hectic Bonaducci home in Belleville, New Jersey, just twelve miles from the Lincoln Tunnel. Yet cold winds of change were about to roll in.

While not having slept since the previous morning, Marietta was refreshed from her short respite, and totally invigorated from her quiet moment with her Creator. Prone to worry and anxiety with her less than balanced childhood, she was reminded of her blessed relationship with Rocky, their healthy children, and the diverse, yet sometimes unwelcome support of his huge family of five sisters, a brother, and multitudes of nieces, nephews, cousins, "goombods" (male friends), and "goomods" (lady friends). Intellectually beyond most in her family, at her best she would chuckle to herself when reflecting upon the menagerie of relatives upon whom she could call. While none were from her side of the family, she would eradicate any self-pity by counting her blessings. She married into a family full of the love of life that was unknown to her as a child. She smiled as she dropped a pinch of baking soda into her simmering gravy. How could she forget her brother, Pete? Indeed, he was a gift and her special friend from God, her fellow pilgrim who made it through a dark childhood with a mother who never smiled or showed them affection.

"Rocky," Marietta yelled up the center hall steps to the bathroom, "We got a busy day today. Cemetery's first, … coffee's ready."

Ignoring his wife's call, Rocky took one last look at his manicured mustache in the mirror, smiled, and gave a Clark Gable smirk that only confused Jo-Jo. With his dad usually a modest person in spite of his good looks, Jo-Jo queried, "You O.K., Dad?"

"Jo-Jo, if Daddy didn't lose his hair in the war, he would've been either real famous or real dead, … and you wouldn't be here. God knows what he's doin." Rocky was always transparent to his kids about how everything works out for the best. He then spun around and said to his second son, "Daddy, go outside and see if Russell delivered the paper. Let's see what football's on TV tomorrow."

Whenever his tone was about to become serious with his sons, Rocco Bonaducci would always call them, "Daddy". It was as if that address signaled the reference to a subject that his sons knew was as close to their dad's heart as could be possible, or something to which they should be particularly attentive. Certainly, Rocky was about to speak a truth when he addressed them as, "Daddy". Principles of life, stories from the streets of Newark to the sands of Iwo Jima, football tales, family issues, or tips on dating; … if it was important information, Rocky would begin his conversations with his sons with …"Daddy".

Opening the Bonaducci front door was always a feat of patience and forearm strength. Jo-Jo did not mind the challenge. It tested the effectiveness of his recent exposure to weightlifting against the perpetually warped house entrance in retrieving the reward waiting on the front doorsteps, … *The Newark Star Ledger*, ably delivered by his four-eyed friend, Russell Giardella. With aspirations to exceed his older brother's schoolboy football notoriety, Jo-Jo was confident many *Ledger* headlines would be about his achievements at Belleville High in the coming years.

With the door finally ajar, Jo-Jo knelt down to reach for the paper lying on the ice-topped steps. He was frozen for a moment, spooked by the invisible wind intruding high in the front yard trees, as if boldly demanding his attention. His haunting trance was not to be understood. He grasped for the partially frozen paper and fled inside.

Marietta had poured hot coffee for everyone in the family. While both Bonaducci sons were outstanding athletes in town, it wasn't because their mother or father was particular about their eating habits or the idea of adolescent coffee drinking. After all, "scadall" (escarole) and beans every Monday night took care of the eating and drinking vices that were cherished traditions in Italian American families in this part of northern New Jersey. Donna even looked forward to her "light and sweet" early morning eye opener. With Marietta now washing last night's dishes that the boys had "forgotten" to do, Frank was busy toasting white "American bread", as it was known at 711 Belmont Avenue. Practically a whole pound of butter would be gone in an hour, as Rocky and his sons put both elbows on the kitchen table to devour almost an entire loaf.

"Rocky, here's what you gotta do," said Marietta. "Before we can start thinking about your mother's tonight, go to the cemetery, stop at Charlie's to pick up "riggaut" (ricotta cheese) and gravy meat, go to my mother's to get some wine, see if Pete wants to come tonight, exchange your sister Bella's gift at Vicarisi's, drop off a gift for Dalla at Giordano's Bakery, and get the bread there, too." (Dalla Della Pella was Marietta's childhood friend and maid of honor at her wedding.)

Her husband was laughing out loud by the time she was finished. "First of all, Marietta, I need money for gas," retorted Rocky who actually could not wait to start the "run" with his two boys that would take them to the graveyard on Central Avenue in East Orange, then through the streets of his old Newark neighborhood, and finally to the Silver Lake section of Belleville.

"And...?" asked Marietta, knowing that her husband had more to say.

"Well, you know that Pete won't be around, 'cause the boys on Bloomfield Avenue probably have him runnin' all over Newark to make their collections for the end of the year. And you know how your mother hates to part with her wine, even if it is for my father. And Dalla will never be workin' at Giordano's today, because she's probably gettin' ready for her parties tonight".

Rocky's remarks about his wife's best friend and her active single life always disturbed Marietta. "Your mind's always in the gutter," she scolded. " Dalla's serious about her new friend."

Maybe Dalla's newest boyfriend was the one, but Rocky also knew her to be an incorrigible flirt. Not being able to deny Dalla's loyalty to his wife, he answered, "O.K., I'll look for her at Giordano's."

As always, Marietta had to have the last word. "What about your sister Bella's reputation over the years. Talk about dancin' till all hours of the morning. Thank God Emil showed up in her life! I mean, I love her, but talk about the life of the party!" (Emil Bruno was Bella's drug store manager of a husband.)

Frank's eyes darted to catch his father's reaction, as Jo-Jo now entered the conversation. "Ma," said Jo-Jo. "You always talk about Aunt Bella like she was pretty wild, but she's my favorite." Always slightly titillated by the stories of Rocky's second-oldest sister, Jo-Jo prodded his father, "Really, … how wild was she, Dad?"

"Let's stop this conversation now," said Rocky in half-hearted rebuke that put a smirk on Marietta's face. But he continued, "Even though Aunt Bella always enjoyed life, she's a good girl. She and Aunt Josephine lead an entourage to visit the veteran hospitals even to this day." (Josephine, who was five years younger, was as religious, snobby, and proper as Bella was not.) Rocky concluded, "And Aunt Bella's the first one that guys lift to pin the money on Saint Gerard at each feast."

Frank cringed, knowing well his mother's next reaction. After all, even he could not ignore the voluptuous showgirl figure and glamorous style of Aunt Bella.

Marietta did not disappoint. "Oh, I'm quite sure the honor guard from St. Lucy's fought hard over who would grab her first, … and where!" Then Marietta laughed. She knew how much she was indebted to her husband's generous older sister, but she'd never been too talkative about her appreciation. If there were another person on the earth who worshiped Rocky as much, if not more than his wife, it was Bella.

Marietta would have loved to tease her husband further about his provocatively sexy sister, but Jo-Jo had just returned to the crowded kitchen table from the TV room on the other side of the hall stairs. "Hey, Dad, we better call Gary Gubitosi over to fix the TV, 'cause it's like a snowstorm on the screen; only the sound's working."

"Marietta, take care of it while we do your list," Rocky requested, and then slowly added, " But didn't he just fix it? God, sometimes I think Gary would rob an ol' lady if no one was lookin'." Quickly changing the subject, he said, " Frankie, go warm up the car."

"Dad, Dad, let me do it," pleaded Jo-Jo.

As his father nodded OK, the boy grabbed the car keys and darted into the hall closet for his weathered Barringer High School baseball cap and his brown leather bomber jacket (another Uncle Pete purchase from … "some guy who knows his leather"). Sprinting back through the kitchen, he faked a stiff arm to his amused older brother and leaped down the kitchen stairs, bounding through the backyard door and onto the patio. He jumped into the decaying family automobile, which had been eternally embarrassing to the Bonaducci boys because of its … "cancer on the sides".

Jo-Jo grasped the two-door '49 Chevy's steering wheel firmly, turned on the unreliable ignition, and began to dream. Maybe someday after a big game as the county's best high school running back, he and his girlfriend would drive to Rutt's Hutt in Clifton for hot dogs, and then after getting his due praise from all the guys and gals from surrounding high schools, they would head off to Eagle Rock Reservation in West Orange to make out. Just the kind of thinking his mother was praying against. But his dream would never come true, … at least not with Rosemarie Masino.

Back in the house, as Rocky and Frank prepared to join Jo-Jo on their trek around Essex County on this chilly, snow flurry-filled last day of '58, the next offering in the 711 Belmont Avenue symphony was about to commence. With the banging pipes all but a memory, Ritchie Valens succeeded the Dell Vikings with his romantic, "Donna". Bonaducci child number three was in the boys' bedroom, and nothing was going to stop her from playing her favorite hit. The perking coffee had long since ceased, but the smoke of the burnt toast from the ravenous breakfast onslaught of Rocky and his boys still enveloped the entire house and everyone's nostrils, while the teenage idol from the Southern California barrios was flooding the home in Jersey with his love song to his girlfriend.

As Rocky and their two boys finally drove away, back in the house Marietta had quieted down to the sound of the eighteen year old Philco radio, a shower gift from

12

Dalla, and now tuned to "The Make-Believe Ballroom", with William B. Williams on WNEW in New York City. "My Frank Sinatra," as Marietta would say, was about to do his thing.

While Marietta knew Rocky was the one the Lord had picked, "Ol' Blue Eyes'" voice always would send her on a romantic escape from her troubles every time he sang. As she wiped the kitchen table with a wet dishcloth that served too many purposes in the cluttered Bonaducci household, she was unconscious of the smile that had come over her face. The Cole Porter lyrics and the Nelson Riddle arrangement from "I've Got You Under My Skin" were beginning to mesmerize her. She and Rocky agreed little about Sinatra other than this was his greatest song.

No one in the house could complain now about Sinatra and Ritchie Valens competing for listening time. Little Donna was upstairs, mouthing Valens' smash in an innocently seductive manner as if he had written the lyrics for her. At seven years old, her imaginings were as pure as the white snow falling outside. She was in her own world.

Marietta had drifted back to simpler times as a young woman, when the sounds of Sinatra ushered rare and enchanting notions of romance. Dancing alone, her tired body glided through the haze of smoke from the burnt toast, parting it as the sun accentuated the reality of its presence. She clutched and hugged the soiled "moppeen" (dishcloth), as if desperately clinging to days gone by. Her painted nails dug into the cloth. Slight traces of blood from the assembly line handiwork coated her cuticles, particularly on the fingers with broken nails. The turned up volume had disrupted Donna's own journey with Valens, causing her to tiptoe down the stairway. By now Riddle's climactic big band entrance seemed to be escorting the song into every nook and cranny of the house. Peeking around the center hallway, Donna beheld her mother in a rare, relaxed smile, eyes closed, and surely focused on a scene of pleasure. The sun in her face temporarily lifted her wrinkles and tightened her soft skin. It was Rocky in his Marine dress uniform, and it was the Waldorf Astoria Grand Ballroom. While the '55 hit was out of place with the post-war crowd of celebrants, Marietta's poetic license easily compromised the conflict. To her and her husband, "… Under My Skin" had become timeless; it had become their song. Her face had taken on a glow, a youthful beauty that Donna had never beheld before. It was too personal a time for Marietta to be anything but alone, and her curious daughter seemed to understand as she quietly retreated back upstairs. Marietta glided across the scuffed wooden dining room floor, refusing to allow time to reenter her life for the three minutes and forty-three seconds of Sinatra's masterpiece. But then it was over. The sound had vanished with the smoke of the toast. She opened her eyes. Still hugging the moppeen, Marietta thought she had been alone for a few glorious moments. It was time for her to continue her day. She had to open the cans of anchovies.

Rocky, Frank, and Jo-Jo returned from their own diverse chores around Essex County by two o'clock that afternoon. "Well, we made it to the Central Avenue cemetery before the snow started to stick. But ya know what?" said Rocky, his voice pitching higher in frustration. "The Christmas wreaths were already gone, Marietta." Aware of the tension mounting for blacks on the Newark-East Orange border, he had his own ideas about the disappearing grave decorations. "The colored kids from East Orange made a pretty buck sellin' those wreaths to their kind. They probably made their move after we left last time."

Having served black families for years from behind her family's butcher shop counter on Bloomfield Avenue in Newark, Marietta defended the alleged graveyard culprits. "Rocky, the wreaths probably blew away. Besides, if they did take them, they needed the money more than my father and my uncle needed the decorations."

Rocky was surprised. "Oh, <u>now</u> she sees the light about all these wreaths and the multiple trips to the graves at the holidays. Christmas time is when you celebrate <u>life</u>, not death. See, we spend all this money on the dead, and some colored kids run off with the goods."

At only thirty-five, Marietta's father had died from a massive heart attack when she was an impressionable eleven year old. Her father's brother, only fours year older, died one year later, … the same way. She changed the subject. "Did you guys say a prayer?"

"Of course, Ma," answered Jo-Jo, in modest disbelief she would even imply they'd forget.

Hardly listening, and taking off his motorcycle boots on the cellar stairs just beyond the kitchen, Frank declared, "We froze to death, Ma. Daddy's heater's not working again."

Rocky shook his head, waiting for Marietta's imminent rebuke. She was starting to think too much for Rocky's comfort. "I thought I gave you a twenty for Henry to fix it at the Shell station. You didn't spend it on art supplies, did you Rocky?" quizzed Marietta, making reference to her husband's undisciplined love of painting, a skill she ironically wished he had developed over the years.

"Marietta, you know it's a '49 Chevy on its last leg," said Rocky. "But Henry did guarantee the work. I'll see him after the holidays."

The room became quiet. Staring into the backyard, watching the snow get heavier, Rocky knew another car could never fit into the Bonaducci budget. He didn't have to convince his wife.

Jo-Jo broke the spirit of oppression that always lurked around Marietta when she would begin to feel sorry about money challenges facing herself and her husband. "Hey Ma, at least we got home safe, and snow wasn't coming up through the floor," he said, referring to the hole in the back seat floorboard that was little Donna's favorite disposal shoot for anything when she was a passenger.

"By the way, Marietta, I was right again," said Rocky, referring to his prediction that his mother-in-law would not part gracefully with her dwindling reserve of homemade wine.

Anticipating the worst, Marietta interrupted, "Rocky, you got the wine for your father, didn't you?" She loved her father-in-law and wanted to treat him with one of her mother's homemade bottles of red.

Disbelief and disgust engulfed Marietta's face as Rocky replied, "Nope." He went on, "I told you so. She changed the subject when I mentioned it. Then Pete wanted to come tonight, but she went into one of her cryin' jags about bein' alone on New Year's Eve. I reminded her that she's invited, too, but she made believe she didn't hear that either."

Rocky never once called his allegedly wealthy mother-in-law, "Mom", "Margarita" (her name), or anything else other than "she" or "her". With his having been raised in a loving family that defended and supported all members to a fault, the only indication of her warmth and love he ever witnessed was directed at her grandchildren. In his nineteen years of knowing her, Rocky never once saw his wife or brother-in-law receive any form of affection from her, nor receive any advice worth following. On top of that, it was she who ultimately discouraged Marietta from supporting Rocky in his bid to play football at St. Bonaventure after the war.

Both Frank and Jo-Jo were rolling their eyes and nodding their heads in confirmation of their father's report. Not wanting to dampen his disbelieving wife's holiday mood further, Rocky said, "Well, anyway, I picked up the bread at Giordano's.

Dalla hasn't been to work in a week, ... sick or somethin'. I left her gift with Angie Giordano. Even she's givin' up on her."

A childhood friend of Aunt Bella, Angie was the oldest of the Giordano family kids who all worked the busy holiday hours at one of Newark's most famous Italian bakeries. She had her own reasons to be upset with her party-animal part-time worker. Rocky quoted her: "I can't believe Dalla is Marietta's best friend. Your wife's so loyal and faithful. This floozy seems to schedule everything around the loves of her life."

Rocky added, "I know, Marietta, she's gonna marry Goomba Vic's kid. But even Angie doesn't trust her."

As usual, Marietta defended Dalla. "Angie should talk. She was always out dancing with your sister, Bella."

"Here we go again," said Jo-Jo.

Although totally committed to his high school sweetheart, Frank could honestly admit, only to himself, that Dalla and Aunt Bella would turn on any red-blooded male in all of Newark's First Ward, or anywhere else in New Jersey for that matter. After all, Frank thought, *Hadn't it actually happened to the young Italian priest at Saint Francis Church after the war? Supposedly he was willing to leave the cloth to marry my Aunt Bella!*

Continuing the preparation of her New Year's Eve antipasto dishes that would soon feed thirty-five people at Mama's, Marietta subtly changed the subject by assuring the boys that they could watch all the football they wanted on New Year's Day. Gary Gubitosi had been by when they were out, to fix the TV, ... at no charge because of his previous misdiagnosis. Marietta was well aware that her husband was never a fan of talkative Gary and his wife, Rosa. Rocky was suspicious of, and never trusted people, who tried to be too friendly. Also, he always wondered, *How could Gary always have a wad of cash in his wallet?*

Marietta sheepishly glanced up from opening her fifth can of anchovies. She even seemed to want to share something further with her husband about their enterprising backyard neighbors, but she decided to remain silent.

Rocky was still in contemplation. *How could Gary always have more money on him than his TV repair business and his "night job" as a printer could possibly provide?*

The afternoon was moving quickly. Finally, Marietta took a break from her cold cut ensemble of "gabagool" (capocollo), salami, boloney, Italian provolone, mozzarella, sun dried tomatoes, vinegar peppers, the depleted supersod, anchovies, pickled mushrooms, pepperoni, eggplant, olives, deviled eggs, and lettuce and tomatoes. With WNEW's "Make-believe Ballroom" still spinning the year's top hits for her exhausted enjoyment, Marietta quietly melted once again into Pete's leather recliner to drift back into memories of her youth. Her boys subconsciously applauded when their mom took a break, because between the graveyard shift and her household chores, she rarely retreated to the sidelines.

By now, Frank was on the phone with his girl friend, Maria, confirming her presence at 711 Belmont Avenue for New Years' Day. Jo-Jo was reminded by his brother's call that he, too, had to check in with his heartthrob, the one that some had thought had turned him into a love sick little puppy dog. Donna warned both of her brothers that after Jo-Jo's call to "that little flirt", she had to call her own friends. While Marietta's mother did not part with any of her wine for Rocky's dad, she had poured a couple of glasses for her son-in-law. Not a big drinker, Rocky had to take a nap, … "to get ready for Pop's".

It was already 4:30 PM, and the family would leave for Grandpa Bonaducci's in an hour. The house on Belmont Avenue was quiet now. The New Year's holiday had begun with a symphony of sounds that came alive with a flip of a red furnace switch at 7:15 AM. By now, even the "…Under My Skin" inspired euphoria experienced by Marietta had dissipated.

As she rested and thought ahead to the imminent family celebration, little did Marietta dream that her life at 711 Belmont Avenue was about to change. And, it had begun with the Belleville-Nutley High School football classic, as a prelude to unpredictable possibilities for the coming year.

CHAPTER 2

"PREGAME WITH UNCLE PETE"

Several weeks before the holidays of 1958, an early winter snowstorm had blanketed northern New Jersey and New York City. On the morning of the first Saturday of December, the snow had changed to rain. Later that day, Frank Bonaducci made a choice that would affect his life, and those of many others, for years to come.

Having just arrived home from her Friday shift, Marietta was startled by a violent knocking sound, seemingly at the backyard kitchen door. It was only 7:30 AM. She looked out from the alcove and was surprised and confused to see the stocky stature of her older brother, Pete. *Why's he here this early on a Saturday morning?* she wondered. *His usual arrival time is 9:00 AM sharp, every Saturday in the fall, for the last four years.*

Peter Frassa was only five feet eight inches tall, but his large round face, enormous torso, and meaty hands convinced you … "this is a big man". A butcher by trade and his sister's senior by two years, he would eat at any excuse. He <u>had</u> to weigh three hundreds pounds. In spite of being alarmingly overweight, he was always smiling and usually well groomed, even though he wore clothes that never seemed to fit properly. But the one aspect that truly distinguished his appearance from all others was … his shoes. Pete had such wide feet and wide girth; he never seemed able to find a pair of shoes that fit comfortably. His only solution to his pontoon boat-like pins was to carefully carve out a cross on either the big or little toe side, depending which extremity was experiencing the most pressure that day. While the slice on either side did not prove to be a total distraction from the rest of his haberdashery, the butcher store sawdust that always caked in the openings,

19

did. Nevertheless, his gentleness and considerate ways still made him particularly popular with children, dogs, and …the ladies. Dark bags under his soft puffy eyes gave him a sad countenance at times, but his incessant desire to make others laugh caused this aspect of his aging to go almost unnoticed. A clear, milk-white complexion contrasted with his jet-black straight hair, and his round nose and pencil-thin mustache above his wide, thick-lipped mouth further enhanced him. However, after thirty-seven years, Pete was still a bachelor. Perhaps, if he had only listened to his sister, "…Pete, just lose a hundred pounds!"

Pete's Jackie Gleason and Oliver Hardy imitations were legendary to his niece and two nephews. To Rocky he was an "angel with a dirty face"; to his sister and her children, he could do no wrong; to his stern mother, he did nothing right; to the "boys" at the Social Club on Bloomfield Avenue at the junction of Fifth Street and First Avenue, he was known as "Petee Five Corners". The Frassa family settled there in the early twenties, and the five street corners and Pete's three hundred pound body seemed synonymous, … big intersection and big man, … thus, "Petee Five Corners".

Perpetually in search of attention and affection he never received from his mother, and a spitting image of his hard-working and fun-loving father, Peter Sr., Marietta's only sibling never recovered from losing their dad. Always a practical joker, Pete was forever looking for short cuts in life that could make up for mistakes of his past and the time he felt he had lost. While his sister skipped two grades in graduating with highest honors at Newark's famed Central High at only sixteen, Pete dropped out of Barringer at fifteen to work his late father's butcher business.

If the hole in Pete's heart, blown open by senior's passing, ever came close to healing, it was only because of his sister and her family to which he was unselfishly devoted. Not only Rocky's heroism in the South Pacific, but also being a two-way end in football in high school, at Bergen Junior College, and on weekends with the professional Paterson Panthers, kept Pete in constant awe of his brother-in-law. Most of all, he respected Rocky's honesty and commitment to family and doing the right thing, qualities Pete was convinced he could never perfect. While he would never recover himself, the pain he felt for his younger sister losing their dad haunted him. He vowed to always help her in any way he could, and showing up each Saturday morning during football season was just one of his many selfless acts… but, before 7:30 in the morning?

"Pete, what'a ya doin' here so early?" asked Marietta, as she took the filet mignon that her brother had neatly wrapped in wax paper at the butcher shop. Sheepishly following her to the stove where he placed the dozen giant eggs he had carried

20

under his left arm, Pete's left hand still tightly held his own favorite pre-game meal, … a dozen mixed breakfast buns and donuts, still warm from Kielb's Bakery on 6th Street, across from Steven Crane Village on the Belleville-Newark line.

"Madiett, is Frankie up yet?"

"I dunno, Pete, I just got home."

Pete took a seat at the kitchen table. Twiddling his thumbs, seemingly impatient for the events of the day to get started, he turned to his sister. "Got *The Ledger* yet?"

Already beginning the steak and eggs breakfast and fatigued from her full week of nights at work, she asked, "Hey, how 'bout gettin' it on the front steps. I was too cold to pick it up when Mary and Nick dropped me off."

On his way to the front door, Pete's eyes darted about, looking for Blackie, the black mutt, too active and frisky to relax in any one place too long. Pete had delivered the dog to the Bonaducci's the previous year. One of a litter of three born at the Yarborough household on Orange Street in the dominant black section of Newark, Blackie was given to Pete by tiny Jerome Yarborough, whose dad had helped Pete out in the butcher shop until he was killed by a hit and run on Central Avenue in 1957. Pete had since made sure the widow and young Jerome would never be without a meal. Only a ten year old, Jerome gave the puppy to the butcher as an expression of appreciation and because he loved "Mr.Pete".

"Hey, Mr. Pete, what's ya gonna call it?"

"I's thinks he's gonna be 'Blackie'," answered Pete in his favorite Kingfish imitation from "Amos and Andy", which he knew would never offend Mrs. Yarborough who was well aware of the size of Pete's love for her family.

"Why's that, Mr. Pete?"

"Cause youse and he's black, and youse both beautiful," said Pete as he picked up the little boy, smothering him in kisses that would leave skin irritation from the chubby butcher's day old beard growth. "And ya know what, Jerome? Every times I sees him, I's gonna think of you."

As anticipated, Blackie ran into Pete just as he made his way through the living room and followed on his heels to the porch. Pete suddenly became surprised at how cold the room was. While the temperamental house heating system had just kicked in, Pete was sweating as he always did from his overweight condition. He reacted to cold air rushing into the closed-in area by way of the broken window at the base of the front door that notoriously stuck.

Shrugging off the low temperature, at his first attempt Pete couldn't budge the door, nor on the second, third, and fourth tries. Blackie found a warm corner in the front room as his perch from which to view the event. Pete's frustration gave way to cramping in his arms and chest. Remembering his weak heart and his family coronary history, he stopped to take a breather that led to an idea. The broken window had a jagged opening that seemed big enough to stick his arm through. Slipping his hand and forearm carefully through the cavity as he bent down on hand and knee, he groped for *The Newark Star Ledger* already frozen by the rain, snow, and ice coating the steps.

Pete halted his plan, pulling his right arm back as he readjusted his kneeling position. Then, he paused for another moment, as a vicious gust of the premature winter wind appeared to be trying to discourage his chore at hand. His respite seemed prolonged as he contemplated the joy of his participation in his sister's family life. He clutched at his fleeting moment of contentment. Yet, the contrasting frustration of retrieving the newspaper was beginning to anger him. If only his hand were smaller, or if his wrists a bit stronger, he would already be reading the sports page on the table back in the warm kitchen.

The wind vanished. Its sudden absence forced another momentary reflection. The cold air was refreshing to Pete's lungs as he inhaled the pure elements, the moist hairs on the back of his neck welcoming the cooling effect of the December morning. However, he could not tarry any longer. The assignment at hand stole the fleeting seconds of peace and returned him to reality. He was still on his knees. Behind him, Blackie's high-pitch groaning reflected Pete's mounting discomfort.

"Blackie, youse is useless," said Pete in that King Fish voice he thought the mutt understood best. "If little Jerome was heres, he'd be helpin' Mr. Pete out. Youse is just spectatin'."

Twenty feet to the right of the porch was Pete's Cadillac with its engine still groaning to keep its waiting occupant warm. Dozing from the carbon monoxide fumes and another sleepless night caused by his incessant smoker's cough, Greenie Delaney opened his eyes to now see the imprisoned Pete with his hand stuck in the broken doorframe. "Jesus, he's gonna cut his arm and freeze at the same time!" mumbled Pete's childhood friend and his "official driver" in bad weather. He kicked his driver side door open and burst into a slipping and sliding sprint to Pete's rescue.

Almost going head over heels, he wildly vaulted up the four broken brick steps, just grabbing the doorknob in time to prevent falling. "Pete, ya nuts? Ya not gonna get the paper that way!"

"Great observation, Greenie. And, ... how may I ask are you gonna help me?" Pete was being classic Ralph Kramden.

Standing in the cold, sporting only his blood stained butcher's apron over his gray tee shirt, Greenie unconsciously became Ed Norton. "Boss, sit tight, ...I mean kneel tight. Pardone to my misdiagnosis of your situation...or kneelulation. I'll break the window."

"I could'a done that from the start, genius!" said Pete.

Greenie paused, contemplated for a few moments, and then, putting his hands on his hips, stood tall and announced, "Looks like I'm in charge, Pete. Just relax, and I'm gonna remove the cracked window, ... gently I might add, ... free your arm and that 'fat' hand of yours, and deliver you the paper through the door panel."

Blackie was watching and listening to the dialogue, his little black head and sincere eyes darting from Pete to Greenie as the strategy unfolded. He seemed incredulous as if to be saying, *"Nobody's gonna believe this."*

Hoping for no reprisal for his "fat" reference, Greenie had little trouble removing his best friend's hand and forearm. Pete licked the blood from the tiny cut just above his wrist. Greenie struggled prying the paper from the ice, and then proudly delivered it through the now glassless opening.

More embarrassed than grateful, Pete offered no thanks. "Greenie, I'm gonna hit ya with this paper. Now get back in the car before Rocky comes out."

Greenie asked, "Hey Pete, how ya gonna hit me with the paper? Ya gotta open the door first, boss!" Greenie loved to tease his lifelong friend. Climbing back inside the toasty car, he could not see Pete's smile. Next to his sister's family and Jerome, Pete loved no one more than Greenie.

Finally making it back to the kitchen, Pete opened to the sports page. Without taking his eyes off of the sodden paper, his fingers searched into the bag of baked Kielb goodies. Quiet, yet fidgeting and anxious more than usual, Pete did not look up as he informed his sister that the weather forecast for the day was not good. He pushed some crumbs from his crumb bun off the table so that Blackie could satisfy his sweet tooth. "Snow's gonna change to rain, and the kids'll have a slush and mud mess. Think they'll postpone the game, Madiett?" Pete was concerned.

Without looking up from her preparation of Frank's pre-game breakfast, Marietta replied, "They'll play no matter what. Just pray, Pete."

The bathroom toilet above the kitchen flushed, and Pete instantly knew that his Adonis of a nephew would soon be joining them. The steak was frying in its own fat and Marietta's heavy-handed measure of butter as another ritual of Saturday game day began. Frank's favorite album was given its football Saturday pass to precede any of Jo-Jo's favorites, particularly "Come Go With Me". In fact, it was Jo-Jo's responsibility to cue up the music. Small talk between the two brothers was quickly drowned out when Dion and the Belmonts began their 1958 hit that almost sounded hillbilly at its outset to the most inexperienced listeners of the music of the day. On the other hand, to Frank, a quiet devotee to the sound of the handsome group of Belmonts, the music was pure mid-fifties and a fuel to his passion for the times and the opportunities of his young life.

"Don don don don don don donda donda daaaa, donda donda naaaaat, know why I love you like I do, don donda donda naaat, know why I doooo; don't know why I love you, don't know why I care, … I just waaant your love to share. Oh, I wonder why, I love you like I do…" "I Wonder Why", Number 1 on the contemporary charts throughout the New York area for many weeks in '58, was now waking up the whole neighborhood, let alone Rocky and Donna, still trying to sleep in their beds. Marietta took a break from her silent praying and cooking to smile in approval.

As she watched Pete nervously await his nephew, Marietta saw a grown man in almost immature hero admiration. Blackie was sitting opposite him on the chair closest to the kitchen door. Frank's fan club was ready for his entrance.

"Ya know, Pete," Marietta said. "That's Frankie's favorite group. Not only the music, but they're from Belmont Avenue in the Bronx…like our Belmont Avenue here in Belleville. He hopes to meet 'em someday."

Frank was taking his time in getting ready for his final high school football game. Jo-Jo pestered him with all types of questions about the tough Nutley team taking on the Bellboys. Staring into the mirror as he towel-dried his black hair, Frank was not as much ignoring his brother, as he was getting lost in Dion's upbeat doo wop that had motivated him throughout his final season.

Next year, Belleville's top scholar athlete would be playing college ball somewhere. But since he first saw James Dean in "Rebel Without a Cause" back in his freshman year, Frank would venture into the seeming freedom and power of juvenile delinquency in how he dressed and saw himself only on game days. His father would not allow otherwise. Frank pulled the pure white tee shirt over his broad shoulders and hairy chest. Stepping into his skin-tight blue dungarees, he took a deep breath, flexing his upper torso as he zippered up the Levi jeans.

With Jo-Jo still prodding and at times answering his own questions about how prepared the Bellboys were, Frank slipped on his white sweat socks and then sat at the edge of his lower bunk bed to complete the final act of his personal ritual. Perceiving himself as a quiet, tough teenager who would intimidate Nutley with his high-stepping running style and ferocious hitting on defense, he began pulling on the black leather motorcycle boots that his father would only allow him to wear on special days as these. The game day wardrobe was now complete, ... except for the matching black leather motorcycle jacket, hanging in the hallway closet downstairs. It was a surprise "Uncle Pete gift" back after Frank began his "Rebel Without a Cause" infatuation. Today, the all-around athlete faced his own imaginary gang war.

Frank squinted into the mirror. He finally heard his brother. "Ya ready, tough guy?" asked Jo-Jo, slightly sarcastic and fearing no retribution.

"Cuz, I'm ready." The music, the James Dean look, and the unspoken mission that only Frank could be aware of had prepared him mentally for the challenges of this rivalry game. He was in another world.

Beckoned by the delectable aroma of the best steak Uncle Pete could cut, Frank strutted his muscular frame to the hallway stairs, his heavy motorcycle boots testing the strength of the steps. Rocky, having lit up a Lucky at his bedside, yelled out, "Frank, ya ready?"

"Yep."

As Frank entered the kitchen, now cloudy with the smoke of the burning fat and butter-soaked steak, Pete pushed from the breakfast table and walked to his nephew. Blackie was right behind. Momentarily shedding his detached James Dean look, Frank brightened. "Uncle Pete, one more time, thanks for the steak and eggs. You're too much."

Supplying Frank's pre-game meals had become Pete's ritual since the fall of '55 when his nephew, as Captain of the Belleville High Freshman football team, broke the school's scoring record. Pete could not have been more proud.

The two embraced, Frank, now several inches taller than his uncle. Pete planted his trademark juicy kiss on his embarrassed nephew's left cheek. However, unlike many times before, Pete would not release his grasp. Usually clean-shaven, his rough, prickly beard against Frank's soft face accentuated the moment for the teenager. At first uncomfortable with the long hug, Frank acquiesced and relaxed in his uncle's grasp.

Still enwrapped by his uncle's chubby arms, Frank glanced over to his mother at the stove. Witnessing her sad-sack brother's act of admiration, awe, respect, and love, Marietta could not prevent a tear slipping out of the side of her right eye. Intuition told her that Pete didn't want the teenage years of football for his nephew to end. It not only had given Pete so much to look forward to, but also earned him a respect down in the North Ward of Newark that his own deeds could never have mustered. As he continued embracing his nephew, Pete's eyes closed, slipping into memories.

"Petee, Five-C's, your nephew had a great game against West Side. Be proud, Five-Corners!" This was often the Saturday afternoon accolade to Pete from the boys on the corner, themselves honored to know someone who was a football star on his way to college, and not into trouble. Some of Richie Boiardo's crew of wiseguys would slow their shiny cars cruising Bloomfield Avenue to pay tribute on their way to Saturday night dates. On these late afternoons and evenings at the Five Corners of First Avenue, Fifth Street, and Bloomfield Avenue, Pete and Greenie waved to all as they sat on white, straight-back wooden chairs like they were thrones, leaning them against the sign that identified "Pete Frassa and Son Butcher Shop".

Pete knew that these moments would soon vanish. The joy of his pride for being honored as Frank Bonaducci's uncle was overwhelming him. In his mind's eye he could not dim the images of his holding court on Bloomfield Avenue for the past four years of Frank's high school football experience. The gentle Indian Summer sun always seemed to slow up as it lazily set over the outline of City Stadium on those Saturday afternoons, a couple hundred yards up Bloomfield Avenue. Pete figured the good Lord stretched those unforgettable sunsets as a way to balance taking his father at such a young age. Otherwise, the butcher could not justify these jewels of moments awarded to such an undeserving uncle. With Greenie being there at his beck and call, and with the passing praise of "the boys", Pete would even think that Richie "The Boot" would not receive as much honor and respect, … and Pete didn't have to break any laws to get such attention. He was just related to Belleville High's "Mr. Outside", and he just showed up each Saturday for the last four years with the best steak he could cut at the shop.

Finally Pete released Frank and shuffled back to the kitchen table, wiping his wet eyes. He returned to the sports page. "Frankie, Greenie says that Dorfman and Glicken both pick you guys in *The Ledger*."

Having poured himself his own cup of coffee and being told by his mother to sit for the steak and eggs feast, Frank responded to the two Newark sports writers' vote of confidence with a laugh. "Hey Uncle Pete, they finally agree that we're pretty good. If ever I would like to go in as the underdog though, it's today." He then suggested, "Read it out loud."

"Here it is, Frank. Headlines: 'Bellboys Picked Over Nutley. Only Game in the State. Bad Weather Expected.' Then Dorfman writes, 'Today the Belleville High School football team takes the short bus ride up Franklin Avenue to the legendary Park Oval, the home of the Nutley Maroon Raiders. Hoping to conclude its best season under former Bloomfield High and North Carolina State great, Ed Popalinski, the Bellboys may be facing more than one opponent—the Maroon Raiders and the mud at the Oval. Belleville's Mr. Inside, Gino Babula, and Mr. Outside, Frankie Bonaducci, will find the running tough after this week's snow and rain. Nutley's Bob Scrudato in the backfield and All State lineman, Jack Chuy, will be out to stop the Bellboy 'B-Boys'. Babula will get the TD that makes him Essex's top scorer. We pick Belleville in a squeaker, 6-0.'"

"Sounds good to me," said Marietta.

"Frankie, what'a ya think?" asked Pete, licking his fingers, having just finished off his second Kielb delight, a cinnamon donut. His nephew's answer would mean much to him. Pete had Greenie put five twenties on Belleville.

"I'll take the six to nothin'," said Frank. "We'll win." Frank had an idea that his uncle had a financial interest in the biggest game of the season. And, the thought reminded him to ask, "Hey, Uncle Pete, where's Greenie anyway?"

Before he could answer, Marietta jumped in. "Pete, don't tell me that Greenie's in your car. He's probably frozen by now!"

Pete quipped back, "Nope, he's not freezin, … I told him to keep it runnin'. The heater's on." He didn't wait for a reaction, "Madiett, he's probably sleepin'. Besides, you know how Rocky feels about Greenie." His brother-in-law's righteousness was toward Greenie's alleged "gopher" role for the "family" down at the Social Club next to Pete's shop.

"Pete, ya should've told me." Marietta was genuinely concerned for the part-time butcher whom the entire family had known since Greenie's parents moved onto Fifth Street during the Depression. She called to her younger son, "Jo-Jo, are you ever gonna get up? Greenie's freezing to death outside. Come down and bring him some hot coffee and one of Uncle Pete's donuts."

Marietta's command for a rescue mission out to Greenie made Rocky pick up his pace in making it down to the kitchen. On the way, he encouraged Donna to get out of bed and hurry to see Uncle Pete before he left. While Rocky showed little affection to his generous brother-in-law, he loved him deeply for his family devotion and respect he always showed when he visited 711 Belmont Avenue.

It was almost 10 AM, and Frank was well into his steak, eggs, and toast. Jo-Jo had returned from the frigid driveway, and now the entire family was huddled at the table in the cramped kitchen alcove. Blackie had selected to cuddle up against the silver multi-paint coated radiator. While it was just beginning to hiss, even he knew it would be fifteen minutes before it would really heat up. He didn't want to miss this last Saturday morning, especially with Uncle Pete dropping the monstrous crumbs from Kielb's buns and donuts to the floor just in front of his moist little black nose.

The traditional family Saturday pre-game pep talk would now begin, but not before Jo-Jo reported back on Greenie. "Well, Mr. Greenie hasn't frozen to death, but he did ask if Uncle Pete finished reading the paper yet." He laughed, and Pete smiled, neither filling in the others at the table about the recent newspaper retrieval adventure.

Then Donna started. "Frankie, ya gonna score a touchdown for me today?"

"Yep," answered Frank, glancing over to his little sister and affectionately sticking his tongue at her.

Donna returned the gesture. Her handsome big brother had made her the center of attention at School Number 10's playground all fall. The fifteen other girls of her second grade class were all in love with Frank, as were their young mothers.

Boys in her class followed her around all day, hoping to hear what living with Belleville's standout two-way halfback was like.

Having been with Rocky since his junior year at Barringer and then in the post-war years of college and pro football, Marietta understood the game. She spoke next. "It's muddy, Frank. Keep your feet under you. Do what you've done all year. Listen to Daddy. We can't be more proud."

Feeling himself getting emotional again and because it was close to opening time at the shop, Pete popped up from his seat. "I better get goin'. Hope Greenie didn't suffocate before he froze. He's gotta set up so I can make the kickoff."

Rocky laughed, knowing that Pete would never have invited Greenie in on his own. "Don't let Greenie freeze out there again," said Rocky, surprising Pete with his concern. "It's never been this cold before one of Frankie's games. If he drives you over the holidays, make sure he comes in."

"Thanks, Rock."

When Frank rose to respectfully bid his uncle farewell, Jo-Jo saw it as an opportunity to dip a slice of toast in the steak juices on his brother's dish. With Marietta distracted in scolding him and Donna already having skipped into the TV room to watch Saturday cartoons, only Rocky saw Pete's eyes fill up as Frank again thanked him for the food and for showing up for the ninth Saturday that year.

As they hugged, Pete blubbered, "Ya know, ya make me so proud. For your Dad, too, and my sister, you've been the best. Do good. Tell Gino to run like hell, too. I'll see you in the end zone, OK?"

As always, win, lose, or draw, whatever the weather, whatever the circumstances, Pete had made the commitment to wait for Frank after the game. And Frank knew the one thing he could depend definitely on in his young life was that Uncle Pete would be waiting under the goal post to greet and congratulate him when it was all over.

Pete then made sure he received a kiss from Jo-Jo, Marietta, and even Blackie. He followed with his classic whistle, beckoning Donna from her cartoons. He lifted her, planting a "smooch" on her chubby left cheek.

"Uncle Pete, you didn't shave!"

Pete laughed and responded with another wet peck of affection on her other cheek.

Rocky shook his hand. "Pete, thanks again,… really appreciate it. Say hello to Greenie for me." They both smiled. "See you in Nutley."

Pete left. It would be his last pre-game meal at 711 Belmont Avenue.

Marietta summoned Donna and Jo-Jo to help with the kitchen cleanup. They never refused. Football Saturdays were always Frank's days, and they were happy to be a part of it by helping to get the kitchen back in shape for their mother.

While Rocky finally had a chance to read the sports page, Frank sat by him at the kitchen table to finish his orange juice.

Jo-Jo seemed to have more nervous energy than usual as he washed the dishes. Then he burst out, "Listen, Frankie, when we played the Nutley Midgets in that All-Star game a couple of weeks ago, the Oval was soaked. It was terrible up the middle. It'll be tough for Gino between the tackles today. Pal, it's your day today. Bounce to the outside quick and hug the sidelines. It'll be drier. Today, you end up big, Frankie."

Donna completed her Saturday game day chores by placing her big brother's gym bag next to the stairs leading out the backyard door. Marietta had folded Frank's infrequently used black leather motorcycle jacket over one of the chairs.

It was time to leave for Clearman Field where the Bellboys dressed for their games. First Frank hugged Donna, and then his mother.

"I'll be praying for you," murmured Marietta.

Jo-Jo proudly received a kiss on his head from Frank.

Everyone now turned to Rocky. They were waiting for his perspective, knowing that he would share advice that would be salted with experiences from the streets of Newark, New Jersey to the sands of Iwo Jima. On this final Saturday game day for Frank, his father did not disappoint: "Frankie and Gino are gonna make history today," said Rocky. "It'll be Frankie's greatest moment ever. Just play each play likes it's your last, Daddy. Enjoy every moment. Don't think of yourself. Forget the other games. Forget college. Just focus on each play. Remember, 'Bonaducci' means 'good leader' in the Italian. Be a leader today by doin' everything you can to help your teammates. You're not on Eniwetok in the South Pacific. No injury should take you off the field of battle. You're playin' the great American game of football, not fightin' hand-to-hand combat. This game will get you the best education in the world. Your grandfather will be in the stands. Uncle Pete will be in the end zone with his friends. Mommy and Daddy will be there, Aunt Bella, Aunt Pinky, Uncle Jimmy Quinn, Uncle Caesar, and all the rest of your aunts, uncles, and cousins. Daddy, don't let one guy take you down. Keep your knees high. Stay up. Don't go down. Block for Gino and don't let anybody get behind you on defense. Have no regrets at the end of the game. Leave it all on the field, Daddy."

Frank hung on every word. Rocky was addressing him as "Daddy".

Little did Rocky realize how accurate his first comment was on making "history". From that day, Frank Bonaducci and Gino Babula would be linked inextricably forever, whenever Belleville and Nutley football would be discussed. Those who cherished the value of the cross-town rivalry would never forget this early December game in 1958, and Frank's name in particular would be immortalized and caste in bronze. In future years the uninformed would comment, "But it was only a high school football game." They would fail to comprehend that in some families, a high school football game is all they have.

Rocky shook Frank's hand. Uncle Pete's pre-game meal was now officially over. It was time to go.

CHAPTER 3

"VINNIE'S VICTORY VOYAGE"

By the time Rocky and Frank arrived at Clearman Field on Union Avenue, just a few blocks up from Belleville High, the precipitation was now totally rain, even though it seemed cold enough to still be snowing. Leaves that hadn't fallen because of the unseasonably warm and dry autumn were now flying uncontrollably through the frigid air, the target of icy pellets, making any travel slippery and treacherous. It forced Rocky to bring his fogged in car to a halt. He and his son just sat there, as the fickled engine struggled to avoid stalling.

There was total silence. Both Bonaducci's were wishing for dry weather, yet knowing without doubt the pivotal game had to be played. Postponed since the third week of the season in early October when the Asian Flu had wandered into the New York Metropolitan area, the Belleville-Nutley contest had to come off on this most inclement first Saturday in December.

Belleville had never played this late in the season, while the Maroon Raiders had experienced December glory during the legendary '39 and '40 seasons when they traveled to Florida to compete for the mythical National High School Football Championship. Having won one of those contests, Nutley players and fans always felt that anyone in Jersey who ever challenged them this late in the season would surely be easily defeated. Nutley High in Essex County was, after all, the only New Jersey school ever invited to play for the legendary national title and, thus, considered themselves kings of post-season high school football.

With only a loss to Bloomfield blemishing their record, a win today would be historic for Belleville. Nutley had three defeats to the Tri-State Champs of Montclair, Bloomfield, and Clifton. Therefore, 1958 was a bittersweet season for the Raiders. On the other hand, the true melodrama was set for Gino Babula, the childhood friend who had capitalized on Frank's nagging ankle injury to inherit the majority of the Bellboy running. He answered the challenge in spectacular fashion, being only five points behind Essex County Scoring Leader, Bobbie Haynes—less than a touchdown—with everyone else's season having ended. A dry field would have made it easier for Frank to help Gino make some history against Nutley. Rain, snow, and mud presented complications.

Rocky broke the silence. "Too bad WPIX-TV and ABC-Radio had to choose this game to broadcast," referencing popular Marty Hickman's play-by-play announcing of the High School Game of the Week on TV, as well as its radio transmission.

"Dad, don't get me down now. This is a pretty exciting game to be playing in," Frank reminded his father.

"No, Frank, I was just thinkin' it's gonna be tougher out there than usual. You kids are good, though. You can do it. But I'd love to have Marty Hickman see you and Gino on a dry day."

"Dad, this is the healthiest I've been all year, and you know Gino; nothing bothers him." Frank reached for the door handle to dash for the locker room.

"Wait," suggested Rocky. " The rain's gotta let up."

Laughing, Frank quipped, "Dad, I'm gonna get soaked today anyway. What's it matter?"

Rocky would have the last word. "Frankie, you had a great year. Sure, the sore ankle slowed ya up, and Gino started scorin' all the TD's. But ya had some great games on defense, too. Everybody knows you're the best all around!"

"Sure, Dad."

"Good luck, Frank."

Frank sprinted for the locker room door, dodging huge puddles and carefully avoiding the muddy mounds of dirt blocking his clear path. He didn't want his motorcycle jacket to get too soaked. He pranced like a deer, much like he had on the field all season, albeit less frequently than planned.

Rocky had taken a deep breath when his son left and exhaled only when he saw him make it safely to the locker room door. As Frank disappeared into the small brick fort-like building, Rocky bowed his head and said his regular prayer for his son: "Lord, be with Frank. Help him to do what I could not do. Help him to be what I could not be. Don't let any of my sins hurt Frankie. Thank you, Jesus. Amen."

Later that day Rocky's prayer would be answered.

Because the bus ride to Nutley from Clearman Field was less than two miles, the players climbed onto the ancient Trackless Transit vehicle in their full equipment. As they shuffled around and through the muddy water and slush-filled puddles with the biting wind-driven rain attacking them from all sides, not a word was being exchanged. Their dark blue leather helmets momentarily insured dry heads, as did the bulky canvas raincoats supplied by the loyal Belleville Fire Department. Nonetheless, freezing rain still pelted them mercilessly. The wind seemed to lift each of them onto the first step and into the bus; their cleated shoes already packed in mud.

By the time diminutive Doc Ameo, the team trainer, stepped onboard the already fume-engulfed ark, not only were all of the plastic nose guards and facemasks completely fogged up, but no one could see out the windows. The subtle scents of mentholated rub, rubber laced adhesive, musty old jerseys, and mounting perspiration joined with carbon monoxide to accentuate the memory of the moment. This was the last time these boys would ever inhale such a variety of dissimilar odors. It was the smell of high school football in the fifties.

Doc placed his case full of tape and other medically oriented paraphernalia on the front seat across from Coach Eddie Popalinski. "Everybody here? Nobody missin'?"

No answer broke the building tension amongst the thirty nine-team members, their coaches, and the few school administrators present. This was the biggest game of the season for all. For some, it would be the most important day of their lives.

"Mr. P., I think we're ready to go," said Doc.

Billy "Doc" Ameo was not a medical doctor, but rather a career New Jersey National Guard Recruiter who graduated from Belleville in 1954. Only five foot and three inches tall and weighing just above a hundred pounds, his devotion and experience with Belleville football since his days as the student manager made him an authority figure not to be questioned. When Coach P. was once asked about Doc's contribution to Belleville football and the town in general, he readily responded, "In life, leadership's like beauty. It's very difficult to define, but you know it when you see it. Billy Ameo is a leader, …all sixty three inches of him."

The bus remained motionless until Coach P. finally ordered the driver: "Vinnie, take us to the Nutley Park Oval. We've got a date with history."

Vinnie Giampietro, who had been the bus driver for all of Belleville's games over the last four years, hit his horn, signaling the police escort that it was time to go. Inside the slow moving black and white vehicle with its flashing red lights were two of Belleville's finest, John Lister and Chief Mike Lanno. John had started the midget football league in town, and Chief Mike always took the ride to away games. In their minds, even for these veteran cops, it didn't get any better than this.

Vinnie, now overweight and a chain-smoker, had played defensive tackle on Eddie Popalinski's first post-World War II team. They went 0-9, … not a win. Some shrapnel Vinnie later took in his left hip in Korea made him limp with an ugly forty-five-degree dip to the left with every painful step. But he feared corrective surgery. Driving the bus for Belleville allowed him to forget his handicap. It kept him young. He was part of a team again; this time, winners.

The boys loved and respected Vinnie for his service to their country. The football given to him after their Irvington contest left him speechless. Gino Babula had put on a record-breaking five-touchdown performance, easily establishing himself as "the most valuable player" that day. But instead, "Mr. Inside" quietly suggested to Coach Popalinski that the ball go to Vinnie Giampietro. Gino said he had enough game balls, and Vinnie had always been so respectful of his on the field heroics.

"Coach, this'll make Vinnie's life," said Babula.

Handsome, lean, and muscular as a teenager back before Korea, Vinnie was embarrassed by his limp. He lived alone in the Silver Lake section of Belleville, next to Saint Anthony's Church where he attended mass every morning. The Bellboy's seven wins and one loss that year represented the highlight of his life. The game ball became the cherry on the sundae.

Now, as the bus headed off for the final game, Vinnie wanted to do something special for his Bellboys. He mapped out the journey for that day, having made calls all over town the previous night. Vinnie asked for some favors. He got them.

At the corner of Union and Belleville Avenues, Vinnie yelled to his passengers to clean the bus windows on the left side ... to see Jackie Rego of "Jackie's Lemon Ice", Belleville's answer to Newark's renowned "Louie Ting-a-ling Hot Dogs". On hot summer nights, Belleville kids would swarm to Jackie's for the best lemon ice in New Jersey, according to *The Newark Star Ledger*. Even Jackie's "Italian Abbundanza Dogs", with peppers, onions, potatoes, and the frankfurters, all coexisting at least a day in hot oil, were a match for Louie's and were an experience only the bravest food connoisseurs would endure. The record for eating "Danza Double Dogs", as they became known, went to "Wee Willie" Brindisi. Belleville's bulky senior defensive lineman gulped down ten in one twenty minute sitting. Jackie promised Willie a trophy. He never delivered it.

Now Jackie's establishment was closed for winter, but there he stood, all five and a half feet of him, dressed only in coveralls, dirty t-shirt, thigh-high rubber fireman boots, a coupaleen on his head, holding a white placard urging ... "Go Bellboys, beat Nutley. Thanks for the memories in '58". Most of the players admired Jackie's support, but it was his statuesque, sixteen-year old daughter, Annette, also in jeans, high heels, and her own tight t-shirt dampened from the weather, who got more attention. She was waving with both hands at the boys.

When the comments and whistles began, Doc Ameo boomed out, "Men?!" The wrong juices were beginning to boil. He wanted their adrenalin flowing, focusing on game time, not visions of full-figured Annette. Instantly, you could hear a pin drop.

Frank shook his head. His admiration of Annette wasn't far behind those of the guys who had made futile attempts to get to know her ... in the Biblical sense. He smiled.

Noticing his reaction, Gino inquired of his friend, "What'a ya think, Frankie boy?"

"Bless me Father, for I have sinned," Frank answered with a sigh.

They made the left onto Belleville Avenue, and then another onto Washington Avenue. Chugging through the center of town, Vinnie's green and yellow bus continued to spew fumes as it slowed to a halt opposite the High School. Baffled by the delay with a green light evident, the players again cleared the left side windows. Vinnie waved, which cued the Bellboy band to start belting out their best ever rendition of "Across the Field", Ohio State's fight song that Belleville adopted when Eddie P. took over coaching in the late forties. It stirred the players. They were back to getting psyched for their imminent encounter. Lingering images of Annette Rego evaporated.

Vinnie's next motivational feature was only about one hundred yards further along on the right, ... the ancient Capitol Theatre. Plainly displayed on the movie house marquis was an exciting, yet less than honest request: "Closed for Game. Frank Sinatra wants Belleville win over Nutley". "Pal Joey", starring Sinatra, was the feature that week, and theater owner, Marty Grossman, did not have time to remove the singer-actor's name due to the weather. Marty, one of the few Jewish businessmen to put down stakes in Belleville, gave the boys a two-handed victory sign. The players were impressed. Vinnie's traveling pep rally was working.

Down the road the bus made a sharp left onto Joralemon Street and slowly climbed to its next experience of encouragement orchestrated by its driver. The players caught a glimpse of the popular Milk Bar at the junction of Franklin Avenue and Joralemon. This landmark was where all of BHS gathered every Saturday after games to inhale cheeseburgers, milk shakes, and mingle with the potpourri of teenage life in northern New Jersey in the late fifties.

In the front of the wooden frame restaurant, which looked more like a barn, were the ten owner-members of the Plenge family. Big George, a former Belleville All County center, who graduated from Cornell's famed Hotel-Restaurant Administration School, stood out in front of his parents, brothers and sisters, waving a Belleville pennant. In rain that was slowing to a fine mist, he led his family in an up-tempo of Belleville's alma mater, which coincidentally originated at Cornell. The Plenge's were Belleville's last farming family, owning significant acreage at the Belleville-Nutley line for growing tomatoes and other vegetables, as well as raising cows, goats, and stabling a few horses. George's initial interest in Cornell's Agriculture School changed with the success of the Milk Bar, which his dad opened originally to sell their garden and milk products. It was later converted into the hottest family restaurant and teenage hangout in town. That development led George Sr. to tell his strapping son to apply to the Hotel-Restaurant School since the restaurant business would be his future.

While Coach Popalinski at first questioned himself about Vinnie' route to Nutley, seeing one of his best former student-athletes cheering on the younger Bellboys left him speechless. He then knew that the handicapped bus driver's meandering voyage had surely become the perfect prelude to the big game.

Vinnie had proposed the Plenge Family demonstration idea to George the night before, and there was no hesitation on the part of the former Ivy League lineman. As a grade schooler, George had one football hero, … Vinnie Giampietro. Their paths after high school vastly different, George achieved greatness in the family restaurant business with his Cornell degree. Vinnie on the other hand, would pray ever day at Saint Anthony's that the Trackless Transit brass would not lay him off from his hourly job because of his crippled hip. It may seem strange, but because of his courage and performance during a long-ago winless Bellboy season, it was Vinnie who would always be George's idol.

The bus driver made the right onto Franklin Avenue and hit the gas pedal as they entered the quaint, tree-lined sister town of Nutley. Vinnie took a deep breath and exhaled slowly. His personalized tour was coming to an end. Only five minutes after leaving the Milk Bar behind, the struggling ancient smoking machine rolled to a stop on Franklin Avenue in front of Nutley High School. Vinnie waited for Nutley police to remove the yellow warning barricades so the Belleville boys could make a right into the school parking lot just opposite the south end zone. His destination had been reached. At that moment, he was proud to have given something back to this team that insisted he was one of them, … hoping it would somehow contribute to a victory for his alma mater. Not one of the passengers aboard Vinnie's bus that day would ever forget his trip to the Nutley Park Oval.

CHAPTER 4

"THE MUD BOWL"

The Belleville team could not believe their eyes. It was an hour before game-time, and the rain had only let up slightly, yet the legendary Park Oval was already filled with spectators. TV and radio equipment stood on temporary scaffolds at the fifty-yard line on Nutley's side of the field. This was unbelievable. The Bellboy kids never dreamed any of their games would ever be on radio, let alone on television. *Could this really be happening to us?*

The field, sunken below the street level of Franklin Avenue, was surrounded north, west and south by six-foot cast iron fences enshrouded in a Nutley maroon canvas for every home game. During the pre-war mythical national championship runs, sellouts at the Oval were common, and its conservative Irish dominated Board of Education wanted to ensure that all spectators paid to get into the field to see their cherished Maroon Raiders. No way would they sacrifice revenue to allow anyone to peer through the fences.

Indeed, lines of anxious spectators were hugging each other in the rain under umbrellas and blankets, waiting to buy a seat. However, this canvas "blackout" and strict ticket policy created a new phenomena on this stormy December Saturday. Every dump truck, pick up, garbage truck, and auto that could support soaked fans standing on their roofs were lined up around the perimeter's fenced sections. Many of the Nutley and Belleville loyalists who had been striving in the local excavation, construction, and garbage businesses since the fall of Germany, V-J day, and Korea figured they'd earned the right to get a good view, whichever way they could.

Sal Orechio, Commissioner of local police and himself an ex-Nutley gridder, instructed his men to ignore any Board of Education command to ticket the illegally parked "grandstands" on that day. After all, names on the trucks' sides told a story: C. Corino and Sons, Greco Brothers, R. Luzzi, Angelo Vitiello and Son, Dimenchino Excavation, DelTufo Plumbing, Orsini Construction, Cardinale Garbage Collection, Pietoso Development, Scarpelli Home Improvement, Cocchiola Trucking, etc. Commissioner Orechio's family had first settled in Belleville after arriving across the Atlantic from Calabria in southern Italy. But, soon afterwards, they moved to Nutley where he, his brothers, and sisters were raised. These trucks were owned and operated by ex-Bellboy and Maroon Raider players whose educations had been interrupted by war. In his mind, they deserved special treatment, regardless for which team they rooted.

"Only out-of-town fans pay today," said Orechio. "All Belleville and Nutley people should see this game if I have anything to do with it. They built these two towns. If they're late 'cause they had to work today, they still sit ... or stand somewhere. The Board of Ed. knows where to find me after the game!"

That day not a parking citation was written, and "truck top fans" had many of the best seats in the house. Decades later, the lanky Orechio is still remembered storming up and down Franklin Avenue in his ankle length rain coat and floppy fedora, chasing away any patrol officer thinking of reaching for a ticket book. The first Saturday of December in 1958 was a serious day for the likes of Commissioner Sal Orechio who helped so many Belleville and Nutley families since he left his business to serve in politics in Nutley, Essex County, and in Trenton. By the miracles of television and radio, the whole New York Metropolitan area had its eyes and ears set on the Nutley Park Oval. Sal was proud of both towns.

Belleville players' first look at the field made it seem brown and green, as if totally shielded from the week's snow and rain. Ridges of snow defined the sidelines. But all was not what it seemed. Suddenly, Coach Eddie Popalinski blurted, "Holy crap, those SOB's plowed the field. They said they'd leave it alone and line it with black ashes. Leave it to that nutty Nutley Board of Ed; they made it worse! It's brown water from hash mark to hash mark. Doc, it's gonna be a mud bowl."

More philosophical than irate, Doc Ameo calmly replied, "Coach, Nutley's gotta play in it, too."

"Yea, Doc, but this stops Gino."

Again Ameo quietly assured the unsettled coach. "Gino doesn't get bothered by anything. Besides, I like the green grass outside the hash marks for Frankie. He's due."

Now Doc Ameo was not only small, but his eyesight was always questionable. However, he never wore glasses. The green Park Oval grass he saw was hardly in its glory, with only the top of its blades stretching above two inches of freezing water. Only one thing was for sure; this day would be a mud bath from one goal line to the other.

As he had since his freshman year in the fall of 1951, Doc led everyone off the bus. His stature contrasted oddly as Belleville's biggest and fastest player roster in years followed him out. Cheerleaders, friends, family, and fans formed a line of umbrellas to protect the Bellboys from the drizzle. Belleville blue and gold pennants flapped wildly as the wind picked up. Yellow mums on many of the girls' collars and lapels were limp with moisture. Shiny gold footballs were in the middle of the seasonal flower. For years to come, only the tiny footballs would outlast the garment ornament ribbons that would later fade in many a family album.

As the extra long medal "mud" cleats of the players' high-top football shoes scraped along the asphalt and concrete, the coaches and the traveling administrators followed Doc Ameo in search of the meeting room for today's visiting team. Due to construction on the north side of Nutley High, the Bellboys actually ended up in a small room adjacent to the basketball court, used to store tumbling mats.

Not usually to complain, Doc shook his head. "Where am I supposed to tape these kids?" He was referring to Gino and Frank who both insisted getting taped only at the last minute before the game, because they hated the restriction on their ankles. On the other hand, the room was warmer than most locker rooms the Bellboys had been in late that season. So Doc at least appreciated that gesture of their Nutley host.

Frank sat on the dusty concrete floor next to Gino. Both had removed their helmets and Fire Department hoods. Doc made a last minute check on their equipment.

Frank whispered to his quiet teammate, "How ya feel, Gino?"

"Sick."

"Again?"

"Yep". Gino's habit of vomiting before every game started back in his sophomore year.

"Gino, what'a ya eat today?"

"Same. Cornflakes, juice, … and coffee"

Recalling his full course meal from Uncle Pete, Frank asked, "That's all?"

"Nope," he casually added. "I had a few drags on my mother's Camel."

Gino watched for a reaction, but Frank just smiled at his running mate. Smoking before games further validated for him that Gino was a gifted, though undisciplined athlete, whose competitive spirit was unmatched by anyone more conscientious.

Gino, the five foot ten inch rock of football fury, began to look pale to Frank and suddenly jumped to his feet, yelling out, " Doc, the head?"

Without even looking up from taping quarterback, Gaetano "Guy" Galioto's wrists, Doc pointed across the hallway beyond the door. Gino took off, forgetting he was wearing football shoes, and slipped and slid into the bathroom. Doc, who had seen Gino go through this routine many times, just shook his head. He told Galioto that if it weren't for Gino's low center of gravity and great balance, he probably would have fallen and cracked his head on his way to throwing up, long before this.

Gino was the only child of Silvia and Gino Babula, Sr. His tight, curly blonde hair and blue eyes betrayed his father's Sicilian heritage. But his mother, from Italy's German and Austrian genetic-influenced Lake Como region, was slight and fragile. Herself a stunning blonde, her husband was a bull of a man.

Almost five years older than Silvia, Gino Sr. never took another woman on a date in his life. Quiet and moody, he was naturally muscular, with a barrel chest developed in his youth as an anchovy fisherman. Exported to Newark by his family and under supervision of a special local Padrone, Gino became the envy of all the First Ward kids during the Depression years. Bulging, hairy forearms and his dark complexion made him stand out amongst Jersey's largest city's other immigrant children from southern Italy. His head was large, and his dark brown eyes were surrounded by shadows even in his youth. Black, bushy eyebrows gave him an ominous look, and coupled with not being one to smile much, his inner generosity for the neighborhood's less advantaged was often camouflaged. It seemed he

44

was always on the side of the underdog. Whether on the playground during the Depression, or later in life, everyone wanted Gino, Sr. on his team.

Gino Jr. had his mother's light skin and her movie star looks. On the other hand, his body and his personality were from his dad. A young man of few words, he kept friends to a minimum. Not a good student, his dreams were of football and to start his own construction company. Like his father, he wanted to be his own boss, and he didn't trust many people, whether in authority positions or not.

Throughout his youth Gino had played in the shadow of Frank Bonaducci. Always the blocker for his high-stepping friend, he carried the ball only on few occasions. Then in the fall of 1958, Frank turned his ankle in the East Orange opener. Gino was called on to do the bulk of the running. In only a few short weeks, Gino's explosive inside thrusts became legendary around Essex County. This notoriety was strange to Gino who had been pleased just to lead interference for Frank over the years. His friend's good grades, solid home life, and almost Christ-like demeanor, made Gino always feel it was his mission in life to protect his leaner, studious, more articulate running mate. Now this season, their roles were reversed, as Frank was often used as a decoy in the explosive Bellboy offense.

While Frank's outside speed and graceful style had returned by the season's fourth game against Newark's West Side, Gino had earned the awe and respect of Coach Popalinski along with the rest of the team as its most valuable player. And even though Doc Ameo was Frank's biggest fan, he commented, "The situations of this year did not make Gino Babula, … they revealed him."

True to Frank's modesty and depth of character, he never questioned not regaining the bulk of the offensive plays. Besides, defenses now stacked to stop Gino up the middle, and while seeing the ball fewer times, Frank often enjoyed more running room on the outside. Quarterback Guy Galioto would fake to Gino inside and pitch to Frank bellying wide. But in the end, Gino became the featured back, and it seemed there was no defense on the schedule that could stop him. Over eight games, he had scored eighteen touchdowns, a Belleville High record. His bull-like rushes between the tackles perfectly complemented Frank's lightning sprints to the sidelines. Often embarrassed by how many times Coach P. oredered Galioto to give him the ball, "Mr. Inside" would insist at times that he was too tired to run any more, and to start to feed "Mr. Outside". However, particularly after Babula's five T.D.-performance at Irvington, there was no doubt in anybody's mind who the fall of 1958 belonged to.

The raging, yet controlled violence that molded Gino's running style had more to do with his father, than any conscious effort on his own part. Those who followed City League football in the thirties and organized crime in the forties and fifties knew Gino Sr. as "Sneaks". His first pair of shoes after coming to America were a pair of black sneakers that he never seemed to go anywhere without. And in 1936 "Sneaks" was named the All City tailback in Newark.

Exempted from military service by a congenital back problem aggravated in a fight with some cops on the take when he was only nineteen years old, Gino Sr.'s nickname took on new meaning after high school. "Sneaks" Babula became a mastermind at manipulating business schemes as an underboss for Richie "The Boot" Boiardo, raising him to prominence in the New Jersey underworld during World War II. His interest in protecting the less privileged as a youth slowly transformed into providing opportunity for those who'd rather cut legal corners for personal gain. Feared because of his physical size and corrupted by the broad power endowed by "The Boot", Sneaks slowly made some enemies within the "family". The Newark Police Department, New Jersey State Police, and the FBI claimed to have enough information from Sneak's own crew to lock him up on extortion charges. The rats' names were never publicized. But one week after Sneak's arrest, two thugs with big aspirations in The Boot's family got reassigned to run a couple of the organization's night clubs in Atlanta. They would never return to Newark.

The day Sneaks was arrested forever tattooed on young Gino's subconscious the embarrassment, anger, and confusion that would eventually be channeled into his relentless abilities with a football. Seeing the world of his mom and dad completely shattered did the same to Gino Jr.'s heart. Miraculously, this rage and fury would be vented only on the football field and not against others in the normal course of life. To Sneak's total disgust, the warrant for his arrest was issued in the Babula kitchen on Carpenter Street in Belleville on the Bellboys' opening day in 1957 against the Panthers of East Orange High.

Gino was not totally naïve about his father's dealings in the construction and garbage collection businesses in Essex and Union Counties. But his mother's saintly ways and the high standards that Sneaks set for Gino about how to treat others, twisted the teenager's sense of reality. Gino simply could not believe the allegations against his dad, and immediately sunk into being moody and resentful, cutting off contact with almost anyone.

Frank Bonaducci was different from Gino in so many ways, yet so appreciative for his friend's loyalty as a running mate. After learning the details of Sneaks' arrest, Frank, at the suggestion of his own father, tried to get closer to Gino, encouraging him to focus on football and his grades. It wasn't enough. Gino's classroom results suffered anyway. But with respect to football, even Frank and Rocky became amazed. That's when Rocky dubbed the duo, "Mr. Inside and Mr. Outside", just like Doc Blanchard and Glenn Davis, Army's double Heisman Trophy winners of the forties. Rocky thought it would help Gino not only get a better image of himself as a player, but also distract him from the reality of his ties to Sneaks. Gino never admitted it, but he loved Rocky for labeling him after one of college football's true legends.

In the weeks following his father's arrest, Gino's devastating blocking sent many a would-be tackler of his friend to the sidelines for medical attention. Like a wounded, wild animal, he was a personal bodyguard bent on creating fear within any opponent. When Frank's injury put the ball in Gino's hands the following season, only the Haynes brothers of Montclair High came near matching his running performances. There was no question that facing the reality of his father's dark life style drove "Mr. Inside" to greatness on the Essex County gridirons, particularly in his senior year of 1958.

By contrast, "Mr. Outside" had the heart of a lion, but the spirit of a saint. At the Nutley Park Oval on this wintry Saturday, Gino and Frank would each learn life's true meaning of "giving", a revelation that would set both of them free, ... eventually.

As Coach Popalinski began his pre-game pep talk, Gino returned to sit next to Frank. He looked relieved, and Frank noticed the color had returned to his light skinned round face. Gino gave a deep sigh, as if to say, *We can start the game now. There's nothing left in my stomach.*

Doc Ameo then cued in. "Gino, I taped Frankie. Ya ready?"

Gino waved off his trainer. "Catch me next week, Doc."

Doc nodded in agreement, knowing he could never convince the star otherwise. Then he gave Coach P. the OK sign.

"Men, if we win today, we finish with the best record at Belleville since before World War II when some of your fathers and uncles played. Not long after their careers, they jumped onto troop ships to the South Pacific. Others volunteered to fight Nazi Germany. I knew those guys; they were warriors. I played against some of them. Gentlemen, you're just like them, ... warriors!

"Listen, Nutley's the best 5-3 team in the state. The schools that beat them are Tri-State Champs, … Montclair, Bloomfield, and Clifton, … and you know how we scared Bloomfield; should've won. Well, we can do that today.

"The mud will make it tough, boys, but we have another incentive. If Gino scores one more time, he's the county scoring champ, … a first ever at Belleville."

The Bellboys were now collectively excited, "… way to go, Gino! We'll get it for ya, tough guy!"

The coach continued, "While Montclair's season is finished just like everybody else, one of the Haynes brothers, Bobbie, is still five points ahead of Gino. We want it for Gino, … but we gotta win first.

"You kids are the best group I was ever a part of. That includes when I was at Bloomfield, and even when I played at North Carolina State. Never saw so much heart in my life. Take Frankie Bonaducci; might have been his year if he didn't get banged up early. Never complained. Still had a good season, doing his job on offense and defense. Even Gino knows it could have been Frankie.

"Yep, gentlemen, we got the two best runners in the state. Nobody's stopped Babula yet, and Bonaducci is the best two-way guy I ever coached.

"Nutley's big and strong. I know ya know a lot of the kids, and Wee Willie's even gonna play against his cousins today. But, they can't stand you guys. In fact, they hate us.

"You know what though? Play the way you did all year, and we make history with Gino today."

A roar engulfed every corner of the dusty meeting room, and the fans standing just outside the parking lot exit became energized by the Bellboys' muffled eruption of emotion. As the players finally put on their helmets, Coach Popalinski could only detain them for a few more minutes. "Boys, just one final thing. I want to thank the seniors. I'll never forget yas. You underclassmen, shake their hands as they move outside. Then follow them and form two columns under the goal post out there. Let the seniors run onto the field one by one. But hold up. First I want to mention their names one more time."

Popalinski got choked up, but recovered quickly. He had been around football his whole life and was considered by some as the best broken field runner in Essex

County history. In '36 his 176 points scored in nine games at Bloomfield High was a record no one would break until the last decade of the century. While his coaching record never matched his playing days, today he was speaking from his heart.

Above the bellowing underclassmen's approval, the coach removed his baseball cap in tribute. "In no special order, I love you seniors: Bonaducci, Babula, D'Angelo, Barra, Bartell, McCabe, Kimball, Shoener, Worley, Vitella, Resciniti, Augenbaugh, Riordan, Pinadella, Long, Szep, Metcalfe, Clark, Anderson, Burbank. Underclassmen, lead them down to the field!"

With Doc Ameo's last words of advice to save the adrenalin for the game, the players stormed through the door and across the street to the Park Oval's entrance. The stands now appeared full, but dozens of grammar school kids and family members still lined the path to the ancient concrete steps that would deliver the charged Bellboys to their field of destiny. Guy Galioto stopped the team at the top of the platform overlooking the lake that was once the football field. "Gentlemen, don't forget," he yelled. "Now we form two lines in the end zone so the seniors can make their entrance."

By now it was impossible for the boys of Belleville not to have become totally absorbed into a state of awesome anticipation and euphoria. As they scanned the panorama of blue and gold and maroon and gray, the color and excitement flowing throughout the miniature arena were only slightly dampened by the few umbrellas that were still perched above the wet heads and hats. The bands for the respective schools were competing for the attention of the overflowing crowd. The Belleville's playing of "Across the Field" was creating a dual frenzy on the Bellboy side of the stadium and in the end zone with the players, who were now ready to be led onto the field by Captain Frank Bonaducci, and then Gino right behind him, followed by the rest of the seniors.

The Nutley team had already assembled on the west sidelines, where behind their bench, their loyal band was well into the fabled sound of "The Notre Dame Victory March". With fans still pouring in and around the Oval, the plethora of sight, sound, and emotion was overflowing in everybody's psyche.

Frank scanned the unforgettable scene; from the tops of the trucks supporting dozens of blue-collar locals perched above the covered fences, to the standing room only crowd in the north end zone exploding with anticipation.

Eddie Popalinski put his hand on Frank's right shoulder and turned around to wink at Gino. "Boys, let's show 'em it's our turn this year!"

As Frank led the team out of the end zone toward their sideline, the response was so loud that some younger, less seasoned Bellboys covered the holes on the side of their helmets to protect their ears from the ringing cheers. The upperclassmen were in awe, savoring all that could be absorbed by their young senses.

Frank, the superb athlete, could not have been more motivated to give his greatest performance on this December Saturday. However, he was also a total realist, and by the time he made it to the bench where Doc Ameo sat him down to clean his cleats, he realized he could not slush through a field of mud, snow, and freezing water that day without the Lord's help. Indeed, with normal weather conditions, this could have been the ultimate way for him and Gino to finish their careers. However, with the horrendous reality of mud beneath his shoes, he was reminded life is not always fair. *On this day*, he thought, *a corps of demons must have been in charge of getting the field ready for play.*

At midfield and in the top row of stands on the Belleville side, Rocky Bonaducci also saw that the conditions would make it impossible for Frank and Gino. He thought, *Today, a big play ... or a big mistake will probably make the difference.* Little did he realize how the ultimate result would rest in Frank's own gifted hands.

As Captain, Frank was accompanied by all of the seniors to the center of the field for the coin-flip with the Nutley captains. Fullback, Bob Scrudato, and Jack Chuy, their sure-fire All-State tackle on his way to Clemson on a full scholarship, represented the Maroon Raiders.

The referees huddled to discuss the playing conditions. Frank glanced to the southern end zone where he quickly found Uncle Pete, waving furiously in his direction. Greenie was on his right, and all around him was a menagerie of the boys from Bloomfield Avenue, each less prepared for the weather than the next. Shark skinned suits, pointed black leather shoes, only one wearing an over coat, not one with a hat. Thomas Anthony, captain for the "Five Corner" crew, stood out as the ultimate fashion plate, refuting the very reality of weather suited only for ducks, ... and certainly not the Bloomfield Avenue hoods.

A damp gray cloud of smoke hovered above Pete's entourage, as their Luckies, Camels, White Owls, El Productos, and Hav-a-Tampas hung lazily out of the sides of practically each mouth. Making money gambling, Italian numbers, selling stolen property, and then graduating to the more serious business of Boiardo's empire—these were the plays of their game. Pete "helped 'em out" during the week with catering and other food requests at their social club. But on weekends, the boys were Pete's escorts around Essex County, following his nephew. After all, they had generated big gambling winnings with the Bellboys' uncharacteristic victorious season. On the other hand, because he had a family hero in a game of life called high school football, these wiseguys from mean streets were genuinely happy for Petee Five Corners.

Frank continued his nonchalant 360-degree scan of the packed stadium. Next to his father behind him at midfield, was his mother clutching her cherished prayer card from her father's funeral more than twenty years ago. It vividly depicted the "Sacred Heart of Jesus" and had been with her at every game. Behind her were Sally and Angelo Giardina, the modest, quiet parents of his girlfriend, Maria. Aunt Bella was there looking glamorous as ever in her full-length fur. Uncle Jimmy Quinn and Aunt Pinky were with dozens of their friends from their days at Barringer High. Uncle Caesar Casciano had a handful of his Catholic War Veteran cohorts with him, fresh from their monthly meeting at St. Francis Church, still sporting their now dampened powder blue blazers and caps. Cousin Nicholas Durso and his friends were there only at his insistence. Not being football fans, especially in rain and snow, they'd rather have been in someone's cellar listening and dancing to make-out music. Grandpa Joe was at the center of the Bonaducci crowd. Grandma Mamie had not seen a football game since her Rocky was knocked unconscious as a starting Barringer sophomore up at Phillipsburg in '38. Then Frank smiled as he watched his father's game-time ritual of leaving his seat in the stands to head for the north end zone where he would be traditionally joined by some of the other Bellboy fathers. Only Sneaks Babula was nowhere to be seen. He was "away at college" at ... Rahway State Prison.

Belleville won the coin toss and elected to kick off. An early Nutley fumble in the mud would give the Bellboys great field position. The crowd was delirious in anticipation as the teams assembled on the sidelines. Only the national anthem had to be played. With Nutley's band doing the honors, you could now hear a pin drop as close to 8000 fans from all over the northern Jersey and New York City area stood to honor their country.

As always, Rocky Bonaducci stretched his neck back, his closed eyes facing heavenward. He would fold his arms. For some reason, this position prevented any chance of his crying. Every time "The Star Spangled Banner" could be heard, his mind's eye would drift, embracing the images of his Marine buddies, the ones who never came home from the South Pacific. When it was over, he would refocus upon his son. Yes, he had made it back. The icing on the cake was that Frankie was playing high school football today.

The rain had totally stopped, and the air was getting colder. Belleville's 250-pound place-kicker, Wee Willie Brindisi, dropped his hand signaling the start of the game. He slowly approached the ball from only five yards, focusing his monstrous body's weight into the totally dry pigskin. Trying to ignore the unsure footing, he hit the ball harder than at any time before in this season. The next he knew, he was the first player down in the mud, his huge frame flipping heavenward into an embarrassing flop on his back, obliterating his blue number 55 on the back of his jersey for the rest of the day.

Nutley's junior sensation, tailback Johnny Ippolito, fielded Wee Willie's short kick on his own thirty-yard line. He hesitated a moment, and then decided to try to make it to drier sidelines in front of the Nutley bench. But the mud sucked the strength out of his monstrous thighs, and it seemed as if he was running in slow motion. With the Belleville players heading to him in straight-line waves, he was being hunted down like a wounded duck. Danny McCabe and Bobby Pinadella drove Ippolito into the watery mud, causing a fumble. The crowd went into delirium as Belleville's Fred Augenbaugh recovered. The Bellboy plan had worked, ... first and ten on Nutley's thirty-five!

As the referees dried the ball and set it on a plateau of mud, the stadium became eerily quiet. Everyone watching quickly recognized it was already hard to tell who was who. Maroon, gray, blue, white, and gold had surrendered to black and mud brown. Only the helmets signified differentiation.

Belleville's first series of downs proved to be as horrific as Nutley's kickoff return. Gino slipped on a direct handoff from quarterback Galioto, eventually stumbling for a two-yard loss, without any Nutley linemen touching him. Coach Eddie P. was sending in plays, alternating guards Donny Riordan and Timmy Worley. Working out of the T formation, on second down Galioto reverse-pivoted and quick pitched to his right to Frank. The ball slipped off his fingertips, but Frank dove for it to preserve possession, sliding head first out of bounds and into the Nutley bench. Now it was third down and twenty. Frustrations were starting to mount on both sides of the ball. Light snow had begun to fall. Gino got the call again. This time on a trap off the left hip of his pulling left guard, he saw a moment of daylight, ... only to land face in the mud as he lost his footing again, attempting to accelerate. On fourth down, Coach P took no chances and sent in Lenny Long, Essex County's best punter that year.

"Lenny, don't fumble the snap and keep it inbounds," ordered the coach.

Lenny didn't mishandle Donny Riordan's perfect center, but putting his foot to the pigskin, he met with the same fate as Wee Willie, … on his back for his own mud bath. His short kick gave Nutley possession on the twenty-five yard line, with an official's time out called to clean the ball.

"Gonna be tough today," said Nutley's single wing quarterback, Mickey Geltrudi, shaking his head in the middle of the Maroon Raider huddle.

"Tough for them ya mean, Mickey," retorted Fullback Bob Scrudato. " We've been on the field with tougher teams than Belleville this year."

On the Belleville side, Frank put the defense into their classic 6-3-2 formation, "Hit hard and go for the ball. They'll never hold on."

Nutley would be running their single wing offense for the last time ever in this final game of 1958. Only time would tell if it would be more effective in the mud than Belleville's straight T. Nutley coach, Sandy Philcox, went to his tailback, Johnny Ippolito, on the first two plays, and the Bellboy defense stuffed him twice at the line of scrimmage. While this game should never have been played in the first place, both teams now fully recognized they had to be ready to take advantage of the other's mistake to even have a chance of scoring. Mounting a drive already seemed impossible.

The first half was like an old-fashioned rugby match. Both teams pushed each other up and down the field, without a single first down being achieved. Total frustration was everywhere in the stands, as some of the more experienced fans could be heard yelling out profanities at both school administrations for playing the game in the first place.

As the first half was coming to a close with 0-0 on the scoreboard, Sal Orechio looked at his Police Chief Sam Diminchino and whispered, "Too bad the entire Metropolitan Area has to see these kids on TV at their worst. We should be playing this game tomorrow. It's supposed to get clear tonight. Who the heck gave the 'go'?"

The half finally ended, and each team lumbered to their locker rooms like exhausted water buffaloes. The condensation from their mud soaked and perspired uniforms rose from each of them as they shuffled up the stadium steps. No words were

53

spoken as both teams converged at the top of the edifice. Exhaustion, confusion, and disappointment enveloped everyone.

Local grammar school children, who'd gathered at the locker room doors to see their heroes, seemed to realize that the "supernatural" powers had been drained from the gridiron gladiators. A scoreless tie was in the makings, which would prolong for one more year any bragging rights between the neighboring towns

Outside the men's rest room next to the food stand, Greenie, who'd been in a line so long he figured he'd "never make it", turned to Pete behind him. "Hey, boss. What'a ya think?"

Already on his second pack of cigarettes and in the middle of a puff, Pete didn't hesitate, "Frankie will do something."

Meanwhile, both teams' locker room rest was ignited by identical announcements from their coaches. "New uniforms! You boys who played get dried up and put on these fresh pants and jerseys."

The schools had decided to switch home and away uniforms, which was truly unique in light of substitutes coming off the bench later in the game wearing different color combinations. This "Mud Bowl" was turning into a visual, as well as physical fiasco for all.

Coach Popalinski was anxious. His halftime talk focused on waiting for a Nutley mistake, and then the inevitable feeding of Gino Babula. However, the mud and snow made Gino less a raging bull and more a Bambi whose movements had become paralyzed, as if being frozen in the headlights of a hunter's pickup. On the other hand, Frank had collected close to fifty yards rushing to the sidelines, even though all his runs seemed to end up under the Nutley bench, as he would constantly lose his footing trying to turn the corner to get up field.

The Nutley locker room was quieter. The Raiders were not happy with their performance. Belleville may have been one of the fastest teams they saw all year, but the mud bogged down that advantage. *Why hadn't Nutley's sheer size and power overcome the Bellboys by now* was the question puzzling many.

More of a disciplinarian than Popalinski, Coach Philcox paced in front of his resting team. A cerebral Physics teacher whom the Nutley Board of Education recruited from Scranton, Pennsylvania, … he had an idea. "Boys," he said. "We're gonna get radical. We're gonna start throwin' the ball!"

Assistant coach, Robert "Big Bob" Zwirek, also from the coal mining football factories of Pennsylvania, could not initially believe what he was hearing. But then Philcox continued, "The referees are drying the ball after each play, and no one has thrown a pass." He pointed to Ippolito, his passing and running tailback, "Johnny, make believe its sixty five degrees out there, and we're in the middle of October. You receivers, same vision in your minds. Once you catch it, sprint down the sidelines. The field is dryin' by the minute."

Roger McDonald, whose older brother Frank had been a star at Nutley and the University of Miami in the mid-fifties, smiled, knowing he would be the main target. Their strategy set, Nutley let out a roar. Their coach's positive attitude had become infectious.

The Belleville second half plan did not change from the first. Get the ball up field with Frank to the outside, and then put Gino into the end zone.

Nutley chose to receive the second half kickoff. As Bob Scrudato fielded the ball and drove straight up field, flattening two would-be Belleville tacklers on their backs, the Nutley stands erupted.

"O.K., Raiders, you know what we're gonna do," said quarterback Geltrudi, as he gathered his teammates into the huddle. "Coach Sandy says throw, … and that's just what Johnny Ippolito is gonna do. Wing right, twenty nine-sweep pass. Roger, remember, it's October, and the ball is dry."

Geltrudi broke the huddle and called the signals. Center Charlie D'Piro softed the dry ball into the small hands of Ippolito. The junior tailback ran wide as if to be looking to sprint to the drier sidelines. *Coach Philcox must be a genius. The ball is dry!*

Roger McDonald followed Zwirek's trick advice: "Make believe ya slip, but when ya go down, keep your fists clenched so ya don't soil your hands. Then sprint to the sidelines, and Johnny will hit ya over your inside shoulder. The Belleville kid will take your fake fall and think it's a run."

Frank Bonaducci had not said a word at halftime. A quiet leader, he was also too exhausted. However, that fatigue forced him to wonder what Nutley might spring in the second half. And for all of Sandy Philcox's same reasons, Frank, too, was guessing, *Pass!*

55

As Johnny Ippolito rolled right as if to run, he saw McDonald had regained his footing and was now churning towards the open corner about twenty yards up field. Defensive halfback, Joey Vitella, took the fake fall, and was sprinting toward Ippolito. McDonald seemed destined to be open. Could this be the magic Nutley needed on this impossible day in December of 1958?

Ippolito saw the opportunity and began to slow his approach to the line of scrimmage, as he came face to face with the small, but tough Vitella. Johnny softly lofted the ball in McDonald's direction as he and Vitella collided. The perfect spiral stunned the crowd to silence. *How could anyone be passing today?*

The only flaw with Coach Philcox's plan was that he didn't know enough about Frank Bonaducci. He fully appreciated that on a dry field with a healthy ankle, Frank could be Essex County's finest all-around back. But the Nutley coach had no idea how it was for this youngster to be born into the house of a Marine in 1942, where, when his dad returned home safely to his wife and first-born son, not a day would go by without Frank listening to Rocky Bonaducci talk about football and the U.S. Marines. That kind of home culture has a tendency to develop leaders out of young boys, and, indeed, thinking two-way football players. Maybe Rocky Bonaducci had missed his calling as a football coach and teacher when he prematurely left Bergen Jr. College to earn fifty dollars per week as a butcher with his brother-in-law. On the other hand, his talent to impart his experience and wisdom into his children was never lost or compromised. With that kind of home coaching, Frank might just as well have been in the Nutley locker room at halftime. Now was the time to make some history, and for Frank and others to be reminded once again that God still answers prayer, … but you had better be careful about what you pray for.

Frank played the other defensive halfback position opposite Vitella. With their single wing unbalanced to their right, Frank cheated into the center of the field, guessing that Nutley could never get up enough speed for someone to reverse back to the left. He also was figuring "pass", because nothing else had worked for either team. Also, the ball and players would never be drier than on the second half's first play. Unlike Vitella, he didn't get tricked by McDonald's fall. With all other players slipping and sliding in the middle of the field, Frank sprinted to where he felt the big receiver was headed. Never seeing Bonaducci, Ippolito launched the ball. Bonaducci loped through the mud at mid-field and leaped in front of the taller McDonald. INTERCEPTION!

The dry football in Frank's hands seemed almost surreal, as did the drying, yet frozen grass beyond the hash mark. Frank experienced a moment of spiritual revelation; *God does answer prayer.*

With his foot touching down on Belleville's forty-yard line, Frank quickly looked up field with only the prone Ippolito blocking a sixty-yard sprint down the Belleville sideline. In his head, Frank heard a scriptural quote his mother always recited: "The steps of a righteous man are ordered by God."

Frank also recalled Jo-Jo's pre-game advice: "Hug the sidelines, Frankie."

Ippolito recovered from Vitella's tackle, as Frank leaped skyward, avoiding any contact with the shocked tailback. Belleville fans were delirious. With number 7 heading to the end zone, the Nutley contingent was stunned into a frustrating and helpless silence. The pass was about to become "Philcox's Folly" in the eyes of his critics who felt a better coach would have had the Maroon Raiders undefeated in '58. Indeed, there was nothing between Frank Bonaducci and the red southeast goal line flag at the Park Oval; nothing except his big heart and a vision he could not ignore in his mind's eye.

It seemed like slow motion to many there that day as Belleville's would-be hero headed into a realm reserved only for legends. The spiritual Marietta, watching her first born as the object of eight thousand pairs of eyes, sensed a battle in the heavenlies ensuing, ... a collision of kingdoms. While corps of angels had engulfed the stadium at that moment, answering her daylong call, legions of demons had swooped down as well; a colossal battle was at its climax as her Frank crossed the ten-yard line, now only having to trot to his historic touchdown. Heading directly toward Uncle Pete and his Bloomfield Avenue supporters, who were already tearing down the wooden fence keeping the spectators off the playing field, the lingering image that had secretly been haunting Frank all week was now materializing into its fulfillment. Could this be it? The only score of the day was at hand, soon to give Belleville a convincing edge and the ultimate victory? On the other hand, Frank's vision was not yet of the finality of a Bellboy win. He was not running for a touchdown on this muddy, snowy Saturday in 1958; he was running to legendary immortality.

None of the shocked Maroon Raiders had gained on Frank. Mickey Geltrudi picked himself out of the mud and was at least five yards behind. Paul Pucci, one of Nutley's gutsiest linemen, was approaching at a slight angle from the muddiest center of the field. Left tackle Jack Chuy, destined for eventual greatness in the National Football League, screamed when he saw the interception, frightening everyone around him. Yet, he did not explode toward Frank. He would have had to cross the entire middle of the mud bowl of water and ice. Instead he headed straight up the hash mark on his side, running parallel. He figured that his only chance was the freezing and slightly drier path, even if it was the longer route. Completely crazed, he mindlessly forced his 235- pound frame to steamroll down the gridiron, on the opposite side.

Known to sprint to the back of the end zone for every touchdown since his freshman days, Frank incredibly slowed down at the eight-yard line, even seeming to look back. This move allowed Geltrudi to leap at Bonaducci, only to have the agile running back sidestep the futile tackling attempt, sending Geltrudi sliding head first into the wooden fence. Frank was now completely turned around at the four-yard line, waving the ball from side to side in his right hand. Unbelievable, he had stopped short of the goal line! Belleville and Nutley fans were uncontrollable, with most thinking that he had already scored. Only those immediately on top of the scene at the corner of the field beheld the truth—he had not yet cross over for the touchdown.

More than one hundred yards away at the opposite end zone, Rocky could not believe his eyes. He knew his son would never celebrate such a run by waving the ball. Around him, the other fathers were also confused.

"Rock, what's goin' on? What's he doin'?

Incredulous, he whispered to himself, "It can't be. No, Frank, take it in yourself."

"What's this kid doin'?" fans gasped.

Frank Bonaducci, who seemed frozen at the four-yard line, was scanning the field … for number 22, his friend, … Gino Babula.

Nutley's Pucci hit Frank high, but he shed his tackle, buying a few more moments. The entire Belleville team was rushing at him, some believing he had already scored. Gino was in the pack, but well behind Wee Willie, who now understood what Frank was trying to do, and thought he just might kill his childhood friend, if he got to him first.

By now, Frank's strategy had dawned on Gino, whose heart was leaping in anticipation of scoring and winning the County Scoring Championship. But could he get there before Wee Willie and Jack Chuy, the game's two biggest players, who seemed destined to meet at Frank's chest?

Frank saw Brindisi speeding at him, and he seemed to be yelling, "Get your butt into the end zone, Frankie, ... or I swear I'll kill ya."

Chuy's run over the icy mix and drier turf had given him traction no one had experienced all day. Making a ninety-degree cut at the goal line, he sped toward Frank, who had not even noticed his approach. If Wee Willie hit Frank first, it would be a touchdown, ... if it was Chuy, the score would be prevented. As for Gino, Frank would now have to lateral over the rest of the approaching horde to get him the ball.

All Frank saw were Wee Willie and the out-of-breath Gino galloping his way, as Chuy leaped toward him from behind. At the same time, Brindisi also vaulted at Bonaducci. Like two missiles approaching from opposite directions, each were aimed at destroying Frank and his plan. For Chuy, it was to prevent a touchdown or the lateral to Babula. Brindisi's sole mission was to propel Frank into the end zone himself.

Totally blindsided, Chuy's hit stunned number 7. Then milliseconds later, Brindisi crashed into Frank so hard the ball jarred loose. Close to 500 pounds of Belleville-Nutley linemen careening into his side and chest lifted Frank into the air at the three-yard line, as the ball sailed out of bounds! He went soaring into the wooden fence beyond the sidelines with Chuy still clutching him, like a rabid junkyard dog that finally saw the opportunity to rip apart its intruder. Brindisi had burrowed into the mud, knowing that he had failed in his attempt to bring a sane end to Bonaducci's emotional gesture.

An eerie hush came over the packed stadium. Time was standing still. Chuy, Nutley's finest two-way lineman since Sammy Stellatella of Penn State fame, had surely hurt Bonaducci. Indeed, the bizarre play had come to an end without a score, giving Nutley a reprieve. Underneath Chuy, Bonaducci was motionless. The Park Oval fans stood speechless. His teammates hovered over him. Wee Willie, lifting his mud-caked body out of the four-yard line mire, was disgusted. Gino seemed embarrassed and walked around in circles. The referees called a time out to fully check Frank's condition.

Slowly the volume of human sounds seemed to resurrect as the thousands of witnesses gradually processed what they had all viewed. Whether voicing support for the Bellboy's good field position, expressing disbelief for Frank's decision, or simply Nutley's elation for their good fortune, the common emotion seemed to be that of confusion. As the Nutley fans finally recognized no score had occurred, their band fed their hope with the Notre Dame fight song. After all, they had achieved the impossible—stopping Belleville from scoring when Frank could have walked over the goal line!

Coach Eddie Popalinski threw his clipboard to the ground in despair when it became apparent what had happened. He ran to the crowd of players surrounding Frank's prone body, only to slip on his back, joining the game's other mud hens for the day. Getting to his feet, he quickly recoiled, as if the fall calmed him down. "Boys, get in the huddle. It's our ball on the four."

While Frank did not score, the reality of his interception and Belleville's possession just short of the goal line rekindled hope in the Bellboys. The near perpetual crowd roar was returning to recreate the pandemonium that existed before Frank's interception. Definitely groggy, Frank was helped up by several teammates as the Nutley defense assembled near the goal line.

"We're all right, Frank. First and goal on the four," said Vinnie Szep, the senior two-way guard, gathering his teammates to huddle.

Fred Augenbaugh, Brindisi's fellow tackle, was less charitable. "Frank, let's go, … and don't try that again."

To lighten up the tension, Galioto gestured that he had a "secret touchdown play" to call. The junior quarterback confirmed Coach Popalinski's encouraging thought. "Only four yards to go, boys."

Dragging himself to the huddle, Wee Willie had nothing to say to Frank. In fact, he would never bring the subject up to his battered friend again until late that night at the Victory Dance.

Frank surprised everyone as he regained his senses and composure as the Captain. "We've got four downs to get Gino in. No sweat." Looking to Galiota, he asked, "What play does Coach P. have for us, Guy? Call it, Cuz."

The other Bellboys look curiously at each other with Frank's use of the term, "Cuz". Known mostly for his modesty, his teammates recognized that when Frank Bonaducci referred to someone or a group of guys as "Cuz", he determinedly meant business. Surely, if he was remorseful about what he had just tried to do for Gino, it wasn't showing up in his word choice. This rekindled the speedy Belleville team's spirit. They were now ready for their next play. Unfortunately, Nutley's Maroon Raiders were just as prepared.

On Belleville's sidelines, Coach Popalinski and his veteran assistants kicked around strategies. Athletic Director, Hiram Wilhelm, who doubled as the basketball coach, suggested Galioto fake to Gino and roll right on a quarterback keeper. Defensive coach, Tim Testa, former Montclair High and Montclair State College All American end, was more forceful. "Coach, everybody's expecting Babula. Let's not make the same mistake Frankie just did. Anything but Gino inside here."

Popalinski listened to neither. Sy Dorfman and Les Glicken in *The Newark Star Ledger* had compared Gino to when Coach Eddie was crisscrossing Essex gridirons back in the thirties as the greatest broken field runner in Bloomfield High School history. "No, let's give Gino a chance now," he finally said.

With the wind picking up and snow now falling lightly, a bone-chilling reaction came over Frank in the huddle. *Suppose Nutley stops us? Will this seal my own fate as that Belleville player who took the game into his own hands and threw it away?* Frank shook his head as if to confirm a "no" answer to his own question. No matter what, he was still convinced his sacrifice of personal stardom was the right thing to do. And when right end Don Schoner arrived in the huddle with the play, Frank got back in focus.

That Saturday afternoon in early December of 1958, Coach Ed Popalinski would instruct quarterback Gaetano "Guy" Galioto to give Gino the ball on four straight plays. Failing on the first three, Gino then picked up a huge block from squatty left guard Billy McCabe, and saw daylight to the end zone. Nutley linebacker Benny Hyland hurled his body into a helmet-to-helmet collision at the one, stunning Babula and forcing him upright. The hit was all Manny Vecchio needed to stuff Gino under his chin. The ball and Gino went down with just inches from the goal line. No touchdown!

Nutley would go on to win that game that became known as "The Mud Bowl" by a score of 13-0. They would take control of the contest from the discouraged and smaller Bellboys. The speed, power, and spirit of Belleville's finest had been neutralized by the inclement conditions at Nutley's Park Oval. The glimmer of hope in Frank Bonaducci's interception run had been extinguished by the courage of his selfless heart.

When the gun signaled the end of the game, Nutley's students stormed the field to congratulate the victors. The vanquished Belleville team just stood silent. Wee Willie cried as they quietly filed out of the Park Oval onto Chestnut Street at the north section of the stadium. Few noticed the one player at midfield, crouched on his hands and knees in the cold mud. Caked in slimy dirt from helmet to cleats, steam rose slowly from his drenched uniform and body. Like a wild animal that had met his match in the jungle of life, this fighter was wounded, struggling to regain strength to face the reality that his enemy had, indeed, triumphed. No one was coming to his assistance. Few could distinguish his profile from the brown killing field. While the weather had finally warmed, a steady rain had returned. It was 4 PM, and the darkness of winter was setting in. Frank's body was beginning to cramp as the cold, fatigue, confusion, and frustration took their final toll. Little did anyone know that Frank Bonaducci was not only battling the gut-wrenching moment, but also talking to his Creator, asking, *Why?*

Finally lifting his bowed head, Frank made out three solitary figures under the southern end zone goal post—Greenie, Thomas Anthony, and Uncle Pete in the middle.

"Pete, let's go help Frankie out," suggested Anthony.

Thomas Anthony was not just another of Richie Boiardo's up-and-comers. He was destined for big things in New Jersey's world of organized crime. His Italian surname had been changed from Antonelli when his father arrived in the First Ward back in the early 1900's. Born "Thomas Anthony", his friends called him Tony, and with the new Anthony last name, he became tagged as … "Two Tones". However, this trite reference to his name never diminished the respect he earned "protecting" the five-corner neighborhood of Pete Frassa and his family. Only more prolific than the value of his wardrobe was the flock of females who followed him around Newark like a celebrity. Tall and lean with a thin angular face, he combed his wavy black hair incessantly. A kind, soft, melodious voice betrayed his illegal lifestyle and made him even sexier to the girls than his Hollywood looks. And Two Tone's swagger, even in the Park Oval mud that day, always got people's attention. It was pure Bloomfield Avenue, Newark, New Jersey, … mid-fifties style.

"Two Tones we can't go out there," insisted Pete, who always considered the football fields his brother-in-law and his nephew played on as hollowed and sacred ground upon which <u>he</u> could never tread.

Greenie jumped in, "Hey, Pete, not worried about your shoes are ya? Two Tones' flyweights alone are wert more than your car and your butcher business combined, and he's goin' out dare."

"The kid's hurtin', Five Corners," said Anthony.

Pete nodded.

The trio resembled Bloomfield Avenue's version of the Tin Man, the Scarecrow, and the Lion. Under his mohair coat, Two Tones suit was so shiny; it seemed to reflect the Nutley street lights that were now on. Lanky Greenie looked more like a visiting farmer whose long shirtsleeves jutted out of his butcher shop jump suit. His red Irish face, sagging jowls, and a long cigarette that always seemed to be perpendicular to the ground were his trademarks, along with being fidgety to the point of irritating anyone near him. Always less than courageous, Pete timidly waddled behind.

It was a fifty-yard walk through the mud before the three street guys reached down to help Frank up. Two Tones spoke first. "Hold your head up high, kid. We might have lost money on ya today, but all the guys from the Five Corners are proud of ya."

Greenie added, "You're the best, Frankie."

At this moment, Pete acted more like a mature uncle than the mesmerized fan he had been for four years. "Frank," he said. "Your mother and father are waitin' by the bus for ya. Maria, too. Let's get ya up." As they pulled him to his feet, all Frank could do was shake their hands, … and hug his uncle. Then Pete reminded his nephew: "Ya had a great year. Greenie clocked ya at 101 yards today, … top rusher. No one in the world had a bigger heart than ya did today, kid. Now get to the bus, and let's get ya home."

As he was escorted toward the Belleville crowd gathering around the school buses, Frank was feeling numb, when he looked to see Gino approaching. Other than the odd threesome from Bloomfield Avenue, no one had said anything to Frank since the game ended. He was shivering. The emotion of the day and the moment was forbidding him from focusing. Frank and Gino embraced, but didn't speak, and then hobbled side by side off to the asphalt driveway.

A small group of Nutley grammar school boys were waiting. "Hey, Frank, thanks for givin' us the win."

"Number 7 played for Nutley today, boys." they chuckled.

Deflated Bonaducci had no reaction, but Gino swung his helmet, just missing a couple of the eighth graders. The Nutley police, witnessing the tense moment, rushed to the Belleville backs to prevent any further encounter. Commissioner

Orechio saw what happened and went after his town's youngsters. "If you kids ever have half the courage of Frank Bonaducci and Gino Babula, Nutley will never lose another football game. Now get your fannies home!"

Rocky, Marietta, and Maria stood stoically at the bus door. Marietta first hugged Gino and said his mother had to leave because she was chilled. But she assured that Mrs. Babula had promised some hot soup would be waiting for him at home. Gino sheepishly acknowledged the affection and interest expressed by his running mate's mother. As always with Gino, Marietta was warm, friendly, and almost perky. After all, Sylvia and Sneaks Babula were friends from the old neighborhood. Their absence from the moment hurt the mother's heart of Marietta. In addition, she was hiding turmoil in her for Frank. She was convinced God must have been angry with her and today had taken that out on her son.

Rocky shook Gino's hand, as he tried to encourage the two fallen heroes. "You guys are still the best I've seen since the Key brothers from Barringer, just before me. Gino, great year, kid."

Maria embraced Frank. Drenched in her cheerleading uniform despite the Belleville Fire Department hooded canvas covering, she would wait to talk with him about the drama of the day. Always the practical organizer who would save her observations for a private moment, she coolly informed him she would be waiting with his family at 711 Belmont Avenue. She kissed his cheek. "You OK, Frank?"

He nodded.

While Gino was already on the warm bus, Rocky's Marine Corp grip would not let go of Frank's hand. A lump filled his throat. "They were tough. On a dry day you would'a had 'em. I was talkin' to Orechio. Ya know he's a big fan of yours. Said if it wasn't for the mud, you gain 200 yards, and Belleville wins."

Frank smiled. As tough as he was growing up on Lake Street and Seventh Street in Newark, Rocky was a real softie at heart, and Frank knew it better than anyone. He replied, "Thanks, Dad."

Then Rocky pulled Frank aside, looking around to make sure that no one could hear. "Frank," he said, "it was a great moment, that thing that ya did. Never saw anything like it. You're special."

Closing the bus door as Frank finally entered, Vinnie leaned over and clasped Frank's right hand with both of his. He said nothing, but squeezed as if to say he would never forget him and Gino for what Frank did that day. Vinnie would regard it forever as the ultimate show of love, self-sacrifice, and friendship.

As Frank gazed over his teammates, coaches, and the rest of the staff huddled in their seats, not a word was being said. The stench from the exhaust fumes, adhesive tape, mentholated rub, mud, and sweat almost overpowered Frank as he dragged his weary body down the aisle before Gino signaled his place to sit.

Then Doc Ameo announced, "All right, boys. Vinnie's taking us home."

The Belleville police escort was getting in place in front of Vinnie's vehicle. The other buses carrying the band, cheerleaders, and twirlers were now pulling out. With all precipitation having finally ceased, hundreds of Belleville and Nutley fans were still lingering on Chestnut Street, trying to get a final glimpse of the fallen Bellboys. The completely fogged in bus gave the team the privacy they needed.

Everything seemed interminable to Frank. He could not wait to return to Clearman Field, take a hot shower, and then get to the protection of his home and family.

Quiet talk began to brew. Reaching across Gino, Frank rubbed the window's condensation to get an idea of what was causing a delay. Beyond the faceless crowd, Frank could see his Uncle Pete on the pay phone in front of the Elks' Club on the opposite side of the street. *Who could he be calling now?* Frank wondered. *All the family was at the game. Perhaps Grandma Frassa? But, she's never been a football fan.*

Frank chuckled the more he thought, gaining the attention of the equally exhausted Gino. "The bookies," Frank said.

Gino nodded in agreement.

CHAPTER 5

"... FOR OLD TIME'S SAKE."

Vinnie ground the bus into gear, and it began to roll away. Frank got a closer glimpse. Pete seemed not to be speaking into the phone, but Frank's emotional and physical hurts were too significant at that point to care. He closed his eyes and slowly placed his wet head back against the cracked leather seat.

Finally after ten rings, Pete's call was answered. "Rahway State Prison. Who's dis?"

"It's Petee Five Corners."

"Hold on." The voice on the receiving end asked no further questions.

There was a pause, and then another person could be heard. "Five C's, dat you?" The cooperative prison guard had given the phone to anxious Gino Babula, Sr.

"Mr. Babula, it's Peter Frassa, ... Five Corners."

"It's about time, Pete. How'd Gino do? Did he get it?"

"Mr. Babula, they lost thirteen nuttin'."

Sneaks was shocked, disappointed, and angered. "No way! What happened, Petee, Five C's?"

"They were too tough and too big, Mr. Babula." Pete spoke with respect and formality as if it were the first time the local butcher and the Boiardo underboss had ever talked. In reality, Pete's assignment each Saturday that autumn had been updating the incarcerated father of Mr. Inside as to his son's exploits and that of the Belleville Bellboys. On this day, Pete was fearful of Babula's response. On the other hand, besides Sneak's reputation in the world of wiseguys, Pete knew him as the first helper his father ever hired in his butcher shop back when the young Babula arrived from Sicily. It had been Sneak's only legitimate job, and it was Frassa Sr. who gave Sneak's his first new pair of sneakers. Sneaks served Mr. Frassa honestly and faithfully until the butcher died suddenly one day in the young immigrant's arms. Already a City League star at that time, but beginning to "get involved" with the neighborhood guys, Sneaks promised Frassa Sr. as he lay dying to watch over Pete and Marietta, and never allow his son to leave the butcher business for anything illegitimate. Other than assigning Pete some harmless "chores" around Fifth Street and Bloomfield Avenue, Sneaks lived up to his commitment.

"Give me the rest of the story, Five-C's," commanded Babula.

Pete went on to detail Frank's decision to wait at the goal line for Gino to lateral him the ball to get his touchdown. When he finished, there was silence on the other end.

"Ya there, Mr. Babula?"

"Petee, Five Corners, first of all, start calling me Sneaks. I know you since you weighed under a hundred pounds. That's a long time ago. Second of all, I can't believe what your nephew tried to do for my Gino. God almighty!"

"Well, Mr. Babula, they're both good kids."

"Pete, my name's Sneaks! Sneaks from the old days, … just after the boat." He relaxed, and then continued, "Now, I want you to listen."

Pete held his breath. He was shivering. While all precipitation had stopped, his clothing was limp from the elements of the day. *What's he gonna say?* Pete thought. There was no voice on the other end. "Ya there, Sneaks?"

"Five Corners, how's Madiett?" The benevolent Newark mobster never forgot that cute little girl with flowing auburn curls, always behind her father's butcher store counter with her hand in the jar of pickled pigs' feet. If he ever failed in his commitment about keeping Pete straight, it would be a feisty sister that Sneaks would have to deal with.

"She's O.K., but I don't know yet how she's handlin' what Frankie did." Pete was surprised by Sneak's interest in Marietta. Unbeknownst to anyone, he had been calling the Boiardo kingpin since September, and Sneaks had never once asked about Marietta. Babula always was a man of few words. Pete could never truly fathom the debt Sneaks so strongly felt to his father for fulfilling Richie "The Boot" Boiardo's request to employ his young protégé during the Depression years.

Sneaks paused again. "Listen to me, Five Corners, and listen good." Pete swallowed hard. "You tell your sister and her hard-headed handsome husband that Frankie's college education is taken care of. Hopefully, both kids get full boats. God only knows Frankie and Gino deserve scholarships. But if anything goes wrong, make sure Madiett knows the money's there. I know she's a worrier."

"Jesus, Mr. Babula," was all Pete could blurt out.

"Tell her I'll get the details to her. Then tell my old friend, Rocco, not to be so prideful and lily white on this thing. In fact, Petee Five-C's, tell your brother-in-law that what his kid did for my kid, neither him nor me would do in the old days." Sneaks paused. "Ya hear me, Pete?"

Rocky had played at Barringer after Sneak's big years at Central High, but they came to know each other in the semi-pro football leagues in New York and Jersey right after the war. Sneaks was with the legendary Biase brothers and their Newark Tornadoes club. Rocky split college time with the Paterson Panthers up at Hinchcliff Stadium. They spoke on few occasions during that time. Sneaks was making an off-the-field name for himself in Boiardo's organization within "Capo de tutti capi" Carlo Gambino's powerful crime family. Rocky was playing college ball on Saturdays, pro on Sundays, and attending classes on the GI Bill, as well as making no money with Pete in the butcher business. Common ground for Rocky and Sneaks was football and the Frassa store. Many times Babula tried to convince Rocky that "helping out" on Bloomfield Avenue could make him the real money he needed for his young family. Rocky always respectfully declined. Then in the early fifties Babula tied Rocky to a Carmine Bonaducci of Brooklyn by figuring out this was the Newarker's first cousin. In his relentless attempts to reel in Rocky, Sneaks only once referred to that cousin's involvement in New York's rackets. Rocky walked away, never to speak to Sneaks again.

Pete was overwhelmed with Sneaks' benevolence. "That's <u>really</u> generous, Mr. Babula." Then he chuckled, "And I'll make sure to tell my brother-in-law you were askin' for him." Pete was hoping that the conversation was over. His feet were still frozen with the Park Oval mud.

But Sneaks was not quite finished. "Listen Five-C's, you can't put a price tag on what Frankie tried to do. My family and my people will never forget. And Pete, thanks for all the calls this year. I gotta go."

Pete hung up the phone. Standing motionless, his entire body ached from the wet and cold. But, his emotions were fired up by Babula's gesture. He thought of his sister and smiled. Then an image of the father he so missed, good-hearted and hard working, flashed across his mind, ... and tears welled up.

Pete began to think, *Hey, Pop, you were good to this guy when he was a kid. You didn't ask The Boot questions. Ya helped out, ... out of the goodness of your big heart. As Madiett always says, "What goes around, comes around". Well, Pop, it came around today for the grandson you never got to meet.* He shook his head in awe and choked up with emotion.

The freezing stupor engulfing Pete melted when his Cadillac pulled up with its favorite driver. Greenie rolled down the passenger side window. "Hey, Boss, ya gonna die of pneumonia if ya don't get in my limo. Ya done?"

Pete gave his friend a classic Ralph Kramden look of disdain. "Of course I'm done, Greenie. Do you see me on the phone any more? Where ya been?"

"Pete, ya just finished with Sneaks. I've been across the street watchin' ya all the time," he said, to show he wasn't sleeping on the job. "Service at your doorstep, Five Corners. Jump in, and let's get back to Bloomfield Avenue. We gotta pay up."

Pete smiled and stepped into the car.

The conversation with Sneaks would not be shared with Marietta until several weeks later on January 1, 1959. And apart from that day, Pete would never mention it to anyone else, ... ever.

CHAPTER 6

"POST GAME PLANS"

It was after 5 PM, and the December Saturday's early darkness seemed to usher in spirits of depression Rocky only infrequently entertained. The weather had changed one more time, with gray clouds rushing across the Belleville landscape at Clearman Field, fueled by warmer winds from the southwest. Leaning against his Chevy, trying to enjoy a Lucky, he kept mentally replaying Frank's interception run. While many parents congratulated Rocky on Frank's fine season as they picked up their sons, not one mentioned the play. In spite of his lonely contemplation, the feisty legion of demons could not crack Rocky's spirit of survival and positive expectancy. He shook his head, smiled, and thought, *Maybe Frank's decision was actually the answer to my prayer: "Lord, make Frankie do today what I could not do." Something good will surely come of this!* The spirits of depression and remorse had similar discernment. They took flight to pester someone else.

It seemed Frank was going to be last out of the locker room. As crest fallen Guy Galioto finally made his exit, he walked up to Rocky. Guy was only a junior, but he had been Frank's quarterback almost every year since midget football. Rocky nodded and patted the stocky teen's wet head. "You're gonna have an even better season next year, Gaetano."

Appearing from his car across the street, Rusty, Guy's father, struggled for a positive comment. Not really knowing what to say, he forced out what he truly believed: "Rock, your kid has always set a great example for my Gaetano, especially today. Frankie's gonna do great in college."

Determined to steer the conversation as far as possible from the interception run, Rocky quipped, "I hope so, Rusty. But no matter where he goes, I bet he never meets another red-headed Italian quarterback." Guy's bushy red locks were inherited from his dad who reached to shake Rocky's hand.

Now the Galiotos were gone, and Rocky was growing slightly impatient as he made the short walk across the muddy field to the locker room. At the door, he suddenly came face-to-face with Coach Popalinski whose arm was on Frank's shoulder, apparently reassuring him about his chances of playing football in college.

Caught off guard, Rocky spoke out of nervousness. "Mr. P, it didn't turn out the way we wanted it, but you had your greatest season." Subconsciously, Rocky was also wondering, *Should I try to make some sorta apology for my kid's decision, or should I keep my mout shut to see what Coach P. has to say?*

When Popalinski spoke, it was unexpected. "Mr. Bonaducci, we should start thinking about colleges."

What? Rocky thought. *No mention of the interception run disaster?*

Securing the locker room door, the coach continued, "I told Frank that Yale and Cornell are really interested. His grades should make it. Besides, both schools love our Big Ten Conference here in Essex County. First of all, Cornell appreciates we sent them Georgie Plenge a couple of years ago. The kid really matured up there. And before Georgie, it was Tommy Steffanelli at Yale. So, two plusses for Frank."

Rocky beamed over his kid's name being linked with the Ivy Leaguers.

The coach added other positives. "And ya know what, men? Bloomfield's Tony Pascal and Clifton's George Telesh are doing great right now up at Cornell. And remember that Billy DeGraaf from Clifton, too. He's still a legend up there. I like Frank's chances at Cornell best, Mr. Bonaducci."

"Ya really think he can get in, Coach?" Rocky asked.

"I did tell Frank we better have a couple of backups. Lehigh, Delaware, and maybe my old school, North Carolina State. But my place is a factory. Frankie could get lost down there. Plus, he's Italian; you know what I mean, Mr. Bonaducci."

"Yea, Italian kids from Jersey in the Bible Belt? I don't think so. Like oil and water. He'll be lucky if he makes it on the field." Rocky was incredulous about this upbeat conversation, given the game's result. However, the Belleville coach was not finished.

"Listen, Rock, inside I told your kid that he's special. He showed me things over the last four years I could never do, with or without the football. He must take after his mother, 'cause I don't think you could'a done them either." His one and only comment about the interception mishap then followed the backhanded compliment. "I told him to loosen up in the future and enjoy the game more, ... his life, too. Don't be so serious. Think a little more about himself. That thing today with Gino, ... we all wanted it for him. But, next time do it for yourself, Frank." Frank was head down, staring at his mud-caked motorcycle boots. "You and Gino were my best ever, inside and out. But, I'm telling you to look forward and finish it off strong in college." Turning back to Rocky, the coach concluded, "This was a big year for Gino, but Frankie's got the head for college. No reason he can't make it big there."

Rocky figured he and his son had dodged a bullet. Eddie P. could have gone into a tirade about Frank's play. They all shook hands, agreeing to continue conversation together again once Frank finished his applications and the holidays were over.

The Bonaduccis gratefully walked to the '49 Chevy Rocky had idling. After weeklong cold weather, he didn't want to take any chances it wouldn't start. By now, the car was toasty with the heater at full blast. Settling his hands on the steering wheel's leather covering, Rocky took a deep breath and prepared to give Frank his final fatherly view of the roller coaster day. Before he could utter a word, his son shocked him.

Usually stoic and sometimes high-strung, the seventeen-year old uncharacteristically broke down and cried uncontrollably. His father wasn't sure how to react. His role in the family had always been to teach by telling stories. Rocky needed Marietta who was always more capable at handling situations like this. He just had no words. Frank supplied them. "Dad, what a jerk I am."

Rocky was expecting the first signs of the remorse with which Frank would have to live a lifetime. What he next heard was totally unanticipated by the hardened Purple Heart veteran.

Between sobs, Frank continued, "If I had just seen Chuy. Then I would have made him miss, jumped over Wee Willie, and flipped the ball to Gino. He was right there. Crap, I didn't look left. Where did he come from?"

Rocky sat stunned. His son was still not accepting the obvious alternative of just scoring himself! The confused father thought, *Whose kid is this anyway? The touchdown was his. He looks for his buddy, and they never score. No regrets?*

"We would've lost anyway, Dad. Maybe not if it was dry. But I never got hit so hard in my life."

Rocky knew his son was right. *Maybe if he scored, they still would have lost. Yea, I feel better. They were gonna lose anyway.* Regardless, Rocky had to respond to Frank's crying. "Daddy," said Rocky, "You did what I and few others could do. You did the right thing."

Putting the car in gear, Rocky had been honest with his son, … at least partially. He could never have accomplished what Frank had done. He was being less candid about his added remark, "…you did the right thing." Down deep he believed Frank chose wrongly. For sure, he knew his wife was totally tormented about what their son had done.

The two remained silent as the spunky car slid from side to side on slushy roads. *Maybe we just drop the subject,* thought Rocky, who was simultaneously marveling at how well his vehicle was performing, particularly with its trademark bald tires.

"Hey, Dad, no snow tires on yet?" was Frank's tongue in cheek question about what his mom and dad would never buy.

"Ah, it's early yet," said Rocky. "Never snowed this soon before. Uncle Pete's supposed to drop off some chains tomorrow. We'll see."

Pausing at the hilltop traffic light where Franklin met Joralemon, Rocky and his son glanced over at the Milk Bar on the corner. Even sealed in their car, both Bonaduccis could not escape the aroma of grilling hamburgers, French fries, and fresh coffee wafting out of the wooden barn-like eatery. Salivating, Rocky reached into his shirt pocket for a usual post-meal Lucky to light up after the imagined taste of a juicy burger smothered in onions and ketchup. When he realized he was out of the unhealthy, habitual sticks, his fidgety fingers began to tap the steering wheel.

Not a parking space was in sight, and local teens lined up outside in the cold, waiting for a seat. Belleville High may not have been well known for sending scores of students to college in the fifties, but its reputation was renown for its number of "souped up" cars for which its part-time working male students seemed to be able to drum up the money. Chopped-top Mercs, balloon-skirted and nosed Fords, and a bevy of '56 and '57 Chevys were all over the Milk Bar lot.

Since young George Plenge's return from Cornell with multiple new ideas to try in the family business, the restaurant and grill revenues had been going through the roof. The Nutley crowd's post-game hangout was Rutt's Hutt in Clifton. But all of Belleville would stop in after the game at the Milk Bar to at least nurse a shake while making plans for the rest of the weekend.

Rocky suggested stopping to pick up the gallon of milk Marietta needed. Also in mind was a possible impromptu meeting with George Jr., so Frank might stress his further interest in going to Cornell, possibly encouraging a written recommendation from the Ivy League alumnus. When his father broached the idea, Frank squirmed and started to complain of stomach cramps. "No, Dad, let's get home."

Rocky persistented. "Hey, Frank, if you're hungry as me, you can't ignore the smell of them burgers. At least let's get a couple to take home."

"Dad, Maria's at home, Ma's probably making tomato pie (pizza), … and I just don't want to see anyone yet."

"Maybe you're right." His father seemed to agree. Then, speaking up, Rocky asked, "Hey, Frank, isn't that Gino's car?"

"No, Dad, Gino's Bonneville is brand new." Then Frank reminded Rocky that Sneaks delivered his son a jet-black Pontiac for his five-TD performance against Irvington. "Besides, Dad, when I asked what Gino was going to do after the game, he told me he was so cold, he was heading home to hug one of his mother's radiators!"

Finally Rocky gave up. "O.K., Frank, just thought it might do you good to see some of the guys."

"Not just yet."

Rocky made a left to head south on Franklin Avenue to pick up Belleville Avenue on his way home. Then, again remembering Marietta's milk request, he pulled into

Chet's Candy Store next to Number 10 School where the Bonaducci children did their grammar years. Leaving the car engine still on to keep Frank warm, Rocky hurried inside. The cluttered confectionary depot was where during the week local kids inhaled Lime Rickies, hot fudge sundaes, Chet's "Coney Island Chickens" (hot dogs), Wise Potato Chips, and Top Forty hits on the jukebox. Besides Chet, a couple of the neighborhood's retirees were listening to the radio's wrap-up of the latest Army-Navy game.

"Rock, the kids never should've played today. Army and Navy suffered too," said Chet. "How's Frankie feelin'?" Chet was a big fan of Frank's, having seen him almost everyday since Kindergarten. But because of business, he never attended a game except on Thanksgiving Days.

"He'll get over it," said Rocky, convinced yet again the only thing that travels faster than good news is bad news.

"Hey, Rock, I wondered if Sneak's kid would've returned the favor in a lifetime."

Chet's subtle jibe over the controversial play caused Rocky to pause. Then asking for Marietta's milk, he silenced the stubby storeowner who bore a striking resemblance to Lou Costello, his second cousin from Paterson. "Ya know what, Chet? Gino blocked for my kid for three years and never complained. I know he would've done it for Frankie, too."

On Rocky's way to the door, "Topper" Series, whose son had starred at Barringer High in the early fifties, stopped chewing on his stogie long enough to yell out that ABC Radio had scheduled a summary of the Belleville-Nutley game at five-thirty. "Rocky, ya don't want to miss dat," said Topper. "And tell your kid we'll never forget him."

Bonaducci, with a farewell wave, hoped ABC and others would be as compassionate as Chet and Topper.

Returning to the car, Rocky reached for the radio without mentioning the upcoming broadcast. Not turning his head to speak directly to his dad, Frank politely requested, "Dad, do we have to? Just trying to stay quiet."

Rocky didn't realize his oldest child had actually been praying for strength to deal with the mixed reaction he was anticipating about the game. His mother's quest for a closer relationship with Christ had rubbed off on him more than anyone could know.

76

"Frank, Marty Hickman's goin' to give a summary of the game. We can't miss it."

"Oh, great, … real great," said Frank with a trace of sarcasm.

Then almost immediately, the award-winning New York area sports broadcaster's voice filled the damp, warm car. Rocky was holding his breath for at least a fair analysis by the former metropolitan area pro athlete-turned reporter.

Hickman was sincere: "High school football fans, I witnessed a memorable contest today in rain, snow, and mud at the Park Oval in Nutley, New Jersey. Situated in the hot bed of Jersey's finest football, two bordering Essex County schools slugged it out at the legendary home of the Maroon Raiders. Wow, the bigger team won, but if it were dry, the 'light fantastic' of the Bellboys might have prevailed. Their Frankie Bonaducci saw lots of daylight, while his high-scoring teammate, Gino Babula, couldn't pick up a yard. Better weather would have made this dynamic duo unstoppable. But the sloppy conditions favored the brute strength of Nutley, with senior single-wing fullback, Bob Scrudato, doing the damage. Final score: Nutley 13 and Belleville 0.

"Before I go to the Army-Navy classic, fans, I have to tell you that I saw something today I bet few of you will ever encounter in life. Senior Frank Bonaducci returned an interception all the way to Nutley's four yard line, when…"

Without warning, Frank's frustration finally erupted, and he hit the dashboard hard with his left fist. The radio went silent. Rocky, who rarely ever raised his voice to his son became upset. "Damn it, Frank, get control of yourself. You can't change what happened now. Maybe Hickman was gonna say something good. Guys like us don't have somebody talkin' about us on radio everyday."

Frank was incredulous, saying, "Dad, I told you fifteen minutes ago. I would still do it all again."

Rocky grabbed the steering wheel as if he was going to tear it out. He looked straight ahead without saying a word. Frank could feel his dad's fierce intensity.

Dropping his head, Rocky chose his next words carefully. "Frank, you really <u>are</u> different. Like Coach P. said, 'you're special.'" Still not totally sure where he stood on Frank's play, Rocky relaxed at the wheel. "Let's go home. Somebody will eventually tell us what Marty said."

Frank could not love his father any more than he did at that moment. He rolled his eyes upward to thank God for his understanding dad.

Left off Belleville Avenue and onto the darkness of Belmont, Rocky and Frank got an amazing surprise. The car's headlights revealed a uniquely mixed welcoming committee waiting on the front doorsteps. The warming weather was cooperating to allow this crew to patiently remain outdoors anticipating the arrival of Rocky and Frank.

"You have to be kidding," groaned Frank.

"Well, get a load of this; here's your real supporters, Frankie," assured Rocky, surveying the small, but ever-faithful flock of family and friends.

Embarrassingly, Frank waved through the foggy windows.

Marietta stood on the top step, her arms folded with the right index finger planted firmly into her cheek, still fiercely wrestling with Frank's goal line decision. *God, did you really desert him, or was it some gang of demons that just messed everything up for us?* She would be sincerely attentive to everyone's analysis in the hours to follow. Then, following her usual behavioral pattern that reached back to her childhood, by the end of the night, she would either thank God or curse Him. The Almighty had gotten used to Marietta's routine.

Donna sat on the first step in her oversized snowsuit. Tilley Gretto, the affectionate next-door neighbor, better known as "Aunt Tilley", had babysat for Bonaducci's youngest that day, so Frank's sister had learned about the game second hand. Win or lose, her big brother still could do no wrong. Thanks to him, she had become a celebrity with all her classmates. Whatever anyone might now say, Frank was still the best football player in Essex County to all the under ten year olds. A handsome hero never does wrong, and even if he does, there is always need to forgive him, … particularly if he's your brother.

Between Donna and her mother were Frank and Jo-Jo's closest neighborhood friends. Two sets of brothers, Eric and Davey Thatcher and Bobby and Jimmy Hardy, were always with Frank since their early years in grade school. Eric and Bobby would graduate with him in June. The younger brothers were two years behind. Jo-Jo's buddies were more dissimilar: little four foot three inch Gerald Gretto, Tilley's son; the English accented Harold Bader, a cousin to the Hardy boys, who moved to Belleville from Bermuda; and Roger Bush, already a six foot thirteen year older. At the top of the steps, with her right arm in Marietta's left, was Maria Giardina, Frank's girlfriend.

As Rocky rolled the car past these eleven loyal well-wishers to a stop in the backyard, Frank gave his father another quick, humble glance. Rocky did not disappoint. "Daddy, as Mommy always says, 'People think more of you than you think of yourself'."

Taking her chubby little hands out of the white fur muff given by Aunt Bella for her birthday several days earlier, Donna tapped impatiently on the passenger window. As Frank opened the door and lifted his seven-year old sister, she squeaked, "Sorry you lost, Frankie, but I still love you anyway."

At the back of the pack, Marietta and Maria smiled. Their coaching of Donna had paid off with her flawless, affectionate delivery. Marietta was beginning to finally relax. *Maybe the play wasn't that critical after all.* Maria, an articulate second generation Sicilian beauty, always brought out the best in her boyfriend's mother. She continued to stand by her, still arm in arm.

Next, Jo-Jo greeted Frank with a bear hug. "Sorry I didn't see you by the bus, but who wanted to get mud all over them." He paused, still holding Frank: "Ya know, big guy, at least you stayed to the sidelines like I told ya. But next time, just fall into the end zone." A smile cracked everyone's face.

Although Eric and Davey Thatcher were committed "Frank fans" and had been at all his games over four years at Belleville, they were really baseball fanatics. Their parents both were of English extraction, with genuine Horatio Hornblower blood in their veins. Rocky referred to them as Frank's "Amedigan friends". Their father, Joe, was a milkman whose early morning starts left him much time to teach the game of baseball to his two sons and anyone else who would listen. Frank firmly credited his own modest success as a Bellboy outfielder to Joe. On the other hand, his wife, Antoinette, a Keely Smith look-a-like, was once a brilliant professional ballet dancer who had her career ended prematurely by arthritis in her hips. Not one to mingle much with other neighbors, she became a prolific reader with an also alleged taste for Southern Comfort Manhattans. Frank, who was often in the Thatcher home, and Marietta, who would chat with Mrs. Thatcher on her late afternoon walks with Blackie, were particularly fond of her because of her intellect, wit, and her most interesting life as a ballerina. They staunchly refuted all references to her drinking. "Anyway, if it were true," argued Marietta, "More people should be as wise and considerate sober as was Antoinette, … with a few belts in her."

Eric was a six-footer whose straight jet-black hair tightly cropped his pointed head without a wave. Dark black eyebrows perched over matching black horn rim glasses on his long narrow nose, kind of doubling him for Buddy Holly. Indeed, he was his mother's son. She was tall, lean, graceful, and almost vampy; he, a rangy kind of athlete who scared opposing hitters to death every time he took the mound as Belleville's finest pitcher. Not only Captain of the Bellboy nine, he was also President of the National Honor Society.

Davey was shorter and more muscular. Curly, sandy hair and his incessant baseball talk made him a younger version of his dad. Two years younger than Eric, he was more interested in girls and his baseball bat than anything related to grades. The brothers' big common bond was their friendship and admiration for Frank Bonaducci.

Eric was anxious to talk, and like a sports addicted sideline reporter, he wrestled Frank out of Jo-Jo's grasp. "Frankie, that play will go down as one of the most controversial, yet valiant and selfless acts in Belleville football history! How does it feel to be a legend, my friend?"

"Hear that, Jo-Jo?" Frank said, knowing his younger brother probably felt otherwise.

Spinning of 45 records at neighborhood parties had earned Eric a reputation as the self-proclaimed "DJ of the Belleville airwaves" and its answer to Jocko Henderson, the popular black R&B jock out of Newark. Realizing Frank might not be overly sensitive about the fouled play, Eric quickly switched on his DJ act. "Let me shake your hand, my man, my friend, my hero, and now our own legend." He ended with a weak Jocko imitation: "Ooo popa dee, our hero's Frankie B.!"

"Eric, that was terrible," said Frank, jokingly pushing him aside, trying to get to the backyard door.

"Just didn't want you to think that you're not the greatest," said Eric sincerely.

"Thanks, 'Snatcher'," said Frank. This was Eric's nickname that referred to his habit of "snatching" 45's at parties for taping on his reel-to-reel machine, only to return them next day to their less than slightly irritated owners. "But stick to geometry and calculus, Cuz, cause as a disc jock or a sports reporter, … you'll never make it."

Frank then walked right into one of the Hardy boys. Bob put out his immense right hand, which outstretched, revealed golden hair on his massive forearms. He and younger brother Jimmy were Belleville's best at track and field, with Bobby having broken the school scoring record as only a junior. He hoped to get appointed to the United States Naval Academy next year. Blonde hair and light features gave his muscular six foot two inch frame the appearance of a country bumpkin. This was much out of place in suburban Belleville where DA hairdos, motorcycle boots, and leather jackets dominated fashion and style of the day. Half his brother's size, Jimmy, as a sophomore, had already established himself as Belleville's finest long distance runner.

"Frank, Eric's right," offered Bob, with a smile that meant mischief. Adept at imitating both Les Keider and Lindsay Nelson, the legendary sports broadcasters of the day, Bob let loose even more dramatically than Eric. "Yes, folks, Frank Bonaducci and Gino Babula will be remembered as long as there is the Belleville-Nutley football game. Like the great All-American Dickey Moegle from Rice and that Alabama knucklehead in the Cotton Bowl, their names will go down in history. Moegle's on his way for a 98 yard TD, and this redneck jumps off the Crimson bench to tackle him—instant notoriety!"

Frank nervously interrupted, "I guess today I was the 'knucklehead'."

Catching his breath, Bob continued, "Bonaducci goes sixty yards to the goal line and stops to look for the high-scoring Babula, and he's back at midfield on his face, pounding the mud and pouting that <u>he</u> didn't have the ball."

Everyone but Marietta was getting into the jest of the moment, as Frank corrected his friend. "Hey, you know Gino <u>was</u> right behind Wee Willie."

"Yea, but my story's better, and I don't know if Gino would have done it for you, Frank." Then Bob, like Eric previously, dropped the satire. "Hey, your heart was right, and who thought you guys could not score from the four anyway?"

"Gee, what profound analysts my buddies are," responded Frank.

Still uneasy, Frank could not relax and be himself ... yet. But after shaking hands with Jo-Jo's quartet of pals and getting a hug from Maria, he stopped to sum it all up for Eric and Bob. "Hey, guys, I really appreciate your support. But I'm sure there're lots in town who think I was a jerk to not just take it in myself."

Jimmy Hardy retorted. "Well, you're probably right, Frank. But as far as us guys who understand the true meaning of sport, we're OK with it."

"Quite mature, James, you insincere, skinny miler," said Frank, smiling.

Davey Thatcher, who had yet to say a word, cut to the chase. "Well, truth of the matter, Frankie boy, is that the real knuckleheads are my brother and the Hardy boys because they're all too dumb to utter anything that makes sense about football in the first place. You see, big guy, my mother is <u>the</u> football and people expert. Everything they said, she said when we told her what happened. If you really want an intelligent analysis of events of the day, catch my ol' lady between *The New York Times* and her TV shows. And you know what? Marty Hickman gave <u>her</u> the ideas in his radio wrap-up after the game."

Frank was appreciative, but it was Marietta who finally heard something she wanted to hear—that Mrs. Thatcher had found worth in what Frank had done. Walking with Rocky behind the crowd of kids entering their house, Marietta gave her husband a smile of relief. He welcomed that more than she, as he didn't need to contend with a depressed wife for the rest of the weekend.

With renewed energy, Marietta took charge, making sure Jo-Jo took all of the guests' coats, and Maria orchestrated seating around the dining room table. Now there was new anticipation ... for the dozens of miniature tomato pies Mrs. Bonaducci would soon push out of her kitchen.

Eric, though, wouldn't let go of the game analysis. "Well my mom <u>is</u> a big fan, Frank." Then glaring at his younger brother, he continued. "But, having seen all of your games since freshman year, I must say Nutley did kick your butts. And you know what? That Scrudato guy made everybody forget Babula. How come he could run in the mud, and Gino couldn't?"

Rocky and Jo-Jo put out Brookdale soda bottles and milk, while Donna and Maria were placing paper plates. At least more at ease, Frank provided some insight. "Well, Eric, their line was better today mainly because Wee Willie was so busy trying to beat up his DiGirolomo cousin, that he forgot his other assignments."

Eric listened and then ended all talk of football for the post-game meal. "The fact of the matter is that the game should never have been played in the mud. But I will say this, and this is <u>my</u> own thought, Davey, my jerk of a brother; it will go down as "The Mud Bowl" in school history, ... and the day Frankie Bonaducci waited at the goal line for his friend."

Silence engulfed the room, joining with the smoke from the burned English muffin delicacies Marietta's temperamental stove had prepared. Proudly she entered, unknowingly breaking the heavy quiet. "Just tomato sauce with garlic. Then I have ones with 'allige' (anchovies). And who wants the ones smothered with mozzarella? How about pepperoni, or those with Uncle Pete's sausage?"

As everyone reached for his or her favorite, Marietta insisted on a word of prayer. While Rocky's side of the family was fiercely dedicated as Catholic War Veterans, the Bonaduccis never said "Grace" at the table. But the Hardy boys and their family were "Presbyterians", as were the Baders, and they were comfortable about the idea. Now the Thatchers never went to church, but Eric thought getting spiritual was a reasonable sacrifice to consume Mrs. B's famous Saturday night pies.

As Marietta prayed, Frank could not help but think of Nora and Queenie Baskerville, his mom's unique black co-workers. They talked to her incessantly about a personal relationship with Jesus, which he knew had helped her become more tolerant of life's frustrations, something she seemed to be unable to achieve in her traditional Italian American Roman Catholicism. Frank, himself, knew his own ability to deal with the events of his last game were partly due to his mom's revelations from her conversations with the spiritual sisters at the factory.

Everyone began to inhale Marietta's Saturday night delight when Rocky interrupted to ask the high schoolers when the Victory Dance started. Maria said eight o'clock would be a good time to get there. She was still in her damp cheering uniform, until Mrs. Bonaducci insisted on drying it with her iron before the young couple left for the high school.

At the Belleville gymnasium Eric would be spinning records from his personal collection of contemporary rock 'n' roll hits. "Wow, it's 6:30. I gotta get going soon," Eric said. "And Bobbie will be driving us all in his dad's station wagon, right?"

"Yep," Hardy responded.

"Maria, do we have to go?" asked Frank.

"Don't start that, Frank. We're seniors."

Rocky concurred. "Frank, these are the best years of your life. Forget the game and have a good time."

Frank knew he was outnumbered when Bob assured that he had permission to drive his dad's car, and that he, Frank, and Eric would be "tripling" with their three girl friends.

"OK, we're all set, boys and girls," said Eric. "Victory Dance in Bob's car; my reel to reels are waiting at my house with a bunch of 45's; we pick up the girls; I play the best of Dion and the Belmonts, The Five Satins, Paragons, Jesters, and even a few Connie Ferro tunes, … our own queen of dreamy make-out music."

Jo-Jo's friends' pre-puberty states of mind began entertaining visions of Belleville High seniors cheek to cheek at the gym. Being in the same room with Maria, Belleville's cutest cheerleader, they were bursting with envy of the seemingly romantic night that was ahead for the older teens.

Then suddenly Eric felt he had to make a last prediction of what *The Newark Star Ledger* would drop on everyone's doorstep on Sunday morning. "Glickman and Dorfman write up the game as an upset, with Frankie's controversial play as valiant, but not enough. That's the sport page. Then in the corner of the front page, the state gets a look at the other side of the neighborhood; 'Indictments about to be handed down all across Belleville, Nutley, and North Newark, … massive counterfeit ring is the target of Federal Prosecutor'. Yep," Eric reassured himself, "That's what we'll see."

"Be careful with that stuff, Eric," said Rocky. "Ya know, that counterfeit stuff." Rocky felt that he had to remind the kids that rumors do not necessarily become reality.

Eric did not back down. "Yea, but ya know Mr. B., Lanno and some of the other cops in town are talking up that kind of thing at the local bars."

"Eric, watch who you listen to," added Rocky, asking himself how the kid could be so privy to alcohol-induced stories at local watering holes.

"Well, I'm hearing that it's organized crime out of New York influencing some of the local boys," confirmed Eric, washing down another huge bite of oil drenched muffin pizza with milk.

Milk and pizza? Rocky cringed.

"Hey," said Thatcher, "My ma's the one with all the theories, and she says it's closer than we think."

Rocky saw it coming. Marietta froze with dread, not only of Frank losing a chance at a scholarship because of the Nutley game, but also the sickening embarrassment of this local rumor of bad twenties making their way into the middle class pockets of friends and relatives, ... and even to 711 Belmont Avenue. She needed to have a plan. *I'll go visit Mrs. Thatcher,* Marietta thought. *That's where I'll get the full story. God love her.*

As Frank and his friends were leaving for the dance, the phone rang. "Hey, my famous cousin," greeted cousin Nicholas on the line.

Without asking who it was, Frank answered, "You mean infamous."

"Naa, for what I know about football, no one in Belleville history will ever do, or think of doing, what you did today."

"Is that a compliment?"

"That's all my cousin, Frank, should ever hear—compliments." Nicholas paused and then continued. "See you at the dance."

"I'll be there, Cuz."

Frank hung up; Belleville High next stop.

By 7:45, the Bonaducci household had become quiet. Donna was helping her mother clear the dining room table, as Rocky settled in the TV room to fall asleep as soon as his head hit the broken down lounge chair he'd inherited a couple of years ago when Grandpa Joe moved the family to East Orange. This day had totally exhausted him.

But within fifteen minutes, Marietta woke her husband up. She was buzzing with renewed energy since resolving to get over to Mrs. Thatcher's in the next couple of days to ply any information she had on the goings-on in town, as well as what she thought about Frank's decision in the game. Besides, she and Rocky had promised to take Donna after dinner to Two Guys from Harrison, the local blue-collar department store across the Passaic River. Marietta had to do some early Christmas shopping, and she and her husband could also enjoy a cup of coffee and cigarette there together. Even at her young age, Donna knew this was her parents' way of relaxing on a weekend, without having to spend much money. Her cooperative behavior might just earn her some kind of special gift that night, too.

Jo-Jo, Gerald, Harold, and Roger wandered onto the front porch with nothing else for eighth graders to do but to talk about sports and girls. Thinking he could light up the stolen Camel cigarette from his mother's coat pocket, Roger suggested sitting outside on the damp front doorsteps.

"But Roger, lose the idea of smoking in front of my house," said Jo-Jo. "My father will kill you. And then when your dad finds out, he'll kill you next."

Tiny Gerald Gretto reached up and patted his oversized friend on the back. "Yea, I get it. Big Roger gets killed twice, which means he musta resurrected once. Now Roger's Jesus Bush instead of Roger Bush."

"Gerald!" said Jo-Jo, who could not believe the choirboy's apparent sacrilege.

Gretto didn't stop. "And don't forget it'll stunt your growth, Roger."

"Looks like you been smokin' since birth, Ger," said Bush, deciding to save his smoke for the walk home to Smallwood Avenue.

Roger Bush was a less frequent visitor at the Bonaducci house than Jo-Jo's other friends. A poor student and somewhat mischievous throughout his grammar school days at Number 10, Roger was a spitting image of his six foot five inch dad, "Red". His arms and legs were unnaturally long, particularly accentuated by his short, round torso and full, almost prematurely puffy face. In addition, Roger was considered the neighborhood's "Eddie Haskell". His fine manners in front of families of his friends would turn into the "Leave It To Beaver" TV character's nasty antics, once the adults left the room.

While Jo-Jo was the number one male student in their eighth grade class, Roger filled last place. Their companionship and his carte blanche welcome at 711 Belmont Avenue were due entirely to an incident that occurred in the summer of '57. Playing basketball on the road that separated Roger's house from the Erie Lackawanna Railroad, Red Bush arrived home early from work one afternoon and approached his son and Jo-Jo carrying an Acme super market bag in both arms.

"Well, here it is, boys. Yas got it for two days. Enjoy." Red was being coy.

"Come on, Dad, what is it?"

"Open it."

Roger turned the contents upside down to read printing on its inside, "'Property of Notre Dame Football, Aubrey Lewis'." He took a deep breath. "God, Dad, it's the helmet of Aubrey Lewis."

Knowing more about the legendary Montclair High School football great than his basketball-playing friend, Jo-Jo was speechless. However, Roger had heard his father's praises of the ex-High School All American and first black to captain the legendary "Fighting Irish".

Each boy kept the helmet for a day. Jo-Jo stunned his football-crazy dad and brother when he brought it home. From that lazy summer afternoon on, as different as Jo-Jo and Roger were, they had a common experience based upon Red Bush's genuine desire to impress the neighborhood kids, and Roger's agreement to share the icon's equipment with his friend. Jo-Jo turned out to be the only one the Bushes trusted with it outside of their home, before returning it to Aubrey who by then was out of football. Over the years to come, any of Roger Bush's failings would be overlooked by all the Bonaduccis. They had a genuine love for the gangly basketball center, even when others refused to support him. In truth, if Rocky did ever catch Roger smoking, and they were both alone, the ex-Marine might just have asked him if he had an extra cigarette to spare. Then during their relaxed smoke, Mr. B. would point out the pitfalls of smoking at such a young age, ... with unconvincing and shallow enthusiasm.

The only obstacle between the boys and relaxing on the front doorsteps that night was the temperamental sticky front door. Gerald, the smallest of the bunch, volunteered his short arms. To the amazement of all, he opened it on the first try.

"Luck," said Roger. "Pure guinea luck."

Gretto put his hands on his hips, as if preparing himself to fight his towering opponent in defense of his heritage.

"Relax," suggested Jo-Jo.

Gretto immediately forgot the ethnic slur.

Now, seeing Roger about to sit down on the damp brick doorsteps, Harold suggested spreading some of the old *Ledgers* the Bonaduccis never seemed to throw out from their storage in the corner of the chilled closed in porch. Casually, the frisky bunch each fixed their respective dry seat cushions, but only after respectfully requesting Blackie to find a place elsewhere. Still, the Bonaducci mutt loved to be around Jo-Jo and his friends.

After getting settled, they each lamented the anticipated boredom ahead of what was left of their Saturday night in Belleville. Cars passed 711 Belmont Avenue with young couples romantically close to each other. Heads turning back and forth as if watching a tennis match, the four boys joined in their ritualistic cry of adolescent frustration. More like alley cats in heat than the Four Aces, they would sing out, … "Date Night, Date Night!" With their cherubic faces nestled in their still innocent hands, they imagined where the teenage pairs would be ending up that night; from the Victory Dance, to Rutts Hutt, to the Milk Bar, to the Royal Theatre in Bloomfield, the Franklin in Nutley, or the Capital in Belleville, perhaps even the drive-in up in Totowa. This giggling quartet even offered some alternatives both Gerald and Jo-Jo knew they would have to eventually confess to Father Francis Ignasunas, for having "impure thoughts about someone else's impure actions". On the other hand, Roger Bush didn't hesitate to designate … "the back seat"… as the final destination for most of those he caught a glimpse of in the dimly lit December evening.

"Jeepers peltz, we're all dummies," concluded Jo-Jo. "We should've asked my father to take us to the Capital. Sinatra's in some movie."

"What?" queried Roger, "To watch others make out?"

Gerald answered to Roger's question with, "Well, if Jo-Jo had thought sooner, he could have asked Rosemarie out, and we could watch them!"

Jo-Jo pounced on Gerald with a "German Haircut", rubbing his best friend's small head until he screamed that he was … "takin' it back".

"We all forgot kids that go to Catholic schools never go to make out parties," said Roger as he was about to also pummel Gerald.

"He took it back," waved off Jo-Jo.

"I was only kidding, Jo-Jo, … only kidding. Honest!" swore Gerald.

Jo-Jo then surprised them all. "Well, Gerald's idea is a whole lot better than what we're doing now."

The youngest of the bunch, Harold, covered his eyes and offered, "Skeevy. Skeevy."

"Skeevy?" said Roger, looking at Harold in disbelief. "Wait until you start figurin' out the facts of life, you limey baby, you."

They all shook their heads and laughed, agreeing on one thing—after Mrs. Bonaducci's pizza pies, the rest of the night was turning out to be a disaster.

Gerald stood up to dry his little wet butt with his hands, and then sounded out what had become the gang's theme song on such uneventful occasions. To the tune of "Give my Regards to Broadway", he took the lead:

"What are we gonna dooo?
Just spit in our own two front shoes.
Eric Thatcher and Bobby Hardy
Used to do that, tooo...."

It was bad enough to wake up Blackie, sleeping in the corner of the room.

"God, we're real wastes," concluded Roger Bush, focusing now on smoking that Camel on the way home. "I'm goin'. Got a CYO game at Montclair Immaculate tomorrow."

Red Bush had "bribed" the head priest at the parochial school he attended in the pre-war years to give Roger a Montclair address so he could play basketball for them. A bottle of port wine delivered to the headmaster every weekend did the trick. The game his son loved to play would keep him on the straight and narrow most of the time throughout high school.

"Coming to church with us tomorrow, Jo-Jo?" asked Gerald. It was a weekly ritual to transport Jo-Jo and Donna to St. Peter's Roman Catholic Church every Sunday since Marietta asked the favor of Tilley and Dominick Gretto a couple of years back.

"No, Ger, my mother made my father promise we would go with her two colored friends to their church in Bloomfield on the Sunday after Frank's last game. Sort of a thanksgiving thing." Strangely Jo-Jo was really looking forward to the adventure of another place of worship, rather than the one he attended since his First Holy Communion in first grade.

"Get ready to sing songs all morning with the coloreds, Jo-Jo," said Roger, who knew unexpected things about the tiny Protestant church on West Street. "Oh man, you're gonna be dancin' with those colored girls before the three hour service is over!"

"Thought you were leaving," quizzed Jo-Jo. "How you know so much, big guy? You never go to church; just play on their basketball teams." Jo-Jo was actually a little worried. He had a hard time getting up courage to dance with Rosemarie, let alone someone "different". The idea of dancing in church was … incomprehensible.

Jo-Jo was shaking his head as Roger said, "My father helped build the place." Red Bush was active in excavation, construction, and trucking around Essex County with some other old friends from his hometown of Montclair.

Now, Gerald piped up. "Ya know it's a sin for a Catholic to go to one of those 'holy roller' churches. Dancin' with colored girls …? Straight to Hell."

Feeling guilty, Jo-Jo looked at Gerald and Roger with eyes wide open. What punishment might he be dealt? How could his devoted mother think of putting her entire family in a position to be excommunicated? How were Aunt Josephine, Uncle Caesar, and the rest of the Catholic War Veterans in the family going to react?

Harold Bader cleared the air. Having been through a couple of Vacation Bible Schools at his Presbyterian Church, he took the pressure off. "Hey, Jo-Jo, relax. There's only one God."

Yea, Harold's right, Jo-Jo thought. *If it's a sin, it couldn't be a mortal one.*

The boys called it a night. Harold politely repeated "thanks" for being invited to the pizza party. Gerald offered a "me, too." Roger just disappeared into the night with his cigarette, as, moments later, it became a faint beacon in the fog rolling in on Belleville.

Accompanied by Blackie, Jo-Jo reentered the house after struggling with the ever-troublesome front door. It was only 8:45 PM by the kitchen clock. His parents had left for Two Guys. For the first time since he had turned up the volume on Dion and the Belmonts for Frank that morning, there was a silence that he did not want to leave. Profound peace enveloped the house. He walked off to the TV room and just flopped on the aging, tattered couch that predated the plastic covered variety in the living room. Smokey remnants of Marietta's burnt pizza muffins still hung in the air. Jo-Jo stared at the ceiling, inhaled and exhaled deeply. It had been a confusing a day for him, although not as confounding as for his brother. He was thankful his own buddies never brought up the subject of the game on the doorsteps. *How was the Victory Dance going for Frank?* Hopefully any negative feedback that had to be brewing somewhere would not erupt at the school. Confusion still dominated Jo-Jo's young psyche. His hero in life had done something that would take years for Jo-Jo to justify.

CHAPTER 7

"VISITORS AT THE VICTORY DANCE"

Although there was no Belleville victory to celebrate, Eric Thatcher did his best to encourage its morose crowd of students onto the basketball court to dance. Losing to Nutley had dampened most everyone's spirits. With few exceptions, the girls congregated in the gym's stands, and the boys were like wilted flowers against the walls behind both baskets. The punch and cookies in the hallway were ignored, as was the makeshift banner, pinned to the bulletin board outside the gym teachers' office, thanking the football team for their great season.

Eric went back and forth from a Jocko Henderson imitation, to the smooth style of Allan Freed. He just could not motivate the crowd himself. He needed help.

"Oohh poppa darts,
I've got Lee Andrew and the Hearts.
This next one will bring your love to new heights.
It's called 'Long, Long, Lonely Nights'!"

A few couples were on the floor, cheek to cheek, when the gym's front door burst open. Coach Hiram Wilhelm, one of the chaperones, got pushed aside by a small band of teenagers. Before he could get assistance, six boys were strutting across the court towards Eric. Recognizing the intruders, he raised his hands, pleading jokingly in terrible rhyme:

"Have mercy, boys, you've got to give me a chance,
Just cool off now and find someone to dance.

One thing I ain't is a gang war fighter,
So pick a lady and hold her tighter."

The wiseguy leading this gang of wannabe thugs was Paulie Puccini, a Belleville kid who'd allegedly become a dope addict, two-bit crook, and aspiring mobster from the town's Silver Lake section. Pointed black flyweight shoes and an oversized black suit with pink stitching down the pant legs set him apart from everyone else in the school. An outstanding athlete in grammar school, a knee injury in Paulie's freshman year and some bad influence from a crew out of Newark's North Ward steered him in the wrong direction. Football team members at the dance, seeing the potential confrontation with Eric, started to converge where he was spinning his music.

"Where's Bonaducci?" asked Paulie, his finger in the taller DJ's chest. "I'm gonna beat the crap out of him."

Trying to buy time, Thatcher adjusted his glasses, and versed another rhyme:

"Now, Paulie my friend, I really don't know,
But if you'd prefer, how 'bout a hit from the … Moonglows?"

High on heroin and upset about money he'd lost in the Belleville-Nutley game, Paulie reared back to slug Thatcher. Suddenly a powerful hold from behind paralyzed the disoriented intruder. Gino was driving Puccini's head to the floor, as Wee Willie, Lenny Long, Donny Riordan, Joey Vitella, and a host of other Bellboy footballers made sure none of Paulie's entourage came to his rescue.

"Get out of here, get sobered up, Paulie, and never threaten any of my friends again, especially Bonaducci or Thatcher." Gino was blind with rage. "Listen to me—I make one call, and you're not gonna see your next birthday!"

"He screwed up the game!" ranted Paulie.

"You're not listening to me, you juvenile delinquent! Dope and gamblin' have messed you up, and that's gonna kill you before any of the guys from Bloomfield Avenue." Usually unexpressive, Gino seemed to almost be feeling sorry for dazed Paulie. "The way you're actin', they'd never let you in. The New York guys are not supposed to be pushin' that stuff, and you're even dumber to be usin' it. Get out of here." Gino knew what was going on in the New York and Jersey underworld. His mention of "Bloomfield Avenue" had finally gotten Paulie's attention.

"OK, OK, let me up, … and I leave."

Gino released him. Paulie's friends lifted him to his feet and out the front door. Slightly wearied from the encounter, Gino looked up into the stands where Frank had been sitting with Maria, when Frank raised his hand to acknowledge his "protection". Gino just nodded and dropped his head. At the same instant, he wondered if Paulie's life would be spiraling downward if guys like his own father had said "no" to the call of organized crime.

Eric quickly went back to his microphone and challenged everyone to the dance floor with Belleville's own Connie Ferro's newest hit from her latest movie. When the police later arrived, there was no visible evidence of the incident, and the Victory Dance was finally in full swing.

In the middle of The Five Satins' make-out anthem, "In the Still of the Night", this Saturday night dance took another step toward going down in history when the next uninvited group arrived. Once again, Coach Wilhelm beckoned for help from the other chaperones to deal with the clutter of latecomers. This time, however, a smile on the coach's face signaled Eric Thatcher that there was no need to panic. This mob without tickets had come there just to dance and listen to good music. But particularly for the boys wearing the football jackets and the girls without partners, the person they all wanted to meet face to face was … number 7, Frank Bonaducci.

For the first and last time in Belleville's Victory Dance history, the opposing team politely asked if they could join the festivities. Captains Bob Scrudato and Jack Chuy were complete gentlemen to Wilhelm, who allowed in the Nutley gridders and almost thirty of their friends with their dates—Pucci, Geltrudi, Ippolito, McDonald, D'Piro, Hyland, Vecchio, and a bevy of underclassmen as well. Some headed directly for the refreshments, others to the dance floor, while mutual friends from the cross town rivals began to congregate in the dimly lit gym with blue and gold streamers hanging from every rafter.

"Who invited you, you fat slob?" Wee Willie asked his younger cousin, Alphonso DiGirolomo.

Nutley's junior defensive lineman had completely baffled the three-year Belleville starter all day in the Oval mud. With their mothers being sisters, it was a big hug and a kiss on the cheek from Brindisi that led DiGirolomo to push him away in fun. The mid-court embrace put everyone at ease, guaranteeing that the joining of the sister towns that night would be an unforgettable show of camaraderie for so many of the kids who knew each other since they could remember.

"Fonso", Alphonso's nickname, asked his cousin, "Where's Bonaducci?"

"What for, Fatso Fonso?" asked Wee Willie, still disturbed by Frank's decision, but determined to protect his teammate from any taunting or ridicule.

Fonso looked around before he answered in a high-pitched voice, "Our guys really want to shake his hand. Not to make fun or anything. They really think he's a great back." Fonso added, " … and to wait for Gino Babula at the goal line, … Jesus, … the guys were impressed."

"Don't bust me, Fatso Fonso."

"What I got a new name now?" asked DiGirolomo, who was being sincere about Frank. "Really, Willie, where's Bonaducci?"

As Brindisi pointed to where Frank and Maria were sitting with Bob Hardy and his girlfriend, the cousins noticed a line forming in front of number 7. Baffled, Bonaducci did not know what to expect. However, speaking with Scrudato and Chuy about the game and their futures in college, Frank seemed to relax. He learned of the Nutley Raiders' respect for his decision and their gratefulness that the field condition was so horrible. By the end of the night, every Nutley player shook Frank's hand, and every unattached Nutley girl, much to Maria's chagrin, also got to touch the handsome senior.

A rumor had also begun to spread that Gino was going to receive a scholarship offer to the University of Kansas, and Eric seized the opportunity to end the dance with a special tribute to Mr. Inside: "Eric 'the Snatcher' Thatcher has one final song for you tonight, kids, and it's a dedication to our great running back, Gino Babula. Even though I'm not sure which Kansas City Wilber Harrison is singing about, I figure it's gotta be Kansas tonight, cause that's where a bunch of people want Gino to play football next year. So for you, Gino, … ooh poppa ditty, the name of the song is … 'Kansas City'."

To the sound of the future 1959 hit song, people began slowly filing out of the Belleville gym. While it had seemed earlier in the night that hardly anyone wanted to be there, by 10:30 PM it was as if no one wanted it to end. Years later in moments of reflection, many of the attendees would glance back to this December night in 1958 and conclude that so special had it become, that it would remain as a permanent mural on the corridors of their minds; Belleville and Nutley football teams becoming one, based around a game that should never have been played, and a player who had only wanted to help a friend.

When Frank finally got home into his warm bunk bed below Jo-Jo, the nervous stomach cramps that had bothered him all night were gone. But, he could not fall asleep immediately. He used the time to not only reflect upon the day, but also to say his prayers. As usual for Frank, his spiritual exercise turned out to be more of a dialogue with God. It had been his mother's incessant counsel that birthed in her son the desire for a personal relationship with Jesus. Once he understood her, Frank preferred the "one-on-one thing", as opposed to the formal, religious, guilt-laden, and institutional perspective.

Frank was over his frustration about not being able to get the ball to Gino. But he thought that it would be best to level with his Creator about how useless that touchdown would have been to himself; for Gino it would have meant a lifetime of Belleville football notoriety, rather than a family legacy tainted with embarrassment and trouble. Being a Bonaducci was translating into rich and wholesome experiences and traditions, … *at least* … *so far that's been the case,* he thought. *So, Lord, I did do the right thing, … didn't I?*

Not anticipating an audible voice, Frank meditated further, yearning for a positive confirmation and some kind of encouragement for the future. At least a morsel of hope would do wonders. This made him ponder for a moment if he might be mentioned on *The Newark Star Ledger* All Essex County Football Team, a longtime dream of his. Then he reflected that this slip into self-indulgence could be God's way of reminding him that even in the gesture to help Gino, Frank just might have been looking for a return favor in the future, not from Gino, but for himself from that big Coach in the Sky. While beginning to realize that his evening conversation with God was slowly evolving into more of a debate of his real motives, Frank was spiritually mature enough not to overly judge his own actions, even if they may have been subtly self-centered, at least in terms of … "doing … to get". In the end, the weary teenager took a deep breath and apologized to his Creator for being so absorbed in the alleged act of selflessness and friendship.

Even after his sign off with God, Frank still could not sleep. He smiled, reflecting back on the Victory Dance. *Who would believe the Nutley team would show up and be so respectful to me?* He humbly concluded that while the day was somewhat of a disaster, it could have been worse. No one protested his play to his face, except for the irreverent Nutley grammar school munchkins after the game … and Paulie Puccini.

Over on Carpenter Street, Gino lay awake as well. With no date that night, he had gone to bed early. His thoughts were not of football. He had been embarrassed by the rumor of the University of Kansas full scholarship offer. A smile formed and quickly left his face as he thought of Eric Thatcher taking advantage of the news to dedicate "Kansas City" to him. *How many realize it's going to be a miracle just for me to graduate in June, let alone make it to a college football factory?*

Gino was not feeling sorry for himself. Yes, his father was in jail, but he took pleasure in knowing he had made Sneaks proud this fall. His mother was healthy and supportive, and the two of them were doing just fine alone. Having been in the same backfield for the last four years with a faithful friend like Frank Bonaducci, he felt fortunate.

On the other hand, Gino traced his sleeplessness to the encounter with Paulie Puccini, remembering his stench from liquor and smoke, and the blank look in his eyes. Gino's subconscious mind traveled back to when he and Paulie played Little League Baseball together. Then he gazed upon other scenes that had lain dormant in his psyche. It seemed like yesterday when the Number 10 School kids got together in Branch Brook Park to play football with the guys from Silver Lake. Paulie, Frank, or Gino would always be the first picked on their respective teams. On the freshman squad nobody hit harder than Paulie. Then the knee injury changed everything for him. He got sucked into thinking he could be a big shot with the hoods down on Bloomfield Avenue along the Newark-Belleville border. Gino could not help but feel sorry for Paulie.

On New Year's Eve night, three weeks later, Paulie Puccini was found dead from a drug overdose in his bedroom on Silver Lake's Franklin Street. Needle marks were discovered under his fingernails. His muscular arms showed no trace. Apparently alone when he died, his right hand was clutching a five-inch trophy. Its plaque read, "Paul Puccini, Federal Industries 8th Grade Football Team, Most Valuable Player, 1954."

CHAPTER 8

"MEET YOU AT THE MANGER"

At 5:30 PM sharp on New Year's Eve, Rocky gave the order to pile into the family car. Light snow falling all day coated the black Chevy, and Jo-Jo and Frank attacked it with their leather gloves, clearing the windows. Donna insisted on sitting in the cramped back seat where the hole in the floor would give her a bird's eye view of the snow-covered asphalt between Belleville and East Orange. Jo-Jo had sat in the back as well, cradling two of the seven-antipasto trays. The other five were tucked in the trunk next to the flat spare tire and the inventory of art supplies Rocky kept out of Marietta's jealous sight. She sat cozily between her two youngest, while Frank rode shotgun next to his dad. When it came to cars over the years, the family got what they paid for. Anything could happen anytime with a Rocky Bonaducci automobile.

Inserting the key, the inevitable took place—nothing, … only a ticking sound coming from the starter! The engine would not turn over. A silence followed. No one expressed disappointment or frustration. The Bonaduccis had experienced this many times. Besides, Marietta's five o'clock call to Mary Durso, confirmed she, Nick, and Nicholas weren't leaving until 5:45, … in case his "Norma" needed to come to the rescue. Rocky's second attempt met with even less response.

Jo-Jo's nervous cough signaled one in the group was losing faith. Marietta inhaled deeply. She coughed as well, but it was from the excessive smoking habit she had developed as of late. Not with total confidence, she announced, "We should pray."

While all three of the children were weekly attendees at Catholic mass, they seemed to express their uneasiness with their mom's suggestion by beginning a squirming motion in each of their seats, … almost in unison. Rocky didn't say a word. How could he? He and Marietta's combined take home pay simply prevented them ever considering anything more than the headaches of a used car.

Over the year Marietta had become most obviously personal in her relationship with the Almighty, causing her children, Rocky, and even her very Catholic sisters-in-laws to fear the worst; could she be turning into the holiest of "holy rollers"? *Was she hesitating or just getting spiritually revved up like those other Protestants?* Rocky wondered. *By now the Bishop Sheen Show would have been over and done with. What's she waiting for?*

Frank was hungry, having not eaten since Grandma Frassa cut some hard salami and Italian wheat bread earlier in the day. He encouraged his mother, "Ma, it's good you're praying to the Sacred Heart. Who knows who the patron saint of '49 Chevys is. Just hurry up."

Sounding more like an emotional Pentecostal than the pious, guilt-filled Roman Catholic she had been all of her life, the effect of Marietta working the graveyard shift with those two Black Baptists became clearly evident. Queenie and Nora Baskerville had relocated from Alabama, arriving on a packed Greyhound bus at Newark's Penn Station one hot summer day last August. For some unknown reason, their evangelical fervor irrevocably touched Marietta's spirit. Imitating her new friends from deep in the Bible Belt, she burst out, "God, in the name of Jesus, start Rocky's car!"

Her shout made Jo-Jo let go of the top tray of antipasto with his right hand to grab support from the nearly broken back door handle. Donna was jarred out of her squinted closed-eye focus to sound a quiet gasp. Frank had heard his mom converse with God before, so her atypical enthusiasm just brought a smile to his handsome face. Rocky coiled, hearing his wife remind God that this problem was surely her husband's, since it was his car. Therefore, he quickly responded when Marietta commanded him to, "…start the damn engine!"

This time when he turned the key, amazingly, the Chevy roared into life. Donna cheered. Now Marietta actually seemed frightened. Frank expressed a relieved countenance, and Jo-Jo was incredulous. Rocky, now acting nonchalant, backed the car out the driveway.

As they slipped and slid to East Orange on balding tires, nobody objected when Marietta tested her family's tolerance in yet another prayer request.

"What the heck, Ma, one good miracle deserves another," said Frank, tongue in cheek.

Marietta did not hesitate. "Lord, make this a good last night of the year. May love and family support abound. May we all build each other up, not judging any one."

Everyone echoed with a hearty, "Amen."

Even Rocky chuckled, "Marietta, that means treating Bella with full respect and no attitudes."

"Yes, Rocky. And it goes for you, too, toward <u>my</u> mother tomorrow!"

Believing God had answered prayer, Marietta figured she had His ear right now, so with the destination on Oraton Parkway now in sight, she silently added another request: *... and please don't let anyone badger Frankie about the Nutley game anymore. Lord, you know what he wanted to do for Gino was something you would have done.*

God would not respond with any positive sign to that plea that night. His grace seemed to have been lifted with the starting of the sluggish engine.

Joe and Mamie Bonaducci's home was still lit up with hundreds of colored bulbs one week after Christmas. All the family members took pride with it being the brightest house on Oraton Parkway. Two weeks ago, Rocky and his sons had joined Uncle Nick Durso and cousin Nicholas, as well as Rocky's younger brother, Tony, and his three sons in the outdoor decorating ritual.

Grandpa Joe had been shocked several years earlier when his wife and two of his daughters, enigmatic Bella and conservative Josephine, revealed their desire to move to East Orange. Just retired from his pre-Depression job at the Edison Laboratory in nearby West Orange, he thought he would die on 7th Street and Park Avenue in Newark, where he and Mamie raised their five daughters and two sons. This section of East Orange was home to more blacks than this Italian American clan was used to. But "the respectfulness of the coloreds", was a pleasant surprise to the seventy-four year old native of Lioni, in Avellino, Italy.

Situated just west of the Newark border, this fifteen room regal residence had overlooked an expansive park area dotted with giant trees, bushes, and meandering walkways. But one year after arriving, the Bonaduccis saw the park turn into … the Garden State Parkway. The increasingly popular Jersey Shore had been crying out to give vacationers quicker access. The state capital of Trenton's answer was this modern highway connecting Cape May with the top of Jersey. Grandpa Joe knew the price of his home was undoubtedly discounted by this drastic alteration to his new neighborhood's ambiance. However, the worst part of his silent disgust for the change was the presence of the same sick feeling he had watching the politicians tear down the cherished First Ward of Newark, the cultural nest of all Italian Americans who had settled in the state's largest city. Still, completely bald and somewhat rotund, Joe Bonaducci was proud of the large home. And on this last night of 1958, he stood in light snow at the top of the front porch steps to greet his arriving family. Not quite as tall as his older son, he smiled with approval as Rocky's car pulled into an open parking space. The elder's dark suit, white shirt, and tie signaled to all that this was an important family holiday.

The warmth Rocky felt at seeing his healthy, aging father turned suddenly ice cold when he realized he was parking behind his brother-in-law, Caesar Casciano. He truly loved his sister Millie's husband who had made sure Rocky had a job at Jergens when he had to quit college back in 1947. It was seeing Caesar's brand new 1959 cream and white colored Pontiac that upset him.

"Hey, Rock, you son-of-a-gun, you. I pay all this money for a brand new Bonneville, and your engine's purrin' better than mine."

Was Uncle Caesar just being sarcastic? Rocky's exiting passengers were puzzled.

"Yep, Rock," he continued, "Henry at the Shell Station must really be takin' care of you. Don't tell Nicky Durso, but I think she sounds better than Norma too! Ya know, you could be savin' some money if you'd just put the car in the garage. Al Matte's motorcycle rent keeps your Chevy in the snow, gettin' cold and full of rust-cancer. And you just keep givin' more and more money to Henry to fix the chiverin' little thing. Those two guys have you comin' and goin'. Al's rent goes right to his best buddy at Shell."

His brother-in-law hardly knew how much Rocky and Marietta needed the extra cash. Besides, Henry Davidson always gave him a break on the Chevy's maintenance, so Rocky figured he was ahead of the game. "Caesar, you just take care of this prima donna car of <u>yours</u>, and let me worry about motorcycle rent, Al and Henry, and my little Chevy."

Then Donna let out a cheer, "Yeah for Daddy's Chevy!"

Under his breath, Frank whispered, "Yeah for Ma's prayer, you mean."

Marietta made the sign of the cross and blew a kiss heavenward as Rocky shook his older brother-in-law's hand, wishing him a Happy New Year and also making sure he did not enter the house empty-handed. "Caesar, don't go anywhere until you grab a tray of 'andibast'."

"Madiett's 'andibast', with lots of 'allige', I hope," complemented Caesar, referring to her heavy hand with the Sicilian tag for anchovies. Uncle Caesar was born in the states, but spoke Italian with a southern dialect as much as English. Staunchly patriotic and a veteran of the European theatre, he never hid his Italian heritage.

All of the Bonaduccis kissed Aunt Millie. While Mary and Bella were older, Millie was third in line, just three years ahead of Aunt Josephine. Carmela, the baby sister, was fifteen years younger. Millie was the quiet "straight man" for her energetic, practical joker husband who fulfilled each of her needs and those of their only child, Margarita, called Margie by all.

Everyone entering the house lovingly greeted Grandpa Joe, "Hey, Pop, Happy New Years."

Rocky reached for his father's hand, who drew him closer and strongly patted him on the back.

Caesar light-heartedly saluted his father-in-law as the head of his Millie's family. "Come sta, Il duce? Bona fortuna millenovecento cinquanta nove." ("Leader, how are you? Good luck in 1959.")

A traffic jam was forming as Aunt Bella led Grandma Mamie and Aunt Josephine in their hugs and kisses just behind Grandpa in the screened-in porch. Then cousin Nicholas, the same age as Frank and also a senior at Belleville High, appeared from inside and pulled the football star aside. He pointed out a legendary element of the Bonaducci seasonal celebrations—the Christmas figurines staring at everyone from the corner of the chilly porch. "Hey, Frankie, take a look at the nativity." Traditionally the family erected a Bethlehem scene complete with paper mache mountains, rubber trees, and bushes borrowed from a discarded miniature train set. " It's grown since Christmas Eve when we were here last."

"Very observant, Nicholas," said Frank, who loved and respected his cousin's musical talents, popularity at high school, and for his sincere support of Frank's academic and athletic prowess. There was not a jealous bone in Nicholas' body. They were presidents of each other's fan club.

"Aunt Josephine must have found a sale in Bamberger's toy department," Nicholas continued, speaking so softly only his cousin would hear. "Now there're four Josephs, twenty wise men, seventeen shepherds, eight donkeys, twelve sheep, and seven angels. Still only one Mary and one baby, but look, ... she must have gotten a deal on a new infant Jesus. Only problem's that it's bigger than any of the four Josephs! 'Madawn', ... what a delivery for Mary, huh? And Aunt Josephine must have bought another can of fake snow, 'cause it now looks like Jesus was born in a blizzard." Nicholas did not take a breath. "The final touch though is the new visitor to the manger. Can you believe the cute little Santa Claus hiding behind that huge angel?"

"You taking inventory, Nick?" Frank said, broadly smiling at his cousin as he pushed him into the vestibule so he could finally break the jam of Bonaduccis.

At the back of the pack finally now making its way into the warmth of the enormous house, Rocky took a glance back outside over his father's shoulder, seeing the many family cars. Darkness was almost complete, but it failed to dim Rocky's image of a scene thirteen years before. Then in 1945, a seemingly endless entourage of Newark police vehicles, yellow cabs, horse-drawn carriages, buses, fire engines, autos, and dump trucks greeted the triumphant GI's returning to Newark's Penn Station from all corners of a war-torn world. It was an unforgettable moment in the sun. Now as he entered the peace and security of his father's home, tears of joy and thankfulness filled Rocky's eyes. *How did I survive the horror of those stinkin' beautiful atolls in the South Pacific? I was treated like a hero when I got home. Now the family's all together, healthy, and my two kids are playin' football. I don't deserve all this. God's been too good to me.* Then he pulled the heavy oak door shut.

A kaleidoscope of holiday celebration greeted all who had just arrived. Now the rest of the family and friends, who were already busily preparing and participating in the year end festivities, poured into the packed vestibule where coats were being passed to be hung in closets, and snow boots discarded by the hearth of the roaring fireplace. The monstrous center hall colonial had been created to host this motley crew of Italian American celebrants, and tonight its atmosphere and space would be respectfully tested.

Many originally asked how Grandpa Joe could afford the house's mortgage. Any further into the suburbs of Essex County, it would have been totally out of reach financially. It featured six bedrooms, seven bathrooms, a finished cellar complete with knotty pine walls, a "dumb waiter" off the kitchen, and a TV room. Spread over five floors, there also was a furnished attic, numerous tiny studies and sitting areas, a mahogany-wall vestibule, and dining and living rooms at the house's heart. Outside, a vine-enshrouded wall surrounded the entire backyard that was perfectly suitable for even bigger family summer gatherings, despite Joe's special garden. Then there was that screened-in porch which wrapped around Oraton Parkway to welcome the late afternoon sun.

The retirement pension from Edison Laboratory made only a tiny dent in the Bonaducci castle's monthly bills. Grandpa Joe was able to pay them all because of the help from the rest of the occupants—Aunt Bella and Uncle Emil, Aunt Carmela and Uncle Jimmy Quinn, the single Aunt Josephine, and Francis DeCostanza, "adopted" by Aunt Bella and Grandma Mamie on the Miami leg of a Havana trip back in '56.

At first the air was filled with the sweet smell of Uncle Tony's pipe tobacco, competing with the heavy smoke from Uncle Emil's Parliament, hanging out of an elegant cigarette holder he had just picked up hours earlier at the counter of his Pharmacy down on Branford Place in the heart of Newark. There was also Grandpa Joe's Havana cigar, one of his Christmas gifts from Aunt Bella's last trip to Cuba, still burning fiercely despite his having spent the last twenty minutes outside. However, the aromas floating out of the big house's expansive kitchen overpowered the multi-smoke cloud. There, Grandma Mamie, her "goomod", "Zi Magalad" (her friend, Aunt Margaret from the "Down Neck" section of Newark), and Aunt Carmela worked furiously on the spaghetti pasta with the "red and white" gravy. Heavy garlic-scented "olyule" (aglio e olio, or olive oil, anchovies, and garlic) and the more common Marinara gravy, absorbing its own array of onion and garlic, totally enveloped everything and every one.

Uncle Tony, Aunt Esther, and their three boys were busily rearranging some of Aunt Bella's and Aunt Josephine's week old Christmas gifts blocking the way into the living room. Just off the vestibule and acting as the entrance to the dining room, this smaller living area was featuring the still unfinished Christmas tree that displayed a seemingly crouching angel at it's apex, scraping its plastic head against the just painted ceiling.

"Hey, Rock," was Uncle Tony's greeting to his bigger brother, senior by two years.

Tony was very much the "altar boy" in the family, while as youngsters Rocky was always on the brink of trouble. A Normandy plus six days combat veteran, Uncle Tony now spent his spare time singing in the Sacred Heart Cathedral Choir when not packing boxes in his hourly job at the Acme off of Newark's Orange Street. The war had stolen from these creative brothers. Rather than go to arts or music school to discover their destinies, they went to work to make a living; Rocky the portrait artist, Tony the singer, and both took home less than $90 per week in their labor intensive jobs.

"Ant, Happy New Year's," said Rocky. "Ant" was his special rendition of his slightly built and angelic looking younger brother's birth name, Anthony.

"Rock, come here, " Tony beckoned over the other room chatter.

Intrigue gripped Rocky. *What's so important?*

"Rock, 'the Feds' are in Belleville," whispered Tony, knowing how his brother had a career interest in the FBI when he was first discharged from the Marines.

"What'a ya talking bout?"

"Not now!" said Tony, with all of the kissing and hugging around them. They'd talk after dinner and get with Caesar, who was really privy to the situation.

Caesar, already in his dining room seat with a white napkin under his Adam's apple, tried to wave Frank over, as the table filled up with Marietta's antipasto trays, bottles of red and white wine, beer, and soda. Graded cheese still awaited the appearance of the pasta.

Frank, locked in chat with Uncle Jimmy Quinn, Aunt Carmela's six foot four inch Irish husband, tried to ignore assertive Caesar, who interrupted from across the room anyway. "Hey, kid, ya hear from Yale or Cornell yet?" Then before his nephew could answer, he went on, "Don't worry 'bout the Nutley game, it won't cost you a scholarship. I been talkin' to a couple of scouts in the area. It'll probably help!"

While silently wishing Caesar would drop the subject, Frank recalled his mother's vocal prayer and decided: *God doesn't answer all prayers the way we want Him to.*

In the midst of all the jockeying for seats at the large oak dining room table, a gift for the house from Aunt Bella and Uncle Emil, the telephone rang. One of the few houses in the family to have more than one phone, Grandma Mamie picked it up in the kitchen, now hectically full with volunteer servers. On the line was Grandpa Joe's nephew, Carmine, his elder brother's oldest son, calling from Brooklyn. This was where Grandpa Joe and his brother, John, had originally been placed from Ellis Island. The nephew was paying his respects. "Aunt Mamie, Happy New Year. Where's Uncle Joe?"

As Mamie returned the greeting, she thought her usually enthusiastic nephew sounded tired. She made sure her husband came into the kitchen to speak to Carmine, and also for Bella to follow suit in greeting her favorite cousin.

Bella knew Carmine well, visiting him every fall in Havana, Cuba, where he had significant business interests. "Something's wrong, Carmine. I can tell. Talk to Rocky."

She handed her brother the phone.

"Carmine, Happy New Year!"

Then after simple chatter about family, Frank's fine football season, and the holidays, Carmine told Rocky his companies were suffering big problems in Cuba, … and lots of money was at stake.

Always careful about never embarrassing the family name in Jersey, Rocky walked the phone as far into the hallway outside the kitchen as he could, so no one would hear. "Carmine, how many times I told ya 'bout some of your friends, and what good you could do with clean people, if only you'd wise up."

Since the war, Rocky had never bought his Brooklyn cousin's stories about being in legitimate businesses in New York and Cuba. The conversations always ended respectfully. As this was a holiday, Rocky promised to call Carmine after the first week of the New Year to see how Havana was panning out.

Returning to the dining room, Rocky quietly announced that the Brooklyn Bonaduccis were OK and sent their love. Without thinking, Bella shook her head, hanging it prayerfully. Only she and Rocky sensed the real nature of cousin Carmine's business career. Others had hunches, but there was an unspoken pact that if there were ever any bad news about anyone in the family, it would be patently denied and quickly swept under the rug.

By now, Marietta's antipasto was being passed around while Mary, Millie, and Carmela were still in the kitchen dumping pasta into their multicolored china serving bowls. Grandpa grunted to Millie to lower the volume on the record player. Being New Year's Eve, the ritual since the boys arrived home from war was to fill the last night of each year with the sounds of Glenn Miller, Tommy Dorsey, and some of Sinatra's earliest music. It was a reminder they had survived tougher times, and tonight they should celebrate the many blessings that life without war might deliver.

Grandpa Joe waved Mary out of the kitchen, and she knew her father was officially requesting her as oldest in the family to lead the dinner prayer. Least religious of all the girls, Mary made the sign of the cross, gave thanks for God's blessings in 1958, and then requested that He return the same favor in the coming year. Afterwards, she stuck her tongue out at her son, Nicholas, as if to say, *You didn't think your mother could pray that well, did you?*

The feast began. As always with this Italian American family, everybody was talking while they were eating. Only Nicholas and Frank, sitting next to each other as they usually did, were speechless, just marveling how this human menagerie somehow mastered the art of speaking and chewing simultaneously. Heads, hands, and upper bodies all moved in different directions. As they passed dishes of several courses, it was miraculous no one ever ended up with a bowl of something in their lap. Both cousins, the family's first to go to college, including the Brooklyn bunch, glanced at each other and knew this passion for abundant living could never be duplicated in the atmosphere of higher education they were headed for next Fall, ... particularly the Bonaducci's medley of sounds led by Glenn Miller, and introduced by Uncle Caesar as, "... now transmitting from high atop the Glen Island Casino on Long Island in New York, ...for your listening pleasure..."

"You know, we young folks might prefer Dion and the Belmonts, Buddy Holly, the Platters, or even our cute, little Belleville babe, Connie Ferro, who's fast becoming a national recording sensation, ... may I add, " suggested Nicholas.

All the adults ignored him. Glenn Miller was simply essential to a Bonaducci New Years Eve.

The main dining room table was extended into the living room by several plywood sections over wooden horses from the cellar. Special guests, sitting next to Grandpa Joe and Mamie, were "Zi" Magalad and Goomba Vic (her husband), the friends from the First Ward who had been displaced to Newark's Ironbound section when the Projects almost snuffed out the beat of the city's Italian American heart.

Frances DeCostanza, the Bonaduccis' "adopted" daughter now living upstairs in one of the fifteen rooms, felt honored to be at the table. This buxom Hahne's perfume sales girl had been traveling alone when she met Bella in Cuba, and later "joined" the family in Miami. Adventurous Bella had made it a habit of taking in "stray" animals, let alone Jersey gals lost in Havana.

Carmela and Jimmy Quinn, who were celebrating their first New Year's together, would remain tenants until they could afford to go out on their own. Jimmy never saw so many people at one table.

The younger children, scattered around the living room and vestibule, were eating off card tables that always seemed to have a slight tilt. At least one cousin a year would get promoted to the dining room because they were ... "old enough now". Besides the swaying tables, the real motivation for moving up to the big dining area had to do with appetite. While the delectable dishes were overflowing when initially handed to Grandpa Joe at the head seat, by the time the food made it to the kids, there could be a fight for a final single olive rolling out of control, or too little pasta that would even insult Blackie the dog back in Belleville expecting left-overs the next day.

Marietta had been quiet since she arrived. Despite all the accolades about her "andibast", she was upset that her mother and brother were alone on Fifth Street, as well as disturbed with her mother for not having sent over the homemade wine. She would surely straighten that out tomorrow when "Grandma Frassa" came to 711 Belmont Avenue. Additionally, she was pestering Rocky about the FBI reference she overheard. And, she would not look at her brother-in-law because of Caesar's comments about college in Frank's future, and the Nutley game in his past.

"Frankie, you and Gino Babula made All County. That's great!" said cousin Anthony. Between Jo-Jo and Frankie in age, he hoped to be on the Belleville High baseball team in the spring of '59. Unknowingly, Anthony had opened up a can of worms amongst the Bonaduccis.

A barrage of questions about that last game then pummeled Frank from all directions. His other younger cousins, Aunt Josephine, and even Goomba Vic, chimed in. The tiny bricklayer, who seemed to be sucking on a wet stogie since the day he got off the boat, had never seen a game and didn't know the difference between a football and a meatball. Yet a few glasses of wine turned him into the Italian immigrant version of Lindsay Nelson, adding his few cents about what little he'd heard about Frank's play. Uncomfortable moments faced Rocky, Marietta, and their Belleville football star.

Just before things about the Nutley game heated to a boil, Marietta was enjoying her own selection of her antipasto extravaganza. Elbows on the expansive table, she began to consume the virgin olive oil of the famed Bartolini family of Palermo, Sicily, competing with Grandma Mamie's house vinegar dominated dressing poured over her selection of soppracetta, provolone, sun dried tomatoes, crispy lettuce, and anchovies. As was always her style, much to the amusing embarrassment of Frank, she placed the index finger and thumb of her left hand in position to assure every element in her dish was escorted fully to that waiting fork in her right hand. Most of the time a piece of Giordano's, Calandra's, Vitiello's, or Zinicola's hard crust bread would guide the oil drenched antipasto members. Even though everyone had brought their own favorite Italian bread from all over Newark, Belleville, and Nutley, tonight Marietta did not wait for the "pane" to get to her. She always ate with two hands when she wanted to rest from her problems in life, when her family was around her, and when the food that <u>she</u> had prepared was in front of her.

Rocky knew Marietta's clock was running. It would only be a few moments before his sensitive wife would react to one of the opinions. After all, since that rainy, snowy first Saturday in December, Marietta had thought of little else. She reached for a red and white-checkered napkin to wipe her left hand, also patted her lips, and then carefully folded and placed it on her lap. A look of disgust, frustration, or anger from his wife would signal it was time for Rocky to speak up. That cue ultimately came.

"Well, it's history now," was Rocky's initial response, as everyone quieted to listen, but few stopped eating. "Nutley was tough that day. They knew how to stop Gino and Frankie. The mud ruined everything. But all our kids played their hearts out. At least it's great to see Gino make All State."

Cousin Anthony, who had innocently started the ball rolling before a single anchovy was swallowed, broke the tension building over the holiday feast. "Frankie, let's face it. If it weren't for your sore ankle, you would have scored all the points this year."

Frank did not look up from his dish of "gabagool" (capocollo) and eggplant. "Thanks, Ant, but Gino deserved all he got."

Then Nicholas, sitting next to Frank, felt compelled to declare that while Gino did have a great season, it would take a miracle for him to graduate on time with his class. Aunt Josephine, particularly proud of Frank's academic record, chimed in, "And my nephew's going to an Ivy League school!"

Playfully sarcastic Nicholas replied, "But Aunt Jo, you remember me, don't you? I'll be going to The University of Dayton on a music scholarship." Few in the Bonaducci family were as personally secure and mentally healthy as Nicholas.

Caesar Casciano half-heartily chastened Nicholas: "Ya pineapple, ya! She's talking about Frankie."

Nicholas, enjoying his aggravating affect, answered, "No kidding, my dear Uncle Julius ... oops, excuse me, ... I mean Uncle Caesar."

Caesar could have made it off Marietta's list of villains that day if he'd shut up then. Instead, he catapulted the conversation to its climax. "Frank, the lateral idea to Gino would've been the play of the year in the state. The mud and those Nutley guys were too tough anyway," repeating his earlier back-handed compliment, "Besides, my sources tell me it'll help you with a scholarship, kid."

The word, "scholarship" gave Marietta a hot flash. *Could Frank's attempt to help Gino win the county scoring championship backfire on him, ... eliminating a chance for a scholarship?* Without financial aid, the first-born pride of her life would follow in her husband's footsteps—high school football hero, but no college career, and just factory work to follow.

Esther, Tony's wife and the other sister-in-law to Rocky and Tony's five sisters, offered, "Madiett, Frankie's grades alone will get him money. Don't you worry, honey."

Marietta gave a modest smile and nodded.

A conversation on a different subject would be welcome between the antipasto and the pasta. Suddenly, Tony's "secret" about the FBI visiting Belleville police all seemed less confidential to him now.

"Hey Caesar, I told Rocky about the Feds," reported Tony.

Uncle Nick Durso remarked, " Feds in Belleville? What'a ya talkin' bout; to catch up with a few guys runnin'numbers?"

Caesar, who was very close with Mike Lanno, head of Belleville's Police Department, knew more. "Chief Mike mentioned somebody's passin' bad bills in Essex County," Caesar said. "They got some Nutley and Belleville leads. They'll get those gavvones."

Marietta dropped her fork. The hot flashes were now accompanied by cold sweats. Her mind drifted … Rosa Gubitosi, twenties, and a promised explanation? Eyes darting from Rocky to Caesar, she was now all ears.

Uncle Emil Bruno, a twenty-year veteran of Petty's Pharmacy on Branford Place where Newark's finest stopped for coffee twenty-four hours a day, provided his own inside scoop. "My good buddy, officer Angelo Longo, says it's bigger than Essex County." Emil was general manager at the all night drug store in the bowels of Newark. While not a licensed pharmacist, there was not one thing he could not provide. "Some of Gambino's boys from Brooklyn are involved. Longo says Richie's upset because it's his territory."

To many around the table, Richard "The Boot" Boiardo, while allegedly being the area mobster kingpin, had been known as a constant help during the tough Depression and war years. Everyone still talked about the "great deal" he gave Mrs. Frassa so Rocky and Marietta could marry at his Vittoria Castle on Newark's Clifton Avenue. There were also standing "job" offers in his "crews" that he would never reneg on. Then there were the memories of his being an advocate for legitimate opportunities as well, ... favors owed by "unconnected" people he had helped out. And overall, there was the guaranteed protection of Boiardo and his "family" against anyone who looked down on Italian immigrants as less than worthy of achieving their own American dreams.

Jo-Jo was happy for his brother and his parents' sake the conversation had finally shifted from the Nutley game to this possible counterfeit ring in Belleville. However, it was Nicholas who was looking for an opening to give his own intellectual take on the less than legitimate means of earning money. Except for Frank, Nicholas's unsolicited analysis would catch everyone by surprise. Being in several classes together, Frank knew to expect the unexpected from him.

"Ya know, it doesn't surprise me," Nicholas started, acting like a seasoned private eye relishing the mystery. The tallest of all the grandsons with lanky arms seeming to stretch to his knees, he looked more Swiss than southern Italian with his thin, straight dirty blond hair that constantly fell over his right eye, requiring a regular sweep of his left hand. "Look, it's all around us. Our family's always worked hard. Now it's payoff time with Frankie and I going to college. But, ya know what? There is an easier way with numbers, the union jobs, no-show jobs, the garbage business, and the protection in some of the neighborhoods."

Nicholas's emphasis on "easier way" backhandedly paid tribute to the strong and law-abiding work ethic of all the Bonaduccis in Jersey. On the other hand, the family faces were full of surprise and confusion. With his relaxed, irreverent demeanor, Nicholas almost seemed like a thirties gangster film character. "Now I don't mean that it's right. But it is easier, especially for those without an education, or who feel somebody owes 'em something. So many people we know think this way. Even politicians hand out jobs because of favors. That's accepted. The other's considered bad. These political no-show jobs help certain people and take advantage of others." Nicholas knew he was a sitting duck for a "shotgun blast" from Uncle Caesar or Aunt Josephine. But, he would not give up. "Now fake money is another subject. I can see normal people compromising for a few bucks; their way of getting back some tax money they should never have parted with, … like all the government money to tear down the First Ward to put up projects that no decent colored people even want to live in."

Nicholas's father wasted no time. "What'a ya talkin' 'bout, you pineapple? Breaking the law is breaking the law. That's no way to live. And there's no excuses to get back at government or politics, or whoever people think have taken advantage of 'em. In the meantime, my college-bound genius, that's no way for you to talk. Grandpa set your mother and us all straight a long time ago. So, stop soundin' like a wiseguy in front of your family!"

Only four years older than her nephew, Carmela never hesitated to add fuel to the fire. "Now, my oldest brother-in-law, please understand my little nephew, your only child, is doing an excellent job critiquing our wonderful state's contrasting cultures. I really want to hear more about the 'easy way'. That sounds good to me."

Having known his sister-in-law since her birth, Nick Durso showed no mercy. "Pinky," using her high school nickname, "Mind your own business. Your husband will show you the 'easy' way! Right, Jimmy, boy?"

The handsome Irishman just nodded, knowing he should stay far away from any conversation questioning Italian American work habits and ethics.

113

Marietta, who loved her nephew for being such a sincere friend to Frank over the years, broke in. "Now, Nicholas, it's a little more complex than that." Increasingly agitated, she hoped this would end it.

"Oh, Aunt Marietta, I've only been kidding'," said Nicholas. "I really don't think much about this stuff." He paused, and then craftily jumped right back into it. "Ya know, though, I gotta tell ya, … I can't believe how much time people think about takin' short cuts."

Mary, who had not yet said a word, found her original interest with her son's revelations was now making her feel sick. She erupted, "Nicholas! When are ya gonna shut your mout?"

Unperturbed, Nicholas took a deep breath. "People printing money in Belleville, Nutley, and North Newark for a little extra cash, …bad idea for some, especially us. But good idea for others. Now, I'm done."

"Nicholas, I'm surprised at you!" said Aunt Josephine, the family keeper of religious purity, as well as the head cheerleader of the Bonaduccis'self-indulgent perception of having impeccable reputation.

Answering her stern look, Nicholas assured, "Aunt Jo, just a college guy makin' conversation," at last delivering the final punch to his take on organized crime in Essex County.

The ladies began picking up the pasta dishes as Aunt Bella, who only cooked one thing a year, diverted to … "Bella's stuffed peppers, anyone? The only ones with honey and raisins."

But Nicholas' mischievousness was not over. "Just one question, Auntie Bell. What province in Italy would ever think of raisins in breaded, honey-drenched stuffed peppers? Must be a Sicilian or some North African thing."

Everyone seemed to ignore Nicholas. Not only had he been on stage a few moments too long, but any inferred connection between Italian roots, albeit Sicilian, and Africa was tantamount to blasphemy.

"Mother of God, forgive my oldest grandchild," whispered Grandma Mamie.

"I love my Aunt Bella's stuffed peppers," was all Frank said to get a big kiss on the cheek from Bella. The real motivation for his comment was not for the brownie points, but to rescue too talkative Nicholas from almost certain death at the hands of more than thirty proud Italian Americans of all ages, outraged by the subtle reference of any influence on their cherished Mediterranean homeland borders by the great unwashed of Africa.

"Perfect Frank," said Nicholas, oblivious to the possibility of his violent demise.

By this time Marietta had completely lost her appetite. Frank's questionable act of selflessness, the counterfeit twenties in Belleville and Nutley, Nicholas's totally shocking defense of the subculture that could support such lawlessness, his unconscionable implication of black blood sneaking into Italy through Sicily; all was overwhelming her. But, perhaps the biggest factor was knowing Rosa Gubitosi's twenty was still folded in Marietta's bedroom dresser.

Attempting to lighten the family exchange of information, Bella informed, "Cousin Carmine's back from Havana. He's all safe and sound, but it's too bad his businesses are suffering."

Rocky reacted sternly and unexpectedly to Bella. "Best thing that could happen to the Bonaduccis from Brooklyn ... and all of their wonderful 'associates. I told him to stick to business projects in the states."

There was silence around the table as Rocky thought, *Why complicate life with selfish decisions and desires for power?* He was not alone in his thinking. The other family members always suspected their Brooklyn relatives had made some "easy choices" for personal gain.

Although the youngest sister in the family, Carmela could very well have become its best cook. Her chicken scapparello, flanked by mixed vegetables and her masterful garlic bread, was now coming to center stage as the main course climax. A multitude of desserts would follow a brief break. Then there would be cold cuts afterwards, ... "if anybody was still hungry!?"

Goomba Vic's homemade red wine was, as expected, mellowing most of the adults out. However, there was an unspoken thought still haunting many. It would be tested to its limits in the coming year: *They're all "good boys" over there in Brooklyn, aren't they? Rocky's always too hard on 'em, ... right?*

Finding it impossible not to speak up, Uncle Caesar offered, "There but by the grace of God, go us."

Aunt Bella now felt obligated to quell any further cousin-bashing. She had, over the years, taken the most advantage of cousin Carmine's generosity, accepting trips to Havana for her, her girlfriends, and Grandma Mamie. (Grandpa Joe always sternly refused with a respectful, "No, gratsia." Uncle Emil, her husband, never went on vacation with his wife.) She stood up, statuesque and as breathtakingly attractive as always, even in her gravy-stained apron to declare, "We all have so much to be thankful for in 1958, … especially the achievements of all my wonderful nieces and nephews."

Aunt Josephine nodded in righteous agreement. Bella had artfully swept the subject of the cousins from Brooklyn and anything else dubious about the Bonaduccis under the rug once again.

Nicholas and Frank, when it was clear no one else would have a word at this point, asked to be excused to the TV room at the back of the house. The only thing more voluminous in the room than family pictures from Avellino in Italy to Lake Street and Seventh Street in Newark, was a collection of long-playing records, deposited by all of the Oraton Parkway inhabitants. Big bands of the forties and family idols, Sinatra and Perry Como, were joined by Johnny Ray, Eddie Fisher, Frankie Lane, Louie Prima, Rosemarie Clooney, Peggy Lee, and Italian tenor icons Lanza and Caruso; no Elvis! And certainly no rock 'n' roll groups of the mid-fifties. But, there was one exception—the newest albums, lying on top of the black and white TV, of Connie Ferro, their homegrown female vocal sensation who appealed to all the kids as well as their parents. Her rendition of "Mama" made everybody cry.

Jo-Jo and Uncle Tony's boys joined their older cousins in tuning the television to the clearest station to broadcast the midnight falling of the ball in Time Square. As they were jockeying for seats, Jo-Jo tweaked Nicholas, "Congratulations, big guy, you sure got their attention!"

"You kidding me, Jo-Jo? That wasn't me. Just imitating Eric Thatcher. Heard him practicing this term paper presentation in his basement last week." Eccentric in some of his views on politics, religion, and sociology in the New York area, Eric's house was always the listening studio for the latest 45's. "I had to come up with something to get the subject off the Nutley thing," Nicholas continued. "You'd think somebody at least would've talked up the Giant-Colt game on Sunday. Greatest game ever, and the Bonaduccis are all focused on Frank and counterfeit twenties. Unbelievable! Hey, the black influence on putting raisins in meatballs was my idea though. God, if looks could kill, Aunt Josephine would've been the first President of the Catholic War Veterans Auxiliary on death row. Can't believe I went that far to save Frankie's fanny."

"Really proud of ya, Nick," said Jo-Jo. "Quite the actor."

Sitting next to Nick, Frank would only smile.

The interlude between dinner and dessert was now in full force. All the ladies helped washing dishes, pots, pans, and glasses. The men remained at the table, sipping wine, beer, scotch, and rye. Nuts, figs, prunes, and Italian Perrigino candy now got priority. All the men picked on Struffala bow ties and balls smothered in honey. Anisette, blackberry brandy, and Goomba Vic's grappa now competed with the other beverages. Indeed, talk had surrendered to post-dining "pickin' and sippin'"… and more smokin'! Grandpa Joe stuffed the stub of his slow-burning Havana into the bowl of the hand-made pipe Aunt Josephine gave him after her last trip to Italy. No way would he sacrifice the last perfect puffs. Clouds from Lucky Strikes, Camels, and Uncle Tony's aromatic Cherry Blend pipe tobacco again took over the dining area.

In the corner of the room stood Jimmy Quinn, stretching his lanky six-four frame. Already a year since he married Carmela, he still was not comfortable sitting for multiple hours, eating, drinking, and talking at the same time. His wavy black hair pompadour looked like it had been styled on the set of "Rebel Without a Cause". A cavernous face accentuated high cheekbones, making his square jaw look even more powerful. His green Irish eyes had paralyzed boy-crazy Carmela into finally settling down to one guy. He was quiet compared to the many Italian-American boyfriends she brought home from all the high schools in the City League over the last couple of years. Unlike these faceless numbers, Jimmy passed the test when he went face-to-face with the Father, the Son, and the Holy Ghost—Grandpa Joe, Rocky, and Uncle Tony.

Jimmy Quinn was particularly grateful for his father-in-law allowing him to live at the Oraton Parkway home until he could save money for his own place. After all, he was the first and only Amedigan to be part of the Bonaducci clan since Grandpa Joe and his brother, John, arrived at Ellis Island. Still keeping his Irish pride, Jimmy found the regular flow of homemade red wine, constant pasta, and life with the very sexy, little daughter of an Italian family not too hard a take.

Jimmy grew up not far from Carmela's childhood home on Seventh Street and Park Avenue. In fact, the Quinn's two-family house on Lake Street was next door to the home Grandpa Joe had originally purchased when he and Mamie relocated from Brooklyn. His neighborhood extended from Barringer High on Ridge Street, up Park Avenue past Bobbie Fritz' Parkway Lodge Bar, through Branch Brook Park, and along Park Avenue to Roseville Avenue, just east of the East Orange line. On the north side was Bloomfield Avenue. The south bordered was the extinct First Ward, thanks to government's minorities projects. Part of a gang of Italian and Irish kids from Barringer, Jimmy and his buddies' biggest actual vice was hanging in local lounges and barrooms in Newark and Belleville, hoping to impress a Saturday night crowd with one of the a cappella groups they either followed or belonged to. Having been a faithful Sacred Heart Cathedral altar boy since he was eight made Jimmy untouchable with Carmela's older sisters and Mamie Bonaducci. .

The most petite of the Bonaducci girls, Carmela was the most overtly aggressive when it came to boys. Outside of the family, she was known in Barringer High's halls and on street corners as "Pinky", because she never left home without a pink satin neck scarf to go with her black satin jacket. Rocky always felt that his little sister was simply rebelling against the double standards of her older religious and self-righteous female siblings. A member of a bevy of Barringer girls called the "Satin Dolls", Pinky, along with the scarf, was also never to be found not wearing black ballerina slippers and a close-fitting sweater. And not unnaturally, the tighter her pedal pushers, the more attention she received. But all her dates soon found out she was a "good" Catholic girl, who would make for an even better wife and mother. When Jimmy entered her life, her "Natalie Wood" looks and attitude seemed to turn more conservative. She wasn't about to do anything to cost her the best looking Irish kid at Barringer, with his immaculate, red '56 Chevy.

Although no athlete, Jimmy got all the similar notoriety he could handle as lead tenor of one of the local singing groups. Lenny Latore and the Four Loves were Newark's most popular rock group, with the best a cappella in Jersey. Superb harmonizing skills honed in the bathrooms of Barringer High, the five singers were the best white team of their kind, second only to Dion and the Belmonts on the other side of the Hudson. Lead singer, Lenny, was Jimmy's next-door neighbor. Only five foot four inches, he always knew he could count on his towering friend for protection in Newark's tough First and North Wards. He and the other three in the group welcomed Jimmy as a member two years ago because of, first his Irish tenor voice, and then his good looks.

While Jimmy dreamed of national pop stardom someday to match Dion and the Belmonts, his new wife made sure the smoky bars and lounges of Jersey and New York City did not become a habit for her naïve husband. Girls, booze, smoke, and drugs would not tempt Jimmy as long as Pinky had anything to say. It was either

her, or harmonizing. At the beginning of '58, Uncle Caesar made a few calls to the Public Service Company, landing the likeable young man a job as a lineman. He was twenty-three years old. His heart may have been into singing, but he reluctantly resigned from Lenny and the others at the end of the summer.

The day before, Jimmy told his wife, "Ya know, Carmela, no body sings falsetto like Lenny. Some day he and The Four Loves will be famous. He's a natural baritone, but his three and a half-octave range can become unbelievable falsetto in less time than it takes to eat a Louie Ting-a-Ling dirty water hot dog with the woiks on it." Jimmy could not have been more accurate or prophetic.

Like so many of his friends who grew up in the post-war years, Jimmy had his heroes, and brother-in-law, Rocky, was his favorite. When they talked about anything in life, Jimmy would hang on to the ex-Marine's every word. So, when he had something he really wanted to say, Jimmy thought it out completely. "Ya know, Rock, the boys at Guys and Dolls up in Belleville, and the others at Bobbie Fritz' and The Red Door up on Heller Parkway, all go along with what Frankie did." Even Barringer alums who hung out with Jimmy had made a big deal about Rocky's son's controversial decision. He continued, "Just about everyone feels that Frankie's a real swell guy for doin' what he did."

Loosened up by a couple of glasses of wine, Rocky exposed his hurt for the first time. "Well, James, not everyone agrees."

Both first floor bathrooms were occupied, forcing Frank to trek up to Aunt Bella and Uncle Emil's private suite just beyond the landing above the vestibule. He took his time climbing the stairs. His ankle was still sore from the game. This delayed by a week the start of his playing basketball, as well as hindering his conditioning for the Belleville team. Frank's thighs seemed to also burn with each step. Brooding from the dinner conversation, Frank paused at the first plateau, midway between floors. Here in this alcove area, Aunt Josephine had placed the prayer bench given to her by the nuns at Saint Francis Xavier Church across from City Stadium. As National Director of the Woman's Auxiliary of the Catholic War Veterans, she received benefits like this from time to time.

Frank surveyed this sacred area. While a small nativity provided a seasonal touch, it hardly distracted from the variety of framed photographs mingled with devotional candles, 365 days per year. First from left to right was a picture of his father as the victorious hero in the end zone of Newark's City Stadium. On Thanksgiving Day 1940, Rocky's extra point kick tied the game, stunning the previously undefeated East Orange High State Champions. On his right was his immigrant father whose hand rested proudly on Rocky's shoulder. Joe's usual stern face could not hide his unspeakable joy. Barringer cheerleaders and fans surrounded the big right end, but not enough to block out the five foot four image of diminutive Judge Leroy Liloia, Grandma Mamie's cousin, who had risen from being an aggressive prosecuting attorney, to the Federal Court bench. He also "stood tall" on Rocky's other side. Indeed, it was a moment to be savored—proof that Joe, Leroy, and their sons were making an undoubtedly positive impact in their adopted country.

Next, Frank beheld the image of Uncle Tony, holding a Nazi flag, captured in a tiny French farm village during the hellfire combat of the Normandy invasion, plus six days.

Aunt Josephine and Uncle Caesar, a most unlikely couple, were next in the line of these moments frozen in time, standing behind a podium that read Waldorf Astoria. That night in New York City these in-laws, only slightly fond of each other, were posing with legendary Bishop Sheen, as they both were presented "Catholic War Veterans of the Year" awards. Frank smiled, recalling the often-repeated rumor that on one snowy night at the Seventh Street house when Caesar and Millie had lived with the Bonaduccis, a few extra scotches with the boys at the Megaro-Cundari Association Christmas party had him inadvertently climb in bed with prudish Josephine, not Millie, … until his still single sister-in-law screamed. No one ever denied the story.

The lineup of images featured the classic painting of Christ by Pompeo Batoni, exposing His "sacred heart", at center stage. Another of the Virgin Mary, standing atop an earth-like globe, flanked it. President Eisenhower and First Lady, Mamie, were next, waving to a crowd at Newark Airport that happened to include the Bonaducci's own … Grandma Mamie. Congressman Peter Rodino, sitting at his desk in D.C.; Perry Como, on stage at Newark's Symphony Hall; and a forties shot of Sinatra, added to the collage. The patron saint of all Bonaduccis, Ol' Blue Eyes', had only one detractor. Rocky considered him "another wiseguy who just happened to know how to sing".

The final shot, the largest of the all, included the most unlikely subjects. Renowned comedians, Jimmy Durante and Milton Berle, were standing with Aunt Bella, Francis DeCostanza, and Grandma Mamie. Taken at the Fontainebleau on last September's trip back from Havana, the picture reminded Frank of how much work Aunt Bella and her mother put into erasing the tough times of the Depression and the war, by enjoying each moment to the fullest, because tomorrow cannot be predicted. *And, perhaps they were snuffing out vanishing dreams*, Frank thought.

As Frank turned to step up to the next landing, another display took his breath away. This time on a tiny table, also in the flickering light of its own candle, inside a single glass frame was a *Newark Star Ledger* sports page headline: "Haynes Boys and Belleville Duo Lead All Essex Football." The subheading read, "Babula and Bonaducci Bellboy Stars." Frank looked down at the floor as if to say this was much to do about nothing. While alone, he was embarrassed. He gazed back upon the alcove below him and then revisited his own family accolades captured in a headline. Frank pondered how life is really so simple—*a matter of choices, thousands of them, good and bad, each made every day of our lives. Like seeds scattered about a field. It's just a matter of whether good or bad seeds had been planted. Only the eventual harvest would tell. Perhaps my family's choice to take time to pray, live humbly, follow the rules, work hard, love family and country, and enjoy the good times was all that was required for a good life. Sometimes I get it, ... but then it seems I'm never really satisfied?*

Frank's last step to his aunt's bathroom sent a sharp pain shooting through his still weak right ankle, reminding him of his own decision that determined his team's fate in the Nutley game. His stomach muscles immediately cramped, and an ache erupted deep in his heart. *What seed did I plant that day? What will the ultimate harvest be?* He sighed. It was 11:45 P.M.; 1959 was arriving shortly.

At 1:05 AM on January 1, 1959, Rocky's car started like it was ready for the Indianapolis 500. By the time he pulled onto Oraton Parkway to return home, all his passengers were sound asleep, ... except Marietta. She was up front with her husband. She had not enjoyed the holiday. Her mother's selfish absentmindedness with the wine and her brother's absence made her feel sorry for herself. She wondered what life would be without all the Bonaduccis. For a moment she forgot her blessings were sleeping in the back seat. She felt alone. The Belleville-Nutley game episode, the possible counterfeit scandal, and cousin Carmine being seemingly "involved" had given her a headache. Just as she had feared earlier in the day, 1959 was not going to be as good as the other years since the war. She contemplated, *What harm could Frank's decision against Nutley do to his quest for a college scholarship?* She could not fathom friends passing bad money and her naiveté about it. *Could I be implicated?* To hear that Carmine, who had been one of her favorites, was not the man she thought he was, ... *This is all too much.* She was scared and worried, just what her husband constantly counseled her against.

The Chevy drove like a charm, even with a couple inches of snow on the roads. Then, as was often the case with Marietta, she perked up, driving away the demons by reminding herself that she had to be a better mother to her children than her mother had been to her and Pete. Forgetting that the kids were asleep, she burst forth with a remark that should have woken everyone up. "Frankie, just don't forget. People think more of you than you think of yourself. Your heart was right in the Nutley game. You were totally unselfish. All God cares about is your heart. If anybody criticizes you for what you did, you just let them know it would've been a lot easier to score. You made a tough decision. Most people don't have the guts to do it. Let me tell you, Gino and his father will never forget it."

Instantly, Rocky glared across at Marietta. "Why did you mention Gino's father?"

"It's true," she spoke back, her look piercing through Rocky.

Her husband said not another word.

Frank, in and out of his early morning sleep, heard little of what his mother had spoken. He had been dreaming; it was a cold Bethlehem night, and he, too, had stopped at the manger out of respect for its transient occupant. However, he did not tarry. A long journey awaited him and his companions. It was time to start 1959.

CHAPTER 9

"BROKEN WINDOWS AND BREAKING NEWS

With Marietta being off work and still in bed that first day of the New Year, the ensemble of sounds and scents that usually awakened the Bonaducci household at 7 AM were limited. On the other hand, a very unwelcome phenomenon that had occurred a couple of times in '58 had returned to the slumbering abode. It was the uncommon marriage of a cry resembling that of Porky, the portly friend of Tommy from the Lassie TV show, with the sound of breaking glass, ... "Kee Yaw Kee!" This was a sure sign that Russell Giardella had just tossed *The Newark Star Ledger* toward 711 Belmont Avenue's front doorsteps and through one of the porch door panels, ... again.

In their room in the front of the house, both Bonaducci brothers' heads popped up in disbelief. Jo-Jo immediately knew his father would find it hard to forgive Russell, the eccentric, yet affectionate oldest of the seven Giardella children. The pain-in-the-neck biggest fan of Jo-Jo had broken the fourth window in less than twelve months.

Still a bit groggy, Frank was not lost for words to make his brother feel worse. "Well, I can see you never practiced with Russell the underhand motion for his daily *Ledger* tosses that Dad suggested."

Jo-Jo's only response was, "Oh, man."

Frank didn't let up. "On the other hand, Jo-Jo, maybe the headlines are so noteworthy that your 'current events expert of a buddy' may just be giving us a cue that the world is about to end, or something. Perhaps we had better get our fannies out of bed and retrieve the lethal weapon he just tried to throw directly onto the kitchen table without the normal stop on the front steps."

Once or twice is excusable, but Jo-Jo was completely baffled that Russell could be so careless for a third or fourth time, whatever it was. "God, that dummy probably went back to his overhand throw," Jo-Jo concluded. "Damn, Dad should charge for this one. Just hope it isn't me he asks for the money!" *This was not the way I wanted to start a new year,* thought Jo-Jo.

Jo-Jo sprinted downstairs as if the speed of his picking up the paper and the scattered glass would somewhat defuse his parents. "Crap, there's glass all over," was his first observation. "… and I'm in my bare feet."

Blackie, who was bounding along next to Jo-Jo, then slid through the broken glass over the wooden floor slick with the snow that had come through another one of Russell's previously shattered panels overnight.

Jo-Jo ignored Russell's wave as the dubious *Star Ledger* deliverer vanished around the corner on his rusty Roadmaster, still crying, "Kee Yaw Kee", in as irritable a voice as ever. Jo-Jo slipped himself, trying to help Blackie, but managed to break his fall with his left forearm. "God, you OK, little fella?" he asked his curious matted mutt. After making sure that the black puppy was not cut, Jo-Jo finally reached for the paper, which amazingly had survived without a tear.

Anticipating some kind of unique news, given his friend's overpowering toss and quirky early morning cry, Jo-Jo ripped off the elastic band surrounding the paper. Almost trembling, Jo-Jo's eyes widened.

"Rebels Moving on Havana. Batista's Cuba Being Overthrown".

New Jersey's most circulated daily was about to introduce Jo-Jo and his family to the commencement of a period they would never forget.

Wow, just what Mrs. Angus predicted, thought Jo-Jo. Being the outstanding student that he was and having deified his eighth grade teacher, he was immediately drawn deep into the article.

"U.S. business interests being overtaken by forces loyal to Fidel Castro …"

Jo-Jo's respect for his devoted mentor was now skyrocketing. *Is she psychic or something? Mrs. Angus called the whole thing. Unbelievable!*

Little could Jo-Jo realize how close to home the Cuban Revolution was. Only his Dad and Aunt Bella really knew the gravity behind last night's call from their Brooklyn "cugino" (cousin), Carmine.

Standing in his bare feet, now beginning to freeze, Jo-Jo impatiently turned to page 3. So engrossed in the news out of Cuba, he missed the local headline on page 2: "Federal Prosecutor to Hand Down Indictments. Counterfeit Ring To Be Exposed." Frank would be the one to discover that article later, while it would be Rocky, over his morning cup of coffee, who would turn to the stunning story of Paulie Puccini's death, deep in the inside pages of the paper. Indeed, 1959 had arrived at 711 Belmont Avenue with a fury, and it had only just begun.

By the time Jo-Jo made it to kitchen table, Frank had already cleared it off. One of their firm New Year's resolutions was to guarantee a clean kitchen every time Marietta returned from work.

"Jo-Jo, the paper better have some unbelievable news so you can defend Russell 'Dingbat' in 'Rocco's Court of Law'," said Frank.

Jo-Jo sat at the table, still damp from Frank's sweep with the soiled moppeen. Without looking up, he fired back. "Hey, football hero, when you read the paper, you'll wonder why Russell didn't deliver it by hand. Unbelievable!"

Frank grabbed *The Ledger* from him.

Jo-Jo moved over to the sink to clean the coffee pot as Frank's eyes glued to the smudged, damp newspaper. Their parents' guidance over the years was to be as familiar with current events as possible to increase their chances for A's in history, geography, and civics. "Straight A's, that's all I want," was Marietta's passionate requirement. Rocky would simply remind them to do "…not as I did; do as I say—study, read the papers, and when you have the ball in your hands, keep your knees high and don't go down."

Frank was a speed-reader and a quick study on everything he encountered. "Jo-Jo, put the radio on ABC. This article's probably outdated now. Seems they're assuming some things here at press time." Frank was correct. The news on the Philco confirmed that a charismatic rebel by the name of Fidel Castro now was in charge of Cuba, and millions of American dollars were being lost by the second.

As Frank gazed out the kitchen window, he said, "Well, one good thing, Jo-Jo. We won't have to go down to Penn Station to see Grandma and Aunt Bella off to Havana anymore."

Jo-Jo smirked, "Oh, great. That'll be my answer when Mrs. Angus asks the significance of the fall of this capitalist economy, ninety miles off Florida."

As Frank continued to finger through to the sports page, Rocky arrived with his first Lucky hanging out of the left side of his mouth. He wondered why the boys were so alert and chatty.

"Dad, you better sit down," suggested Jo-Jo, "because we got lots to tell you. And, the morning's still young."

Jo-Jo was going to confess to his friend's errant throw through the window, and then promise he would negotiate with Russell about free *Ledgers* until the glass bill was paid off. Certainly less of a businessman than Frank, but more of a salesman, Jo-Jo figured he had nothing to lose with that strategy. He took a deep breath and updated his dad about the broken glass.

"Are you serious?" asked Rocky. *Russell could not have done it again.* With the boys expecting anger, Rocky caught them both by surprise. "Jo-Jo, the Giardellas need the money, or the kid wouldn't be workin'. He should've been playing football with you this fall. Ya didn't tell him to start throwin' underhand?"

"Forget it, Dad. He can't hear that well, and he surely can't see," said Jo-Jo in no defense of the world's worst paperboy.

"Just do the shoppin' with him, and I'll give you the money." It was a new year, and Rocky did not want to start off playing hardball. "Tell him I'm rethinking our tippin' policy with him though. And no guarantees on dinner left-overs either."

Every Friday, when Russell collected his paper money from the Bonaduccis, Marietta made sure he stayed to eat. He loved her food, and she knew that was why he had always made 711 the last stop. Russell also enjoyed the peace and quiet there compared to the organized chaos at his house full of seven children and his parents.

"Get it done in a week," ordered Rocky.

Having heard Russell's delivery yell, which routinely meant big news was in *The Newark Star Ledger*, Rocky asked Frank what was wrong.

"Dad, Cuba got overthrown. And the radio's confirming everything."

Much to the boy's surprise, instead of anxiety about cousin Carmine, Rocky began to think out loud. "Good news and bad news. Rebels take over Cuba, but my cousins will have fewer problems in the future with the Feds. They lose everything. Good lesson." The boys were stunned by their father's frankness. His left hand fingers tapped on the kitchen table. Lifting his coffee cup with his right, while still holding a smoldering cigarette, he went on. "Boys, study hard and run hard. Get a college education. Don't think there's short cuts to making money. What you want is to be able to sleep at night and be healthy. That's all. Listen to your mother; she's the smart one in the family. Never break the law. I left a lot of buddies back on the islands fightin' to keep our freedom. And that freedom needs laws. We got a good name here in Jersey. My cousins in New York have their reasons for messin' up. Respect them at family affairs, but don't think their money buys anything but heartache and aggravation. Your educations will bring you all that you need in life. Football will help you, but grades are what's most important."

As Jo-Jo opened the Wonder Bread to start the toasting onslaught, Frank looked up from the paper. " Hey, Dad, look at this." On page 2 was the article about Sal Giantempo's impending indictments on organized crime's alleged involvement in the area's counterfeiting activity. The Federal Prosecutor based in Newark had made it clear on the last day of the year that his office would be issuing warrants to dozens of area residents for their part in distributing illegitimate twenty dollar bills.

Rocky snatched the paper out of Frank's hand, but immediately apologized, adding, "Damn it, a lot of guys are in trouble now. Can they get any more stupid?"

"Dad, what have you been hearing?" asked Jo-Jo. "You didn't say much last night."

Rocky mostly refused to be too judgmental about indiscretions by the neighborhood "boys". On the other hand, there were those in his life that he … "would not give ya two cents for …", and he suspected those degenerates were amongst the potential counterfeiters.

"Your mother's gonna get sick with this one," said Rocky.

"Why?" asked Frank, determined to discover what obviously had bothered his mother the night before.

Rocky hesitated. "Well, you know how Ma worries about Uncle Pete. Then there's Greenie and Two Tones. She loves those guys down on Bloomfield Avenue. But she also knows they're close to ... 'a lot of stuff', particularly Two Tones. And he's been protectin' that corner for years."

"Don't tell me Uncle Pete," said Jo-Jo.

"Forget Uncle Pete. The guys keep him out of trouble," assured Rocky. "Besides, he knows he'd have to face me if he did anything wrong. Don't get me wrong; he's no angel, but he doesn't break any laws. And he's still the best uncle youse guys will ever know."

The toast began to burn, bringing Marietta and Donna downstairs. The kitchen came alive with "Happy New Year" wishes from the ladies of the house. Marietta was particularly bubbly, having just prayed in bed and committed to start 1959 as upbeat as possible. Besides, she was hosting the holiday meal today, and she needed all the positive energy she could muster.

The boys would not dare relate any of the current events to their mother yet. They figured they would give her a chance to have her first cup of coffee. They loved when she displayed a cheery countenance. It was infrequent, and her self-deprecating sense of humor that would often accompany it was something to savor.

Rocky put the paper down, slouched in his wooden hard-back chair, put out his cigarette, and placed both hairy arms behind his head.

"Dad, what's wrong?" asked Frank. He knew his father had been dealt a blow that he was now trying to determine how to communicate it to the others.

"There's bad news here!" announced Rocky.

"What, Rocky? Read it to us," demanded his wife. Marietta was sick with fear almost immediately. She walked over to her husband, squinting to read the paper.

"Daddy, tell us," pleaded Donna.

The boys were quiet. How did they miss this article?

Rocky ordered Marietta to sit, and then slowly told his family of Paulie Puccini's tragic death. Everyone was stunned. Frank pushed away from the table and headed up to his bedroom. Jo-Jo, face in his hands, stared at his dad, listening to every word from the article. Donna sat paralyzed.

"Oh, no, I know Jean Puccini," groaned Marietta. "She lost her son. Sacred Heart of Jesus! Her husband died the year after Paulie was born. She couldn't do it all herself." Her voice breaking, she went on. "Oh, God, take me first. Don't ever take my kids before me. How, Rocky, how?"

"Marietta, you're not listenin'. It was drugs."

If his wife was upset now, what about when she reads the bad money article? A tough day at the house was looming.

Upstairs, Frank was silent. He'd grown up with Paulie, but after getting hurt his freshman year, Puccini seemed to vanish, missing classes and getting into trouble. Frank, sick to his stomach, spoke to God. "Take care of his mother, and I know it's late, but have mercy on Paulie." Frank learned from Marietta's black Baptist friends, Queenie and Nora, that praying for the dead was not in the Bible. *It's when they're alive that you should try to help them out. After death, it's too late. Pray they come to repent and know Jesus when they're alive.* He could hear his mother reciting her friends' many scriptural teachings. That was the "holy roller" stuff his family had always stayed away from. This idea of it maybe being too late for Paulie made Frank upset. It did not seem fair … because Paulie could not have a second chance, … and because Frank never had prayed for Paulie Puccini when he was alive. "Forgive me, Lord," whispered Frank. "But, there but by your grace go I. Give Paulie a break. He never got one here."

Back four years ago, Puccini was an important part of Belleville's freshman football team. Thinking of all his own injuries and disappointments over the years, Frank fully admitted any success he achieved would have never happened without both his parents. He could not imagine how he would have handled the serious knee injury that Paulie experienced, … *and to come home to an empty house without a father, and a mother who was always working to make ends meet.* Frank's biggest fans were always Rocky and Marietta. Poor Paulie had no one to lean on. He wasn't religious. While his mom loved him, she was just one person. It was the wiseguys from the neighborhood who swooped down on Paulie and gave him some kind of identity and opportunity to separate himself from others, just like football and school had done for Frank. *God, if it weren't for the knee, he would have been a madman on the football field.* Frank almost felt guilty. His family support system was so strong, and Paulie's was non-existent.

Silence ruled the kitchen table. Marietta had called Pete, and Paulie's fate was news to him. Pete did remind his sister how uncontrollable Puccini had become with some of the crew on Bloomfield Avenue. Drug and alcohol abuse, combined with his natural aggressiveness, had concocted an overly expressive Paulie. He just seemed to talk too much for the mature mob lieutenants controlling the area. Pete admitted to Marietta to overhearing Two Tones expressing concern, somewhat fatherly, for Paulie's growing lack of dependability and control. She did not share this conversation with Rocky, working on another Lucky and his second cup of coffee.

Donna was busy looking for cartoons on TV, while Jo-Jo slouched, seemingly in a trance on the couch. No one seemed interested in the burned toast.

Marietta now fixed herself at the stove to begin preparing her famous fresh ham New Year's Day dinner. In addition to her mother, Pete, and Frank's girl friend, Marietta, much to Rocky's chagrin, had invited her best friend Dalla at the last minute. She had not appeared for work at Giordano's Bakery on New Year's Eve, but Marietta had tracked Dalla down to make sure she was O.K. It seemed she and her fiancé, George, had been arguing since Christmas. And she refused to be with him and his family. As was usually the case on holidays, either at the Bonaduccis or at her mother's house, Marietta or her brother would invite a "stray" person in some kind of need. For Pete it was usually some black kid like Jerome from the neighborhood, or down on Orange Street or Central Avenue where he picked up some of his meats. The late Pete Frassa Sr. got his two children into the habit of always sharing their food with the less fortunate on holidays.

Frank always felt the mystery guest list added a little extra to the celebrations. Returning from his bedroom, he asked, "Who'll be this year's surprise visitor, Ma?" Frank was hoping tiny Jerome would be the lucky one. He had come to love the miniscule black kid. However, Marietta had selected her sexy Maid of Honor. Both boys, fighting raging hormones, were not overjoyed about Dalla showing up in her pump heels and low cut blouses.

Meanwhile, Frank jumped on the phone to call around the town to see what others had heard about Paulie's death. In most cases, he was breaking the news to his friends. Becoming restless with the gloom and heaviness in the air, Jo-Jo returned for the sports page, and within moments, loudly announced it was time to figure out how the men of the house were going to watch all four bowl games without offending Marietta, Grandma Frassa, and Dalla. Donna, who loved football, would be leaving the dinner table early as well to fight for a seat in front of the TV.

"We got the Sugar at 12:30, Cotton at 1:00, Orange at 2:00, and the Rose Bowl at 4:00," proclaimed Jo-Jo. "God, you think these games could be scheduled so we could at least watch two of them all the way through."

No one responded, so Jo-Jo began searching for Sy Dorfman's column on football. *The Ledger's* high school football writer since when Rocky played, Dorfman had now added college to his portfolio. "Bowled Over by the Bowls" headlined his column that day. Halfway through, Jo-Jo froze. His brother's name was there! This did not feel good.

Dorfman had crafted a fascinating review of college football's most bizarre plays, two of them having been highlights in bowl games. Most fans knew about "Wrong-way Riegal", that University of Southern California player who scooped up an opponent's fumble, got spun around, and sprinted up the field to the wrong goal line, to be tackled short of the opponent's end zone by his own teammate. Then there was Rice halfback Dickey Moegle's run when a passionate Alabama player jumped off the bench to halt a sure TD. Apart from bowl game snafus, there was the famous "Fifth Down Game" back in 1940 against Dartmouth that cost Cornell the national championship. The Big Red lost a post-season appearance chance because their winning touchdown was scored on a fifth down. Later, walking off the field as winners and with only lowly Penn last on the schedule, the "Fifth Down" came to be revealed. Cornell forfeited the victory, literally ruining their season. Penn upset them the following week.

Reading the next paragraph made Jo-Jo's mouth go dry.

"Speaking of Cornell, it seems local All Essex halfback, Frank Bonaducci, could be headed for the Ivy League institution, nestled beautifully in the Finger Lakes region of western New York State. And when it comes to bizarre plays, the Belleville senior fashioned one on the last day of New Jersey's high school football season."

Jo-Jo swallowed hard, … *"the play"*.

Dorfman first mentioned Babula's quest for the scoring title. Then: "Well, Bonaducci, a pretty good student at Belleville as well, did not run the wrong way. But, did he do the right thing? The jury is still out on that one. The question is whether the likes of Cornell and the other schools recruiting him will hold against him his decision to wait to lateral to his teammate. If so, the kid looses the kind of coveted scholarships he and Jersey's best are seeking."

This is really bad, thought Jo-Jo. *God, it's horrible timing with the rest of the news.*

Dorfman then signed off with a surprise final opinion: "In the end, Belleville's Mr. Outside was thinking of his teammate, Gino Babula, surely one of the state's most explosive Mr. Insides this year. And, it was still early in the game. The Bellboys may have gone down to defeat at the hands of bigger Nutley, but I think Frank Bonaducci earned a name that will only honor him in the future. 'Wrong-way Riegal' made an honest mistake. The Cornell's players and coaches were gentlemen offering their 'victory' back to Dartmouth. That Alabama kid had too much Crimson blood flowing in his veins. 'Faithful Frank' from Belleville was just trying to be a loyal teammate and friend. Isn't that really what the game is all about?"

Jo-Jo closed his eyes and sighed in relief. His brother dodged a bullet, … the day's first bit of good news. Thinking too quickly for his own good, he jumped up to tell everyone. Excited, Marietta urged Frank to finish his phone conversation with Maria, … "to hear what Mr. Dorfman has written about you".

As Jo-Jo read to everyone, Donna hung on her brother's shoulder trying to read along with him. Reaction from his parents and brother were unique. Rocky nodded at every word, being a huge fan of Dorfman who had crowned him a high school football hero for his '40 Barringer-East Orange feat. Frank was disinterested, consistent in his convictions to others about his game time decision. Marietta, anticipating only complements, gasped at the mention of the scholarship issue.

Rocky sought to reassure her. "Marietta, this is a sportswriter. He doesn't know how positive the college coaches are with Frank."

"Ma, the schools recruiting me give out financial aid anyway," assured Frank. "They aren't talking about big football scholarships like the ones talking to Gino." Frank was impatient with his mother's naiveté and obsession with the money issue. He had seen that all over her face at Grandpa's the night before.

Jo-Jo concurred, "Ma, Frank's right. Gee, to be mentioned in a college football column is great. This is good, Ma, really."

"I don't know," said Marietta, hesitating. "It's just the way this day started. I prayed so hard this morning. I guess you guys are right."

Then, Rocky offered priceless wisdom. "Marietta, life will always have its difficulties. Some of us will have more than others. It's how we react. Choose to have a good day today and just count all of our blessings, ... please? This article's OK. The guy complemented Frankie."

The morning had gotten off to a dubious start, but conversation now seemed to brighten the room as much as the first warm sun of the New Year which engulfed the kitchen, clouded by cigarette and burnt toast smoke, competing with fighting the sweet aroma of seasoned fresh pork roasting in the oven, and complemented by the garlic and meat laced gravy getting its warm-up for Marietta's holiday lasagna. Her heavy hand with parsley for the ricotta cheese added a subtle freshness to the buffet of smells. The cold winter day outside was in sharp contrast to the cozy warmth that had slowly become a balm to the spirits of all the inhabitants of 711 Belmont Avenue.

Jo-Jo was on the phone with Rosemarie, while Frank and Donna were making sure the temperamental television would be ready for the network bowl game telecasts. Rocky saw the moment as the best to tell his wife the rest of the bad news. "Marietta, Giantempo is gonna indict lots of people on this counterfeit thing."

While a couple of years behind him at Central High, she readily knew and understood Sal Giantempo's aggressiveness as a law enforcer and a politically hungry powerhouse in Newark and Essex County circles. "How close, Rocky?" she asked, indicating an intuition that familiar names would be mentioned.

"Well, first of all, don't worry about that thing with Rosa," whispered Rocky, referring to their backdoor neighbor who slipped Marietta a twenty several weeks ago in exchange for a four dollar supersod, ... perhaps one of the most idiotic deeds Rocky could ever imagine. Why would his righteous wife have ever fallen for this gesture from Gary Gubitosi's spouse? He added, "And, don't let the whole thing drive you nuts when people we know get collared. Stata sitta (be quiet), Marietta. Especially with the kids around."

Then Marietta abruptly turned to him, "What about Pete?"

Rocky assured his wife, as he had his son earlier, that from what he could glean from last night's conversations with his brother and brother-in-laws, Pete had been "protected" once again, no one even mentioning his name relative to the alleged area counterfeit scandal. She changed tact. "Rocky, God forbid Rosa is involved and mentions my name. That will embarrass us all, … and, God, … Frankie's scholarship opportunities!"

Rocky was losing his patience. "Marietta, where's this faith I hear you and your colored friends talkin' about. Damn it, <u>you</u> didn't do anything wrong. I'll tell ya though, Gary and Rosa can't be trusted, and sometimes you're dumb about that. With you, everybody's a good person. Well, that's simply not true. I never liked Gary. Always trying to make a quick buck. Now, I can't trust Rosa."

Marietta knew she had to shift focus. Not responding to her husband's mild tirade, she concentrated on checking the ham in her temperamental oven.

The morning's harrowing roller coaster ride for all the Bonaduccis made time pass quickly. Maria was their first dinner guest to arrive. Her dad, Angelo Giardina, popped his head in the back yard door to wish everyone Happy New Year, and handed Rocky a bottle of Seagram's rye. The families had known each other for three years, and since the sweethearts started to date, both fathers had become very fond of each other.

Marietta was particularly appreciative of Angelo's gift, insisting he return that night with his wife, Santina, for leftovers, fresh ham sandwiches, and dessert. There was no one more hospitable and generous than Marietta Bonaducci. Maria seemed excited about the invitation and encouraged her dad to convince her mom. Their presence later that night would prove more valuable than Marietta could ever imagine.

Maria had met Frank in their freshman year at Belleville. At first, when she quickly glided through his morning cafeteria study hall, Frank thought she was a teacher, as she seemed so mature and sophisticated. Her tight, short, brown curly hair, round face, high cheekbones, perfectly tweezed eyebrows, and cute shape initially resembled Annette Funicello of the Mickey Mouse Club. After their first date in October that year, they became inseparable. This seriously disappointed Frank's female admirers, as well as Maria's own following of Belleville boys on the prowl. Later, her dark Sicilian complexion and long pointed nose would eventually have Frank proudly describe his girlfriend as a Sophia Loren look-a-like to his college buddies in the years ahead. Frank always would see himself as totally lucky in love.

Reaching for the moppeen, Marietta made sure her hands and arms were clean before she planted her patented multiple kisses on both Maria's cheeks, hugging her like her own daughter. Any potential girl friend, she told Frank, would only pass the test after the Bonaduccis met her parents. Indeed, Frank had found the right family. Maria's natural beauty and intelligence … " were simply an example of God's grace …" according to his mother.

As Maria and Donna assisted Marietta setting the dining room table, Pete's jovial "Happy New Year" could be heard from the back door. Frank quickly jumped up, knowing he'd be requested to help carry in armfuls of Calandra desserts, Giordano bread, homemade wine, and anything else his big-hearted uncle had gathered to enrich his sister's dinner. No one but Marietta knew he supplied all the gravy meat of pork sausages, pork necks, the chopped meat for the meatballs, and even the fresh ham. What he had in his arms at the back door was only a portion of his holiday contributions.

Following behind him was a most contrasting sight—the stern, round faced Grandma Frassa, popping out of her oversized black, ankle length coat, … and the glowing presence of Dalla Della Pella. Like most women of her generation, Dalla did not drive, so Pete did the favor of picking her up.

Marietta's girlfriend was thirty-five years old and still single. And she oozed sex appeal. On the other hand, when she opened her mouth with her wholesome and sincere interest in all whom she met, any errant fantasies dancing on the conscious mind of the beholder would disappear, as if doused by a pail of cold water. However, the reality of her appearance could not be diminished. Her flowered felt hat, padded shoulders, knee length coat, heels, and seamed flesh colored stockings could not distract Frank from her cleavage subtly peeking out from behind her silk scarf. He softly uttered, … "Jesus". Impure thoughts racing, Frank respectfully accepted his mother's childhood friend's wholesome hug.

Frank could have easily put out that fire by simply greeting his Grandmother more quickly. Heavy jowls and puffy eyes seemed to hang without end from her unyielding face, until her oldest grandson welcomed her. A black hair net that never seemed to leave her head acted as a winter hat. In her arms was the white and red wine that was her umbilical cord to the past when her husband, Pete Sr., would spend hours in the cellar beneath their two-story walk up on the corner of Fifth Street and Bloomfield Avenue. With it being nearly twenty five years since her spouse's passing, the beverage of her heritage would only appear when she would scold Pete harshly enough to demand his descent into the bowels of their cellar to concoct a few gallons of the staple.

Wearing black as long as Frank could remember, Mrs. Frassa's dresses always loosely draped her round body in such a way that no one ever knew just how large she really was. Not unlike the extended posterior style of Victorian female royalty, Grandma's backside and hips seemed to extend all the way back to Newark. It was not the framing of the dress or the extra layer of the coat that broadened her figure; it was <u>all</u> Mrs. Frassa. Jo-Jo, looking from the TV room window, thought Uncle Pete surely had to be hiding a couple of colored kids from Orange Street under his mother's coat.

Holding the door open for Pete and Dalla, Frank reached to hug his mother's mother. "Grandma, Happy New Year."

While none claimed to ever see Mrs. Frassa show any sign of affection to either of her children, her genuine love for her three grandchildren was undeniable. "Frankie, come sta, velo bello (how are you, my handsome one). Grandma hasa soma wine for you and soma udder tings for you and your brotha and sista." She always gave cash for any special occasions to all three young Bonaduccis. Naturally pleased by such generosity, Marietta often wondered when her mother might send some financial help in the direction of her and Rocky who could certainly use it. Indeed, her mother seemed to totally avoid the subject of the potential cost of Frank's college education if a scholarship was not available. For weeks, Marietta had hinted she might need some assistance, but the elder Frassa would just suggest to … "waita".

Nonetheless, Marietta respectfully hugged her mother, as Jo-Jo took her coat, still convinced at least one tiny guest had to be hiding under his grandmother's dress. While he liked Jerome, he was glad that no one peeked out. Jo-Jo did not feel like entertaining "some colored kid all day". Today was a day to watch college football.

Rocky simply shook his mother-in-law's hand and nodded.

"Rock," she responded.

Mrs. Frassa was famous for one-word comebacks, and Rocky for never having addressed his wife's mother by name, or any family title. It was because he could not fathom his mother-in-law's constant coldness toward Marietta and Pete. On his side of the family, love and encouragement knew no bounds. Once when he expressed his frustration to his own father, Grandpa Joe replied how a small segment of Italian immigrants abided by a perverted philosophy of not having their children accomplish more than their sacrificing parents. "… 'fesso chi fa I figli meglio di lui' …" or "… 'stupid is he who makes his children better than himself …'"

That day dinner went well. Marietta was pleased to be with Dalla to whom she gave advice between courses about how to become indispensable to her fiancé, George. Her mother's constant fussing over Donna showed some warmth and goodness in her, even if Pete and Marietta never remembered similar affection coming their way.

Jo-Jo made sure the Cotton Bowl telecast was on highest volume so Lindsay Nelson's play by play could clearly be heard in the dining room. Between the multiple conversations at the dinner table and the blaring TV, the Bonaducci home was full of peripheral sounds. To top it off, Marietta refused to shut off the WNEW radio presentation of all-time musical hits. Her ear was waiting for Sinatra. Indeed, another organized madness of sight, sound, scent, and salivation was being produced for anyone who might have inherently been in search of peace, simplicity, and quiet. Not at 711 Belmont Avenue. For at least the duration of this smorgasbord of life, a new year was being welcomed in, no matter how dubious some already saw it becoming.

Throughout dinner, Dalla stared at Jo-Jo. He picked up on the glances, momentarily entertaining an unspeakable fantasy that he could not even possibly fulfill at thirteen. Back and forth trips to the TV room to catch moments of the game helped cool off his adolescent desires.

But Dalla did have something on her mind. Assisting with some dish washing, she said, "Marietta, Jo-Jo is so handsome, and he's growing right before our eyes."

"Oh, thank God, Dalla. He's following in Frankie's shoes, getting good grades, and Rocky tells me that he should be just as successful in football as his older brother." Marietta glowed when hearing complements about her children. They were her passion in life. She had long abandoned any of her own dreams. The mission that did remain for her was her emptying herself totally into her offspring so they would never be faced with the late bills, intermittent unemployment, the graveyard shift, and general frustration that seemed to characterize her total existence.

Dalla then added, "Marietta, I've been staring at Jo-Jo all dinner. He's gotten so muscular and mature. But I don't like what I see on his neck."

Marietta was now curious and disturbed. "Dalla, what?"

"One side is bigger than the other."

Without hesitating, Marietta called her son from the TV room.

"Ma, later. The game!"

"Now!" Fear was growing in Marietta. Her friend would not have mentioned anything like this, if there were not something to it.

As soon as Jo-Jo made it to the kitchen, both women began examining his throat area with caring hands. Naturally he objected. But both their faces showed genuine concern. Their probing fingers on the right caused Jo-Jo to sense soreness.

"Ma, I've been lifting. My neck's getting bigger. That's the reason."

Rocky was called in, followed by Frank and Uncle Pete. Their consensus, too, was that Jo-Jo's neck growth was definitely uneven. Something existed just to the right of his Adam's apple.

Wringing her hands with the moppeen, Marietta wiped the top of her nose that always perspired from anxiety.

"Ma, he's been lifting a lot," said Frank. "This kind of thing happens. He might have just pulled a muscle."

Dalla remained silent. Donna wanted to check her brother out herself. Jo-Jo was convinced there was nothing to worry about, but Rocky made it clear that he would travel with his son to Dr. Ciccone down on Roseville Avenue in Newark that week. The doctor had delivered all three Bonaducci children.

Grandma Frassa had fallen asleep in the TV room's spacious recliner a few moments after devouring Marietta's fresh ham. The homemade red wine surely contributed, too. The impending Rose Bowl kickoff woke her up, so Pete told her about the kitchen commotion. Still groggy, she shuffled in and insisted on examining her grandson herself.

"Manedge diaola! (Damn the devil)." Mrs. Frassa scared even Jo-Jo with her violent and abrupt cursing of Satan. Jo-Jo had a problem. She was convinced.

"Ma, just stay out. We'll take care of this," replied Marietta. Tension instantly began to build between the two.

"Stata zitta (Be quiet)," Pete said to both. He was worried, too. He just didn't want anyone to know.

A knock came at the back door, as simultaneously the telephone rang. Angelo and Santina Giardina, Maria's parents, had arrived for dessert. And Aunt Bella was calling to wish everyone, "Happy holiday".

Mrs. Giardina, Sally, as her friends called her, was apprised about Jo-Jo almost immediately. To calm Marietta, she enthusiastically told her about her younger brother who had the same kind of swelling in his neck twenty years ago. In the end, he had a harmless cyst removed.

Donna had answered Aunt Bella's call and gave the phone to Rocky who returned his glamorous sister's holiday wishes. But she instantly discerned his mind was elsewhere, and wanted to know what was wrong. He updated her. Bella immediately assured Rocky that she and her husband were coming to Belleville. She hung up without any emotion and apprised Emil of the concern. Her medically adept husband, who always saw himself as more than a pharmacy general manager, was anxious to help. They arrived in less than twenty minutes.

As she did anytime she entered a room, Bella Bruno immediately became the center of attention at 711 Belmont Avenue. She opened the backyard door without knocking, announcing, "Auntie Bell's here". Wearing a full-length mink coat that could not have been bought only with her husband's salary at Petty's Drug Store and hers as a shoe sales girl, she glided across the kitchen's cracked linoleum like Loretta Young. While Dalla was a coquettish beauty, Bella had sophisticated glamour that had been crafted from years of an adventurous life aimed at making it in the theater. Maria took her mink. Bella's red silk blouse gently caressed her broad shoulders and healthy bust line. Dalla needed padding on the shoulders of her dress to portray her outdated style. Bella's natural contours were all she required to stop any admirers in their tracks. Her backless high heels from the legendary "Footnotes" in wealthy suburban Millburn, where she'd been general manager since the war, put the finishing touch on her provocative style and attitude.

Donna and Frank quickly acknowledged her presence with hugs and kisses. Pete had always been in awe of Rocky's Rosalind Russell look-alike of a sibling. She was a close friend of Greenie's younger sister, Katherine Delaney, the only true love of Pete's life. His mother had quenched that back when they were in their twenties. Bella had lobbied for the couple, but to no avail. He never forgot her sincere effort to play Cupid.

After embracing everyone, Bella called for Jo-Jo and got right down to business. "Quanda si bello … (so handsome), your mother's cheekbones and my brother's smile. Jo- Jo, sit down next to Aunt Bella and Uncle Emil."

Marietta was fussing with expresso and scotch for Emil and his dynamic mate. The fresh ham sandwiches and the other leftovers and dessert would have to wait for the examination by the pharmacy manager-turned doctor and his Florence Nightingale of a wife.

"Jo-Jo, sit up straight," commanded Emil. Never having set a foot in a college biology or pre-med course, Emil Bruno, in his brown tweed suit and starched dress shirt with matching brown speckled yellow tie, could have fooled anyone that this was the family physician paying a visit. He did not apologize for his impersonation.

Bella was confident in her anticipation. Everyone else in the dining room was quiet, waiting for his diagnosis. Marietta was squeezing the moppeen, … hoping for a good report. Dalla, who had often gone out dancing with Bella when she was still single, stood arms folded in the kitchen alcove.

"There's surely something there. But it's soft. It does go deep though. That's the only problem. Feels like a cyst to me. That's good." Emil was staring at the ceiling rather than the surrounding crowd.

"What's the bottom line, Emil?" asked Rocky, wanting to hear it from the brother-in-law he respected as the only man in the world who could have ever tamed his sister. Had the two never met, Bella was destined for the Broadway stage or some burlesque hall. So, Grandpa and Grandma Bonaducci worshiped the ground Emil walked on. A first generation Italian American daughter should be working or pregnant, not traveling the country as a singer and dancer.

"Rock, forget Ciccone," advised Emil. "My friend, Marvin Rinzler, further down on Roseville Avenue, is the guy to take care of Jo-Jo. He's a Jew boy—the best eye, ear, and throat specialist in Jersey. No nonsense." Emil took his hands off Jo-Jo's throat and knocked down the double scotch. He relaxed.

Not a word came out of his audience, until Bella spoke. "We'll all be OK."

Emil looked to Marietta. "Now, mother, forget cancer. Not this kid. It's not on either side of the family, and he's on his way to big things. God is good." He then began to sip the expresso as Bella put a bottle of anisette within reach. "Look, I don't know what he's gonna say, but I can tell you this. Rinzler's face is angelic. So is his disposition. His hands are beautiful. If I didn't know he was a Jew, I'd say he was Jesus himself."

Frank corrected his uncle light-heartedly. "Jesus was a Jew, too, Uncle Emil."

"Just a minor detail, Frankie." Emil laughed.

Rocky was still unsure. "Emil, has he worked on anybody we know?"

"Well, Rock, you know how The Boot's boys stop by at Petty's at all hours?" Knowing his brother-in-law's distaste for wiseguys, Emil tread softly. "They told me a couple of month's ago that Benny "Bad Boy" Badalamenti from Gambino's New York crowd needed some work on his voice box. Rinzler got recommended."

Frank, still in a joking mood, added, "Well, Uncle Emil, Jesus healed all they brought to him, ... and he hung out with some questionable people, too." The heaviness in the air was vanishing.

Emil concluded, "You'll be pleased with him, Rock. Anyway, just like I said, it's too soft to be a tumor. I'll call Rinzler later, and he'll take you tomorrow."

A collective sigh of relief gently enveloped the room, now smoky from the cigarettes of Rocky and Bella and warm from the crowd of family. Everybody knew the game plan for the week—pray and hope for the best.

Frank and Jo-Jo had seen a side of Aunt Bella they never had before. In the midst of uncertainty she was as driving and strong as she was physically attractive. As amateur as her husband's examination may have been, the mood of the night had been turned around by their visit.

In the end, the presence of Aunt Bella, her husband, and the Giardinas helped to divide the concerns of the day. Marietta, who always set the mood for the house by virtue of her handling of life's challenges, was being as brave as she could. She did not want her mother to perceive any weakness. On the other hand, the day had been overwhelming to her, ... from Paulie's death, to the article about Frank, to the discussion of the counterfeit ring. She could care less by the end of the night if Rocky's Brooklyn cousins were involved in the rackets and losing everything in Cuba; but, now her son.

Pete had been quietly observing everything unfolding that January 1. The happy years of Frank's football career were now over, and even ever-hopeful Pete felt changes evolving. It was time to end one of his sister's worries. Before he left with Dalla and his mother, he would tell her in private about Sneaks and his promise to pay for any college need Frank might have. He invited Marietta to join him for a cigarette just outside the kitchen back door. By that time, darkness had set in. Neither was wearing a coat, but the emotional day had been too charged for brother and sister to be concerned about the outside chill.

When Pete revealed his post-game telephone conversation with Sneaks, Marietta could not believe her ears. Her jaw dropped. "Pete, how could Sneaks be so generous? The years with Poppa?" Pete didn't answer. "Frankie's plan to help Gino against Nutley?" He just smiled. "That's it, Pete! Oh my God! My son, ... my perfect son."

Pete had delivered the perfect antidote for her doubts about Frank's Nutley game decision. Her eyes could not have gotten any bigger. A euphoric look overcame her countenance. She took a deep breath of fresh air. After exhaling, she quickly and nervously placed the Lucky between her lips. As she blew her smoke heavenward, it married her breath condensing in the evening cold. It dissipated into the dark, and as she watched the elements disappear, she beheld the millions of stars above. She wondered why the good Lord had waited to the end of the day to finally allow her to hear some good news. She anticipated some type of audible answer from above. There was only silence.

Now Marietta could face Jo-Jo's problem. If there were no scholarship for Frank, an old friend would take care of the money problem. She felt a weight being lifted from her back as she pondered how to handle Rocky's inevitable objection about the source of the money. Then, she violently turned her head to Pete, to make sure again it was true. When he smiled and touched her shoulders, his face became her father's ... with Sneaks by his side during the Depression at the back of the butcher shop. *That's it,* she thought. *Sneaks is just returning the favor.* Sighing in relief, her mind then raced to the image of her son's selfless act in the Nutley game.

While the morning breaking news on January 1, 1959 had broken a glass panel on the front door, by the end of the day, Marietta's spirit had been renewed. In fact, by midnight, like a mother eagle in flight, she was soaring with renewed hope for her family, thanks to a benevolent and grateful jailbird, ... named Sneaks.

CHAPTER 10

"FROM BASKETBALL TO BACKSTAGE JOHNNIES"

The year's first week of school was anything but normal for Jo-Jo and Frank. As he promised, Uncle Emil Bruno had made a home phone call to Dr. Rinzler before leaving the Bonaducci's on New Year's Day night. He set up a time for him to see Rocky and his son the next day. Rocky's other brother-in-law, Caesar Casciano, let him leave Jergens an hour early to pick up Jo-Jo for the 4:30 PM appointment. On the other hand, Frank would have his own appointment with basketball coach Hiram Wilhelm about his sore right ankle.

Rinzler took little time in deciding the young eighth grader should go under the knife, and soon. Emil's diagnosis was right. The growth was probably a cyst. But his major concern was its expanding inward toward Jo-Jo's windpipe. Surgery would be at the ancient Children's Eye, Ear, and Throat Infirmary in the bowels of Newark below High Street.

An hour before Jo-Jo's examination, Frank had been called into coach Wilhelm's office. Doubling as the Belleville athletic director, he was concerned about Frank's slow recovery from his football injury. Belleville had won two of its four basketball games in December. The coach had been expecting more from both his team and his lean, but muscular forward. "Frank, you can jump with the black kids from the City League. When are you going to start this season?" Over the last four years, many an opponent in the small Belleville gymnasium had found Frank's patented soft jump shot unstoppable from the left side of the basket.

Bonaducci knew the coach had been complaining about his senior letterman to other teachers and even to some teammates. He wanted to be respectful, but also very clear to the aging mentor. "Coach, the ankle's still bothering me. I'm doing my best. The whirlpool would help if it wasn't broken, but I am soaking it at home."

"Forget the whirlpool, kid," said Wilhelm. "A little more concentration and toughness is all I want." Wilhelm then hit a nerve he should have avoided. "And don't think I'll tolerate what you did in the Nutley game. With me, it's get it done for the team, and forget that sentimental stuff."

Frank could not believe his ears. Having been raised by a Marine to always respect authority, he went limp and slouched back in the wooden chair. His face flushed. Then Frank's seldom seen temper began to boil. He thought, *If my mother were here, she'd eat Wilhelm's eyes out, Bloomfield Avenue style, ... then finish him off with some ethnic slur. Later, she'd ask for forgiveness from Jesus.* While the good Lord had not yet rid Marietta of all her demons, Frank was not going to invite them into this situation.

All at once, Frank went blind. He did not see Wilhelm any more. Not a rage, but rather a soothing vision erupted—that of the green grass of a well-groomed college football field. It took form slowly, as if painted by a brilliant artist. The scene of running the football at a great university danced across his mind, and the kaleidoscope of dreams calmed him.

When the coach's face finally reappeared, it seemed Frank had been absent for hours. He took a deep breath. "Coach, I should have gotten the ball to Babula. The mistake I made was never telling him what I planned." Frank added, "You always coach your players to talk it up between them. Right, Mr. Wilhelm?"

"Right," answered the coach, who was no longer leading the conversation, just wondering where Frank was going with it.

Playing with a basketball in his hands, Frank started to bounce it. He stood up, gave Wilhelm the ball, and shook his hand. "I've played my last basketball game for Belleville High." He left before the stunned coach had any chance to react.

Since he had not yet begun practice that day, Frank quickly changed back into his school clothes without showering. He left the locker room without speaking to any teammates, now already warming up on the court. Unemotionally, Frank was convinced what he had just done was the right decision. Without properly resting his right ankle, all he would be doing in college would be attending football games as a fan. His basketball coach's autocratic and insensitive perspective helped his choice.

By the time Frank got to the school exit door, he was thinking clearly and less emotionally. On the two-mile walk home he'd stop for a haircut. Then he would first inform his feisty mother. Hopefully, she would not write a biting letter to the Superintendent of Schools about how the system should have more Italian-American coaches at Belleville who understood "... how our kids sometimes think with their hearts". He laughed inside. *What about my father?* he wondered. *Maybe he'll be thrilled.* Rocky knew Frank's right ankle was taking too long to repair itself, and that basketball could jeopardize Frank's football future, particularly with any interested recruiters.

As Frank exited the school, a strange and unfamiliar feeling came over him; never in the last four years at Belleville High did he have any time after school. It was always football, basketball, or baseball practice.

Buttoning up his hooded parka, Frank noticed a phenomena involving classmate Craig Francello that he had only heard about since his sophomore year. Craig was being helped on the green and gold DeCamp bus heading into New York City by some of Belleville High's most dazzling female students. Some of the bevy of ballarina-slippered and high-heeled coeds had reputations that preceded them.

God, it's true, Frank thought. *Unbelievable little devil!*

Craig Francello was seventeen and special. Raised in the town's Silver Lake section, from where some of Belleville's toughest kids spawned, he was a victim of cerebral palsy. His large and narrow head always drooped left. Very few people understood him, because they refused to slow down their listening to his laborious delivery of words, sometimes with saliva dripping from his mouth. His motor skills were wanting, and falls in the school hallways were daily events. Always with his book bag, Craig would need help any time he and his homework went flying all over the slippery floors. Whether rescued by a healthy athlete or a tight-sweatered female, Craig would manage a smile, gain his composure, and holler, "Safe". Not safe were the young ladies. Conveniently for him, Craig's flailing would land touches on parts of their most attractive structures.

Four young ladies were involved in the struggle to get him on the bus and pay his fare. Frank stared even harder as the severely afflicted Craig awkwardly pulled out a wad of cash that looked like he could have hosted all his pretty attendants at the 21 Club for dinner that night.

Where does he go in New York City? wondered Frank. *And where's the little cripple get all of that money?* Bonaducci walked in the opposite direction, thinking neither Craig Francello nor any of the girls had seen him.

As Frank crossed over to Joralemon Street to head west to the newly opened "Pentagon Barber Shop", he could not get Francello out of his mind. He knew while Craig did spend some time at the Cerebral Palsy Center on Nanny Goat Hill on the Belleville-Newark border, Francello's parents had received permission for him to be schooled with his contemporaries since the third grade. Four years ago, Frank first set eyes on him and felt he shouldn't even be at Belleville High. While compassionate like his mother, over their first two school years, Frank avoided Francello. Then in advanced Physics in the fall of '57, Frank felt a tap on his shoulder from the person sitting behind him. It was Craig. *A whole year with this kid,* Frank thought with frustration. *Now I have to try to understand him!*

Understand him is just what Frank learned to do. He focused on Craig's lips, listened to every sound, and began to laugh himself silly. Craig was not only humorous, but also intelligent beyond the other students, well read, and, much to Frank's surprise, a big football fan! Craig would start on Mondays after the Saturday games. "Yaaaa run like that again this week, Frankie boy, then Coach P. might give ya the ball a little more. Annnd, maybe IIII could arrange a date for you with Julie Manzer. She only likes guys who scooore … touchdowns that is!"

Frank would just smile and shake his head. It amazed him how Craig would not only be at all of his games, but understand what was going on. And then there were his frequent remarks about Belleville's most voluptuous coed. Frank was honest enough with himself to know a date with five foot ten inch Julie Manzer might get him excommunicated from the church. *Is Craig Francello actually the incarnate Lucifer to suggest such an "impure thought" that would surely lead to an "impure action"? Besides I'd surely lose Maria forever as my girlfriend.*

Craig constantly throwing Julie in his face reminded Frank that the entire high school male population was an envious bunch. Julie was certainly never going to become a nun, but her reputed amorous escapades always seemed to happen with guys from out of town. She never dated Belleville boys. Aspiring to be an actress, her concocted love adventures seemed to extend all over Essex County's community theater scene and even into New York City entertainment circles. Her only tie to Belleville High was that she seemed to fall all over Craig Francello every time she joined him at lunch in the cafeteria, or at one of Frank's games. Craig also rode shotgun in her '57 Chevy with the continental kit that proclaimed, "Tonight's the Night". Neighborhood guys surmised that she, or her dad, had money. He was a Newark cop.

While Frank's relationship with Craig grew in their last two years of high school, he still never learned why he ventured into New York City everyday.

Walking on mostly unshoveled sidewalks, Frank took about thirty minutes to reach the barbershop across from the Milk Bar. The attending haircutter was not the aging Mario Pietoso, who had put all his life's savings into his new location. (His Nutley family called him a "traitor" for moving his business to the Belleville side of the line in early '58.) Approaching the door, Frank squinted and hesitated. While he'd never been particular about his wavy black mop of hair, Mr. Pietoso never made a mistake. *Who's this barber?*

"Frankie Bonaducci, welcome to Mario Pietoso's famous Pentagon Barber Shop, … or hair salon if ya choose, depending on how secure you're in your own masculinity." It was Joe Pelli, known for butchering his English with a bravado-like use of big words and concepts beyond his formal education!

Frank knew Joe by this journeyman barber's reputation for never shutting up during a haircut, so that you either began to nervously laugh, or wanted to jump out of the seat. Frank had never actually met him before. Joe dropped out of Belleville High to pursue haircutting and also an entertainment career, … although his life as a comedian in the New York City and Jersey Shore nightclubs was advancing at a snail's pace. Frank wondered how Joe knew his name, and before he could ask, Pelli continued. "'Mario da Man' ain't feelin' good today, and we've been talkin' about me helpin' out anyway here at da Pietoso family enterprise. Please make yourself comfortable in your reserved seat, Mr. Outside."

Joe's warmth and knowledge of Frank's football reputation got his attention. "You're Joe Pelli, right?" asked Frank.

"Dat's correct, and you and your associate, Gino Babula, were da best tings that happened to Belleville football since I can remember. Sit right down, Frankie, and let's make ya look like a movie star." Joe did not seem to take a breath between sentences.

It became readily apparent to Frank that while certainly a street guy, Joe was a quick study, and very perceptive about nearly any subject you care to discuss.

Slightly overweight with a trace of acne left over from his teens, miniscule Joe was full of life with a sparkle in his dark eyes that signaled optimism and hope for himself and others. Always neatly groomed and stylish, his swagger signaled the inkling of an entertainer, the mob, or a guy who had turned cutting hair into a choreographed performance. He flashed his scissors with quick wrists. The story around the North Ward of Newark and Belleville was that as a comedian, Joe Pelli was a great barber.

After getting Frank's special styling instructions, Joe jumped back into his staccato dialogue. "So, why ain't ya at basketball practice with dat prune-face Wilhelm?"

Frank smiled, amazed at Pelli's astute observation of his early exit to the world of … "no practice after school". So, he told Joe what happened.

"His loss. Da guy should retire," Joe continued. "Flunked me in gym. What'a ya gonna do wit your time?"

Frank outlined his plans to strengthen his ankle, get ready for baseball in the spring, and then college football.

"Dat's it, kid. Stay in school and make Belleville proud of ya." Pelli loved every minute of advice-giving. "Forget this Wilhelm guy. If he wasn't such a jerk, I don't drop out of BHS. Den, I would'a missed my shot, dough. Yea, somebody up der likes me. Maybe Coach Wilhelm really helped me in disguise; helped me get my shot." Joe took a deep breath, stretched his arm out with the scissors, and then brought it back to his lips, playing it like a microphone. "And now, here at Las Vegas' famed Sands Hotel, da critically acclaimed comedy team of Pelli and Benedetto."

Pelli was dreaming, and Frank didn't know whether to laugh or cry. He did know that he didn't have enough money to pay for the haircut and the performance. "What are you talking about, Joe, … your 'shot'?"

"Tell ya, Frankie. Ya gotta do what ya love to do. If ya do, my mother says, 'Ya never woik a day in ya life.' And I don't like to woik. This barber stuff pays da bills, but my comedy stuff? To me, dat ain't woikin', … dat's heaven."

Frank persisted, "But, Joe, come on, tell me about your shot."

"Oh, my entertainment career's got some life. Me and my partner are doin' OK … makin' a few bucks. And we're gettin' to know people in da business. We tell our crowds Jersey stories. Ya know, Italian stuff. The Jews in da audience like when we talk Jersey and get into Italian food. Dey tink we eat "gabootsells" (capozzella, the head of a lamb) for breakfast. Dey laugh. Not Lewis and Martin yet, but we're woikin'on it."

Changing pace, Frank went on. "Then let me ask you something else. How'd you know me when I first came in?"

"Yas a hero, kid," said Joe, embarrassing him. "Just what I wanna become. And, by da way, Frankie, good try wit Gino in da Nutley game. Would'a been a great ting. At least ya had da guts to give it a try. Must of pleased Sneaks and da boys all da way from Bloomfield Avenue to Boot's headquarters down at Vittoria Castle."

"Vittoria Castle" needed no explanations. It was Boiardo's mob restaurant, catering hall, and hangout where the local crime king entertained celebrities like Joe Di Maggio and Frank Sinatra, not to mention also where Rocky and Marietta Bonaducci married.

"Joe, you know Mr. Babula?"

"Before my ol' man croaked, he woiked for Sneaks. Tell ya, Mr. Sneaks and his boys got connections in da entertainment business, and dey opened a few doors. Nuttin' wrong or bad. Just made a call for me wit my fodder bein' dead and all."

All the time, Joe continued to give Frank the best haircut he could remember. Not too short, just right. *Maria will love how it's turning out.*

"Hey, Frank, ya go to the city much wit Gino?"

Frank updated Joe that while the running mates were fond of each other, their differences meant they didn't socialize much together.

Joe then had a suggestion. "Look, ya like rock 'n' roll, da groups, and stuff, right? The Five Satins, Buddy Holly, Connie Ferro, the Belmonts, and da harmony ting. Right? Dat kind of ting?"

"Of course. Especially Dion and the Belmonts and Connie Ferro."

"All right, I'm gonna make ya a 'backstage Johnny', but ya gotta bring Gino, too. My partner woiks at the Paramount in Brooklyn. He'd love to meet yas. He's a

Nutley guy, and a real high school football nut. Ralphie Benedetto's his name. Pick a Saturday night. You and Gino show up where Ralphie B. tells yas."

"Mr. Pelli, please slow down. What's a 'backstage Johnny'?" asked Frank, envisioning a part-time job of sorts. He could use the money, particularly if a scholarship would not be forthcoming.

"Kid, it's just entertainment tawk. My partner gets yas in the back door cause ya know us. We get yas back stage wit da stars, and ya coagulate; ... ya know, ya mix wit 'em. Get a couple autographs, have a couple drinks. Ya famous, kid, cause de're famous. Dion, Connie; ... dale all be dare."

Frank was excited. *Meeting Dion would be the best. Connie will remember me. Now she's the country's top female singer—American Bandstand and everything.*

"Gimme your home number. I'll get some dates from Ralphie. Ya pick 'em."

That day Frank was exposed to a new world and another local character striving to leave his own mark on the neighborhood that had nurtured him. Joe's ticket was his love for making people laugh, even if it made him look foolish. Along the way, he would respectfully turn down cash from running numbers for the local hoods and cut a lot of hair, but never lose his dream of becoming an entertainer. Some day Joe would, indeed, make his imprint on the entertainment world, seemingly by chance, ... and not as a comedian. Frank's promised experience as a "backstage Johnny", complements of Joe, would have a unique dramatic impact on him. They were, indeed, two ships passing in the night. On the other hand, their hoped-for destinations were not unlike. The routes they would take on their journeys would be different, as would be the duration of their respective trips to fame and destiny. And there would be an unlikely fellow traveler on board with them, ... Craig Francello.

Even with his haircut delay, Frank arrived home well ahead of the usual 7 PM after basketball practice. In the Bonaducci home, getting home at set times was gospel. Only work or practice waved Rocky's strict "quarter-to-five" rule.

Finding his mother uncharacteristically waiting on the front doorsteps, Frank was convinced Coach Wilhelm had called and broken the news about his quitting. Then he realized as he entered the icy driveway that he had become so self-absorbed, he had completely forgotten Jo-Jo's neck appointment. That's why his mother was out front.

"Frank, your little brother has to have an operation," said Marietta, adding mater-of-factly, "How was your day?"

"Ma, you OK?"

"The Sacred Heart of Jesus is not going to let him have cancer."

Frank gave his mother a reassuring hug at the front door, observing her almost business like approach to this most recent family challenge. While it was a refreshing alternative to his mother's usual emotional and agitated reaction to most problems that came her way, Frank was uncomfortable with her puzzling aloofness. "So what's the story, Ma?"

Marietta told him surgery was scheduled for next week. A cyst was probably the culprit. Little did Frank realize that Sneak's guarantee for his own education enabled her to focus on Jo-Jo's condition, and not lose control.

Still, Frank decided to wait for his father before breaking his basketball news. Ultimately, the family supported his leaving the team, in view of his weak ankle and the possibility of scholarships from the likes of Cornell, Yale, and Lehigh. Frank never informed anyone Wilhelm's comment about the Nutley game. Why jolt his mom, ... who really just might want to eat the aging Jewish basketball coach's eyes as an early Easter delicacy?

The mood at the house that night was reflective and philosophical, as they all prepared in their own ways for Jo-Jo's surgery in one week. The basketball issue really did take a back seat. Only Jo-Jo asked how Maria was taking Frank's decision since she was a senior cheerleader, and the season was important to her.

"God, I forgot to call her!" Frank realized.

Before he could contact Maria, three straight phone calls would confirm Frank's decision to put basketball behind him.

"Frank Bonaducci?" The voice was deep and business like. "It's Coach Hetrick from Cornell. Good time to talk?"

Usually never lost for the proper words, Frank was nervous. "Coach, Coach Hetrick, Happy New Year."

"Just a routine call, Frank. Want to make sure that all of the application is in."

"Yes, sir."

"Great. How's your dad?" The Cornell staff enjoyed speaking with Rocky, appreciating him for his own football career and his knowledge of the game.

"OK, Coach. He's great. Thanks."

"Listen, as you know, we want you up here. We really do. But after speaking with the other coaches, we want you to know while that thing in the Nutley game was virtuous, you must always think of the team. No big deal. It will probably never happen again. But, you can't do such things at this level. Don't you agree, son?"

Initially, Frank was rattled. *What should I say? Dad's always reminding me to respect authority, the Marine Corp way. But Yale's my first choice anyway.* Thinking quickly, Frank knew this was not a battle he was going to fight, … even though his principles were at stake. "Coach, a one time thing."

"Great, Frank. Listen, keep up the grades and get healthy. I think we'll have some good news by March."

Frank wondered how much Hetrick knew about his ankle, and figured there was no use mentioning basketball. "Yea, Coach, I'm doing some weight training. Looking forward to the good news." Hanging up, he was jittery. *Glad I left basketball. These guys mean business.*

Just as his father tried to find out about the conversation, the phone rang again. It was Hiram Wilhelm. He insisted on apologizing for his remarks about the Nutley game and asked Frank to reconsider quitting. Wilhelm knew he had spoken out of turn, and didn't need any problems with Belleville's Board of Education that considered Frank one of their favorite sons. He let the coach down gently, by confirming college football was his objective, and that the ankle needed rest.

"That's what we'll report," said the coach, half asking, and half telling his player what others ought to hear.

When Frank hung up this time, Donna got into the act. "Frankie, who called? I gotta do homework on the phone with my friends."

Ignoring his feisty little sister, Frank was about to update his parents when the third and most unexpected interruption came. It was Craig Francello, who was actually telephoning him for the first time ever. "Craigie boy, I can't determine what you are saying when I'm <u>looking</u> at your handsome face. Now you expect me to blindly interpret your babblings on the phone?"

Craig slurred his words. "III'm concerned, big guy. I … I have my daily thing to do in New York while you goooo to practice. But not todaaay! I catch you sneaking out. Date with Julie Manzer?" The "Julie" remark was supposed to disguise Craig's deep interest in his favorite three-sport star's break from his usual routine.

Frank decided to play along, and maybe get an answer to the question everybody wanted answered. "So, Mr. New York, you tell me what you do everyday in the City, and I tell you what's up with me."

Francello roared with laughter. "Fooootball, basketball, baseball, and your pretty girlfriend—child's play, Mr. Bonaducci, … child's plaaay. Did you hear meee, football hero?" If Craig were normal, he might be obnoxious enough to be friendless. On the other hand, Frank also recognized how lonely it really must be to be Craig Francello. His sharp tongue was just a façade.

Frank gave him a full update about Wilhelm, the ankle, and his encounter with the colorful Joe Pelli. Mention of the barber excited Craig. "Joe Pelliii, the wannabe comedian, former wannabe gangster, former wannabe hair stylist, former backstage Johnnnnny, former wannabe Mr. Popular of BHS," rambled Craig. "Ugh!! Great company on your first day of entering the real world without sporrrrts." Francello seemed to know more about Pelli than he was telling over the phone.

When Frank told how Joe could get him in to see Dion and the Belmonts and Connie Ferro, Craig laughed again. "Boooy, do you know how to pick your new friends, … Joe Pelli, his sidekick, Ralph Benedetto from Nutley, and a couple of the other New York City boooys!"

How's he know Benedetto, and what did he mean about … "the other New York City boys…"? Frank wondered.

In the end, Craig explained he was calling from New York and had to catch a bus back to Belleville. "See ya in school tomorrow."

Craig never did reveal why he was in the city. Frank would finally get the answer fifteen years later. He smiled; impressed to think his friend with cerebral palsy would care to check up about him. Little did he realize that Craig was also smiling when their conversation ended. But then, … Craig Francello was always smiling.

CHAPTER 11

"AUNT BELLA TO THE RESCUE"

A week later, the weather in the New York City area turned warmer. But the low-pressure system that seemed to have been around since the Nutley game over a month ago had not yet moved on. It was late afternoon as Rocky pulled his decaying '49 Chevy up to the front of the Newark Children's Eye, Ear, and Throat Infirmary. He quipped to Marietta and Jo-Jo that if the rain pelting outside were snow, it would be a blizzard. Attempts to keep his wife's mind off of her son's impending surgery were not working. Her child was about to be cut with a sharp scalpel, just below his chin.

Jo-Jo recognized what his dad was trying to do. "Yea, Dad, and if it was snow, you'd be shoveling forever. I'll be recuperating, and Frankie's always studying or working out. So don't be wishing for that pretty white stuff." Jo-Jo looked for his mother's reaction. The demons of depression had made their appearance, and they had taken Marietta out to lunch.

After parking the car, the threesome scurried into the tenement-like building that had been built by immigrant Italian laborers in the early part of the century. While it appeared to be well behind the times of other hospitals in Newark by virtue of its cracked foundation, torn window shades, and unkempt landscaping, its specialists inside were incomparable in the area. However, there was no ignoring the reality that the Infirmary's dilapidated exterior discouraged entrance for its young patients and their families. In fact, it drew fear.

Jo-Jo grabbed both his parents' elbows as they entered. "Looks like they filmed Frankenstein here!"

It was hard to convince visitors that this was an award-winning hospital. Its dimly lit corridors were uncluttered, but no people to be found either. Paint on the walls and on the light fixtures was cracking. Ancient doors could be heard creaking down the hallways. Holding his nose, Jo-Jo was first to be overcome by stale air heavy with odors of formaldehyde, iodine, and adhesive tape. He was amused. Marietta still ignored her surroundings. Rocky was getting aggravated.

At the end of the center hall, a makeshift registration desk looked more like a card table. Three by five boxes acted as a patient filing system. Just before the wrinkled seventy-five year old female volunteer appeared from inside the small office behind the desk, a voice filled the sterile halls of Newark's Eye, Ear, and Throat Infirmary for children, with refreshing tone and welcome vitality.

"Auntie Belle's here."

Looking as glamorous as ever, she contrasted sharply with the cold, lifeless environment she'd just entered. Her black fur coat was dry, glistening only with the natural texture of the mink that graced her from the top of the neck to just above her ankles. A giant umbrella, held by her lean husband, had repelled the January moisture. Emil's London Fog raincoat was soaked, and his felt fedora was dripping.

"Bella, you guys didn't have to come," said Rocky as he shook Emil's hand and kissed his sister's cheek.

"Bella, you're too much," perked up Marietta. "God bless you."

As Bella kissed Jo-Jo on both cheeks, Emil smiled and pulled his nephew's left ear. She was on a mission, and her co-pilot in life had been her transportation in the inclement weather. She told her husband she wanted to be with her brother and his wife as much as possible before, during, and after the surgery. Intuitively Bella knew they were frightened about the growth on their son's neck.

"Emil and I are going to have dinner Down Neck, so we thought we'd stop by here," she announced. For years the Bonaducci family had frequented the many Italian and Portuguese restaurants in Newark's Ironbound section on the east side of the city. Even so, Bella still wasn't being entirely honest. She wanted to make sure that her brother's family could handle the cost of the surgery and knew that

156

being present at Jo-Jo's registration, she'd get to hear the numbers. But, in the end, Dr. Rinzler's relationship with Emil and modest help Rocky would get from his employer would make the medical procedure affordable.

It was two hours later that Jo-Jo finally got to his hospital room. During that time his parents remained quiet, sitting uneasily on the lobby's hardback chairs. Bella, meanwhile, busied herself making friends with everyone from nurses, to volunteer receptionists, and to young interns strolling in the halls. Since her arrival, the aging edifice had found new life. After the weak-legged senior at the registration desk was so sweet to Rocky and Marietta, as well as reminding her of her own mother, Bella slipped the granny a twenty-dollar bill when the admission papers were finished.

With her nephew finally tucked in at 8 PM, Bella stood at the foot of Jo-Jo's bed, put her hands on her soft hips, stuck her generous chest out, and declared, "I see we have a problem."

Jo-Jo chuckled. His father's sister was always full of surprises. Like his Uncle Pete on his mother's side, Bella, with no children of her own, was forever trying to make life better for all her nieces and nephews. "What, Aunt Bella?" he asked.

"No TV for my brother Rocky's son. Not acceptable. Emil, what are we going to do?" Before her husband could answer, Bella went on. "Emil, your midnight crowd. Don't they always have special deals on appliances?" Bella was talking about the half dozen Boiardo crewmembers who always met at least a couple of times a week at Petty's Drug Store. Between coffee, hot fudge sundaes, grilled cheese sandwiches, ice cream sodas, and cigarettes, Emil would make sure that his soda jerks treated the "boys" with respect, as well as to "forget" to charge for what they ordered. The mobster tips were a good incentive.

"Bella, don't start there," said Emil. "They can get you anything you want. But we're a respectable family. The guys are good to me, but we want to keep our distance."

In Rocky's presence, Emil was being a bit more self-righteous than the usual when he and Bella would talk about his midnight customers. And even she only knew half the stories. Emil would overhear everything from "inventory reports" on men's suits, TVs, cigarettes, and fur coats, ... to whispers about Gambino's organization doing "too much" business in Jersey. Then there were smirks about call girls and the booming cash from prostitution that the aging heads of the New York area crime families insisted did not exist.

Emil would never forget one night when Benny "Bad Boy" Badalamenti showed up. A Gambino lieutenant from Brooklyn, he'd moved to Newark's Forest Hill section in the mid fifties. Loud mouthed and brazen, Emil thought this thug was as ignorant as he was daring. Richie Boiardo objected about the move to Carlo Gambino himself, but the New York boss convinced The Boot that Badalamenti would be kept on a short string. But the real thorn in Emil's side had to do with Badalamenti's quest to make Bella his wife in the years before she married Emil. Bad Boy first met her at cousin Carmine Bonaducci's home before the war, when she had "run away" as "Bella LaStarr" to make it as a dancer and singer. While she kept fighting Benny off, the money, lifestyle, and his entertainment connections were increasing bait to becoming ... Mrs. Badalamenti. In the end, it was Grandpa Joe who stopped any of her lingering thoughts about becoming an underworld wife.

Bad Boy's one night trip to Emil's pharmacy even bothered the Boiardo wiseguys already there. He'd had too much booze. He talked incessantly when he was sober, but after half a dozen "Seven and Sevens", no one could shut him up. Badalamenti babbled on about a counterfeit strategy he thought fool proof, and then about the drug traffic into New York City, and how he had convinced Gambino to join in. The Newark boys were trying to quiet him down with as much black coffee as he could take, when beat cop, Eddie Manzer, showed up. Emil remembered it well.

"Everything all right here, Mr. Bruno?" Manzer asked, ignoring, but also knowing, each of the sharply dressed customers, ... until he spotted Bad Boy. Inflating his chest and clutching his nightstick, the cop demanded, "What are you doing in this neighborhood, Benny?"

Many considered Bad Boy insane, but he was not nuts enough to utter to the law what he was really thinking. He wanted to say, "What I'm doing here ya flat foot is lookin' for your eighteen year old tease of a daughter; figure it's time she learned the ropes from a pro." Without any doubt, with that statement, Manzer would have killed him.

The fast-moving images dancing across Emil's mind disappeared as Bella broke his trance. "Emil, you can get a nice TV for Jo-Jo, can't you? Legitimate, of course, my darling."

"Yea, yea."

"OK, loves, it's all set. Aunt Bella will be back for the big day tomorrow."

Bella and Emil never made it to Ferry Street for the sangria and seafood extravaganza. Instead, he drove her back to East Orange and the Bonaducci mansion they shared with the rest of the clan. Then, it was back to the heart of Newark to start his graveyard shift.

On the way home, he and Bella spoke few words. He had his assignment, and she knew he would get it done. She dozed, and her mind wandered back to by-gone days. The feel of a warm Caribbean breeze lapped at her soft face, tossing her black hair gently in the Havana night. She was on the balcony of the Americana Fiesta Hotel, a faded beauty of a building her cousin Carmine and his company were trying to buy. The view from on high of the dimly lit city and the handful of fishing boats moving on the darkened waters was like gazing upon a collection of Van Goughs. It was only several months ago, but her mother and she had lived the spirit of Havana so many times since their maiden voyage in the late summer before Pearl Harbor.

Mamie Bonaducci was sitting to the right of her daughter and "Bad Boy" Benny Badalamenti on the left. Already married to Emil for eighteen years, Bella no longer had any interest in the Brooklyn hood. But he always seemed to be around when she visited cousin Carmine, either in Cuba, or at his Brooklyn estate. She easily dismissed any thought of Carmine being involved in illegal activities. But she could not help fantasizing once more how her life might have glittered with fast-moving Bad Boy—the theater, singing, dancing, even Hollywood. She would have convinced him, with her beauty and charm, to go legitimate.

Actually Bella had her chance with Benny just before the war when he was a rising street hood. Richie "The Boot" even called Grandpa Joe to broker the relationship. They agreed to meet at The Boot's Vittoria Castle restaurant one Sunday after mass at the Sacred Heart Cathedral. A surprise guest at the dinner was key to the God-fearing laborer from Avellino's final decision. It was his young nephew from Brooklyn, Carmine. Without asking his reason for being in Newark that day, Joe looked to his older brother's son when Boiardo asked his opinion about a courtship beginning officially. Uncertainty filled his nephew's eyes. At the end of dinner, Joe slowly rose from his plush chair, reached over to shake the benevolent Jersey crime boss' hand, and said one word, … "No." Carmine would later tell Bella this story on one of her visits to Cuba, well after her marriage to Emil.

Havana's attraction for Bella over the years surely was not Bad Boy. The two-week treks with her mother began with the traditional "going away" party that buoyed the emotions of Grandpa Joe and Emil. They both could look forward to imminent independence from their flamboyant wives. The family sendoffs from Newark's Penn Station were reminiscent of the busy transportation hub in the war years. Bella and Mamie knew new friends would be made and old acquaintances renewed, especially with half of each trip spent in Miami Beach. Havana's Spanish influence, island charm, and old world style were the perfect antidote to living in New Jersey the other fifty weeks of the year. But there was something else that drew Bella—her cousin Carmine Leonardo Bonaducci!

The first born of her Uncle John, Carmine's enigmatic success in the New York trades, especially on the waterfront, generated a lifestyle for his family and four brothers that he would share with his Jersey cousins at every opportunity. Whether in Brooklyn at his brick, fortress-like home, or his estate in Havana, they would always be welcomed. What was amazing was that he had no formal education after high school.

On that last stay at the Americana Fiesta in September of '58, Bella asked Carmine to consider Rocky and her younger brother Tony for business opportunities in Jersey. She caught him off guard at a late night reception he was hosting on the majestic hotel's roof that sported pools, bars, and dance floors. A tall, handsome man, Carmine's slightly pocked face gave it a ruddy look that rather than distract, actually added to his tanned, weathered profile. He loved his Jersey cousin's beauty, glamour, love of family, and eternal optimism. He was known throughout the five boroughs as Carmine, "the Artist", because like the Renaissance "Leonardo" of his middle name, he, too, was recognized as a creative, positive thinker, … always "painting" a picture of optimism regardless of the circumstances.

With a couple of drinks in him, and just having heard that his chances of owning businesses in Cuba were now threatened by Castro's rebel uprising, Carmine was uncharacteristically curt. "Bella, so many times I've offered Rocky opportunities in construction, the unions, the restaurant business, … all clean chances to get out from under his ninety dollars a week take home at Jergens. The offers would hold good for Tony as well. But I always get the same, … 'let me think about it'. He's stubborn, Bella. Now I got Bad Boy hounding me about doin' more stuff in the Newark area. But I tell him we can't get the help. Besides, I have to respect Mr. Boiardo."

Attracted to the underworld flamboyance, but somewhat naïve about what it took to fund such a lifestyle, Bella flashed a stern look. He caught it, and quickly recovered in classic Carmine "the Artist" style. "I know the Boiardo family from the many ventures we have together in construction and with union business relationships.

Bella, regardless of the allegations that often come the way of Mr. Boiardo, I have always respected their interests."

Bella had been hoping for some attitude of legitimacy, and Carmine just gave it, although feebly. That's all she needed to continue her fantasy of compromise. "If your father, my Uncle John, were alive, he would be so proud of you boys. Don't give up on Rocky. Remember, he wanted to be FBI when he came out of the service. So he feels funny about some of the people you have to deal with in your businesses, Carmine."

Bella had also had too many martinis. The reality of Carmine's world was all around her. But the alcohol, her double standards, and her family pride made her hear only what she wanted.

"Bella, we're home!" Emil's voice shattered his wife's reverie.

How right she was not to pursue any Badalamenti relationship years ago. Even her cousin's businesses were getting too risky for her or her brothers' consideration. Kissing Emil good night, she accepted that fun in Havana with her cousin and his friends was one thing. But marrying into the mob was out of the question. After all, every Bonaducci in Jersey would have abandoned her. She wasn't sure about her Brooklyn cousins.

At 4 AM that morning, a well-dressed man in a black raincoat arrived at the Eye, Ear, and Throat Infirmary's registration desk. Behind him were two strapping black teenagers, jointly cradling a huge box. Inside was a television set. The man had to wake the duty attendant, seizing her wrist with his strong, yet gentle right hand, sporting a massive diamond ring.

"Listen, don't ask any questions. This TV's for one of your patients, complements of Mr. Richard Boiardo." He looked around. "My dear, how do we get to Joseph Bonaducci's room?"

The sleepy clerk seemed puzzled, as a crisp twenty-dollar bill was handed over.

"Just take us to his room. These two colored kids will do all the work."

Thomas "Two Tones" Anthony had followed orders. He would inform Pete Frassa of The Boot's good deed directed at "Five Corner's" nephew. The family had cooperated with little notice—Uncle Emil, Aunt Bella, Two Tones, and everybody else from Petty's Pharmacy on Branford Place to the "social clubs" along Bloomfield Avenue, … even Sneaks at Rahway.

When Jo-Jo awoke that morning, he and his nurses watched television before his surgery.

CHAPTER 12

"BELLEVILLE CORNFIELDS"

Heavy, dry snows the first two days of February seemed to cleanse the northern New Jersey streets of January's left over exhaust and mud-tainted stains. Marietta felt totally cleansed, too, renewed, born-again, invigorated, and hopeful … about Jo-Jo. His surgery had taken three hours. The biggest challenge was untangling fibers of the bronchial cyst from around his windpipe. With no trace of cancer, he would recuperate one week at home, keep his four-inch scar bandaged for two weeks after that, and then perhaps be able to resume basketball at School Number 10 by middle of the month. Surprisingly, Marietta's mother offered to reimburse Jo-Jo's infirmary expenses. "Beefing up" the bill to cover some of the numerous times Grandma Frassa could have pulled her and Rocky out of family financial jams but didn't, Marietta gladly accepted.

February began bubbling with anticipation at 711 Belmont Avenue. Jo-Jo had been declared healthy. With baited breath, the family awaited replies from schools where Frank had applied. Rocky even got a raise at work, which Marietta and the kids convinced him was worth a least a trip to Rutt's Hutt for hot dogs to celebrate. Furthermore, Uncle Pete had started on a diet. Then there was excitement only she and her brother could share secretly. It was over the account Sneaks Babula had opened at Peoples Bank for Frank. The statement read: "$10,000".

On Tuesday, February 3, 1959, exactly two weeks after his surgery, Jo-Jo rose early for his first day back to eighth grade. He was ready to resume the normal life of a thirteen year old, just as Uncle Emil and Dr. Rinzler had promised. This meant his father and siblings had to endure their daily dose of The Dell Vikings' "Come Go With Me" once again.

Marietta had just returned from work as Jo-Jo entered the kitchen. "OK, Jo-Jo, the Lord has healed you," Marietta began. "Now He expects straight A's for the rest of the year, doing well in basketball, and being good to your family. Pretty simple. You've never disappointed your mother. Mrs. Angus can't wait to see you." Ellie Angus, Jo-Jo's "drill instructor" teacher, claimed no favorites. But in confidence, she assured Marietta that her second son was one of the best she ever had, ... even more so than Frank.

"Ma, don't worry," said Jo-Jo, rubbing his eyes, still swollen from a reaction to Blackie's licking his face when he came home from the hospital.

"A little less with this Rosemarie girl, and a little more studying," ordered Marietta, now cranking on two cups of Medalia D'Oro coffee. "Don't let everything you've achieved in grammar school go down the drain because of a girl. Besides, Mrs. Angus says you deserve better." Marietta would not let up. "Remember how Mommy would study at Central; read a paragraph, think about it, read it again, then memorize it. Simple. It'll get you to college just like Frankie. No butcher shops or factories for you boys."

"God, Ma, ... enough," cried Jo-Jo, as The Dell Vikings were replaced by ...

"I had a girlfriend, Donna was her name. Since she met me, I've never been the same..."

In less than an hour, no one in America, let alone in the Bonaducci household, would listen to Ritchie Valens' love song with the same heart. Marietta has once written a poem on the back page of *The Newark Star Ledger*:

When the heart breaks, it is never the same.
The scars last forever, entombing images—some good, some bad—but all indelible,
... Every one to be viewed, when summoned by emotions that demand a glance back.

The hurt really begins, when the glances turn to stares.

With everyone now wide awake, the muffled cry of paperboy, Russell Giardella, ricocheted through the frigid outside air. Jo-Jo cringed. Marietta was oblivious.

Upstairs, Frank knew the drill. It had called him out of slumber several times before. Rocky would reach for his first Lucky at the sound of the four-eyed monster of newspaper boys.

"Oh no," said Jo-Jo, bracing himself.

Moments after the … "Kee Yaw Kee", … and something that sounded like … "Herb Oscar Anderson", … the nauseating sound of breaking glass again caught every one's attention. Russell had inevitably done it again, and Jo-Jo knew there had better be equally earth-shattering news in *The Ledger* to justify the latest goofy paperboy's toss.

"Ma, he'll pay for it," offered Jo-Jo.

Marietta just smiled. She felt sorry for the oldest of the seven Giardella children who sought attention in so many different ways. She would still feed him on Friday's collection night.

"Jo-Jo, your allowance," Rocky yelled out, from the smoky bathroom upstairs.

Both Jo-Jo and Blackie made it to the scene of the crime at the same time, discovering that while *The Ledger* had not crashed through to the porch, glass was still everywhere. The paper had landed on the doorstep. Scanning it, Jo-Jo felt that old stories were still making headlines. *So why the heads up "Kee Yaw Kee"*? he wondered.

"Well, 'Mr. Know it All' and 'back from the dead' little brother, … what's news?" said Frank, moving slowly to join his brother on the front porch. While his ankle was healing, his newfound obsession with lifting weights had him sore from neck to toe. He liked poking at Jo-Jo's new status; the spoiled, miraculously healed member of the family, as well as owner of a TV, which after making it to Belleville, never seemed to work again. It sat now on the porch with some of the latest slivers of glass on it. Uncle Pete was supposed to deliver it back to Two Tones for an "exchange" somewhere on Bloomfield Avenue.

Frank grabbed the paper, flipping impatiently through the headlines, including the sports page.

"Boy, you're in a great mood," commented Jo-Jo.

Ignoring his brother, Frank concluded, "Yep, musta been something to do with 'Herb Oscar Anderson'."

Jo-Jo also now recalled Russell's strange message. "Got it. Russell wants us to turn on ABC radio for Herb Oscar."

"Yep," agreed Frank.

As soon as the popular New York City DJ's voice, known to millions as the "Morning Mayor of New York", was tuned in, time stopped in the Bonaducci household. Similar scenes were also unfolding all across America.

"Ladies and gentlemen and boys and girls all across the New York City area, terrible news has arrived into our studios from Associated Press and United Press International. Early this morning, a small plane crashed into snow-covered cornfields in stormy Iowa. In addition to the pilot, rock 'n' roll idol, Buddy Holly, teen sensation, Ritchie Valens, and Texas DJ-turned singer, the 'Big Bopper', … are dead. I repeat, … there are no survivors. Our phone lines are flooded with inquiries. Unfortunately, as the 'Morning Mayor of New York', I must bring this terribly sad news to you. Once again, Buddy Holly, Ritchie Valens, and the 'Big Bopper' have been killed in a plane crash. We will bring more details when we get them. In tribute, we now play Buddy's hit, 'True Love Ways'."

Marietta became ashen. Jo-Jo was frozen in confusion. Frank stared grimly outside to the back yard. No word was spoken between them.

Rocky came silently into the kitchen. "I heard it." While never having commented much on popular music other than his appreciation for Sinatra's "wiseguy" voice, it was apparent only the father of the house could express himself. "Those were good kids. Kids like that died in the war. But accidents like this are worse. Gotta be careful in life. Flying's dangerous. Flying in snow is stupid."

"Their mothers!" cried Marietta. She felt their pain. "God, take me first. Such beautiful music. So young."

Jo-Jo added, "Can't believe it. I feel sick."

"Hey, Cuz, things are a changin'," said Frank, attempting to imagine a world now without any more Buddy Holly music. *God, this isn't in the plans. Maybe it's all a bad dream.*

As Donna entered the kitchen, the voice of Ritchie Valens was still rolling down the stairs, and she began to cry. "Mommy, does that mean I can't play 'Donna' any more?"

Marietta was choked up, so Rocky answered, "Donna, he's gone, but his music will live forever."

That day was like no other in Belleville. In the town's grammar schools and at the high school down on Washington Ave., radios were at full volume as girls cried and guys wondered why the stars flew into a snowstorm in the first place. Marietta spent hours talking to Dalla and her mother, whom she reminded in Italian that she should count her blessings, … "nothing worse than to lose a child". She repeated this several times to Mrs. Frassa who usually gave money top priority on her list of daily concerns.

Marietta could not wait to read *The Newark Evening News,* even though she'd cancelled her subscription when their sports department relegated Frank to second team All Essex County in football. *The Ledger* selected him on the first team. The only newspapers to be found in the Bonaducci household were *The Newark Star Ledger, The Belleville Times,* and *The Italian Tribune.* The latter always had a place of honor throughout the Bonaducci families since it featured Rocky's South Pacific heroics in a special article after he was wounded at Eniwetok. But that afternoon, Marietta would make the sacrifice and trek up to Joe Stein's Candy Store on the Bloomfield-Belleville border to pick up *The Evening News.* Loss of the rock 'n' roll icons had to be explained in more detail to her as well.

Ellie Angus had heard the crash report on her car radio during her morning drive from her home in Montclair to School Number 10. A die-hard big bands fan, she was not oblivious to the impact that Buddy Holly and Ritchie Valens' contemporary music was having on the teenagers of America. She loved her country, its children, her Catholic Church, and the history of each. Indeed, some of her students would go on to make their own history because of having met her.

Mrs. Ellie Angus was a childless widow. All her students knew the story. Her naval officer husband was lost at sea after the SS Indianapolis went down in shark-infested waters in World War II. He was a hero to her and became the same to all of her students. Not long after receiving the notification from the Defense Department, the diminutive Ellie's hair turned totally white. That was the only evidence of her grief and shock. It contrasted hauntingly with her youthful figure and cherub-like face. Her steely resolve was to be the best teacher she could, especially honoring her country with her dynamic instruction of American history. She was tough on all the kids that came through her class. Having been in Belleville since the mid forties, she became a surrogate mother to many of them as well. Forever wearing high heels regardless of the Jersey weather, her strut down the school hallways signaled the presence of someone on whom you could always depend, no matter your status as a student or parent. She was the only personal coach many of her students would ever have in life.

Sitting in her car in the parking lot, Ellie said her daily prayer of thanksgiving for having become a teacher, and then added, "… and Lord, help me find something positive to teach these kids today about this terrible plane crash."

There would be no writing, reading, arithmetic, or even history and geography in Mrs. Angus' class that day. She moved directly into the subject of the plane crash, asking the students to express their inner most feelings. Jo-Jo would never forget her effort to make this event a life-long learning experience. "Children, what good lesson can be found in the deaths of Buddy Holly, Ritchie Valens, and the Big Bopper?" she asked, not knowing what to expect.

The class was silent for at least two minutes. Then Elinor Petro, the top female student, raised her hand. "Mrs. Angus, they should not have flown in such bad weather."

Discussion followed about better judgment being required, updated weather reports, and the irresponsibility some people might display in becoming famous. But Jo-Jo wanted to remind everyone that Mrs. Angus had asked for a "good" lesson to be learned. He saw the practicality in the offered answers. *But what's so "good" about what they're saying,… that we can learn something "good" for <u>our lives</u> as well? Maybe there's no good in this event, and it just has to be taken in stride; an example of one of life's terrible turns. God, it always seems that good people go this way,* he thought, remembering his father's stories of how Glenn Miller vanished over the English Channel. A plane crash also took legendary football coach Knute Rockne, and even the great Iowa Heisman Trophy winner, Nile Kinnick, who became a fighter pilot. Now his frustration was turning to anger. He wasn't quite sure yet what he would say as he raised his hand.

Mrs. Angus acknowledged his interest. "Yes, Joseph?"

Words jettisoned out of his mouth. "The only positive here, Mrs. Angus, was that they were doing what they wanted to do, and they were doing that better than anybody."

The class was silent. Even Ellie Angus needed to hear more. "Yes, Joseph?"

"I know that Glenn Miller sorta died this way. His music was the best during my parents' time. No body was better." He paused. "My father always talks about Notre Dame football and Knute Rockne. He went that way, too. Couldn't coach any better than Rockne. Nile Kinnick won the Heisman, ... then got killed early in World War II. He couldn't do any more. These people were the best at what they did, and maybe they could do no more. I mean, maybe God figured they were finished doing what they were supposed to be doing."

As Jo-Jo spoke, Roger Bush looked to the clock, his mouth watering for his mother's famous peanut butter and banana sandwiches. Russell Giardella gazed around the room through his thick glasses, worrying his friend's speech on everybody else but the three singers had lost everyone's interest. Rosemarie Masino, Jo-Jo's girlfriend, squirmed in her seat, chewing her gum, and crossing her legs every five seconds. As always, she was bored if the subject wasn't boys.

On the other hand, Ellie Angus loved what she was hearing. "Keep going, Joseph."

"Well, Buddy Holly and Ritchie Valens had to love what they did. They were both young and famous. Even this Richardson fella had a big hit song. I mean these guys were at the center of rock 'n' roll and, you know, the music that's popular today. Sure they could've done more, but they were on top. And you know what? They were loving what they were doing, and doing it better than anyone. We lose, ... they don't. I mean, if there's a heaven, and if they're going there, ... then they go out on top."

"So what's the 'good' in all that, Joseph?" asked Mrs. Angus, hoping that Jo-Jo could sum up with logic that even his friends could understand.

"Well, Mrs. Angus, if you are doing what you love to do, and doing it well, then regardless of when it ends and what the result is, you did your best, and that's all you can do." He inhaled deeply, as his mind's eye glimpsed his parents. "I mean, if you live to be old, but don't like what you're doing, and you don't have much success, wow, ... that's not good. These guys died doing what they loved to do. That's success, even if we wanted them to be here to do more for <u>us</u>."

Mrs. Angus allowed the peaceful silence that enveloped the room to linger. Maybe their subconscious would tell most of the twenty-three students they'd just had a good learning experience. No one moved until Louise Gubitosi, Jo-Jo's backyard neighbor and daughter of Gary and Rosa Gubitosi, raised her hand. Although not wanting to compromise the moment, the teacher announced a last comment would come from Louise.

"He's absolutely right," said Louise. Jo-Jo was cringing, fearing what attention-craving Louise would utter next. Louise had chased after Jo-Jo like a puppy dog in heat all their youth, only for him to politely lie to her on numerous occasions that his parents did not want him to date until after college. But she continued. "My father's a TV repair man during the day and a printer at night. He did not go to college, but he does the best for us. I hope he never dies, but if that happened tomorrow, he's a success, … just like these singers."

Everyone else in the class but Jo-Jo ignored Louise's contribution. He rolled his eyes and thought, *If her father's a failure as a daytime television repairman, he must even be worse as a printer at night.*

When school ended that day, Mrs. Angus asked Jo-Jo to stay behind for a few moments. She had a book on the Civil War to present to him. It was a gift for his operation. She also shook his hand and additionally congratulated him. "Joseph, four years ago I told your brother, Frank, he would be a success in life. But I reminded him not to measure that in dollars and cents or titles, … when he finds what God wants him to do, to do it to the fullest and not to worry about the results. God will take care of that, and when it should end. Remember in this order, God first, then your family, and finally your chosen work. My Hughie was doing what he loved when those Japanese torpedoes ended everything for him. He was a natural born leader and was fulfilling that destiny in the Navy. To die doing what you love? You're correct, … that's true success! It may be our loss that these fortunate pilgrims are gone at young ages, but it is heaven's gain. By the way they go away, they will always be a part of us. God makes sure we will learn from their lives, … and their deaths."

Jo-Jo Bonaducci would never forget February 3, 1959. Unfortunately, not everyone in his family, and certainly his neighborhood, would benefit from his or Mrs. Ellie Angus' thoughts that day.

Frank had rushed out during his late lunch period to get his own copy of the paper. By the time he left school, he'd read *The Newark Evening News'* account at least five times. Eric Thatcher's car was garaged with a couple of flat tires, so Frank had been taking the bus home for the past week. It seemed on this day more people were traveling on the Trackless Transit Number 98 than ever before. On the other hand, with the <u>News</u> tucked firmly under his arm awaiting his sixth read, he quickly became oblivious to everyone.

The paper mentioned that Dion and the Belmonts were featured with Holly and Valens at this place called the Surf in Clear Lake, Iowa. *God, if they had flown, The Belmonts would have sung "I Wonder Why" for the last time. But Clear Lake, Iowa? What agent would book these stars there? Sure, it was a tour, and this was just one of those stops in some sleepy town with a few crazed teenagers. But, these were the biggest stars in America.* Frank couldn't stop thinking about this bizarre trip across the Midwest. *Any town would have shut the schools to hear Holly, Valens, and Dion's group. Whether it was Clear Lake, or Belleville, or Nutley, the place would be standing room only. Make a stop in Newark, and even the colored kids would turn out.*

"I bet Holly and the boys were having a great time," Frank whispered to himself, imagining the reception the Iowa kids probably gave to the stars. *Wow*, he thought, *a seventeen-year old kid from Southern California, a Texas cowboy, and Dion and his hood friends from Belmont Avenue in the Bronx. And this Big Bopper guy was no slouch either with 'Chantilly Lace'. Talk about an All American team of rock 'n' roll.*

Frankly, Frank was relieved that Dion and the Belmonts did not board the plane. *Talk about "I Wonder Why"!* Frank was wondering why. *Why did they take the bus? Did they have a choice? Maybe only the biggest names went. But that would have been Holly, Valens, and Dion. Maybe the three guys who died became friends. Maybe they had the most money to charter the flight. But why leave the rest of the show participants to an icebox of a bus?*

Staring out the fog-shrouded windows, all Frank's eyes seemed to see was miles of cornfields—snow-covered, separated only by almost invisible asphalt country roads, as howling Midwest winds blew heavy flakes across their worn faces. But these cornfields were covered by stalks of yellow corn, glowing in the blinding whiteness of the storm.

In the distance was a black metal back stage door, ripped open by the wintry blasts raging through Iowa on that fateful night. Inside stood Buddy Holly. Shivering, he was speaking to Dion. "Ya gotta come on the plane. We're the stars, and the stars belong shootin' across the sky tonight, ... so they're not so damn sick tomorrow that they can't sing anymore for the fans."

"No way, man. Can't leave the boys. The Belmonts go with Dion, and Dion goes with the Belmonts."

Buddy wasn't finished. "Look, whoever goes on that bus is gonna become deathly sick anyway. The driver told me the heat's still not workin', and the parts are waiting for pickup in Green Bay, ... or is that Greenland?" Holly was attempting to keep the conversation light. He really wanted Dion to be onboard at midnight. "So here's the reality; I'd rather have the boys in the band losin' their voices, than incomparable Mr. DiMucci from the Bronx. Make a business decision, man!"

"I just did, you Lubbock cowboy. Since the plane can only hold a pilot and three others, I fly the plane with the Belmonts in back." Dion faked a punch at America's Number 1 rock 'n' roll star.

"You can't even drive your ol' man's beat up Buick witout runnin' over some Italian grandmutha on Belmont Avenue back home in 'da Bronx', ... let alone fly a plane," said Buddy, testing his New York City accent on the reigning King of the Bronx Blues. They both laughed.

That's it, thought Frank. *It was supposed to be Buddy and Dion. But Dion could never have put himself before his friends. Just like me and Gino at Nutley. Yea, that's the way it probably happened. Now Dion's still alive to continue to make music. His career's going to explode,* thought Frank. *The "Cuz" put his friends first. Way to go, Dion!*

"Buddy, how much?" Dion was now shaking like a leaf, blowing into his freezing cupped hands. "How much, you rich son-of-a-gun?"

Buddy did not hesitate. "Forty-five dollars a piece."

"Oh, man, too much. My parent's mortgage payment ain't that much higher. Damn, I'll pay ya twenty-five. Let's Jew the pilot down."

"This ain't the Bronx, city boy. And only one Belmont can come. Besides, the pilot's a Baptist, not a Jew."

"Forget the Belmonts and forget me; too much money, Buddy! We'll just have to lose our voices on that refrigerator bus, and you and whoever is as rich as you will have to do all the singin' at the next stop." Dion reflected. "Damn, you're makin' all the money with that hillbilly sound of yours. Can't believe it." The door slammed shut.

172

Yea, maybe that was it. Dion could not afford the money. Even if he had the money, would he have left the Belmonts behind to freeze on the bus? No way.

Blowing open again, this time the door broke its hinges and was swept up in a funnel cloud of pure white snow. Everything else in Frank's sight was black, … except for the glowing, golden ears of corn—just the white cloud, the airborne black door, the pulsating golden ears transmitting their yellow radiance, and the dimly lit back entrance to the building.

"You dumb, tobacco chewin', hay suckin' country boy." Dion was talking. "Takin' a plane the size of a '57 Chevy in the middle of subfreezin' weather… with that frightened, sickly Mexican kid who just happens to have two Number 1 hits in the last twelve months. What 'a ya got horse manure for brains? I ain't that smart, but <u>you</u> are real stupid."

Buddy Holly and Dion embraced.

"Make sure you shootin' stars come back to earth," said Dion, as a tear crawled out his right eye.

"Next stop, Smallwood and Belmont; your stop, Frankie. Ya getting' off?"

No, he could not return just yet. *But, the glowing corn, … life in the midst of death? What could be so alive about a cornfield where three guys and their pilot lay lifeless? Their bodies were planted in frozen tundra like seeds falling from a dying flower. Seeds that had hope, planted in dirt. Golden, radiating ears of corn were resisting the murderous onslaught of an invisible fleet of flying swords savagely diving in from the Northwest, … a birthing in the midst of death. Life was resisting the imminence of eternal termination. Would there be a legacy to follow? Could some kind of good win out over evil? Would there be new life that could come out of this horror? What could be so alive with the loss of these three? Ears of corn glowing in a blizzard, trying to stave off a demonic uprising that would suck the light out of the three shooting stars.*

"Yo, Bonaducci. Home sweet home."

Finally Frank had returned. He politely thanked the driver as always, departed the bus, and gingerly picked his steps through the slush and ice across Belmont Avenue to his home directly opposite the bus stop. As he walked down the driveway, Frank made a decision. Tonight he'd call Joe Pelli to set a date when Dion and the Belmonts might be back in town, … perhaps at the Paramount, the Apollo, or wherever else they performed in New York. It was time to become a "backstage Johnny". Frank wanted to meet Dion. He had a couple of questions for him.

Next morning, Russell Giardella did something for the first and only time as a newspaper boy. He did not toss *The Newark Star Ledger* to the Bonaducci's front doorsteps. Instead, he parked his dilapidated Roadmaster two-wheeler just beyond the front yard hedges and slowly lowered his kickstand. Then he shuffled up the walkway, carefully taking the final four steps to the broken multi-glass paneled Bonaducci front door, reverently placing the paper on the snow-covered cracked brick landing, similar to putting a flower on a friend's grave. With the plane crash finally finding its way to the headlines of the daily that had become a northern New Jersey institution, the eternal finality of the event had touched even the heart of this simple teenager working seven days a week to help his parents raise their growing family.

A tear came to Russell's eye as he squinted to capture the early morning images in his friend's home. Were his feelings for the American recording stars whose lights had fizzled in an Iowa snowstorm? Or was he imagining what it would be like if any of the Bonaducci family would pass on as quickly as these late fifties icons? Jo-Jo was his best friend. Frank was a town-wide hero. And always friendly Mr. and Mrs. Bonaducci treated him with respect and love, consistently generous on Friday collection night … with food and tips. They made their home, his home, and they'd not yet charged him for any of his errant newspaper tosses. He had never seen death take someone he cared about. He was only thirteen. Strangely, the Holly plane crash-landed on his life, even if it was mainly via 45 records and expressive radio DJs. Now he could imagine losing someone he loved. He felt grief for the first time in his life, and it formed a scar in his spirit that would quench his youthful hope forever. Bad news made it to a doorstep, and a thirteen-year old newspaper boy with Coke bottle glasses cried.

CHAPTER 13

"ROAD TRIP... UNAUTHORIZED"

Jackie Carey was a tall, gangly senior at Belleville High. Almost always he wore black. From his shiny flyweight shoes that were as pointy as any ever crafted, and were on his feet 365 days a year, regardless of the weather, to his chino pants whose cuffs were always short, and the plastic comb in his back pocket for grooming his also black, straight greasy hair, ... the color of his days was black. All this contrasted with his white sweat socks and smartly starched dress variety white shirt, or simply his undershirt of the same color. If it were the undershirt, a pack of Lucky Strikes would peak out of the left shoulder rolled up sleeve. With his dress shirts, the cigarettes were to be found in the left chest pocket. An ever-present smile, matched with a warm and sincere backslapping personality, made others ignore his heavily pocked face. Neither athlete nor student, he idolized Frank and Gino.

Having been kept back in third grade, Jackie was one year older than his friends. His passion in life was his "Heavenly Heap", a golden '49 Mercury with its chopped top, bubble skirts, nosed hood, and continental kit. Down payment for the car had been a gift from his sister, ten years older than he, who had been working since she left high school. Her boyfriend sang with the popular "Four Loves", and always was helping out with her younger brother since Jackie's father died when he was in sixth grade. Little did Jackie realize that his Heavenly Heap was about to take a road-trip.

It was early March, and Gino was getting the runaround from the University of Kansas. While they had loved him on film, only a local alumnus visited him. No one from the coaching staff had traveled to Jersey, and their invitation in late '58 for him to visit the campus seemed shallow. It was becoming apparent around college football recruiting circles that Gino might not even graduate high school. So, the All State running back was frustrated.

The University of Maryland, who had won the National Football Championship back in '53, always recruited heavily in Essex County. They overlooked Gino. He leaned towards playing for the Jayhawks of Kansas because they had been so encouraging early on, but the idea of Maryland did interest him. He mentioned this to Sneaks on one of his visits to Rahway. The Boiardo underboss did not say much that day. However, as soon as his son left, Sneaks took quick advantage of his free access to the prison guard phone. Calls were made to his Baltimore-DC associates. One week later, Gino was told by his father to head to College Park, Maryland for a meeting with the Terrapin coaching staff. Either plane or train tickets would be available, or two of Sneak's friends would drive him.

Gino and Frank were not the closest of buddies in Belleville High's hallways, but their football exploits and recruiting experiences were always a mutual point of conversation, along with their impending visit to New York City to "hang out" with some rock 'n' roll legends. But the invitation from Maryland prompted Gino to seek out his straight-laced teammate.

"Frankie, what'a ya think?" asked Gino. "I mean it looks like my dad did his thing. Should I go?"

"Gino, what's the story with graduation?"

"Well, Coach Popalinski, and would you believe, cranky old Wilhelm are talkin' to my teachers. And I'm sure my father's also burning the phone lines to the Superintendent. What's his name?" Gino let slip about the underhand assistance he was getting from cell number 27, aimed at getting him, one way or another, a diploma in June.

Frank knowingly smiled. "So, looks like you will be graduating. Just inform Kansas and Maryland that it's for sure. Then, Cuz, get your fanny down to Maryland to hear what they have to say. It's getting late. Maybe Kansas will get wind of this trip to College Park, and it'll get you accepted out West, too."

"Alright, I'm goin' to Maryland this weekend."

That night, Gino Babula did not make plane or train reservations. But he also reasoned that he could never be caught traveling in the company of two of his father's lieutenants. Instead, he called Jackie Carey ... about the "Heavenly Heap".

After they talked, Jackie was ecstatic. Being the chauffeur for Gino Babula's recruiting trip would be the highlight of his high school career. The idea brightened the disheveled living room of his small Cape Cod home on the Second River in Belleville's Soho section, just on the other side of Nanny Goat Hill.

"Bonaducci goin?" asked Jackie's Irish beauty of a sister with flowing red hair. Elizabeth Carey knew her Belleville High facts. With their mother working two jobs, she was always watching out for Jackie, and she understood Mr. Inside was not the studious, articulate one of the All County running back duo.

"No, Elizabeth, Frankie's goin' to Yale or some utta school for smarta guys."

Because of her boyfriend, Patrick "Patsie" Pratola, who sang with Lenny Latore and The Four Loves throughout the Newark area, Elizabeth knew enough to link the famous Gino to the infamous Sneaks. She was clear to her brother. "Ya know, Patsie sees a lot of guys from Bloomfield Avenue at his shows. And this Gino kid may be this great football hero to you, Jackie, but his father's a big shot in the mob."

"Tanks for your concern, older sis. But when sweet singin' Patsie is applyin' to colleges, den maybe I'll be interested in <u>his</u> opinions. Seems you should be more concerned about who he hangs out wit after his gigs, than who I drive around wit in my car."

Jackie's sarcasm did not disturb his sister, and his simple reasoning quickly changed her decision. "Then just be careful and get home early Saturday night."

While Gino got permission to leave school after lunch that Friday, Jackie simply cut classes for the whole day. The trip down the New Jersey Turnpike was more boring than Jackie could have imagined. Gino didn't say much, so Jackie concentrated on finding Philadelphia radio stations that were playing the current top hits. Other than disc jockeys still lamenting music's great loss in the Iowa crash, Philly groups dominated the airwaves, and Jackie didn't recognize one of them.

"Not bad. Great lyrics, but tough to dance to." Jackie paused and asked, "Gino, who are dese guys anyway?"

When Gino didn't answer, Jackie ignored his silence, not taking it personally. He figured Gino had lots on his mind. Nonetheless, he continued, "Hey, Mr. Inside, how 'bout we crash Bandstand on da way back?" Still no response, so Jackie flashed his patented smile and burst into uncontrollable laughter. He wasn't waiting for his passenger to respond any longer. "Yep, I'm gettin' takin' advantage of, ... just a driver for da football guy. Arrives in my Heavenly Heap, and at least Mr. Babula gets some attention. Now I understand da deal. Your new Bonneville's OK back home, but da <u>real</u> car experts down here know dat mine's a classic already; my Merc makes ya a big deal on campus dis weekend with all da attention; but, dey figure ya don't have your own car, and den dey end up giving ya a scholarship, ... all because of Jackie Carey."

Gino remained silent, but this time glanced over, stretched his eyes wide open, and signaled his chauffeur with a slow nod that this assessment just might be accurate. As different as he was from Jackie, Gino really did appreciate what his friend was doing for him. He just wasn't about to say so. With Kansas seemingly "cold" on him, Gino would take Maryland and Jackie Carey singing his praises any time. His choices had become few and far between.

It was early evening when they reached the Maryland campus. The Belleville seniors had never been on the grounds of a nationally renowned football school before, so they were genuinely impressed. Brick colonial buildings spectacularly lit up as darkness descended upon College Park. They cruised by the ominous Cole Field House and along the college's quiet streets searching for the football offices at Byrd Stadium.

When they arrived at their destination, Gino and Jackie were warmly met by one of Maryland's players from Jersey. He took them on an abbreviated campus tour and then checked them into a Howard Johnson motel just off the grounds, on Route 1. This was a big recruiting weekend at Maryland, and since Gino had not originally been on the candidate list, there were no beds for him and Jackie at any of the fraternities that usually hosted potential football recruits. The schedule for Gino and Jackie after getting refreshed was to meet other players at a party back on campus that night. Jackie could not have been more impressed ... partying with major college football stars, ... not bad for a kid from Belleville who just wanted to get out of high school and become a cop. On the other hand, Gino saw the musty Ho Jo's room as a bad sign.

That balmy night at College Park was one to be remembered for Jackie; the beer flowed, and his golden Heavenly Heap became an attraction for the southern coeds.

178

On the other hand, maybe his all-black ensemble, complete with leather jacket and the cleanest white tee shirt he could find in Jersey, had the Maryland ladies from south of the Mason Dixon gawking, like he was from another world. The girls also did not ignore Gino's light northern Italian features and muscular frame. However, his sullen attitude clearly signaled his mission here was not to find a Terrapin cheerleader, but rather a football team. The forward and friendly ladies got the moody hint and decided to focus on his partner, who thought that this could be the night he might perhaps get to know Bible Belt women … in the biblical sense! Jackie was always dreaming.

About 10 PM, Jackie was shocked to hear his traveling mate snap his fingers, pointing to the fraternity front door. Over Jackie's disappointment, they both had to get a good night's sleep to prepare for meeting the Maryland coaching staff, next day.

"Gino, babe, I'll drive ya back," assured Carey. "But, da night is young and da Southern chicks are inta Jackie from Jersey."

As Jackie was now speaking of himself in the third person, Gino knew the Maryland beer was not watered down as much as he figured, and it really was time to go. "Now!" commanded Gino.

Under Gino's piercing stare, Jackie got the hint, requesting, "Just let me say my goodbyes until da next life, my man. I'll probably never come dis way again."

Gino finally chuckled, as Jackie planted a kiss on every girl that he had met that night, advising them that duty called for him to "…tuck Maryland's next All American inta bed."

But it was not until late the next day that Gino finally met the coach in charge of Jersey recruiting. So, Jackie did not stop reminding him that they could have partied all night with the way things were turning out. Gino just scowled at him. Throughout the morning Gino seemed to be passed from one current player to the next, watching highlight films and hearing all the reasons he should pick Maryland. He was getting a sick feeling, and Jackie was even getting quieter by the hour as he felt his friend's frustration.

Looking to Jackie at one point after lunch in the student union, Gino lightened up. "Ya know, Jack, these guys are OK. I could play with them. They're pretty good. Not that big. Man, would love to talk to a coach, though. What 'a ya think?"

"Ya askin' me?" responded Jackie to something he knew absolutely nothing about. "Well, Mr. Inside, if da players were doin' the recruitin', you'd start tomorrow. But, if I may, permit me to remind ya dat Gino Babula is an Italian kid from Belleville, and dis is da gateway to da Sout down here. No offense, my friend, but when dey ask your fodder's occupation, ya just might have to do some quick thinkin'." Jackie moved quickly to the next part of his analysis, by adding, "I don't want to be pissimistic, my man, but da big question dough is 'where's da coaches?' Don't want to ruin any ray of hope, number 22, but do dey have a coaching staff? I mean dey haven't rushed to welcome us, have dey?" Putting his arm around Gino, Jackie laughed and concluded, "God, maybe dey think I'm you!"

Gino nodded and smiled, as Jackie hit on the same sore spot he was seeing himself. "You're smarter than I thought, Jackie. But, let me tell ya, Mr. Chauffeur, they know who I am. But they really must be wonderin' about me showin' up with this Jersey grease-ball with the goofy car. Yea, that's it. I got it. You're probably the problem."

Jackie wrapped his arms around his idol's neck, faking a headlock. "Gotta be yourself, golden boy."

Later that afternoon the offensive coordinator finally introduced himself. While cordial, he did not seem overwhelmed that Maryland might be landing one of 1958's top football players in New Jersey. His research revealed it might be difficult for Maryland to even accept Gino, because of his poor grades. Gino's ego was bruised even more when he was asked of his interest, perhaps, in a prep school down south, .., Fork Union in Virginia.

"What's a Fork Union, coach?" Gino asked, shrugging his shoulders. "I wanna play college football, not get lost at some fork in the road in the Deep South. Since we won the war, why would I wanna spend time in the back woods of Virginia?"

Wrong answer! Even Jackie winced.

But, surprisingly enough, the coach seemed to ignore Gino's naiveté and instead requested him to stay over one more night. The staff would review his films further, and then all of them meet at breakfast on Sunday. Gino knew he had caught a break, and instantly agreed. Jackie rolled his eyes. There went his promise to his sister who was expecting him back Saturday night. It was out of the question. He'd have problems at home for a month.

A sly craftiness, which in the past few people would have ever detected, came over Gino. "Listen, we got the room, and this is my only shot, Jack. How 'bout getting a couple catabs of beer and some pizza, and we talk it over in the motel?"

Gino's infrequent drinking was well known. The possibility of his finally loosening up encouraged Jack. Now his plan was that with the extra time together, he could convince Gino to head north on Route 95 later that night before it was too late. Little did he know that Gino had a bizarre strategy that would soon get others involved, and ultimately change both their young lives.

Later guzzling beer from soft cardboard containers to wash down College Park's poor excuse for pizza, Jackie said, "It's gotta be da water down here, 'cause da dough's like rubber, and da tomato sauce seems sour. Tank God they didn't screw up da beer." Gino, however, seemed to be pulling back into moody silence, prompting Jackie to ask, "Ya broodin' again?"

"Na, just thinkin'," said Gino. After another bite of pizza, he frightened Jackie by blurting out, "Listen, Jack, we're down here now, so here's what we're gonna do."

Jackie sat motionless and looked at the clock in the room. It was 6 PM.

Staring into his beer, Gino continued, "Listen. These Maryland guys don't want me, ... at least not this year. Me in prep school in the south? Forget it. We're gonna sleep here tonight on them, then leave in the morning."

"Great," Jack said in relief. "Goin' home, ... right?"

Then Gino Babula, Jr. exploded his bombshell! "Road trip to Lawrence, Kansas, Jack. Kansas City, here we come. What'a ya think?"

Jackie Carey didn't hesitate. "I always knew you was nuts, Gino, but not dis nuts. No way! Not in my car and not wit me. Ya want me to get killed when I get home. What about school, your mutter, your fodder, and everyting else? Dis is bad, big boy. Kansas don't want ya neither. Now, let's go home."

Only the cars outside on Route 1 could be heard in the room.

"Gino, ya OK?"

"I'm goin' to buy more beer," Gino replied. He was now in the same zone that made him a ferocious running back at Belleville. He was animalistic, moving on instinct, fueled by a rage brewing deep from within.

Jackie had only heard about his rare, and unpredictable mood shifts. "Gino, slow up. Let's talk. Besides, I got da keys."

Gino was already at the door, his hands jingling the car keys he had confiscated off the dresser when they first returned to the room. Within seconds he was out the door, leaving Jackie to his fears, confusion, ... and the telephone!

Jackie's mind raced. *Oh, Ma, dis has gone from bad to worse. Dis kid's hurtin'. He's gonna do somethin' stupid. Oh, God, get me out of dis. My car, ... my sister. Oh crap!* He was walking back and forth, his black fly weight shoes clicking on the linoleum floors as his stride turned into a strut. Wearing only his white sweat sox and boxer shorts, he was gaining confidence. Then he stopped, sat on the bed, and put his head in his hands. *Who's kiddin' who? I ain't never gonna stop Gino. Wait. Maybe I at least buy some time wit my sister by callin' her.*

Elizabeth answered, still getting ready to drive down to Heller Parkway on the Belleville-Newark border to listen to her boyfriend sing with Lenny Latore at the Red Door Night Club. When she heard the plan, she didn't even hesitate one moment. "Jackie, get your sweet little Irish fanny home, or I'll send Patsie to get you."

"Elizabeth, it's outta my control."

"Ah, ha! Worse than I thought."

Now Jackie was really scared. His big sister's boyfriend, he was convinced, might not only be a mediocre singer, but an even worse wannabe wiseguy. Knowing that nicknames down on Bloomfield Avenue were always well thought out, "Patsie" hit the nail on the head for this guy in his sister's life. However, she was Jackie's good friend and confidant, despite Patsie's constant presence. He was really looking for advice, not her threats, so he decided to tell the whole story. "Listen, Gino wants me to drive him to Kansas." Not giving Elizabeth time to react, he added, "Don't yell at me. Help me."

Jackie had made a mistake. He had caught his sister on her way out for the night, and now in her mind, he was being "kidnapped" by the son of a mobster, who just happened to be a great high school football player and her brother's idol.

"That's it, Jackie, I gotta get involved," said Elizabeth. "I'm gonna see Patsie in a few minutes, and he'll help out."

"God, Elizabeth, dat's a terrible idea."

Jackie had to think quickly. Powerful and familiar, a face popped into his mind's eye. He stopped her runaway train of emotions by saying, "I know, I know. I'm gonna call Frankie Bonaducci. He'll help. Fogettabout Patsie. OK? Ya know dat Frank'll talk Gino out of dis."

"Now you're talkin', little brother. Frankie's a straight arrow who can drive some sense into that hard-headed Italian."

"OK, OK, I'll call ya back later, Elizabeth. Frankie's gonna get involved. Don't worry."

"Ya sure?"

"Yea."

Hanging up, he was sure Frank's name had calmed his sister down. Now he had to get in touch with Mr. Outside. Little did he realize that by the time he would be able to get Frank to call him back, Elizabeth had already alerted Patsie Pratola. The part-time harmonizer and two-bit "numbers" runner from Silver Lake went into an emotional fit, as if he really cared about Jackie. He began talking to all the wrong people at the smoke-filled Red Door about Jackie's "abduction", and his big mouth chatting about thwarting the road trip to Kansas would ultimately set back his standing amongst the Bloomfield Avenue crew.

Frank had just returned from Charlie Bucchino's Italian-American deli after picking up some boloney, cheese, cole slaw, dill pickles, hard Italian rolls and "dadolls" (tarallees) for the family's Saturday dinner, when his mother revealed Jackie had called. Frank jumped on the phone, puzzled by the strange call back number.

Talking slowly, Jackie knew that Frank was his only chance. "He's been drinkin' beer, and ya know dat he never drinks dat much. Gino's just disappointed and depressed. After da big year, he's seein' how his grades and tings are doin' him in, and he doesn't tink he's gonna play anywhere next year. The Kansas stop is nuts, Frank. He just wants to get in my car and get lost. I can tell. His mood is swingin' from pillar to post every two minutes. Ya gotta help; he'll listen to you."

Rocky, Marietta, and Jo-Jo were at the kitchen table, and by Frank's reaction, they knew there was a problem. His mention of Gino's name made them even more attentive.

Frank assured Jackie he would speak with his parents and call back within fifteen minutes. Gino would be returning with more beer momentarily.

Hearing Frank's appraisal of the situation, Rocky kept shaking his head in disapproval as Marietta was wringing the moppeen in her hand. "See, Frank," said Rocky. "Sneaks does what he does all these years. His kid does some good this fall, but it all falls apart because the old man has to be a big shot. Gino's a little messed up right now."

"Yea, I know that, Dad. But we have to help him."

Frank's sincere concern for his friend touched Rocky, who grudgingly nodded agreement.

Marietta jumped in. "We're gonna pray, Frank," she assured her son. But then she turned to her husband with a helpless look. " Rocky, what can we do?"

Throughout tough times during their relationship, Marietta would always look to her husband first, but then quickly roll up her sleeves to tackle their problems. She just couldn't wait too long for Rocky to come up with a strategy, even though many times her initial bold moves would end in mistakes. So when her husband gestured, implying to Frank he had come up with an answer, she felt relieved.

"Frankie, what'a ya wanna do?" Rocky asked.

"Dad, let me borrow the car. I can talk to him. It's only a four-hour ride. I'll be there by midnight."

"God, Frank, I'd let you take it, but the Chevy's been overheatin', and what about the tires? It'll never take the trip."

"Gee, Dad," said Frank. "Uncle Caesar may be right. Stop storing Al's motorcycle and start putting the car in the garage. Besides, you've been going over to Henry's to get it fixed a lot lately."

"Just forget the Chevy," said Rocky.

"I got it, Frank," said Jo-Jo, jumping in. "Remember the times we'd go to see Aunt Bella and Grandma off at Penn Station. Well, the trains stop in the DC area, and that's where they're at! Sleep on the way down, and you're ready for Gino when you get to Maryland."

"Cuz, you're thinking. Not bad for an eighth grader." Frank looked to his parents, "Dad, Ma, what do you think?" Frank needed a quick answer.

"Rocky, let him do it. Sneaks and Silvia would do it for our kids." Marietta would not let Rocky say no, and he knew it.

"Let's go, I'll take you down Newark," said Rocky, already pushing himself from the table. Any of his misgivings about helping a Boiardo lieutenant in trouble vanished when he thought of Sneak's son, whom he respected for getting in as little trouble as a Belleville teen as he did. Over the years, so many people kept expecting him to follow in his father's footsteps. "But what'a ya gonna talk to him about, Frank? Gino's not gonna be a pushover."

Frank looked to his mother, and then boldly stated, " I'll talk to Gino about God! He needs <u>that</u> kind of help, Dad. Not church, but the personal thing Mommy's always talking about with Queenie and Nora."

Marietta smiled at Rocky. Jo-Jo had already retrieved some overnight clothes for his brother and bounded back into the kitchen. Donna remained oblivious to what was going on, polishing off a twenty-five cents bag of Wise Potato Chips and watching "Bonanza" in the TV room. Her journal was at her side, as usual.

"Sounds like a 'foxhole' conversion for Gino. Don't be a fanatic about it though, Frank," said his non-religious father. "I mean, sometimes Mommy and her two colored friends from Alabama are a little too much about that stuff. I know you'll say what's right to help him out."

Before leaving for the station, Frank quickly called Jackie back just to make sure that he and Gino slept in the motel room tonight. Frank's arrival was set to surprise Gino about midnight.

As Frank was boarding the train, Elizabeth Carey had ignited a wildfire at the Red Door, where her boyfriend began whining to anyone who would listen about "… Sneak's kid goin' berserk in Maryland and stealin' my girlfriend's brother's car, …

the one 'we' bought for him." If only the obnoxious motor mouth appreciated that several of the club's patrons that night had a direct line to Sneaks, … at Rahway.

Thomas "Two Tones" Anthony was decked out in his Saturday best, sitting with his date, at the end of the bar. A fixture at the club on the Belleville-Newark border, whenever Lenny and the Four Loves were featured, he was actually rumored to be financing their slow climb to fame. His Hollywood looks and North Ward attitude both helped, and hurt, his attempts to promote them in the area; music people could spot this Newark wiseguy a mile away. Hearing every word that Patsie and Elizabeth exchanged about the Gino and Jackie situation, Two Tones, between sips of his Seven and Seven, calmly continued to draw on his cigarette. Excusing himself from his female companion, he strolled to the table where the singer and his girlfriend were sitting. He stopped and stared at Patsie, and then beckoned him to follow outside, even though it was only minutes to show time.

His cigarette, liquored breath, and a finger in Patsie's face, Two Tones explained silence was golden. And how, if Patsie said one more thing that could embarrass Sneaks, he would never talk again, let alone utter doo wops behind Lenny Latore's falsetto. Realizing he might only be seconds away from taking his last breath, laying in subfreezing weather in nearby Branch Brook Park, Patsie nervously answered all Two Tone's questions. Satisfied, Sneak's loyalist escorted Patsie back inside the smoke-filled nightspot, and then quickly went to the pay phone.

It wasn't long before Thomas Anthony received his instructions to jump into his car with one other person he could totally trust, who would drive. There was no time to lose. First person who came to mind was Pete Frassa. After all, Five Corners' nephew was now involved in this. Then, just as quickly, he thought better of recruiting the rotund butcher. He knew that Sneaks never wanted Pete to participate in anything that could tie him to the organization on Bloomfield Avenue. Next, Greenie Delaney came to mind. *God, no,* he thought. *Greenie would talk me to death on the ride down.*

"Two Tones" Anthony quickly scanned around the club as Lenny Latore and his group were being introduced. No one looked suitable. Then the door slammed open, and "Bad Boy" Benny entered. The Gambino operative, who lived up the street in Newark's Forest Hill section and was never welcomed anywhere by The Boot's people, looked ready for a big night out. *But would this New York wiseguy be more trouble than it's worth? What's he doin' at The Red Door anyway? Perhaps with the ride down and back, Bad Boy would talk enough for me to gather some bits of information why he's always in Jersey,… when he should be working the Boros of*

New York for Gambino. Two Tones knew he was running out of time. According to Patsie, Gino could take off any minute in Jackie's car.

Two Tones approached Badalamenti, and not surprisingly, Bad Boy jumped at the opportunity. He had his own agenda.

Gino took two hours to return with the beer. What took so much time was finding two Italian submarine sandwiches in the state of Maryland. Jackie was praying the food would surely minimize chances of the depressed Babula getting really drunk, as well as buy time to reconsider the trip to Kansas. At least this is what Jackie was hoping.

By 11:30 PM Gino began to doze, despite the late news blaring on the TV. No morsel of food was left, but neither of them consumed much of the flat draft beer from a bar up the street. Still wide-awake, Jackie anticipated Frank's arrival at any minute. He had not mentioned a word to Gino.

Just before midnight, a car pulled up outside the motel room. Jackie slowly peeked through the musty window curtain. Frank Bonaducci stepped out of a cab. Reinforcements had arrived.

Jackie felt peace come over him as he quietly opened the door. However, before the Belleville seniors could even exchange greetings, a shiny black Cadillac pulled up. Official business seemed written all over it. Two Tones and Bad Boy had arrived, … representing Sneaks. Both Frank and Jackie recognized Thomas Anthony. Badalamenti was a new face for the high school students. Jackie thought, *Oh, oh, dis just got confusin'.*

When Two Tones did the introductions, Frank smiled and said, "Hey, Mr. Anthony, we can't go wrong tonight with the four wise men from Jersey in control."

"Ya mean two wiseguys and two kids," said Two Tones, correcting his friend's nephew.

The underworld emissaries were impressed, not offended, by Frank's sense of humor. From his quest for Bella Bruno's heart over the years, Bad Boy had known of Frank's reputation as a student and athlete. On the other hand, Frank's maturity for a seventeen-year old that night would be an enigma to them and Jackie. He had brought some friends in high places with him on his rescue mission. However, their names were not Bad Boy, Two Tones, or Jackie Cary. In fact, they had not yet been introduced.

"Mr. Anthony, if you don't mind, I have a plan to get Gino back," said Frank. "If you could stay outside with your associate, we'll get the job done in here."

"First of all, you can call me Two Tones, Frankie boy. We made more money on you and Gino down on Bloomfield Avenue this year than ever. We should be addressing you guys as 'Mr'."

"Thank you, sir. Then I can take over from here?"

"Rock 'n' roll, Frankie."

"O.K., Two Tones, here's the plan," said Frank, hardly addressing his uncle's friend as a smooth Boiardo family member in charge of the Five Corner-area on Bloomfield Avenue.

Frank Bonaducci was as prepared as ever to convince Gino to get a good night sleep and return to Belleville the next morning. On his exit from his Belmont Avenue home in Belleville just under five hours earlier, he had dispatched Jo-Jo back up to their bedroom to retrieve his black leather motorcycle jacket and his boots. The white tee shirt tightly hugging his muscular frame was draped with the silver studded coat that might look better only on James Dean if he was alive. If Frank's thoughts could have been heard, his three cohorts would be assured that he <u>was</u> in control. The Ivy League hopeful was flying in a different realm, on a foreign frequency, and ready to do battle of a type that no one physically present on the mission could yet comprehend. His three visible comrades saw neither Frank's supernatural associates, nor the enemy legions infiltrating the room and surrounding the environs about the broken down motel.

While concerned that Frank was a bit overconfident, Anthony was willing to give him the freedom he wanted. As the strategy was being detailed, Two Tones thought, *"Kid, you <u>do</u> have a plan, don't ya."*

Frank understood that if Two Tones and this other hood were present in Maryland, then Sneaks, back at Rahway, knew what was going on and only wanted the best for his son. Frank was convinced only he had that answer. "Mr. Anthony, honestly, … you can relax. Here it is. You guys stay out here. Jackie and I will go inside. We'll wake him up, keep him calm, and then I'm going to give him some instructions to help sort out everything that has him so upset." Getting no reaction from anyone, Frank looked to Badalamenti and patted the New York mobster's shoulder. "Cuz, just be patient."

The aging street hood, Jackie, and Two Tones all waited for Frank's next show of strength and control. Bad Boy had become impressed. "Kid, ya got it together."

Two Tones nodded agreement.

"Listen," said Frank. "We'll keep the door cracked so you guys can hear. Just stay quiet."

On the train down, Frank had prayed as his mother always instructed, …to the Sacred Heart of Jesus. On the other hand, his idea had been meticulously crafted more as a result of the instruction of Nora and Queenie, than the Bonaduccis' Roman Catholic background. The full gospel spirit of this black duo had forever changed Marietta in the mind of her oldest child. She still battled her daily demons, but with new confidence that the power of God was working in her. That strength had transferred to her devoted Frank. Gino would now be the first to see it.

Entering the room, Jackie suddenly became jittery, blurting out Gino's name, which woke him. This was just the approach Frank did not want.

Clearing his eyes, Gino was shocked to see his running mate. "Oh, God, what are you doin' here?" He looked to Jackie. "You are dumber than I thought, Jack. Frank, what's up?" Gino lifted himself to a sitting position on the bed, using his bulging forearms for balance.

Frank was ready. "Gino, you know you and I have been pretty tight, even though we don't talk much about it. And you know what? Jackie really respects you. He called me about your plan to head to Kansas and all that. I thought I should come down to give you a geography lesson."

Gino smiled. "Yea, I was never good at geography,… or any subjects for that matter." He shook his head. "Where the heck is Lawrence, Kansas, anyway?"

At least Gino was conversational. With Jackie biting his lips, Frank continued, "Listen, Cuz, first of all, you have to believe that you'll be playing college football somewhere soon. You just have to stop getting so up tight about where or when. You're going to drive yourself, your parents, and on this occasion, Jackie a little nuts. His 'Heavenly Heap' could never make it to Kansas. Besides, State Troopers would feast on you guys all the way out with those mufflers, the continental kit, and the Jersey plates."

"Frank, how'd you get down here?" asked Gino, trying to stall his friend. "Fly?"

"Sort of," said Frank, who now believed there had been enough angels on the train with him to have jet propelled the steel rail hugger to the stop in Greenbelt, Maryland.

"I was drinkin' tonight, Frank. Believe that? I had Jackie worried that we would take off tonight. He's still a nervous wreck, aren't you, Mr. Limo driver?"

"Gino, we're goin' home, right?" asked Frank, testing the waters.

Frank got the conversation with Gino moving along smoothly, and Jackie was thanking God that Frank showed up. But, too quickly, Jackie began jumping to conclusions. "Great, guys, we can leave now, can't we?"

"Jackie, relax, ...in God's name," commanded Frank. The last three words he'd never used before with his friends. However, having been almost a year now around his mother and her two Baptist companions, the "church talk" surprisingly just rolled off his tongue. It was an hour later before Jackie was given permission to speak again.

Outside, the two wiseguys adjusted their plastic chairs, leaning at a 45-degree angle against the motel room wall, just as if they were on Bloomfield Avenue in Newark on a lazy Sunday afternoon in the summer. They wanted to hear as much as they could, so Two Tones could report back to Sneaks. As a New York City soldier living in Essex County, Badalamenti was persona non grata everywhere from the Vittorio Castle down on Park Avenue all the way up to the Vesuvius Restaurant in the North Ward of Newark. So, getting so close to the Boiardo family that night thrilled Bad Boy.

Frank had become oblivious to everything around him. He continued, "Gino, what's bothering you so much that you want to head to Kansas, telling no one, ... when the furthest west you've ever been is Trenton?"

"Frank, I know some of these coaches here aren't as interested anymore, but when Kansas hears I'm gonna graduate in June, plus when I get to meet them personally, I know I'm in." Gino was lucid and hopeful. "I gotta get to meet the backfield coach at Kansas. He played at Hackensack ya know."

"O.K.," said Frank. "That makes sense, except for one thing,"

"What?"

"You don't call on coaches without an appointment. If it's meant to be, let's get Coach P. to call this week, and hash it out on the phone. It's getting late. You can't waste the ride across the country with Jackie's car, and you don't want to offend Kansas by just showing up. Pretty presumptuous, …don't you agree?"

"There he goes, the first word I can't understand," said Gino, looking to Jackie who definitely was not going to give a reaction. An invisible power would not permit his further participation in the conversation.

"Come on, Gino. What's really bothering you?" asked Frank.

For the next hour, Gino talked about his mother and father, how great they've been to him over the years. On the other hand, his father's organized crime activity had become an embarrassment. He appreciated more the peaceful and guilt-free benefits of good clean, hard work, … an example set by Frank's dad. Gino had heard stories of how Rocky could have easily gone the other way like so many guys who came through Central and Barringer in the pre-war years. Gino reaffirmed hopes that football could get him an education, in spite of being a poor student. With so many of the colleges that had originally contacted him backing off, even his All State selection was beginning to seem hollow. Maybe the only one to blame was himself, but he wanted to make a last ditch effort to get somewhere next year to play football. In the end, Frank saw that Gino was beginning to feel sorry for himself. Being an only child, having no girlfriend to be proud of, the son of a Boiardo kingpin, and now getting the runaround from Maryland as well as Kansas, Gino flatly pointed out that maybe he now had good reason to rebel and take off. *Hadn't so many people in town always figured I'd go the wrong way? My only salvation was football, and now even that's slippin' away. My enemies could be right after all.*

While Thomas Anthony strained to overhear what Frank and Gino were saying, "Bad Boy" Badalamenti would not stop trying to open up dialogue about "business" in northern New Jersey. Two Tones was getting impatient, and at one point stopped mid-sentence to question about the rumors of a counterfeit scam in Essex County. Two Tones instantly made it clear to him that a lot of people in Newark were upset it could be happening under The Boot's nose, without the Jersey head's sanction.

Fidgety at first, Bad Boy then began to speak in future tense about how a joint counterfeit operation could benefit organizations on both sides of the Hudson. Two Tones let him speak, but knew most of what he proposed was probably already in place. If so, because Bad Boy was notoriously unorganized and impetuous, the plan was probably already vulnerable to law enforcement. Two Tones was sure this loose cannon from New York was going to hurt Boiardo's Jersey operation, and it was too late to prevent it. He dropped the subject. Besides, he needed guidance about it from Sneaks.

Back inside, Frank asked, "So, Gino, you're feeling pretty crummy now, right?"

"Crap, Frank, me drinking beer and tormenting Jackie to drive west. Yea, ... feel like crap. None of these coaches are giving me a straight answer."

"Suppose I could show you a way to take the load off of your shoulders, and still get what you want, Gino? That would make sense, right?"

Gino raised his head. "What'a ya talkin' about?"

Frank took a deep breath. "Listen, you know this was a tough year for me, ... the injury and everything?"

"Yea, and a jerk like me scorin' all the T.D.'s that should'a been yours."

"Gino, you were unstoppable. You were ready. God's been setting you up for this season for a long time. You'd served as the best blocker for me long enough. When I went down, you were ready. Your humility had prepared you, Cuz, ... your humility."

"Man, I've been called a lot, but never humble."

"All right, let's just say a little prayer together," said Frank, as serious and assertive as he'd ever been with his friend.

"Frank, now you're soundin' like one of those religious freaks. You're still Catlic, right?"

"Cuz, don't worry about those details. How did you think I made it through this year? God healed me and helped me make the most of what I had. Man, he answered all my prayers. We had a great year, you make All State, and I make All County. I was facing disaster, without Jesus. Jealousy of you, frustration, anger, and all the rest would have otherwise choked me. Cuz, I gave those things up, and looked how it all turned out."

"Yea, and then the Nutley game, … you waitin' for me at the goal line. My old man still can't get over it. What made you do that, Father Bonaducci?"

Frank wasn't threatened by Gino's remark. "Listen, you would have done the same for me."

Gino did not immediately reply. "But what kind of prayin' you talking about? I ain't gonna become an altar boy or anything. I don't even go to church. Besides, first I tell my old man that I don't ever want any part of his friends and the businesses. Now, I tell him my friend's trying to get me to do something that's doesn't sound Catlic?"

"Gino, this isn't Catholic, or Protestant, or Jewish, … or any kind of church thing. You don't need religion, you just need a relationship."

"Yea, a relationship. But, with who?"

Frank then quoted the New Testament about how the simplicity of Christ's plan for salvation could give Gino a more victorious life. He explained the Trinity of the Father, Son, and Holy Ghost. These were familiar terms, but putting Jesus on such a pedestal was not sitting well with Gino.

"Cuz, I had the same problem when I first heard this stuff. I still go to the Catholic Church. But you know what these colored gals told my mother that convinced her, … and me when I heard it?"

"What?"

"Well, Jesus is either who He says He is, … or He's the biggest liar that ever lived. That would make him more of a criminal than some of the guys we see hanging out on the corners, … worse than some of your father's crew, let alone the punks that do all the dirty work to become 'made men'. After all, more people have died for Jesus than guys getting killed on orders from Gambino, Genovese, or the Jersey boys."

"Heavy, man." Gino liked the simplicity of the logic. "Talk about a real 'capo', huh?"

"Praise da Lord and halleluiah!" exclaimed Jackie as he saw a stern look reel off from Frank. "Frankie, sorry. I'm supposed to be quiet."

Gino, too, scowled, figuring Jackie was making fun of what was going on.

"No, Gino, dis is good. I mean it," stammered Jackie. "I mean, man, if ya don't let Frankie help ya here, <u>I'll do</u> what he's tellin' ya to do. Give your problems to God or one of da utter tree guys, … or whoever, and just stop worryin' bout tings. I feel better already. Forget my car, listen to him."

Frank corrected him. "The Holy Trinity, Jackie, … not the three guys."

Outside, Badalamenti had fallen asleep in the leaning chair. Two Tones had been as attentive as Jackie, hanging on Frank's every word. *At least that would get the kid home, and Sneaks would be happy,* he thought. *But what if Gino did understand Frank, and asked Jesus to step into his deal? Then Sneak's kid would never become part of this way of life. Who's kiddin' who? The mob puts the guys and their businesses before their own families, let alone some God they couldn't see. Nothing else could merit more favor. Yea, they donated lots of money to churches, and some even went to confession, but we're still part of a thing that's as ungodly as anything could get. Yea, the numbers and some protection around the neighborhoods are harmless, but extortion, robbery, and the inevitability of murder make this way of life ugly. Now everybody's talking drugs and prostitution. A little counterfeit? So what. But all of* these other ways of making money are sickening. Sure Two Tones liked expensive suits and women he could get with a wad of hundreds, jewelry, and his big car. But why did he always have a stomachache? The price was getting too high. *Yea, the Boot and our group helped a lot of people over the years, but behind closed doors, only demons were present. No one would ever say that. There's surely not the peace that's here in this motel room in Maryland. This organized crime ritual of induction isn't too different from what Frank's pitchin' to Gino, … surrender and commitment. But the benefits Frank's talkin' about are better, … peace, someone to talk to all the time, forgiveness, and even a shot at some favors, as long as the Boss was in agreement. Look at this kid, Frank,* thought Two Tones. *It got him through a tough football season, and now he's helping his friend for seemingly nuttin' in return.* Two Tones suddenly recognized that if he had the same chance that was being given at Gino's age, he knew what direction he would go, … and not toward Bloomfield Avenue and the meetings at the Vittoria Castle. Thinking to himself, the words were loud and clear: *Go for it, kid, don't make the same mistake I did. Go with the Father, the Son, and the Holy Ghost. Forget The Boot, your father, and this cursed "Cosa Nostra" way to live. Listen to Mr. Outside!*

That night Gino prayed with Frank for God's forgiveness and peace. He put his hand in the hand of someone he could not see. Not fully understanding what he'd done, and still resistant to the less than traditional approach Frank had taken, it would be years before the seed planted inside him in that motel room would fully blossom. But, it did convince him to trust the Higher Power with his challenge to play college football. In addition, much to the pleasure of Jackie, Two Tones, and Frank, Gino also made another commitment to return to Belleville the next day. And when Gino and Frank said "Amen" at the end of their prayer, the Irish kid with the golden car, and a street guy with the funny name from Bloomfield Avenue echoed the same, "Amen".

The two thirteen foot angels on guard at the entrance to the motel room spread their wings and rocketed skyward in celebration. The legion of frustrated demons fled in disgust. Bad Boy, on the other hand, remained just that. He was still asleep, turning out to be an unworthy cohort in the satanic assignment that had Kansas City as its eventual destination. Frank had not come alone to the University of Maryland, … he had brought some friends from higher places, and even their Boss of bosses was present by His Spirit. An unauthorized road trip finally turned out to be a heavenly voyage, … at least for four guys from Jersey.

CHAPTER 14

" APRIL FOOL'S DAY"

April Fool's Day finally determined which colleges would welcome the two outstanding running backs from Belleville High. The neighboring town of Nutley was buzzing about Clemson accepting both Bob Scrudato and Jack Chuy. At the local hangouts of Plenge's Milk Bar, the Guys and Dolls pool hall on Washington Avenue on the Belleville-Nutley border, and Rutt's Hut in Clifton, debates raged amongst teenage patrons all winter as to whether Belleville's Mr. Inside and Mr. Outside would ever get into schools of their choice or not.

Yale, where he really wanted to go, rejected Frank. Delaware and Lehigh offered full scholarships, but Cornell's acceptance had a financial aid package less lucrative than the other two schools. On the other hand, a dishwashing job in one of the fraternities could make up the difference.

Kansas never even processed Gino's application. Although Maryland had initially been encouraging, their future interest was predicated on his enrolling at Fork Union Military Academy. A good year in football and proof that he could sit down to study would then make him eligible for the big time college game.

Frank had foregone his senior year of baseball in favor of track at the suggestion of assistant football coach, Tim Testa, who was also the head track coach. "Frank, ya got the heart of a lion and the spirit of a saint," said the coach. "Now we gotta put some thunder in those thighs, and lightning in those legs. Forget baseball. Play football in college and make friends for a lifetime. That's your game. You're a leader, and football requires your kind of leadership." Testa, who had questioned

Frank many times about his Nutley game decision, loved the student-athlete and wanted him to play in the Ivies.

When Frank came home after track practice, about 5 PM, Rocky, Marietta, and Donna were sitting at the kitchen table with envelopes from the four schools.

"No one opened them up yet?" Frank asked, as his family held their breaths.

Donna was anxious. "Hurry, Frankie, we can't wait."

Frank shuffled through the pile quickly. "Well, the lightest and smallest is Yale's. That's history. Looks like the others want me."

Frank instantly thought back to the Nutley game. Out of all the schools where he applied, Yale said the least about his controversial play. Originally, that encouraged him. Then, he quickly dispelled any further thought about that emotional day in the mud. He knew it was useless.

Marietta really didn't care which school accepted her son. She just wanted him happy. Besides, she was privately harboring the knowledge of Sneak's bankroll set aside for Frank. She was philosophical and spiritual. "Frankie, thank God you still have such nice choices. We are very proud of you."

"You and your cousin, Nick, ... the first Bonaduccis goin' to college, ... countin' the Brooklyn Bonaduccis, too. Great job, Frank. You did it," said Rocky, choking up. Marines know about experiencing the grace of God.

"Frank, you have an idea of which one you want?" probed Marietta.

"Not just an idea, Ma. I know where I'm going." Frank opened each package carefully, studied them, and then looked out the kitchen window.

The back door burst open, with Jo-Jo storming in. "Where's Frankie going? Did he hear?" Breathless, he'd run all the way home from grammar school baseball practice, and as soon as he looked into everyone's face, Jo-Jo froze in his tracks.

"Well, everybody's here," said Frank, taking a deep breath. "So, it's ... Cornell! Yep. The Ivy League thing and School of Industrial and Labor Relations, plus, the coaches want me, and they're offering a part-time job that will mean you won't have to pay, Ma. You know Yale was my first choice. But, Ma, just like you and the

Baskerville girls taught me, I prayed, … 'God have your way.' Well, He has, and I'm fine with that."

Marietta reached over for her son and hugged him. She was thinking, *My coaching has paid off, and the Good Lord is blessing my son.* As they embraced, her ever-active mind wandered. Sentimentality and regret could have overwhelmed her as she flashed back to her own fleeting college opportunities during the war. Her mother had coldly quenched any thoughts of Marietta's continuing with her education, insisting that work and pregnancy were more acceptable options for a first generation Italian American beauty whose family was in a struggling butcher business. Swallowing a rising lump of self-pity, she wondered what she could do with Sneak's endowment, now that it may not be needed.

The Cornell choice set Rocky rattling off names of previous Jersey stars that had ventured up to Ithaca, New York, on the shores of Cayuga Lake. "God, you follow some great ones, Frankie. Bird Legs Murphy from Glen Ridge High… caught the famous 'Fifth Down' pass back in '40. Sneaks Babula's cousin from Garfield, … tougher than Sneaks and Gino. Freddy Wesphal from Barringer. As a kid on Lake Street, I'd watch him practice with the Big Blue in Branch Brook Park. Man, what a pair of mitts; best two-way end I ever saw. Then there's Billy DeGraaf from Clifton, … the dairy family's kid; ranks amongst their greatest quarterbacks. And let's not forget Georgie Plenge, one of Belleville's best, …first kid from the neighborhood to go to Cornell. Also, you got Bloomfield's Tony Pascal who's up there now with that Telesh kid from Clifton. All good company, Frankie. Grandpa Joe and everybody are gonna be proud."

"Yea, Dad, and I'm sure Frankie will be playing with a lot of farm boys," teased Jo-Jo, referring to his father's constant talk over the years about playing for Barringer against "farm boys" from Phillipsburg. Rocky, who never wore a facemask, would confirm the rural athletes' abilities, chronicling their toughness as well when he faced them later, on the football field at Camp Pendleton when he was with the Fallbrook Marines before heading to the South Pacific.

"Jo-Jo, you're right," said Frank. "I finally get a chance to play with the farm boys. Cornell's Agriculture School will supply lots of them. Just hope they don't stop me from starting when I get there."

The telephone rang, and Jo-Jo picked it up quickly.

"Jo-Jo, your brother there?" asked Gino.

"Yea. Ya hear yet?"

"Just put your brother on, Jo-Jo. Ya won't believe it."

Frank came on the line. "Gino, what's up?" asked Frank, who had become embarrassed over the last couple of weeks by ending up with more college opportunities than his running mate.

"Frank, ya sittin' down?"

"Go ahead."

"I'm goin' to Fork Union next year! Ya believe it?"

"Gino, you OK with that?" asked Frank with disbelief.

"Listen, you started it with me, altar boy. So last week I just prayed God would make the best decision for me. And ya know what? He did. Maryland says do good down there, and I get a full four-year ride next fall. If it's OK with God, it's OK with me."

"Gino, you mean that?"

"Hey, Mr. Outside, Mr. Inside doesn't have any other choices. I made it easy on the Boss of bosses. And ya know what else? My old man's OK with it, too. Says he's gonna be gettin' out soon, and is lookin' forward to the road trips to Virginia. Sounds like he's got some business down there, ... if ya know what I mean."

"Gino, if you're happy, and your dad's all right about it, then great!" said Frank, to whom Gino's humble acceptance of the final outcome of his desperate college hunting was definitely a minor miracle.

"And what about my running mate?" asked Gino.

"Cornell!"

"Great, just great! Congratulations. What you did for me, ... what ya done for all the guys, ...ya deserve the best, Frankie."

"Hey, cut the sentimentality, Gino. We'll celebrate this Saturday in New York, right?" Frank was already thinking about his upcoming debut as a "backstage Johnny" that would lead to his "dream" of meeting Dion and the Belmonts.

"New York? ...Oh yea, Joe Pelli's thing at the Paramount for us. Yea, we'll celebrate we finally know where we're goin' to college, ... OK. But what kind of celebration we gonna have when you don't drink, ...ya got a girlfriend. I can't have more than one beer, ... and we don't know what the heck's gonna happen in the first place?" Gino added, "By the way, Mr. Social Chairman, you figure out yet what a 'backstage Johnny' is?"

"Who knows? Hey, Pelli says Dion's definite, plus Connie Ferro, maybe Frankie Lyman and Jackie Wilson."

That night Frank called Joe Pelli to confirm who else he would be taking to the Paramount: Jackie Carey, in his golden Mercury doing the driving, with Gino riding shotgun; Eric Thatcher and Bob Hardy would join Frank in the back seat; cousin Nicholas Durso had to take a pass. He had a date.

The lineup amused Pelli. "I know da Carey kid. Patsie Pratola's goin' wit his sister. Right, Frankie baby?"

"Yep. You know everybody, Joe."

"He ain't no atlete, dough, Frank. Ya know, I told my buddy, Ralphie Benedetto, I got dese Belleville studs comin' backstage. Dat's how he got the tickets. Ya know there ain't much room backstage on a big night like dis Saturday. Dis Carey kid's a greasier version of what I been representin' to my people in the City. After all, the audience'll be filled wit enough Jackie Careys. We don't need any of dem backstage wit the stars, " declared Joe. He had the totally naïve seventeen year old on the hook.

"Look, the kid's a good kid, Joe. He helped Gino out of a jam a couple of weeks ago. Besides, he knows Brooklyn. Gino can't take his new Bonneville. So Jackie's our only ride."

"Only puttin' ya on, Frankie boy. Just kiddin'," said Joe. "I know all about the Maryland ting. Besides, Lenny Latore and the Four Loves just might be gettin' a chance to open up before Connie. Ya know, ... 'cause of the Newark-Belleville ting. Talk about some grease from da neighborhood! So, Jack's dopey intended brother-in-law could be singin', if ya can believe dat! Jackie Boy will fit in real well," assured Pelli.

"Great, Joe. Thanks again. Seeing Connie again will be OK. But the guys are really excited about Dion and the Belmonts and Frankie Lyman. Jackie Wilson will be there, too. Right?"

"Don't know. Will let youse guys know before Saturday. Just remember, it's the back stage door, and you're askin' for … 'Ralphie B. from Nutley'. Dat's your ticket. Ralphie will take care of everyting from dare. Meet the stars, have a few drinks, … a good time on Joe Pelli."

"Joe, what we owe you by the way?" asked ever-respectful Frank.

"Nuttin'. Maybe dough, when ya play in college, ya get Ralphie and me a couple of tickets … and a couple of dates. Ya know, some coeds who might dig older guys from Newark. Den, we're even."

Frank hesitated. "Gotch ya, Joe. Won't forget."

On his recruiting visit to Cornell, Frank recalled hearing that the football players had to make weekly road trips to find female companionship. So, he hoped one part of the payback request would later slip Joe's mind. The Ivy League school was known for brainy women, … but just a handful. And beauty pageants were not on their college agendas. Matchmaking these two wannabe entertainers with a couple of townies from Ithaca that he'd have to hunt down, made Frank shake his head in amusement. He could not see Joe Pelli fitting in very well at a Cornell fraternity party either. On the other hand, he knew one thing for sure, … not too many Cornellians would be able to define a "backstage Johnny".

CHAPTER 15

"BELLBOYS IN BROOKLYN"

Jackie Carey was proud of himself. He had masterfully negotiated Gino back on the sanity track, just as it looked like they were going to be derailed in Maryland. Of course, Frank Bonaducci helped. However, he smiled at the thought that his "persuasiveness" with his sister, and then Frank, proved that he was a natural to fulfill his future as a community cop, ... the perfect peacemaker and compromiser in the name of law and order. But then being honest with himself, a lot of it all had to do with the unforgettable prayer exchange he witnessed between the two football stars, ... a moment that changed both of them, as well as Jackie, and even Two Tones.

"Old Jackie Boy, ya gonna be OK," he assured himself.

His inner peace since Maryland was far too real for him to ignore. Sitting in front of the Bonaducci house waiting to pick up some of Belleville's finest athletes and students, Jackie concluded he was now part of the BHS elite inner sanctum, and that was a miracle, too. But most of all, he felt everything in his life would now start working out. He didn't feel alone and afraid as much as before. Even more new experiences were about to overwhelm Jackie and his friends on this night, ... with the birth of a couple of "backstage Johnnies" from Belleville.

When Frank and his two closest neighborhood friends, Eric Thatcher and Bob Hardy, came walking out, they all quickly piled into the golden Mercury's back seat, totally ignoring Jackie. Miffed, he looked back. "Well, what would youse guys ever do witout da ever-dependable Jackie Carey and his 'Heavenly Heap'?

Yea, … great guys. Youse all just sit in my legendary back seat wit nobody up here, actin' like yas swallowed your tongues."

With a matching English accent, Eric made a pompous waving gesture to the front of the car. "Drive on, Mr. Jack. The theater awaits your distinguished riding clients this evening."

"Here we go," retaliated Jackie.

Eric continued, "Yes, Mr. Jack. Here we go, … off to retrieve our illustrious Mr. Inside, … Babula, by name. He'll reside in the front seat with you. On to Carpenter Street, Mr. Jack. And toot sweet, I might add."

Jackie again jabbed back. "Hey, Eric, cut it out. Besides, your accent is almost as bad as your Jocko Henderson and Allan Freed imitations. And dey stink. Eric 'the Snatcher' Thatcher, … I mean, how ridiculous is dis nickname of yours?" His sense of humor was wearing thin.

"Jackie, you're the best, … the best driver that is," quipped Bob Hardy.

Then Frank tried to get Eric and Bob under control. "OK, guys, let's get serious."

"Yes, very good idea," agreed Jackie. He continued, "Hope we can still have a good time tonight, boys, because so far youse given me da same feelin' I had a couple of weeks ago when one of 'your kind' was trying to commandeer me to Kansas? So, just everybody relax. Ol' Jackie Boy will take care of youse. After all, if I don't get yas dare, youse never get another chance at becoming a … 'backstage Johnny'. So who's really da boss here?"

Once Gino had been picked up, the trip to Brooklyn took only about an hour. Conversation seemed to settle down to college, picking up New York City girls, and Dion and the Belmonts. Not to be left out, Jackie kicked in about getting into the Police Academy. That was all Gino needed. "Man, I better tell my ol' man to stay at Rahway, with Sherlock Holmes here packin' a gun. Hey, Jack, what would you do if you had to go after one of The Boot's' crew, … and it probably being somebody ya know. I can just hear ya: 'Hey, Crazy Louie, how ya doin'? Heard da new song by da Belmonts?' Yea, they'll all be scared of Jackie Cary from the Belleville PD. Sure."

"Oh, Gino, dose guys are in Newark," said Jackie.

Stretched over the seat to see the other's reaction, Gino added, "Oh, this is great. Jackie thinks gangsters stop at the Belleville line. He forgets my father lives on Carpenter Street when he's not in Rahway. Innocent people of this world are in trouble with Jack wearing the blue of Belleville's finest. Don't ya think, fellas?"

Jackie returned the volley. "Ya should talk, Mr. Inside. Maryland likes ya so much dat dey send ya to some reform school in da woods down sout. Fork Union versus the Police Academy? No comparison, big guy."

Eric interceded again with his English accent, to drive Jackie even nuttier. "Jack, my boy, you are almost correct in your assumptions. The fine University of Maryland does have a genuine affection for the player of football by the surname of Babula. But your assessment of their official's enthusiasm is a bit off. You see, they want Mr.Gino so badly; they require immediate matriculation at the Fork Union facility. The point is, Mr. Chauffeur, they want him there tonight. And you and your spoiled little vehicle are going to get him, and us, there." Transforming from his rendition of the King's finest English into his combination of Jocko Henderson and an Orange Street, Newark, black hood imitation, Eric recited:

"Ya gets us down to Virginia by night,
Or your skinny Irish butt gets kicked in a fight.
Brooklyn ain't where we wanna go,
Ya best head sout on the Pike, … bro.
Ya sista can't help ya and neither can Frank,
Just sit back and drive, it's only a prank."

Then, much to Jackie's relief, Eric changed focus. "Relax, Jackie, only kidding. Hey, Frank, let's get down to business. As resident DJ of the Smallwood Avenue Ballroom, when are we going to get our audience with Dion and his Belmonts?"

"Pelli says his friend, Ralphie, has everything worked out. We'll find out when we get there."

Bob Hardy broke his silence. "And when, may I ask, do we have to endure Connie Ferro?" While her rise to pop fame helped put Belleville on the map, the future Midshipman was not a big fan. "When she showed up at the football dinner to honor our two big heroes here, I thought she was gonna maul you, Frank, right at the podium."

"God, that <u>was</u> embarrassing, wasn't it?" Frank shook his head. "If I didn't turn away in time, she would have kissed me on the lips!"

Jackie jumped back in. "Yea, and I was dare. Did youse see Maria's reaction? Man, if looks could kill, Frankie, ya would'a been dead, and so would'a America's favorite female singer for da moment."

"Ah, Frankie's a one-woman guy, fellas, … and it ain't never gonna be Connie Ferro!" offered Gino. "Let's just hope that for us guys who ain't so henpecked as perfect Frank, there're some hot New York City chicks there, … who'll love our Old Spice."

"Gino, Old Spice? What happened to your Canoe?" asked Frank, jostling Gino from the back seat.

"Jackie came over the other night, and drank it on me."

After parking the Heavenly Heap at a Brooklyn lot recommended by Pelli, the boys followed his directions to the backstage door of the Paramount. A huge bellied security type, dressed in a flowered shirt that was more like an African ceremonial blouse as it draped nearly to his knees, greeted them in a surprisingly high-pitched voice. "The Bellboys are here. Follow me."

Walking behind their behemoth host, the boys could not see where they were going. People coming in the opposite direction would squeeze around the gentle giant and rush on by as if the show were about to start.

The hallway had a distinct odor. The air's mustiness and scent of stale beer reminded Frank of Sundays after church in the early fifties. His dad would drag him to Charlie Fritz' Parkway Lodge on Park Avenue, just down from Barringer High, where, after the war, a bunch of the First and North Ward boys who had made it back would hang out any day of the week. After mass, Rocky would always baby-sit his first born at Charlie's to review the City League football games, one by one, during the fall.

"Where's Big Boy takin' us?" asked Eric, not expecting their giant guide to hear.

"Looking for Ralphie B. from Nutley!" the bouncer amazingly answered in his almost comical high-pitch. "Lookin' for Ralphie B. from Nutley," he then repeatedly screamed out.

The huge physical presence with the "Tweetie Bird" vocals prompted Jackie's inevitable whispered query. "Hey, Frank, ya tink dis guy is really a real guy?"

206

"You ask him, Mr. Inquisitive."

Thankfully, the next voice they heard belonged to Ralph Benedetto. "Thanks for helpin' out, 'Tiny.'"

Approaching from the opposite direction, Ralph embraced the big escort. Now Benedetto was not small himself, but he vanished into the clutches of arms that were more like two meat hooks covered with overlapping layers of human flesh. Tiny then turned around and wished the boys an enjoyable night. All five managed to politely smile back. With a name like "Tiny" for a six-foot, four hundred pounder, "unusual" was hardly the adjective to describe their first impression of the "backstage Johnny" experience.

Appearing to be in his late twenties, Ralphie B. was as dapper and as magnetic a personality as Joe Pelli had represented to Frank. He immediately made them feel at ease by mentioning something he already knew about each one. A real sports fan, he bet at all levels of competition with his bookie on Bloomfield Avenue. But his delight to be meeting the Belleville athletes was truly sincere.

When he greeted Jackie, Ralph also made it clear that he was wired into the Jersey scene. "And you're the guy with the Mercury in Maryland, ... Pratola's girfriend's little brother."

Jackie meekly nodded.

The boys could see how Ralph Benedetto's affable and outgoing personality made an attractive complement to Joe Pelli's edgy, but comical ways and appearance. Bigger than his show biz partner by at least eight inches, Benedetto's impeccable dress implied the entertainment business, ... or the mob. Nobody was seeking answers tonight. Tanned from a recent gig in Miami, his long, handsome face was crowned by wavy black hair streaked with some premature gray. He stood out in any crowd. So, the boys from Belleville felt comfortable Joe had set them up perfectly with a most capable host for their unfolding night to remember.

"Guys, follow me into this room here," said Ralph. "You'll mix with some of our other guests, ... lots of food and drinks. Have a good time. I'll be back with some of the stars before show time. You all look like real 'backstage Johnnies from Jersey'."

"God Almighty, what's dis 'backstage Johnny' supposed to mean?" Jackie whispered in Gino's ear.

Ralph opened a metal door and patted each of the boys on the back as they entered. He then vanished as his guests fully absorbed the smoke-filled room, laced with the scents of cheap perfume, alcohol, and overheated food. They had just entered the world of "backstage Johnnies". At first, they were glad to be there.

It was standing room only, cramped with approximately twenty-five chattering people and a couple of couches. Tables were full of cold and hot snacks, with two bartenders making drinks, non-stop.

Jackie was first to utter any reaction. "Oh, God. Jackie from Jersey comes all da way out here to Brooklyn wit his beloved Heavenly Heap to hang out wit a bunch of utter Jersey people. Don't tell Jackie dat half of Belleville and da Nort Ward is here, 'cause he just might trow up. We might as well be at da Red Door by da Park. And I could've walked dare." None of his companions was starry-eyed either, but rather felt disappointed astonishment. Carey's raw view was hard to refute, as he went on. "And now I gotta listen to my sister's boyfriend sing in Lenny Latore's group? Yep, Patsie's here, cause nobody could look like him. And dat means my sister's here, too. Oh, what a night dis is gonna be for Jackie Carey. I risk my 'Heap' for another Four Loves gig?"

Lenny Latore and his Four Loves were drifting in and out of the crowd, excited about their unexpected New York debut after Connie Ferro asked them at the last minute to open for her. It was obvious that night that Patsie Pratola was acting more and more like the group's lead singer than its tenuous bass. He was drawing disparaging looks from Lenny, who had been more than serious over the years about taking the group to national stardom. Latore's falsetto voice was fast becoming the rage to teenagers around the metropolitan area, but he remained humble about the group's modest success, as he dragged them in and out of smoke-filled nightclubs and musty Jersey Shore bars. The egocentric Pratola was clearly getting on Lenny's nerves. He just needed one more excuse to send Patsie back to Bloomfield Avenue, where Lenny felt he really belonged, … running numbers. Latore really wanted to bring back Jimmy Quinn. But Frank's uncle was not going to disappoint his feisty wife, Pinky, who had made sure Public Service would be her husband's employer, and not some aspiring singing group that had grown up from Steven Crane's Village on the Belleville line to Lake Street in Branch Brook Park.

As Patsie continued to mingle like some fast-rising mobster, Lenny bit his tongue to avoid a scene in front of the fans and New York music crowd intent on hearing the Four Loves' Brooklyn Paramount debut.

The five new "backstage Johnnies" from Belleville dropped their jaws as their eyes opened wider and wider. They simultaneously beheld the oddest couple in the jammed room. Like seeing a ghost, their necks quickly snapped back and forth towards each other. There, oozing sex in a tight fitting red dress and black blouse, stood steamy Julie Manzer. The tops of her trademark black stockings showed underneath her dress hem, accentuated by a pair of patent leather high heels. And she was fawning all over... none other than the infirmed Craig Francello! There they were, Belleville High's two most extreme personalities, seemingly more at home in the star-crazed crowd than anyone.

"Well, Joe Pelli's got some sense of humor, doesn't he?" remarked Eric Thatcher.

"Now this is really turning into a mystery thriller," added deadpan Bob Hardy.

Frank just shook his head in disbelief.

Jackie summed it up. "Yep, I got it. We're not a bunch of 'backstage Johnnies'. We're a bunch of 'backstage jerks'. Craig and Julie? ... Here? ...Tonight? ...What are da odds?" Then he pointed to the other enigmatic character who made up the bizarre trio, ... Julie's dad, Officer Eddie Manzer. "Now I get it," Jackie observed. "Julie's old man is here for security for da Loves, and to make sure his lethal daughter gets discovered by some agent or some theatrical honcho. I wanna pewk. If I didn't know he was a Newark cop, I'd say he was some sleazy gangster. He looks and acts more like a wiseguy when he's out of uniform than Boiardo's boys do when they're wearin' dare thousand dollar suits. Great image for up and comin' flatfoots like Patrolman Jackie Carey."

Jackie's wide-eyed companions could not refute his heartfelt opinion.

The evening's bizarre dissent into disillusionment continued as a familiar face appeared behind Gino, and whispered in his ear. "Mr. Inside, welcome to the Paramount and the music business."

Gino never appreciated anyone that close to him other than his saintly mother. It was "Bad Boy" Badalamenti, the New York hood that the Jersey family wished would stay east of the Hudson. Sounding like his father, Gino reacted, "Why don't you just vanish, Mr. Badalamenti, 'cause I'm getting' sick of seeing ya."

"Ah, Gino, your father would want you to be more respectful, …or haven't ya seen him lately?" Bad Boy's sarcastic remark had Sneak's son close to spitting in his face. But, Gino said nothing and turned his head away.

Remembering Badalamenti was "Two Tones'" partner on the Maryland trip, Frank distracted him with a gentle shoulder tap. "Man, fancy seeing you here, Mr. Badalamenti. Business or pleasure?"

"Frankie Bonaducci, Gino's guardian angle. Good to see ya, kid." Badalamenti stared back at Frank. "Yea, that's it. Here for business and pleasure. Ya know, lots of ways to make a buck and have a good time, …all at the same time." While only half his age, Frank could never muster an ounce of respect for Bad Boy.

Jackie leaned over to Eric and Bobby. Referring to Badalamenti, he said, "Another grease ball rolled in, and even Bloomfield Avenue hates dis guy."

Finally, two people, who represented some hope for the evening, rushed over to welcome the teens, … Jackie's sister and Two Tones. Although smiling, Elizabeth Carey could not avoid mothering her brother. "Hey, Jack, you never told me you were going to be here."

"And ya never told me, sis," said Jackie, reaching for Two Tones' hand. "Mr. Anthony, how ya doin'?"

Any semblance of class in the Boiardo crew that infested the North Ward was definitely Thomas Anthony, … particularly for Frank, Gino, and Jackie after the Ho Jo experience in Maryland. They had become big fans of the handsome, suave, and strangely considerate Two Tones. With his being such a protector of Pete Frassa on the Five Corners at 5th Street and Bloomfield Avenue, Anthony was not unaware of Frank's positive feelings toward him. "Hey, Frank, I tried to get your Uncle Pete and Greenie Delaney to come with me. But Greenie's sister was making them some Irish stew. Feed those two guys, and they're in heaven."

"Yea, except Greenie gets skinnier, and my Uncle Pete gets fatter."

Two Tones' undisguised dislike for him made Badalamenti silently vanish into the maddening crowd. Frank introduced Thatcher and Hardy to Two Tones. His sincere warmth was welcomed, but surely a surprise when Gino later related what Thomas Anthony mostly did for a living. However, his financing and management of Lenny Latore's singing future certainly gave him some extra credibility with the teens. "Guys, get something to eat and drink," suggested Two Tones. "Ralphie from Nutley is gonna have Jackie Wilson and Frankie Lyman in here soon. So make yourself at home."

"My brother's not drinking, because he's driving," was Elizabeth's stern message to Jackie.

He hit back. "Oh no! Jackie Carey's sister has to show up on his one time chance at bein' a 'backstage Johnny'. Not only is drinkin' now out for him, but also she'll be watchin' his every move wit da New York City girls."

As they all laughed, Two Tones added, "Hey, when's somebody goin' to inform Jackie here that Brooklyn girls are not New York City girls?"

Elizabeth snapped. "Alright, Tommy, I don't want you educating these boys on this girl thing, so that's enough."

Frank tried to defuse Elizabeth. "Hey, Jackie's of age in New York. Besides I told him I'd drive home. So, don't worry, I'll be in charge of getting the boys and the Heavenly Heap back safe and sound."

Elizabeth squeezed his cheeks, "Ooohh, if only this kid was a couple of years older."

While Frank blushed, Jackie gave the victory sign. "OK, boys, da drinks are on me."

"Just don't get drunk. Remember, Jackie, you're gonna try to become a cop after graduation," Elizabeth warned.

Two Tones then changed the subject. "Listen guys, there've been some changes in the show. But you won't be disappointed. That's obviously why I'm here with Lenny and the Loves. Connie, Wilson, Lyman and his group are all set. But the bad news is … Dion's a no-show. He and the Belmonts had a schedule conflict or something."

Just as Two Tones finished, Ralph Benedetto reappeared and patiently got everyone's attention, except Badalamenti. Bad Boy had discovered Julie Manzer and was all over her. He'd already forgotten his wife of fifteen years back on Heller Parkway in Newark.

"OK folks, here's the new deal," said Benedetto, emphasizing that Connie Ferro would not join her supporters until after the show. However, Frankie Lyman and the Teenagers and the incomparable Jackie Wilson would enter the room shortly. But, the reason he gave for Dion's absence was sickness, not a schedule conflict. Then Ralph made a wildly applauded surprise announcement: The legendary disc jockey, Allan Freed, who was the guest master of ceremonies, had agreed to visit with…. "the Jersey crowd" after the show.

For Jackie Carey, his one "Seven and Seven" was already having effect, and alcohol meant his immature sarcasm would elevate to the nth degree. "Well, boys, ya did it to me again. Jackie Carey exposes da Heavenly Heap to Brooklyn traffic, and now it's all official: Lenny Latore and da Four Loves stand in for Dion and da Belmonts; a couple of hoods from Newark are here to protect 'em and look important; I have to see Julie Manzer hangin' all over Craig Francello just as she does in cafeteria study hall; and, … we all get to meet a bunch of colored guys who sing like girls. It's official, … I'm now a 'backstage jerk'."

"Jack, you're finished drinking if you don't quiet down," said Frank.

"Honestly, Frank, Julie Manzer and Connie Ferro are more in my dreams than you, and I really shouldn't be complainin'. On da other hand, it would've been great to talk to Dion."

Frank agreed. "Man, that's a bummer, isn't it?"

Jackie put his arm around Frank. "Listen, buddy, don't pay too much attention to Jackie Carey. He really appreciates bein' here. Price is right, and da fact dat Patsie Pratola is here is not your fault. Besides, da night's young. Wait until dose New York City girls, …I mean Brooklyn Babes… discover Jackie from Jersey."

Frank affectionately pushed Jackie away.

And so, in the last half hour before show time, Frankie Lyman and Jackie Wilson did make brief appearances, cordially signing autographs on request. The five Heavenly Heap riders continued to filter into the crowd, renewing acquaintances from the Five Corners of Bloomfield Avenue to Steven Crane's Village. But then, one final unique character took center stage.

Sean McMahon was a red-faced, plump saloonkeeper from the Astoria section of Queens, New York. A barrel chest contrasted with his small head, shining brightly from perspiration and featuring a hairline that was vanishing too soon for a man in his early thirties. Long, thin legs made it apparent that being overweight was probably due to drinking as much of the bubbly as he sold. But his jolly, expressive disposition clearly supported his reputation for being a classic Irish storyteller with a wit as sharp as any, particularly after a few Irish whiskies.

Eric Thatcher first observed Sean sitting between Craig Francello and leggy Julie Manzer, while Bad Boy was making a fool of himself around her, acting like a dog in heat. Eric nudged Hardy, who immediately began his own analysis of the trio's chemistry.

Alternately, McMahon became glued to Craig and… Benny Badalamenti. Eric's big ears and Bob's keen insight discovered that McMahon might have made a living as a local bar owner, but his real love was being a stand-up comic and writer. In fact, he could be the center of attention at any gathering… in a New York minute. Despite irreverently joking about Francello's labored speech, his affection for the ever smiling, yet complex cerebral palsy victim was just as apparent.

Both Bob and Eric several times overheard McMahon say, "If they all understood you, Craig, you'd be getting more laughs than me. Craigie boy, I'm gonna make you a star. Your sense of humor is as twisted as your running style, Francello."

Craig and Sean McMahon's relationship obviously preceded this night at the Brooklyn Paramount. But, whenever Badalamenti poked his head into the trio's space, Sean went quiet, as if he and Bad Boy had business of a less than comedic nature.

The Paramount show turned out to be a huge hit with both the Brooklyn patrons and, of course, the horde from Jersey. While Connie Ferro caused a sensation with the #1 song from her beach blanket movie, and Frankie Lyman, the Teenagers, and Jackie Wilson all drew standing ovations, it was Lenny Latore's falsetto voice and the harmonizing background of his Four Loves that totally stole the limelight. Even Jackie Carey joined the standing room only crowd's frenzy for an encore. Then after the curtain finally was allowed to come down, Ralph Benedetto encouraged all of the original guests back to the jammed reception room.

When Connie Ferro finally entered, her Jersey dominated fans were jubilant about her presence and the smash success of the Four Loves. The night had turned into a Jersey love fest, and if you were in the room and not from the Garden State, you just might have been joining Jackie Carey in threatening to run to the bathroom with an upset stomach.

Connie's graciousness in mixing with everyone surprised the five Bellboys, who were only three years behind her at Belleville High. On the other hand, her stout and stern mother, who acted as her manager, was as tough as ever as she accompanied her daughter through the throng of supporters. While her mother was acting more like a Sicilian bodyguard just recruited from Palermo, Connie escaped her grasp enough to make sure she met everyone. Raised in Newark's Ironbound section, but now living in the heart of Belleville, she was more relaxed than usual.

When Connie's eyes spotted Frank Bonaducci, she no longer was a national star who'd just signed a major studio contract to appear in multiple teenage rock 'n' roll movies. She felt herself melting into the lonely woman she was fast becoming because a close, personal relationship with any man had become almost impossible, and certainly, increasingly, difficult. She remembered Frank from her guest appearance at the Belleville football dinner. Connie could never forget his blue eyes and black wavy hair, as well as his warmth and gentleness when they were first introduced. Little did she know, as an incoming freshman at Belleville, he had had a crush on <u>her</u>. But, when Frank met Maria Giardina, Connie quickly disappeared from his wish list.

Frank couldn't forget the podium kiss Connie planted on him the night of the awards banquet, because the smell of alcohol on her breath made the surprise move a bit distasteful. And, his friends never let him forget the incident. Tonight, Connie brushed past everyone just to greet him. Frank knew that he had better think fast, not to insult her. He thought of his mother and offered up a silent heavenly request. *God, let me say the right thing.*

Connie Ferro had been born Concetta Ferragamo at Columbus Hospital in Newark. During grammar school, her angelic voice could be heard throughout Catholic churches from Ferry Street Down Neck, to Saint Lucy's in the doomed First Ward, to the Sacred Heart Cathedral in Branch Brook Park, and on to Saint Francis' on Bloomfield Avenue across from City Stadium. Success on youth talent shows in New York City paved the way for her first recording contract at only thirteen years old. Her mother had been the mastermind behind the rush to national fame. Mrs. Ferragamo made sure that while contemporary rock 'n' roll, with wholesome teenage love themes, would be Connie's primary focus, singing classic Italian standards would win over adult audiences as well. As the family bank account swelled rapidly, this formidable matriarch moved her husband and other daughters to Belleville in time for Connie to enroll as a freshman. Despite her exploding career, the disciplined songbird graduated as Valedictorian of the Class of '56.

Short and curvaceous, Connie's auburn hair was tightly curled. Her round face, full lips, and deep brown eyes were framed by thick eyebrows and long lashes. In a flowered peasant dress, her southern Italian beauty would wow any male whose name ended in a vowel, … or who grew up along the Passaic River in Essex County, where so many immigrant families had settled since the late 1800's. Her bright eyes spoke as loudly as her satin voice revealed her love for music.

As she reached to caress his face in her soft hands, reality hit Frank. This was a woman in full bloom, wanting to be loved for herself as a person, not as a public figure. Frank's knees weakened. He was already perspiring. Any image of his mother or girlfriend back home was now being overtaken by his own manliness. She lightly kissed his left cheek.

Absorbed by their every move, Jackie Carey leaned over to Gino. "Hey, Mr. Inside, your buddy needs a cold shower, … and quick. Let's see if he can break dis tackle."

Faking jealousy, Gino replied, "Ya know, … she obviously likes the dark Italians."

"Well, sure," agreed Jackie. "You're just as studly as Frankie. But she must tink you're some Nazi, or whatever, wit dat blonde hair all over your body."

Then a different distraction entered the room. The inimitable Allan Freed stormed in unannounced. Eric not only immediately sought an autograph, but also introduced himself as the "Dean" of uncertified DJs in Belleville, New Jersey. Freed was not impressed, … until "The Snatcher" went into his Freed, and then Jocko Henderson imitations. At that point the national figure roared. The ultimate complement of being mimicked by this obviously creative teenager was not lost on Freed before he moved on into the crowd. Eric looked to his fellow "backstage Johnnies" for approval and saw Frank in the middle of his Connie encounter. The naïve and potentially vulnerable Bonaducci clearly was in need of Eric rescuing him.

When Thatcher went over to recruit Bob's help, his friend snapped, "Saw it all 'Snatcher'. Spare me the Freed details for later. Our saintly buddy over here is about to become a sinner, … if we don't step in."

"Listen, Bobby, you have to know the details," shot back Eric. "My 'sources' tell me that Concetta Ferragamo here is on the rebound from Bobbie Darwin. You know, the self proclaimed 'Mr. Everything' of rock 'n' roll, who even thinks he's a band leader."

"Eric, I know who Bobbie Darwin is."

"Anyway, ol' lady Ferro wouldn't let Connie get involved with him because she thinks he's like us."

"Like us? What are you talking about?"

"You know how Rocky Bonaducci calls us Frankie's 'Amedigan friends'? That's what Connie's mother thinks Darwin is."

"And...?"

"Well, Darwin is more Italian than Mario Lanza. But Mrs. F. figures because his name doesn't end in a vowel, he's an Amedigan, ... and, therefore, not good enough for her olive-oiled little girl. The battle-ax simply couldn't figure out that he changed his name. Can you believe it?"

"That's one way to screw up your kid's life," reacted Bob. "Give her advice based on dumb and wrong information."

Eric caught his breath. "So, little Miss American Bandstand is hotter than those peppers Mrs. Bonaducci grows back on Belmont Avenue. And our little Saint Francis is really being put to the test by this five foot two bundle of sugar and spice."

"Don't get carried away, 'Snatcher'."

By the time Bob and Eric clawed through the crowd to Frank, they figured they were too late. His focus on Connie seemed unbreakable. They thought if Frank Bonaducci was going to fall from the grace of God, as well as disappoint loyal friends who always looked to him as a shining example of morality and temperance, tonight was the night. However, it was actually Connie who broke Frank's concentration ... by asking the identity of four-eyed Eric and rural looking Bob, now lurking over the couple like star-crazed fans.

"Just two Belleville High seniors testing the world of 'backstage Johnnies'," commented Frank, casual as usual, his impending seduction at least put on hold in the minds of his panting, alleged rescuers.

First to speak, in a formal manner, was Eric. "Hi, Connie. Let us introduce ourselves. This is Robert Hardy, the most prolific track and field star in BHS history, ... also soon to be, I might add, Belleville's first midshipman at the United States Naval Academy, ... a celebrity, indeed. Just try to ignore his Levi's. He doesn't own dress pants."

Bob laughed. He wasn't embarrassed.

"Most impressive," Connie responded politely, although certainly uninterested at that point. Then, she could never have anticipated what happened next.

"...and I, my dear, am Eric Thatcher,
 DJ host of 'Summer Sunday Specials ... with the Snatcher'.
My tribute to all the tunes that are a spinnin',
Introducing the stars of rock 'n' roll just beginnin'.
Making sure the kids of Belleville ner' forget their own Connie Ferro,
The Dell Vikings, Belmonts, and even the Dominos.
For these are the times of our lives,
Spinning 45's and eating tomato pies."

Bob Hardy was now very embarrassed for himself and Frank. Eric was making a fool of himself in front of the famous Connie Ferro. However, Frank roared approval, now seemingly off the hook of being a young man about to fall for the tiny flirt's romantic lure.

Surprisingly, Connie, too, had become impressed. "Well, Mr. Snatcher or Thatcher, or whatever your name is. You're not bad. Career in the music business somewhere?"

Although impressed with himself, Eric quickly changed characters. "Oh no, Miss Ferro, it's college baseball and psychology for this Belleville product. I'm sure I'll soon outgrow this infatuation with the sounds of my adolescent generation."

Wondering whether transformed Eric was really being sincere, or just continuing in his effort to cool down Connie's desire for Frank, Bob reached out to greet America's rock 'n' roll sweetheart with a respectful, formal handshake.

Frank gained control of the situation, and stunned his friends. "I was just telling Connie about Cornell, Yale, and that stuff. You know, my plans to get engaged to Maria, get the degree, and then get married right after graduation. In fact, I showed her this picture." Frank reached for his wallet. "Connie agrees that my Maria could be a double for Annette Funicello. Connie knows her well."

Their hero had dodged a bullet. There was no doubt in Eric and Bob's minds that Connie was coming in for the kill, one most red-blooded American boys would welcome. And what does Frank do? He talks about his Mouseketeer look-a-like girlfriend! That surely cooled simmering Connie down. Indeed, when Gino joined the group, Connie gave her goodbyes. But, her brown eyes still held a glimmer of amorous hope for Frank's interest. "Boys, enjoy the rest of the night." She paused in reflection. "Unbelievable, …Bellboys in Brooklyn. This was unforgettable." Nodding her head, bewildered Connie disappeared, her mother resurfacing as her escort into the masses.

"My man could'a made out with Connie tonight, but he resisted. I watched the whole thing," said Gino, patting Frank on the top of his head.

Jackie came out of nowhere. "OK, backstage bellboys, or jerks, or Johnnies, or whatever we're supposed to be. Who's gonna drive the Heavenly Heap, cause Jackie C's smashed. But don't tell his sister."

"Yea, as if your sister couldn't figure that out, you drunk," said Gino, trying to fan the stench of alcohol between him and Jack. "Frankie will be in the driver seat, … and you'll be throwin' up all over the Heap."

As they each gazed upon the group still left, the five Bellboys could not help but reflect on their evening as "backstage Johnnies". Frank, at first naïve and innocent, appreciated Joe Pelli letting him see part of the heart of America's rock 'n' roll scene. Maybe Elvis wasn't there, but Frank believed he and his Belleville friends could not have been given a more intimate glimpse of the fame, fortune, and fun of the music business, as well as the unexplained diversity of humanity surrounding it. *Why was Badalamenti, the aging New York City underboss, who was closer to the top of Gambino's organization than anyone could have imagined, lurking all night. Why would Belleville's own poster child for fighting Cerebral Palsy, Craig Francello, be joined at the hip with this Sean McMahon who followed Bad* Boy *around like a puppy dog? Two Tones was there simply because of his relationship with Latore and his group. Julie Manzer, BHS' aspiring actress, had her father to simultaneously guard her, as well do whatever PR it took to get her "discovered". Talent agents must have been wandering around. Ralph Benedetto? Pelli's comedy partner was just trying to pick up a few extra bucks as host, staying close to the entertainment business he and Joe were trying to break into. That made sense.* Silently, Bonaducci lipped his final take on the night: *Wiseguys, well-wishers, fans, family, celebrities, and wannabes of all sorts. Feel good I resisted Connie. Could have never done it without saying a prayer. Glad I'll never be in this business.*

As Frank's eyes scanned the room in search of his friends who had scattered yet again, his mind suddenly recalled the absence of Dion and his Belmonts and all the questions he still had. "Jeepers peltz, Dion, what the heck happened up in Iowa in February anyway?"

Frank's trancelike conversation was cut short. "Jeepers peltz? Now, Mr. Outside, just where did ya pick up dat language? On one of your trips to Cornell?" Jackie's slurred voice asked.

"Jackie, chew some gum or something. You going to be alright?" Frank questioned, who'd just whiffed the breath from hell.

"Listen ol' buddy. You're da best … to take us out here tonight. I mean, what chance do I have to meet all dese stars, … and to mix wit 'em, too?"

"This doesn't sound like the same Jackie of a couple hours ago."

"Well, Frank, ya see dat after a couple of drinks I get more loveable." Jackie had to grab Frank's shoulder to stop swaying. "Get me a couple of cups of black coffee on da way back to Belleville, and I'll be as sarcastical and obnoxical as da true Irishman dat I am, buddy boy."

Seeing Jackie's tipsy state, Gino put his arms around him and Frank. "I got a couple of things to say. First of all, Jackie, if you have any plans to get sick, do it here in Brooklyn and don't you dare do it in the car. Understand?"

"Yesssss, sirrrr." Jackie saluted, fighting a sudden desire to collapse in sleep in the middle of the party room floor.

"Now Frank, don't you think you have to apologize to us tonight?" Gino continued. "See, I know you, buddie boy. I mean it was pretty exciting. After all, we almost saw you take a drink, almost saw you get jumped by the world famous Connie Ferro, and almost saw you get upset about no Dion."

Bob and Eric had now wandered back to the group, ready to exit. "All in all, we had a good time celebrating college decisions and Jackie getting ready for the police academy," said Thatcher, slapping Bob's back, as if to capture everyone's attention. "Yep, Gino, in a most unorthodox way, we took a night in the City and had a good time. High school is soon behind us, college around the corner, your reform school in the South, ...and walking our beloved Washington Avenue in downtown Belleville at midnight will be our own Officer Jackie Carey. And, we add a term to our vocabularies, ... 'backstage Johnnies'." Eric paused to take a long breath. "Allan Freed finally gets to meet me, and Connie Ferro gets turned down by Mr. Frank Bonaducci once again." Unable to resist switching to his English accent, Eric looked to Bob. "But I must turn to our dear Dr. Watson once again, to give us his most objective analysis of the diversity of humanity in attendance this night. Dr. Watson, your take on the bizarre evening, my good man?"

"I'm confused," said Bob, shaking his head. "But I do have one thing to say: the lyrics of the music were great, but it all was a little too tough to dance to." It was a feeble, elementary attempt at humor, so everyone ignored it.

"Well, my friends, Dr. Watson is, indeed, right on. The North Ward is here for the Four Loves; Belleville types for Connie. Mr. 'Two Tones' runs Latore's group from a business perspective. However, confusion does enter in with this Bad Boy fellow, young Craig with his disability, sexy Julie with her slimy father, and then this Irish barkeep, ...McMahon by name; quite a bizarre potpourri of people."

Gino was getting impatient. "Eric, ya finished yet? 'Cause we can talk about this in the car."

"No need, my good man," said Eric, still the English gent. "I, too, am confused, and, therefore, must take this case to my beloved mother, the bohemian Antoinette Thatcher. Ah yes, this astute mystic will solve the puzzle by the time young Jackie sobers up on the morrow."

Frank seized the moment. "I think Eric's finished, guys. Now let's thank Ralph from Nutley and get out of here."

Uneventful best describes their trip back to Belleville. Frank drove with Eric up front, and the other three slept on in the back seat. Thankfully, Jackie was not as crocked as he seemed. But he was dead to the world. A stop to sober up with coffee at the Schuyler Diner in Lyndhurst was shelved. It was after midnight. *Just let me get everyone home,* thought Frank. He would drop each of them off, finally getting Jackie to his doorsteps. From Mill Street Frank would make the one-mile walk to his house. He announced the plan to Eric who was wide-awake, and when he mentioned his home on Belmont Avenue, Eric perked up. "Ya know, Frank, the Belmonts not being there were a big thing for all of us. Don't get me wrong, ... still a night to remember. But I know you're the big fan of Dion, what with their music before your games, the Belmont Avenue connection, and for all of us, the plane crash."

"Yea. Well, I guess you can't have it all. Meeting Dion definitely would have been great."

"What would you have talked about?"

"The night of the crash. Did Buddy ask Dion to take the plane? If so, why'd he refuse? Ya know, all that kind of stuff." Frank seemed to focus even more on the road as they sped over the Pulaski Skyway to the Belleville Pike.

"May never find out, my friend."

"Cuz, I have some thoughts though." Frank went on, wanting to continue the discussion. "I think my little brother has the answer. Yep. You know, Mrs. Angus asked his take on the whole deal the morning we all heard about it. And, apparently what he said was so mature and thoughtful, she wrote my mother a note."

"Jo-Jo, the philosopher, or Jo-Jo the brown-noser?" chided Eric.

"He said it was their time to go, but not the others. If my brother's right, I figure Dion's work's unfinished."

"Don't get religious on me, Father Frank."

"No kidding, Eric. I mean Dion and the Belmonts are big in New York. But Holly, Valens, and the Big Bopper were top of the charts nationally. Can't get higher than that."

"OK, I buy that."

Frank wasn't finished. "I just would've liked to have learned why Dion said 'no' to the plane. I mean what his reason was, … the one that basically saved his life for bigger things in the future. Eric, the big question is: what's Dion's purpose here now since being given a second chance."

"That's not the biggest question, Cuz," replied Eric. "Here's the real query, if you will: If there is a special purpose for Dion, that means we've got a special purpose, too. Are we all really programmed to fulfill some destiny in our lives, … like Dion?"

"You know what, Eric?" said Frank. "I'll tell you what I really think, Cuz. While we have all of our lives to discover what we're supposed to do, most of us miss it." There was silence in the car. "Just hope Dion doesn't miss it now."

"Forget about Dion, I hope we don't miss it," concluded Eric.

The weeks ahead in northern New Jersey would require some of that proverbial wisdom to understand disturbing events coming up on the horizon. In fact, at 9 AM on the morning of May 14, 1959, a press conference at Newark's downtown Federal Building at least would give a possible explanation to some of the enigmatic relationships seemingly witnessed at the Brooklyn Paramount, three weeks earlier.

CHAPTER 16

"ROLL CALL"

Sal Giantempo was Essex County's very politically savvy federal prosecutor in 1959. A cum laude graduate at Notre Dame, he received his law degree from Harvard. Not only named Valedictorian of the Central High's Class of 1937, but he was also voted "most likely to succeed". However, the "most popular" member of that class was All-City Football selection, Gino "Sneaks" Babula. Little did others realize, revenge and justice were unlikely bedfellows flowing through Giantempo's veins in all that he did. Having sat four years on the bench as backup tailback to Sneaks in Central's explosive single wing offense, Giantempo never forgot his frustration at watching the Sicilian immigrant emerge as the football star. On the other hand, he rightfully gained his notoriety in the classroom. But knowing Babula's relationship to Richie Boiardo, Giantempo made his life's goal to not only stifle the Italian mob's growth in Newark, but also to put Sneaks permanently on his own bench, … for life in some penitentiary. Giantempo's only mistake was ignoring how much his well-publicized quest for justice really camouflaged his envy and jealousy for Boiardo's benevolent underboss.

Next to Giantempo in the Federal's meeting room on High Street, stood Jane Bateman and Quincy Braxton. Two young attorneys, a woman and a black male, combined with a first generation Italian American, surely represented a formidable and well-balanced assault on whatever injustice Giantempo had uncovered. Strangely absent was brash and gritty Bobby Zarcone, Newark's district attorney. Was Giantempo making a new political move to get all the thunder? Sal certainly knew he didn't need popular Zarcone picking up another victory boost to his own law and order ambition. This was Giantempo's second mistake in the about-to-be announced case. First revenge and jealousy, now one-upmanship with a potential political rival, … Giantempo could not fathom the challenge he had set up for himself.

Flash bulbs went off as television cameras and radio microphones jockeyed for best position. Relishing every moment, Sal Giantempo walked slowly to the podium. He'd lobbied tirelessly for this vital opportunity. He unfolded several papers from his suit pocket, and then read the statement that he thought would propel him to the pinnacle of New Jersey political popularity:

"Ladies and gentlemen, beginning at 4 AM this morning, personnel from the Federal Bureau of Investigation, in cooperation with the New Jersey, New York, and Georgia State Police, as well as the departments of Newark, Belleville, Bloomfield, Atlanta, Georgia, and Queens, New York, arrested the following individuals for the federal offense of counterfeiting: Benjamin 'Bad Boy' Badalamenti, Heller Parkway, Newark, New Jersey; Thomas 'Two Tones' Anthony, Roseville Avenue, Newark; Sean McMahon, New York Avenue, Astoria, Queens; William 'Greenie' Delaney, Fifth Street, Newark; Gary and Rosa Gubitosi, both of Smallwood Avenue in Belleville; Henry Davidson, of Montgomery Street in Bloomfield; Al Matte, Rocco Street, Belleville; Chet Costello, King Street, Nutley; Vincent Giampietro of Heckle Street in Belleville; Craig Francello, Cuozzo Street, Belleville; Michael Manzer of Union Avenue in Belleville; Patrick 'Patsie' Pratola, of Steven Crane Village, Newark; Gino 'Sneaks' Babula, Sr. of Carpenter Street in Belleville, presently incarcerated at Rahway State Prison; Hiram Wilhelm, Ratzer Drive in Wayne, New Jersey; Leonard Malafatano and Richard Lisa of Atlanta, Georgia; and Louis 'Crazy Louie' Montana of Bloomfield Avenue, Newark.

"These eighteen people are presently being processed and will be arraigned in one week. With the exception of Babula, Sr., already behind bars for other convicted offenses, they will be eligible for bail. My office is also cooperating with the previously named law enforcement departments relating to the death of one Paul Puccini, eighteen, of Franklin Street, Belleville, on New Year's Eve this past year. Further charges are forthcoming. We believe stellar police work yielded these suspects in this alleged network of organized crime, corruption, and murder.

"My friends of the press may now ask questions."

While the Federal Building was buzzing from the surprise announcement, two of the early morning arrests were already old news at Belleville's 711 Belmont Avenue. The Bonaducci household had been woken at 5:30 AM. Pete had telephoned, overwhelmed with emotion after a call from Katherine Delaney that

Greenie was now at Newark police headquarters. She'd no sooner hung up than Two Tones' mother wanted Pete's help over the sudden arrest of her son. The most loyal friend of both Greenie and Two Tones, Pete was never known for being effective under pressure. Before hanging up on both ladies, he assured them that he and his brother-in-law, Rocky, would be back to them with help.

When Rocky ultimately heard the full story from Pete, he lit up a Lucky Strike and wondered how his wife would react to the arrests coming so close to home. But, Rocky didn't seem upset.

"Rock, what's wrong with you? My best friends just got arrested for somethin' they didn't do. We need help, Rocky," pleaded Pete.

Rocky explained himself. "First of all, Pete, thank God they didn't pick you up. Your sister would have a heart attack, and your mother would have killed you with that monster frying pan of hers before the cops got you downstairs to their wagon. Second of all, Greenie's too dumb to pass bad twenties, and Two Tones is too smart to be involved in petty stuff. Lastly, The Boot will get your two buddies the kind of legal ammo they'll need. Don't worry about them. Just thank God they didn't pull you in, too."

"But, Rock, I wouldn't do that kind of thing."

"I know that, Pete. But you know what? You're lucky, brother-in-law. You and Greenie are two innocent moths, who've both been flying too close to the fire. And now Greenie gets burned."

Marietta arrived home from her night shift right after Pete's call. Even without being told the complete list by her husband, she began to wring her hands, and lit up her own smoking spree that would last the whole day. As her sharp mind mulled over the Gubitosi's involvement, she began to wonder if even she might be targeted because of having "temporarily" accepted that twenty from her backyard neighbor. At this time, of course, Pete knew nothing about who else had been arrested, or the threatening murder charge. Rocky and his wife only had a portion of the whole messy story. The front page of *The Newark Evening News* later that day, plus *The Newark Star Ledger* the following morning, totally filled them in. And Rocky's light response would become vastly more somber. Marietta would resume chain smoking, also brewing up a couple of pots of coffee for whoever dropped by to hash over the disturbing and embarrassing black eye for the whole neighborhood.

Throughout the day rumors flew around Belleville High about the absence of both Craig Francello and Julie Manzer. When Craig arrived at school after lunch, more BHS students took time to listen to him than ever before. Frankly, he loved their attention, as he held court in the parking lot after school got out.

"So dat's why we can't find ya after school, Mr. Francello. Printin' counterfeit bills?" Jackie Carey, leaning against his Heavenly Heap, yelled at Craig, who had been propped onto the hood of Julie Manzer's powder blue '57 Chevy.

Craig could only be understood by the most loyal of his friends who had labored over the years to learn to interpret his answers. "Yea, Jackie. Yoooou got it," stammered Craig. "Taaaake the 'ol 32 DeCamp to the city to deliver bad bills every daaay. Then I come home, do my hooooomework, go into the print shop in my bedroom, and do my thiiing." He roared with laughter at himself. "IIIII can't write a sentence, but I'm supposed to operate some printing press. Yeeea, that's it. IIIII'm the way I am because I got caught in some printing machine when we started this scheeeeme, ... back when I was five years old. Is that a great story or whaaat?"

"Hey, Craigie, da mob should be so lucky to have <u>you</u> running one of dare businesses," quipped Jackie.

Craig responded, "By the way, Mr. Careeeey, I read that one of my money-making colleagues is your brother-in-law, 'Patsie' Pratooooola. Boy, does your sister have exquisite taste, or whaaaat?" Craig was speaking extra slowly to make sure everyone surrounding him understood.

"He ain't my brother-in-law yet, man, and after dis news, my sister won't even take one of his calls." Then Carey added, "Mother Superior Elizabeth Carey? Are ya kidding me? She'll never marry dat turd."

While Craig and Jackie's cut and thrust between each other certainly loosened up their fellow classmates, Julie Manzer was still all nerves. "Craig, how can you be so relaxed and joke about this whole thing? My father's reputation is at stake."

"The PBA will protect your daaad. If they arrested <u>meee</u>, there have to be other holes in this case."

While Julie looked more like a Las Vegas show girl than a High School twirler for the last four years, her friends were many and totally supported Francello's encouragement.

As Gino passed through the crowd, Jackie grabbed his arm. "What I tell ya, Gino, … Manzer's a bad cop."

This spring Gino had stopped throwing the shot put for the track team, to try to make sure he actually would graduate in June. "Shut your big Irish mout," he said. Jackie had stupidly forgotten "Sneaks" was also named in the paper. "Don't worry about my father," continued Gino. "He's already in jail. Dis thing with all the other people, though, …they never been in trouble before. That's really bad. Craigie here, … then Pete Frassa's friend, Greenie? These are good people. And Two Tones? Crap, I like that guy. My father's upset about that one. This jerk from Gambino's crew, Badalamenti, …he's got the right name, … 'Bad Boy's' bad news. He should rot in jail some day for all I care."

"All right, all right, Gino. Sorry," apologized Jackie. "Hey, but isn't it unbelievable? Dat night in Brooklyn … I mean, dey were all dare."

"Jack, shusssshhhh, for God's sake," insisted Gino, wanting to grab his friend by the neck. "Keep quiet about that stuff before you end up with all kinds of visitors at your house. And some of 'em ain't gonna be cops just askin' questions."

Jackie froze in his tracks. Gino had pressed a button in his brain, and he instantly reminded himself: *Keep ya stupid mout shut from now on, Mr. Future Flatfoot.*

Rocky left the Jergens factory early to pick up *The Newark News*, getting home as soon as he could to spend time with Marietta. He was uncharacteristically as thoughtful and honest as he had ever been with his wife as he read her all the names of the arrested. While they hoped most were mistakenly caught in the counterfeit net, all of them could still be tainted for life. Guilty by association was still, in every day living, a major crime. Some obvious "connected guys" had been reeled in, but Rocky was puzzled by the extent seemingly common folk were involved, and how close many of them were to his own family. Indeed, Marietta felt implicated, and every moment oppression gained a stronger foothold in her spirit. Silently, <u>she</u> was really Rocky's concern.

"OK, we can figure that Badalamenti's involved," concluded Rocky with his reading glasses on. Leaning forward with both elbows on the kitchen table, he went on. "Thank God Bella never ran away with that dope." Inhaling on his Lucky, he allowed the smoke to escape as he mentioned the next two suspects. "Tommy Anthony and Greenie, … well, great friends of Pete, and fans of our Frankie, and all that. But after all, Two Tones is part of the crew down on Bloomfield Avenue,

… as much as we try to ignore that. And stupid Greenie's always runnin' around for 'em. You become part of those guys in the smallest ways, and things like this happen to ya."

"Tommy's mother's probably makin' buttons," said Marietta. "And Greenie's sister, Katherine, … we'll pray to the Sacred Heart of Jesus for all of them, … and all of us." Marietta folded her hands in front of herself and took a break from her own pack of Luckies for the first time that day.

"Marietta, what do you mean, 'all of us'?" Rocky asked. "Yea, thank God they didn't pull Pete in. But don't include us. You didn't do anything wrong when Rosa was here. Stop it now. You won't even be questioned. Who's to know?"

Totally unconvinced, Marietta answered, "Oh, Jesus, they're sure to call me downtown. Oh, how embarrassing for all of us, Rocky?"

"Forget about that stuff for God's sake," said Rocky, continuing down the list. "I don't know about this Queens guy, McMahon. But, my brother-in-law, Emil, always told me about Manzer. 'With bad cops like him, who needs the racketeers?' Emil's been saying that since Manzer started showin' up late night at Petty's. He's always got a gang of wiseguys in tow."

"Rocky, this is really close to home," continued Marietta. "His daughter's that beautiful twirler in Frankie's class."

"Close to home, Marietta?" said Rocky as he lifted the paper. "Well, keep prayin' and don't get upset, 'cause it's good you're sitting down." Marietta held her breath. "OK, just as we thought, Gary and Rosa are on the list." She gasped, but Rocky did not slow down. "I don't know this Pratola kid, but listen to this: Sneaks, Malafatano and Lisa, his old buddies in Atlanta now; that 'Crazy Louie' kid that scares your brother to death every time he come into the butcher shop; and now the most surprising, … Henry from the Shell station; Al Matte, our own motorcycle garage renter; Chet from the candy store by the school; Vinnie, the football bus driver for Frankie the last four years; and the two most unbelievable, … Craigie Francello, the cerebral palsy kid, and Mr. Wilhelm, the high school athletic director! God, this is bad."

Marietta was stunned. "What do we do?"

"I thought you were prayin'. And know what? If you are, get those two colored Baptist friends of yours on their knees with ya. There's gotta be some innocent people in this bunch. So, real prayin' is gonna be needed. And make sure the cops stay away from Pete," warned Rocky. "Yea, that should be your first prayer request."

Rocky knew he'd have to work overtime to stifle his wife's fear of Pete's reputation being tainted by any of this. Since surviving the horror of war, few things in life now surprised him, let alone disturbed his peace. But he was wrestling with totally unexpected ideas that seemingly innocent friends and acquaintances of his committed crimes. He simply could not fathom their involvement with the possible murder of Paulie Puccini. But fake money was no little matter either. Al Matte, a former Navy pilot with a crew cut, had served in Korea, and as wholesome as they get. His only crime was that he seemed to worship his Harley Davidson more than his fiancé whom he was scheduled to marry in only a week. The motorcycle was in the dilapidated back yard garage of 711 Belmont Avenue, … and Rocky Bonaducci was the landlord! Al's best friend was Henry Davidson, who owned the Shell gas station at the corner of Belmont and Smallwood. For 365 days a year, the station's bells would ring across the neighborhood that Rocky called "home". And Henry was the hardest worker he'd ever met. Another Korean vet, this ex-Marine had much in common with Rocky. But it was Al Matte and Henry who were inseparable. Their only point of disagreement? As tough a leatherneck as Henry had been overseas, he was frightened to death of Al's motorcycle, and always refused to jump on for a ride. How could these man-mountains be involved in what Rocky saw as a cheap way to make a few extra bucks?

Inside cellblock 27 at Rahway State Prison, Sneaks Babula was furious. Not a man to show emotion on most occasions, his anger did not result from added problems caused by his indictment as a counterfeit and potential murder conspirator. It was rather because he perceived these new aggravations to be politically motivated. "All Giantempo did was throw a net out, and any fish swimmin' in the wrong place got pulled in," said Sneaks, holding court with whatever other inmates and guards cared to listen. "This guy hasn't changed since Central High, … always lookin' for limelight, and he's more ordinary than my dirty underwear. So smart, he ain't got no common sense."

"Sneaks, pick up the phone. It's your attorney," said a friendly prison guard.

"Don't waste your time, counselor," Sneaks blasted. "I'll be my own attorney on this one. Can't wait to go opposite my old teammate. At least I'll get back to the old neighborhood for a few days."

When Vinnie Giampietro finally answered the door to his two-room apartment on Heckle Street in Newark's Silver Lake section, his visitor could see the limping bus driver had been crying. Sneak's son gave him a big hug. "Gino, what am I gonna do?" asked Vinnie. "I need my job. I'm not involved in this stuff."

The younger football star encouraged the loyal former Belleville lineman. "My father is no role model for any of us, Vinnie. But he knows about this kind of thing, and he told me to tell you not to worry. He'll get you help, … legitimate job and all until it's over."

After track practice, Frank stopped at the Pentagon Barber Shop for his haircut. Although Joe Pelli was always excited to see his handsome customer, that day there was only one subject on his mind. "Frankie, see what I tell youse kids, … stay out of trouble. Look at what da Feds are doin' to some of da boys, … dough I gotta tell ya, … dat group is more mixed up dan my mudder's 'chambought'. (Giambotta, a traditional Italian dish that includes every type of meat, vegetable, potato, and whatever amount of leftovers the chef can find; nothing to be wasted. It would be a sin!) Bad twenties. Can ya believe dat?"

"Joe, who you know?" asked Frank.

"Know? I know all da guys and kids ya know. Plus, some I hope ya don't know."

"Like who, Jo?"

"Like Malafatano, Lisa, and 'Crazy Louie' Montana."

"Know what, Joe? They're the only ones I don't know."

Now Joe became fatherly, although Frank was only four years younger than him. "Let me tell ya, Frankie," he said. "I mean my fodder was 'involved' before he died. Not big time or any ting, but numbers and such. Well, I start woikin' for da boys down on Bloomfield Avenue. Ya know, runnin' around. And one day I go into da back poolroom at The Belmont Bar over on Heckle Street. Who's in dare beatin' da day lights out of some guy? 'Craaaazy Louie' Montana. I mean I tink this guy was dead when I got dare. And ya know what? When Louie looked up to take a bret, he looks at me. I'll never forget his face. And ya know what I did?"

"No, … what, Joe?"

"I went to the badtroom in my pants, … and I didn't do number one." Frank burst out laughing. Joe was serious. "Let me tell ya, kid. It was da best day of my life."

"What?"

"Yep. Scared me so much, dat I told my ol' man I was finished wit da crew; gonna become a comedian. Rather make people laugh than watch 'em get killed. Ya know what I mean?"

"God, Joe. Great story."

"Yea, if it wasn't for Crazy Louie, I wouldn't be in da entertainment business today, but just another dumb mob guy from da neighborhood."

"What about those other two guys, Joe?" asked Frank.

"Let me tell ya, Frankie. Dey were two of Sneaks' street lieutenants. Some of da guys say de're in Atlanta wit dese nightclubs, … 'cause dey were makin' good money for Sneaks and The Boot. Others say dey were rattin' on Sneaks and helped get him locked up, … dat The Boot really sent 'em down sout to buy some time to see if de're really rats. And if dey are, dey ain't never gonna see dis counterfeit trial, … if ya know what I mean."

"My Lord."

"Yea, tank God for 'Crazy Louie'. Chased me right to a legit business. Not makin' much money yet, but I got no one tryin' to kill me, and I sleep at night. Gonna make it big, too. You just watch me and Benedetto."

Across Belleville on the King Street side of Nutley, Chet Costello was explaining to his wife and three daughters that with all the cash his soda shop and candy store handles, it's inevitable some bad money would get into his cash register. "You know, kids, a few gangsters, who like to gamble and always have cash in their pockets, stop by to get candy for their own kids, or cigarettes for themselves. Some just hang around at daddy's store, just smoking cigars and drinking coffee, … all day! Don't worry. I'll be OK." Chet did all the talking. His wife and the children believed every word.

Eddie Popalinski made the first call to coaching colleague Hiram Wilhelm's home. "Hiram, you OK?"

"OK? Those greasy guineas trying to get me involved with their filth? I'll tell you coach, their kids are worse than them. And I'm gonna get my chance to tell them."

"Kids, what are ya talking about? Calm down, Hiram. You're innocent. It'll turn out OK."

"That stinkin' Puccini. I'm glad the kid croaked. Him and his slimy goombas, always asking change for lunch, … buying seats at all the games. I should've seen it coming. And they involve me?" Wilhelm could not relax. "And that weird little Francello and that leggy Julie girl. At every game I'm selling them tickets, hot dogs, soda. You name it. Where the hell do these kids get all their money? Now I know, Eddie."

"Listen, Hiram. Everybody knows you don't belong with that group in the paper." Then Popalinski added, "On the other hand, you'll be at home in the court room."

"What are you talking about?"

"All the wiseguys will have their Jewish lawyers with them," laughed Eddie, trying to loosen up Belleville High's only Semitic administrator.

The athletic director hung up.

Another telephone conversation commenced late on Thursday night. Lenny Latore wanted to speak to Jim Quinn. "Pinky, that you?"

"Yea, who's this?"

"It's that little pain in the butt that still thinks your handsome husband should be doing backup for me with the Loves. He there?"

The feisty former Pinky Bonaducci did not appreciate Lenny treating a sore subject lightheartedly. "Hold on, Lenny." She handed the phone to her husband, convinced there was no need to coach Jim's response. The case was closed on singing with an a cappella group. Public Service Gas and Electric paid the bills, and more importantly, Jim would have a pension at sixty-two years old. Security was preferable over the dream of making Lenny Latore famous.

Lenny informed Jim he was severing his relationship with Patsie Pratola. He wasn't sure of Patsie's innocence, or lack thereof, to the counterfeit indictments. But he was thrilled to now have a strong excuse to get rid of the mediocre singer and wannabe Bloomfield Avenue wiseguy. Next, Lenny updated Jim on his pending contract with Zircon Records. A cross-country tour also was being looked at, after a potential American Bandstand date in early July. Finally, he made the statement Jim was yearning to hear. "I want you back with us, Jimmy."

Goose bumps climbed all over Quinn's six foot four inch frame. His mind's eye peered through rose-colored glasses that were ignoring all Pinky was thinking. He began to imagine the exciting days in a record studio, … those moments in front of TV cameras at the Philadelphia studio of Dick Clark's national show, and the raging fans that would surely be lining up to hear Lenny's unique falsetto and the harmonizing echoes of his faithful Four Loves in the background. He was oblivious to his wife standing rigidly behind him and Lenny's silence on the other end of the phone, as they both awaited some response. *Gettin' back into the Loves' turquoise blue tuxedo jackets would be like heaven for me. Man, I can feel the smoothness of my silk cummerbund.* Dirty, size twelve work boots, with the strapped, knife-like daggers to lift him up telephone polls like a monkey, were furthest from his mind. Looking down at his feet, he saw only his patent leather flyweights, pointed almost as sharply as his Public Service issued pole-climbing footwear, but in the direction of an adoring audience that was buying millions of the Four Loves records.

"Jimmmmm?" Impatient Pinky was stunned her husband was taking so long to say, … "no".

It made Latore try harder. "Listen, Jim. I know how Pinky's thinking, but Two Tones is guaranteeing this contract, and he's getting me more involved. That's good, because with his new problem, I'll have more say, which is the way it should have always been anyway. So, we're goin' in the right direction, and you can be right there with us. With Holly and Valens goin' down last February, the kids out there are clamoring for something different, … and our sound is it! Let's rock 'n' roll, Jimmy Quinn. You gotta be there when we make it big, 'cause you were there at the beginning. It's a second chance, you overgrown leprechaun, you. I gotta have a least one Amedigan in my group, Jimmy. Not everybody's gonna go for five Italian meatballs from Newark."

"Let me call you back."

Pinky represented everything Jimmy had ever hoped for in a woman. She was shapely, spunky, and full of life. Her great Italian cooking, loyalty to her husband and family, as well as her desire to have as many Irish-Italian kids as Jimmy cared for, were a paradox in light of her Barringer High School years as leader of the

Satin Dolls, North Newark's only female gang. With both her hands on her hips, accentuating her shapely legs that fit into her skin tight peddle pushers like no other female he'd ever met, Pinky stared at her husband. Wearing her ballerina slippers that had withstood her conversion to conservative homemaking since their marriage, her black curls hung lazily on the front of her trademark pink sweater that highlighted her healthy bust line.

Jimmy didn't have to ask his question. He knew Pinky's answer, … the one he had to give to Lenny Latore.

As midnight struck on May 14, 1959, many lives in Essex County would never be the same again. Jimmy Quinn's was not one of them.

CHAPTER 17

"... A QUARTER TO FIVE"

Fast-pedaling Russell Giardella was going to be late for school. Coming up Belmont Avenue, his headline announcing "Kee Yaw Kee" sounded perfect, but today's paper toss to the Bonaducci doorstep was never more inaccurate. His speed sent *The Ledger* skyrocketing right by the cracked brick stairs, and over the budding evergreen bushes, left of the broken window panel front door.

Waiting in the kitchen, Frank had been nursing his mother's first cup of coffee.

"He's finally here." Still incredulous to what had been revealed in *The Newark News* the night before, he had to see *The Ledger* to be sure the list of indictments was for real.

Friday, May 15, was as clear and sunny as anyone could remember. Spring 1959 was in full bloom in northern New Jersey. It could have been one of Frank's favorite days. A gentle wind chauffeured the scent of seasonal flowers popping up all over Belleville. The early morning sun gently warmed and caressed his face as he walked to Smallwood Avenue to get his ride from Eric Thatcher. He should have been at perfect peace. Cornell's football team was awaiting his arrival at the end of August. His grades were highest ever. His new track experience had met with instant success. His speed increased, and the injured ankle had healed perfectly. He was also saying his prayers every day. But, waiting for Eric, Frank's stomach began to ache. The bad news in the paper was disturbing, ... and he missed baseball. The day before, Eric had thrown the first no-hitter in Belleville history against Nutley, and for the first time since they were kids, Frank was not in the outfield. Still, he had so much to be thankful for, … yet he could not shake the gloom beginning to overtake him that crystal clear morning.

School passed by quickly that day, and with Saturday's scheduled important duel meet with Nutley, Coach Tim Testa let his track team go home early. When Frank walked slowly down the crumbled, worn asphalt driveway into the backyard of his home, it was 4 PM. Putting his books and gym bag on the patio, he sat in the rusty beach chair. Along with the nearly torn, tasseled hammock, it represented the Bonaducci family's total outdoor furniture package. Back in April, Uncle Pete told Marietta he had something "on order". The truck from the Carolinas had just not delivered it for them yet.

Resting in the chair, Frank was nervous about the Nutley meet. Having left the basketball team, he had not competed against the arch- rival Maroon Raiders since that stormy December day. He prayed those bratty, taunting little grammar school fans from the Oval would not be there. Then he laughed to himself because his spirit again told him he had done the right thing. On the other hand, his senior year at Belleville was ending hardly as he had dreamed. Yes, hard work on the football field and in the classroom had clinched Cornell, but Yale was his first choice. Track experience might make him a more complete running back in college, but it could not replace the sound of a leather hard ball against a brand new Adirondack bat, with Mickey Mantle's name on it. His parents didn't have to worry about financing his college education. But now they were consumed with how much they could be drawn into this counterfeit case, with so many friends and acquaintances being suspects. While Rocky was adamant Marietta would never be called as a witness, Frank knew how his proud dad feared the Bonaducci name would somehow appear in *The Ledger*. It was never spoken about at home, but the mature teenager knew the enterprising cousins from Brooklyn had their hands into all kinds of businesses. Rocky understood mob territorial jurisdiction, but also that nothing would stop cousin, Carmine "the Artist" Bonaducci, from testing some "new venture" waters in Essex County. Then there was the reputed relationship between Badalamenti and his Brooklyn cousins, not to mention the lingering memory of Paulie Puccini. Did someone actually kill him? *Yes,* Frank thought, *the kid deep down had a good heart. But he had become a big-mouthed, drug addicted wiseguy wannabe. He was one of the toughest hitters in football. Then the injury, bad friends, and the rest became history.* So, Frank decided to pray for Mrs. Puccini who was now alone. *Maybe I should go visit her with my mother, Queenie, and Nora.* The more he pondered Paulie's short life, the more Frank thanked God for his own, as different as it was becoming from all of his own plans, dreams, and prayers.

"Anybody home?" Frank called to the kitchen window above him, smelling brewing gravy and so believing his mother must be inside.

"We're home, Frankie," yelled Donna from the top floor bathroom. "Me and Mommy."

"What's for dinner?"

Marietta announced her "masterpiece" of a meal. "Eggs in the gravy with peas. Uncle Pete dropped off some Giordano's bread. If it's not enough, we'll order tomato pies before I go to work."

Frank hated sunny side up eggs in tomato sauce. But he detested even more that his mother had to work from midnight to 7 AM. The "depression" meal served two purposes: cheap and easy to make for his weary mom.

"What time is it, Ma?" Frank never wore a watch.

"Almost a quarter to five."

Frank was startled by someone appearing at the foot of his reclined beach chair. It was the Bonaducci's garage tenant and most recently indicted ex-Navy fighter pilot, Al Matte, who left the teenager both startled and lost for words. One of the newly infamous eighteen alleged counterfeit conspirators was standing silently over him.

"Frank, your dad home?"

"Not yet, Al."

"No problem. Just tell him he'll get the rent check next Friday, but I won't need the garage anymore for the motorcycle."

Figuring the accusations were already changing Al's life, "Sure," was all Frank could utter.

"Yea, good news. Tell him I'm getting married next week, and it's time to get rid of the cycle. My fiancé doesn't want any part of it."

"Well, great, Al. Congratulations." Frank was relieved.

"And, kid, tell that Marine father of yours I was never involved with this other thing. Tell him I'd never embarrass the United States Navy like that."

Frank reacted slowly. "I'm sure he knows what kind of guy you are, Al."

"Thanks for the vote of confidence, Frankie."

Al turned away to the garage to retrieve his motorcycle for the last time. He stopped suddenly. His back to Frank, as if thinking what to do next, he then turned. "Hey, Frankie, how 'bout takin' the last ride with me. You're goin' off to school. At your age, me and your father were goin' off to war. Get some wind in your face. Nothing like it. Maybe you'll want to become a pilot like me some day."

Frank's spirit soared. He had never been on a motorcycle, but he always loved riding his souped-up Roadmaster bicycle before he had to abandon it for girls and cars. Of course, he had one girlfriend, Maria, and his dad's weary Chevy. But, God, he thought, hardly adventurous. Bicycle riding at seventeen was just not cool. Those motorcycle boots he so infrequently wore because of his conservative dad, just might finally get baptized for their real use. He was speechless.

"Well, I think I have your interest," said smiling Al. "Go get that leather jacket of yours, ... and those boots."

Is Al reading my mind? A euphoric feeling came over Frank, not unlike the one that overwhelms him every time he sees Maria in heels, and thinking this extraordinary, beautiful woman someday may very well be his wife. *Oh, God, I really want to go, just this one time.* Accepting the ride might be exactly like satisfying the feelings that come over him on those infrequent times when Maria's being her naturally feminine self. *Surrendering to that urge would be sin, but riding on a motorcycle isn't sin.* Frank was maturing enough spiritually to figure that out. Then he jumped up, and all at once the tempting urge left. "It's almost a quarter to five!" he said.

"A quarter to five? What's that mean, Frank?"

"Yea, I can't go. It's almost a quarter to five. I have to be ready to eat when my father gets home at a quarter to five."

"You're kidding."

"No, Al, but thanks anyway."

The Bonaducci "quarter to five rule" was rarely breakable.

"Alright, kid. Give my regards to Rocky."

Having given up on trying to convince Frank, Al retrieved his cycle, walked it out the Bonaducci backyard, started it on Belmont Avenue, and quickly rode it to Henry Davidson's Shell Station on the corner.

The young Bonaducci picked up his books and gym bag and entered the house, shortly before his father arrived home. As Donna and Frank sat at the table, Rocky appeared. Marietta was cutting the hard-crusted Giordano bread, when Jo-Jo came busting through the backyard door. Out of breath, he looked at his father washing his hands at the sink, nodded to his brother, kissed his mother, patted his little sister on the head, and glanced at the tilted clock between the two windows, above the kitchen table. It was … a quarter to five … on Friday, May 15, 1959.

Everyone's plate was empty by the time Jo-Jo requested to be excused. Dinner had taken more than an hour. Only Rocky and Marietta really cherished the meatless Friday dinner, with the Giordano's bread making for some delectable dish cleaning of the yoke and tomato sauce. The children, who would have preferred some alternative menu, had at least honored their hard-working parents by leaving no trace of food. On the other hand, the meal was a journey back for Rocky and Marietta with every mouthful to their youth in the Depression years, even though it was now some twenty-five years later.

The peace and quiet at the table was in sharp contrast to the fear and anxiety that had earlier filled everyone's day because of the indictments. Uncle Pete had visited his sister earlier and discussed how fortunate his name was not mentioned in the news releases. After all, he handled a lot of cash at his butcher shop, much of it from "connected" customers. Their mutual verdict was also that Greenie and Two Tones were never part of the mess. Rocky would rather forget it all. But his silence was really hiding his concern. Rose and Gary Gubitosi were backyard neighbors, and that was turning his stomach. Each of the children avoided the subject because they knew how close it was to their very lives. After Frank conveyed Al's plans, Rocky just nodded. Only the sound of Jo-Jo taking a shower upstairs could be heard as the rest of the Bonaduccis slowly pushed away from the cluttered kitchen table.

Just after 6 PM the sound of sirens rang out. Unknown vehicles sped past Belmont Avenue toward Bloomfield. Other fainter sirens could be heard throughout the neighborhood.

"Sounds like a multiple alarm fire," suggested Rocky.

"Clara Maas ambulance and Belleville cops!" yelled Jo-Jo from the bedroom. "Heading to Belleville Avenue up in Bloomfield."

Curiosity pulled Rocky and Frank to the front porch. They hurried out the door and could see people running at the junction of Willet Street and Belleville Avenue.

"Dad, let's go take a look," Frank urged.

Walking to the top of the hill that divided Bloomfield from Belleville, the two Bonaduccis could see ambulance and police personnel two hundred yards up blanketing two bodies. Something had happened about a half hour before.

Faceless spectators walking away from the scene revealed to concerned Rocky and Frank, "Two guys on a motorcycle!"

Rocky's mind froze. Frank's whole body went numb. Both men reached for each other. Then they saw the shocked, ashen face on Mark Brunello being walked up the street into Joe Stein's candy store.

"Markie, what's what?" asked Rocky. No response came from Henry Davidson's trusted mechanic.

Rickie Murray, who garaged his custom '49 Ford at the Shell station, was holding Mark up. He reached to touch Rocky's shoulder as he passed. " Motorcycle must have hit a rock or somethin'. They're gone. I think Markie's in shock here. It's Henry and Al. Both dead."

While he'd lost buddies in the South Pacific, Rocky had not known a fellow Marine longer than Henry Davidson. It had been almost nine years since Henry befriended the Bonaduccis when they moved to Belmont Avenue. The handsome tattooed Korean War veteran was always a gentleman to Marietta, passing by on her way to the Acme up the street. And each of the boys knew they had a sincere fan in the football-crazy Henry, who played at both Bloomfield High and later with the armed forces. In fact, he had started a collage of all of the neighborhood boys' headline heroics on the back wall of his station. To Rocky, he was that quiet giant of a man who would allow him "forever" to complete payment of his many car repair bills. So, for someone of his presence and integrity, his inclusion in the list of counterfeit indictments had to be a mistake. However, what they all remembered most was Henry's constant ridicule of motorcycle riding. He feared nothing, … except that! Now it had killed him. His good friend, Al, had somehow convinced him to take the last ride.

Rocky and his son returned home and broke the news to the family. Mentioning Al's name, Rocky had to stop. As Marietta saw his reaction, she was inspired to speak of how … "God is already talking to both men, welcoming them through his heavenly gates as they entered with thanksgiving and praise. He's giving them his final and merciful judgment"

Jo-Jo was doubtful. "Ma, how do ya know they're in heaven? Not everybody gets there, right?"

"Yes, Joseph, but they each responded to the Gospel," said Marietta, feeling confident and righteous.

"Ma, you kidding?" said Frank.

"Frank, I'd see each of them practically every day. So, just like with my family, and just like Queenie and Nora taught me, I helped them make their peace with God. Your father knows."

Rocky recovered from his grief. "Yea, your mother has a habit of preachin' to veterans."

With that subtle complement, Marietta began to sob. As if her husband's regained composure gave her permission to assume her usual role of carrying a heavy heart, she needed the cry. Al and Henry had always made her feel like a lady, who should never doubt her pride in her war-hero husband and their three children. But, for more than any of her family, the last twenty-four hours had finally overwhelmed her.

As the five Bonaduccis huddled together, Gerald Gretto was calling outside for Jo-Jo. "Let him in," said Rocky, trying to lighten up emotions.

"You guys hear?" their four foot eight inch next-door neighbor asked. "Boy, my parents are so upset. You all OK?"

"We're getting better, Gerald," said Frank, wondering if it was time to share the secret that would surely divide their current grief. "Well, there's no good news in what just happened, but everybody sit down for this."

241

"What, Frankie?" probed Marietta, who knew her growing understanding of God still wasn't mature enough to handle another setback.

"Well, I was supposed to be on the cycle with Al, … not Henry!"

Rocky immediately responded, "Frankie, what'a ya talkin' about?"

Over the next moments, as Frank detailed his conversation before Al wheeled his bike out the driveway, everyone was speechless. Then, Jo-Jo asked the question Frank knew was coming. "What made you refuse, Frankie?"

"I had to be home … at a quarter to five ... for dad."

As Rocky dropped his head, Marietta jumped to hug her oldest child. Donna began to cheer. Jo-Jo patted his big brother's back. Gerald's eyes, as wide open as they ever could be, knew about the "Bonaducci rule", too.

Marietta was slowly on the rebound. The day's unbelievable events had now climaxed in what she interpreted as God's total grace by sparing her son, and were generating excitement in her soul she could not conceal. How could she express the peace and joy beginning to overwhelm her, forcing the confusion, grief, and oppression back to its hellish roots? She took a deep breath, silently asking God what He would want her to say or do. Marietta began to speak softly, choosing carefully words she believed she had heard from above. "Rocky, look. So much has happened today. I'm gonna call your sister, Mary. I'm gonna tell her what happened and suggest we take the night off. I'm gonna order some tomato pies, have her, Nick, and Nicholas come over. Call Bella, Pinky, Caesar, and the rest of your sisters, … and your brother, too. Tell them to drop by. I'll call Pete to pick up the pies at Napoli's. What'a ya think?"

Everyone looked to Rocky. There'd be lost income, plus the cost of feeding the whole family. On the other hand, his philosophy of life was always to have a party any time something good happened. And it had taken years for his wife to truly embrace that concept. To lift the tragedy of the accident from everyone's heart, Rocky could only agree. After all, his son was still alive. Besides, he had a thought to which no one else could have been privy.

"Listen," reacted Rocky. "We should invite Maria over, too, with her parents. Mr. and Mrs. Giardina should come."

Rocky's suggestion caught Frank by surprise. "Dad, we don't have to," said Frank, not wanting three more mouths for his mother and father to feed if it wasn't essential, … particularly his girlfriend's parents.

"No," Rocky insisted. "I want Angelo Giardina to tell you another 'quarter to five' story. It says a lot about the way we all live in this area, … ya know, Newark, Belleville, and Nutley. Family, respect, and all that."

"OK, I'll call them, Dad."

For the first time on this Friday, Marietta was smiling. "Great. Jo-Jo, check the TV to make sure it's working. We'll watch the Friday night fights and get a couple of pools goin'." She looked to Gerald Gretto who seemed to be in a trance from the unbelievable, emotional roller coaster ride he was on, … from grief to acceptance, and then breathtaking thanksgiving for Frank's decision, …and now it all being triumphantly celebrated with an imminent family gathering. Marietta hugged Jo-Jo's dwarf-like buddy. "Tell Tilley and Dominick to come over, Gerald. And bring your brothers and your little sister."

Frank was shaking his head. Decisions were being made at a break-neck speed. He anticipated the night turning more into a kind of Irish wake … for Henry and Al. What a switch from the usual Italian-American lifestyle. But, there was strong reason to get together. Then he paused. Another 'quarter to five story'; what was his father talking about?

By eight thirty that night the Bonaducci home was overflowing. The mood of family and friends was respectful for departed Al and Henry. Talk was reserved, but constant. Pete got Rocky's permission to bring Greenie, in spite of his indictment. He also walked in with little Jerome Yarborough on his shoulders. The black Orange Street munchkin toted a box of cannolis Pete had picked up from Calandra's bakery. Hugs and kisses were plentiful, particularly when everyone eventually learned about Frank's decision not to go on the tragic motorcycle ride.

As his guests seemed to be settling in, Rocky got everyone's attention. "Listen, it's been a rough day. But we're still all alive, have our helt, and have each other. What happened to Al and Henry is terrible. They were good kids. What's in *The Ledger* today, … not so good. Lots to learn. But, before the fights start on TV, I want Mr. Giardina to tell a Belleville story. I heard about it back in '46. He reminded me about it when we first met, after Frankie and Maria started datin'. It's a story 'bout all of us, … a story 'bout today. Thank God we still have Frank. Angelo, come over here and tell the story."

Giardina slowly lifted his stocky frame to stand at the head of the dining room table, next to Rocky. The room was full, overflowing into the living room and adjacent kitchen and TV room. A cloud of cigarette and cigar smoke hung around respectfully from the chandelier above the food and drink. Tomato pie was still being enjoyed, along with the homemade wine Pete had wrestled away from his mother. Marietta and the other ladies had already brought in dozens of Italian pastries that would now go untouched, … until after the story telling.

Uncle Anthony sensed the heaviness of the moment, and in his softhearted style began to clap for Giardina. "Angelo, good to see you. Everybody welcome Maria's father." Rocky's younger brother was a prince of a man, softer than his Marine Corp sibling, always looking for the good in people and situations. At last getting everyone's attention, he said, "Go ahead, Ang."

In his early forties, Angelo Giardina was no more than five feet six inches. Heavy jowls and weathered face made him appear older. His hands were huge, his wedding band lost in the thickness of his fingers. Premature gray made him look distinguished, in spite of daylong stints he and his four brothers and father spent in, on, and behind their dump trucks excavating and paving all over Belleville, Nutley, and Lyndhurst, fifty-two weeks a year. He took care of the books for the family business, but was a laborer at heart. He'd never met a wheel barrel he'd refuse to push. Having left Belleville High at fifteen to work with his dad, his only later schooling was with the US Army in England. He was a flight controller, responsible for sending hundreds of planes over Germany in World War II. Having shared many a beer with American pilots on English soil, he often cried himself to sleep on learning they went missing over enemy lines.

"Rocky asked me to tell you this story, because of Frank stayin' home this afternoon, rather than goin' on the motorcycle. Well, he added another … 'quarter to five story' to the neighborhood."

Silence spread throughout the house. Giardina began. "When we were kids in the thirties, they were tough times. But we had good times. There was always food on the table. The front door was open for anybody to come in. It seemed each of our families were having 'coffee and …' any day and at any time, for anybody stopping by. My best friends were twins, Enzo and Emmanuel DelTufo. I called them Enzo and Manny. Their mother was a Casale. Now, I'm goin' back, way back; they were distant cousins, but it would take too much time to explain that. Ya know, same paese (town, region) back in the old country. We'd play all day together, … stickball, box ball, buck-buck, football with a stuffed sock, basketball, marbles, ball and jacks. Now I'm goin' way back. Well, because Enzo and Manny's dad worked down in Newark most of the time, he'd get rides from friends, hitch, take a trolley, or sometimes walk. But what he always required his two boys was to be sittin' at the dinner table at … 'a quarter to five' when he got home. Now Enzo and Manny were swell guys, … good friends, good brothers, and good sons. But we had other friends, too. So when we all weren't together, and the two of them were playin' with other kids or doin' odd jobs in the neighborhood to make money, … well, they would whistle to each other as a signal their dad was due home on time, … or if they sighted him comin' up the street."

Angelo, a modest man, looked at Rocky and back at the group. "Am I borin' youse?" They roared back their desire for him to continue.

"They lived on Forest Street over by Number 5 School, and their father would usually be comin' up Greylock Parkway from Washington Avenue. Ya see, they had one whistle for 'hurry up, Pop's gonna be on time'; one for 'Pop's late'; and one for 'you're late, … and you're gonna get the belt'."

The laughter was soft. The only other sound was Blackie barking in the back yard as he chased the Gretto cat.

"Now the thirties weren't as bad as a lot of people think. But then came the war. We all went off, … me and my brothers, … all the guys from the neighborhood. Enzo and Manny went, too. After Pearl Harbor, we all went in. We wanted to. Well, here's the story: Enzo was in 'Normandy, plus six' and was chasin' the Germans to Berlin. Manny was on a troop ship off the coast of Italy, waitin' to join Patton comin' up from the sout. Now, these boys were swell guys, and they loved each other, if you know what I mean. They always wrote to each other, tryin' to stay up on where they were, and tellin' each other they'd get together during, or after, the war, just to see each other. Ya know, have a beer, celebrate, … whatever. Then Manny gets notified on his ship that Enzo's missin' in action … somewhere in France. So, he somehow gets off the ship and somehow gets into France and the front lines, determined to find his twin brother. The Good Lord must' a been with him, because somehow he runs into this Irish kid from Brooklyn who says he'd help him with this Jeep to find his brother. Nuttin' was gonna stop Manny. So, him and this Brooklyn guy start comin' up on dead Germans, GI's, cows, whatever… bridges, farmyards, the stench of death, … gasoline, diesel, gunpowder, … everything. So the kid stops the Jeep and looks at Manny. 'Now what?' he asks. Manny doesn't say nuttin'. He just gets up in the Jeep, and starts whislin'. He's whistlin' the … 'quarter to five' whistle. Nuttin'. It's quiet except for artillery in the distance and other Allied vehicles movin' into the area to collect bodies and such.

Then the driver asks again, 'Now what?' Manny tells him to drive further into the battlefield. The kid thinks he's nuts. 'Keep goin', says Manny. They go another two hundred yards, and Manny gets him to stop the Jeep. He stands up, takes a deep breath, and whistles again, the same … 'quarter to five' whistle from Forest Street in Belleville. At first, nuttin' happens. He tries again, and ya know what? The same … 'quarter to five' whistle comes back."

Angelo stops, choked up. Around the table, jaws drop, as handkerchiefs and paper napkins dab tears. Marietta hugged her moppeen, and no one was eating any more tomato pie. Glasses had been placed aside. All eyes were on Angelo, who continued. "Yep, he found Enzo under a dead German. He was in bad shape, but he heard the … 'quarter to five' whistle from Manny, … and the tough little kid whistled back. They got him. They picked him up. They brought him back."

"Damn it. Can't be. God bless 'em," whispered Uncle Nick Durso.

Giardina was not finished. "The war ended, and they came home. *The Newark Star Ledger* wrote about it. They married sisters. Can ya believe that? The Landolfi girls; they're related to us, too. Same paese. They've been in the plumbin' business together, … the brothers. Always find them at the Italian mass every Sunday morning at Nutley's Holy Family Church, … 5:30 AM sharp. They moved down by us, next door from each other on King Street after the war. Live in Nutley now, … right on the Belleville line, … Big Tree section. Their boys both will play football for Nutley next year. Enzo and Manny are swell guys. Bein' home at … 'a quarter to five' saved them, … just like it saved Frankie today."

By now the haze of smoke had been ushered out the side windows of the house as the mid-Spring breezes enveloped the humanity inside. No one was moving. The ultimate "…quarter to five" story had been told. Uncle Caesar Casciano could not contain himself.

"Listen, this has been quite a day; … miracles, but loss. It's great to be alive. How's 'bout we end it with 'God Bless America'? My Irish brother-in-law, James, is here. I'm sure Pinky won't mind him singin'. It'll be good for all of us."

Nicholas looked to Frank and rolled his eyes to the back of his head, as if to say, "Enough with this emotional stuff."

Frank returned a gentle smile, blessing his patriotic uncle's gesture.

Jimmy Quinn needed no further coaxing. He walked to Rocky's side, looked at Pinky, smiled, and then asked everyone to stand, as his voice rang out.

Jerome Yarborough had mostly experienced the night in the soft lap of Bella Bruno. As the prayerful lyrics rang out, he could only gaze around the room at the strange blend of family, patriotism, and love. It was many miles from the crowded apartment his mother kept on Orange Street in Newark. He looked up at his host, Mr. Pete. The chubby butcher could not sing, but his tears were a symphony of praise for the good events of the day. Next to him was Greenie. Never known for carrying a tune, he was singing louder than anyone, maybe because it was the first time Rocky had invited him into the Bonaducci home.

Frank's head hit his pillow at 11:55 that night, but he was restless. Sleep wouldn't come easily on May 15. He reached for Dion and the Belmonts' new 45 that had yet to be played …until now. "Teenager in Love" was speeding up the national charts, and Maria had purchased it for her boyfriend earlier in the day. Listening to the boys from the Bronx's unique harmonizing sound, it suddenly dawned on Frank that Dion and he now had more in common than just growing up on streets named Belmont Avenue. On the night of February 3, 1959, Dion made the decision not to take the fateful plane ride. He had to stay with the Belmonts. On May 15, 1959, Frank made a decision not to take the motorcycle ride. He had to be home for his father … at a quarter to five.

Downstairs, Marietta was alone as she wiped her kitchen table with her tattered moppeen for the final time that evening. Prayerfully, she was thanking the Lord for his grace with every one of her strokes across the wobbly wooden furniture.

It was the last Friday Marietta would have off that year. However, its memory kindled within her and all the others at the Bonaducci house a renewed reverence for their heritage, families, and traditions. It would motivate them to keep going in life, no matter what the circumstances. Embarrassment had come to the neighborhood on the heels of the indictments, followed by tragic death. But, a glance back to the past during a somber celebration of life had provided all the reason to keep going forward, regardless of the odds. The … 'quarter to five' discipline … took on meaning that day that became a foundation for many people, … for many years to come.

CHAPTER 18

"AND THE WINNER IS ..."

Graduation night was a classic June evening with Belleville Municipal Stadium surrounded by clear skies and a purple hazed sunset on the horizon. Dozens of American flags lined the football field, flapping in the soft early summer breeze that welcomed family and friends of the 364 candidates from the class of 1959.

The event was particularly triumphant for the Bonaduccis. As class president, Frank would lead everyone in the Pledge of Allegiance, while cousin Nicholas Durso, as featured pianist, would play "May the Good Lord Bless and Keep You" for the class' end of ceremony exit.

Throughout the day Frank and his friends ribbed each other about who would receive the greatest ovation when the Belleville Board of Education would award the diplomas. Some favored brainy valedictorian, Myra Fortunato. Other bets were on June DiBella, the salutatorian, who was also captain of the cheerleaders, as well as clearly the more popular of the two.

Jackie Carey thought differently. "It'll be Julie Manzer, da subject of every boy's dreams who has ever seen her. Plus, dare fodders will surely chime in, witout dare wives knowin' da deal. Bunch of dirty minds. Too bad her rotten cop of a fodder will tink da claps are complements."

Eric Thatcher pondered the question when on the phone with Bob Hardy in the afternoon. "It'll be Gino Babula. Yep, he'll get the biggest hand."

"Gino, the jock?" challenged Hardy, veiling his own ego that he merited a strong chance, being a track star, an outstanding student, plus the first of Belleville's favorite sons to receive appointment to the United States Naval Academy.

"That's it, Ensign Hardy. And it has nothing to do with his eighteen touchdowns," replied Eric, convinced by his clairvoyant mother who nominated Gino when he asked her opinion.

"No way," Bob said.

"This crowd will give him a standing ovation as a weak gesture of respect, adoration, ... and fear of Sneaks." Then Eric explained, "After all, Bobby, guess who'll be in the stands, sitting on the 50-yard line with his Rahway guards and State Trooper escorts? You got it, ... the Sneaker himself. Who got jobs from him and The Boot, ... who grew up with him, ... who feels sorry for him with this new counterfeit thing, ... all that stuff. He'll be like a Roman Emperor, watching the spectacle with scores of faceless supporters cheering around him."

"Don't think so," insisted Hardy.

They were all wrong.

The ceremony was early into recognition of the Honor group when the name of one of the achievers caused a sincere and thunderous frenzy, ... Craig Francello! As the tribute echoed through the packed stadium, everyone rose in admiration for the cerebral palsy victim whose family insisted on his being mainstreamed with his childhood friends. Arms flailing, head tilted left, and the broadest smile he could muster, the recently indicted seventeen-year old dragged his delinquent legs onto the platform and waved his leather-bound diploma. For several minutes, Craig held center stage. All eyes fixed on the student warrior whose high grade point average, sharp sense of humor, and quick mind had made believers of anyone who took the time to listen to his slurred, but amazing insights.

As the volume of applause slowly subsided, Jackie Carey, sitting behind in the next row, tapped Frank on the back. Without turning around, Frank said, "Jack, don't even comment. He deserves it."

"Soooo sorrrry, Mr. Nice guy," said Jackie, knowing it was not the time for any humorous sarcasm.

Then, as Craig struggled off the platform, Wee Willie and Gino jumped up to help. Craig reacted, lifting his hands referee fashion, signaling a touchdown. And one more time, the Belleville crowd erupted.

Frank could not stop staring at Craig. It was as if he was being compelled, … as if God was trying to make it apparent that the Higher Power was far from finished with Craig Francello, … or Frank for that matter. Only the years would tell the rest of the story.

CHAPTER 19

"ONE SUMMER NIGHT"

With Frank's graduation now behind them, a constant tension tightened its grip on the Bonaducci household. The counterfeit indictments and a possible murder conspiracy came to increasingly dominate everyone's thoughts, particularly when Uncle Pete made his daily phone call. But not totally, … Frank was still anticipating a couple of trips to Seaside Heights with his friends to show off their new weightlifting-induced muscles on the beach, as well as take on any challengers at touch football games on the sand in front of the Surf Club night spot. For Donna and Jo-Jo, Rocky and Marietta could only promise daytrips to Asbury Park and the lakes along Route 23 in Passaic County. After all, Rocky's car did have its limits. Destinations beyond Exit 100 on the Garden State Parkway, or past Butler, were far beyond its capabilities. At least that's what he and Marietta claimed, although more likely it was the usual problem of cash flow, than the much-maligned black Chevy with the hole in the back seat floor.

For the past four years, summers in the blue-collar neighborhood bordered by Belmont and Smallwood Avenues, and the Lackawanna Railroad at its southern most perimeter, had become almost euphoric to its young inhabitants. Sunday evenings the thumping sound of endless freight trains heading for destinations unknown would sorrowfully compete with Eric the Snatcher's "Sensational Sunday Sounds", or whatever he called it. When not playing baseball or studying to maintain his Honor Society status, the wiry Buddy Holly look-alike would tape any Jocko Henderson or Allan Freed radio show, … even American Bandstand telecasts that were spinning 45 sounds of the mid to late fifties. The fourth Sunday in June kicked off the '59 summer edition. But its significance would be beyond anyone's comprehension.

Jimmy Hardy and Davey Thatcher were helping get meticulous Eric's classic reel-to-reel system in place on the back porch of his family's tiny brick house, when his mother came out. Antoinette Thatcher piled her *Sunday Newark Star Ledger, Newark News,* and *New York Times* for her final perusal, as she plopped into a wooden kitchen chair just outside the door. Her flowing silk bed robe at 7 PM only slightly distracted the youngsters. Her subtle, often bizarre personality was particularly appreciated by Marietta, the few times the two mothers had met. Antoinette enjoyed the neighborhood kids' appreciation of Eric's two-hour hit parade, especially now that several Southern Comfort Manhattans were making their way through her blood stream. This would inspire her loud vocal requests for a few Glenn Miller sounds, which Eric deftly refused. Taking the hint, the avant-garde, yet compassionate mother soon vanished into her cluttered home with the three newspapers tucked sloppily under both her arms. Most usually she'd be muttering something about her belief her generation would be the last great one in American history. But the smile on her face signaled her genuine love for the purity of youth gathering in her backyard, and her yearning for her own vanished years of adolescent innocence.

As Mrs. Thatcher took a last glance over her shoulder, she smiled internally at seeing Jo-Jo, sitting on the crooked ranch style fence, holding on with both arms as Gerald Gretto periodically tried to unbalance his next-door neighbor. A bit more aggressive than his older brother, Jo-Jo would have loved to toss Gerald to Bloomfield to teach him some respect. But that might mean forfeiting use of the three-foot plastic pool in the Gretto family's backyard. So, it was "be nice to Gerald night". Roger Bush, too tall to sit comfortably, leaned against the fence's decaying maroon stained wooden posts, and constantly tossed his basketball skyward. Harold Bader was trying to get his three buddies' attention on two familiar cars at the Shell station, with Rickie Murray and Mark Brunello in the drivers' seats, their questionable-reputation girlfriends hanging all over them. However, view of the "one night stands" heavily made-up faces by the four hormone-bubbling pre-teens was blocked by fuzzy dice hanging from both cars' rear view mirrors. Rickie and Mark still might be recovering from the tragic deaths of Henry and Al, but these young ladies squeezing close in the '49 Ford and '57 Chevy would tonight help the two Bloomfield High grease-monkey dropouts forget the May 15 accident. After Eric personally invited them to stop by to listen to his newest tapes, Rickie and Mark saw an obvious opportunity for a cheap, early date night.

Frank had arrived earlier in Jackie Carey's Heavenly Heap, with Bobby Hardy in the back seat. Jack insisted on backing into the Thatcher driveway so they'd all have a panoramic view ... of Thatcher on his porch, Rickie and Mark making out with their dates, and Belleville Avenue's shopping center, where the other neighborhood girls promenaded. Sporting "short-shorts", they earnestly hoped to be waved over to join the Snatcher's Sensational Sunday Sounds by any attracted male wearing dungarees. But the anxious wait did not stop these beauties from sticking their noses any higher in the air without breaking their necks. Their haughty glances toward the Thatcher backyard confirmed that boys from twelve to eighteen were rapidly gathering, and that's where they wanted to be. Indeed, Jackie Carey was bubbling with amorous anticipation.

Frank, who had promised to visit Maria that night, was always asking Jackie for the time. But Bob kept urging him to forget his girlfriend just this once. With all plebes being expected at Annapolis by the end of the week, this would be his last Snatcher Show.

Slowly pulling his immaculate new Pontiac Bonneville up to the Thatcher driveway, Gino Babula made a rare visit to the neighborhood. Wee Willie, Billy McCabe, Donnie Riordan, and Guy Galioto were with him. It was a cool June night, and each was wearing his blue and gold football letter sweater.

Frank made his decision to stay for the duration of Eric's show when his cousin, Nicholas, pulled up in his father's Packard, the Norma Desmond. There was never a moment that Frank did not enjoy his articulate cousin's presence. Nick's most current female admirer, Cheryl Austin, was his passenger. She had been taking piano lessons almost as long as Nick. Their love of big band music and jitterbugging, as well as the sound of a great piano, seemed to make them a natural couple. But they contended to be "just friends". "Frank, you are very obvious without Maria at your hip for this special sock hop." Nick loved to tease his cousin about being a bit henpecked.

Now his decision to cancel his night with Maria got to Frank's conscience. "You really know how to make me feel guilty, you pineapple, you." Although they talked regularly by phone, the two cousins actually spent little social time together. Nick was busy with his music, dancing, and partying, and Frank was tied into sports, school, and his future bride.

Frank cringed even more when Jackie jumped out of his car and beckoned a half dozen of the female teens, making their way down the street, to be his guests at the "record hop". "Jack, Rosemarie Masino's in that group," Frank reminded. Jo-

Jo had broken up with the overly mature eighth grader after his first ever less than scintillating parent-teacher report, and his older brother sensed her being there might make things uncomfortable.

"Frank, Jo-Jo's over it," said Jackie. "And let me tell ya. I hear little Rosie's enjoyin' nightly dates at da Totowa Drive In wit dat Marty Gilrain."

"Marty Gilrain? Cuz, you have to be kidding."

Bobby added, "Yea, Frank, we didn't want to tell you guys. Man, Marty's got to be twenty years old."

"Yep, and he could end up in jail." Jackie paused, and then adding, "Oh, man, I'd give anyting to be in his shoes."

"You're disgusting, Jackie," said Frank. "What about being a cop who makes a living locking up those cradle snatchers?"

"Well, I know dat God must be blockin' it for me," said Jackie, "cause I'm at home every night, and that Marty Gilrain is at Totowa wit dat little honey. But don't forget dat I ain't protectin' da world yet wit a trusty night stick."

Suddenly everyone's attention switched to Eric taking center stage, sitting behind an unstable card table full of notes and a 45 record player for special requests. The inaugural 1959 edition of his "Sunday Sensational Sounds with the Snatcher" began:

"Hey guys and gals and kids of all ages,
It's The Snatcher here, the sage of all sages

With our 4th season of rock 'n' roll,
Just come on over and enter the fold.

We're playing those hits that are sweepin' the nation,
It's pure sensation and teenager elation.

I got Freed and Henderson at my side,
We'll listen to the sounds that'll give you a ride.

As we all take off to rock 'n' roll heaven,
Just sit on back, the time is seven.

Our first selection's a special request,
So we're giving our tapes a little rest,

What 45 could we possibly hear?
It's "One Summer Night", by the great Danleers."

With Eric's volume dials turned up as high as they could go, the chart-topping hit blared across the neighborhood. But there would be no complaints. Still reeling from the counterfeit indictments, Paulie Puccini's death on New Year's, Henry and Al's motorcycle accident, ... and few forgetting February 3rd, too much change was occurring in many lives. So the romance and hope of youth was otherwise welcomed by all within hearing distance of the sounds of the hit songs being played. On the other hand, the Snatcher still had critics, and Jackie Carey was one of them.

"Not for nuttin', guys," said Jackie. "I mean I love all Eric's preparation and stuff, and I don't forget da price is right showin' up here. But, will one of youse guys tell him dat a poet he ain't. I mean, it's gettin' worse, da older he gets."

"Jackie, you goofball, don't be so critical. You'd be home watching Ed Sullivan with your mother and sister if Eric wasn't doing this show," snapped Bob Hardy, quickly shutting his friend up.

After the first song, Eric went to a taped Allan Freed introduction of "Oh Rose Marie" by The Fascinators, at the same time catching sight of Rosemarie Masino, ... his chance to make Jo-Jo squirm. "Mr. Freed and The Snatcher dedicate this one to Jo-Jo, ... as his lost teenage love arrives at the Snatcher's Sensational Sunday Sounds. And now, boys and girls, ... 'Oh Rose Marie'."

To Gerald, Harold, and Roger's giggles, Jo-Jo, still ignorant about her new romantic experiences, turned red as his ex strutted by with her entourage of friends. His embarrassment was minimal compared to the reaction that would come later.

Eric continued other dedications throughout the evening: "In the Still of the Night" by The Five Satins, for Gino, his favorite; "Tonight, Tonight" by the Mellokings, for Jackie Cary, reminding everyone of his seemingly daily prayer for a young lady to come into his life, always hoping it would be ... "Tonight"; and, of course, all waited for "I Wonder Why", the '58 Dion and the Belmonts single, to be sent out to Frank. Eric did not disappoint:

"For my friend, Frank, … it's 'I Wonder Why'.
As we all know, he's a real special guy.

So just sit on back, as the Belmonts appear,
Before every game they'd catch Frankie's ear.

And then he'd wow us with his high-steppin' moves,
Leadin' the Bellboys into the groove.

He's off to college where we know he'll soar,
'Cause Gino's history, and Frank will score."

Gino waved his amused approval over at Jackie's car where the ever-modest Frank made a circular motion on the side of his head with his right hand, in his synopsis of Eric's latest zaniness.

Jo-Jo caught the subtle exchange between Mr. Inside and Mr. Outside, and left his friends to visit Gino and the other Bellboys. "Gino, working out yet?" He always talked football around Belleville's All State running back.

"What, ya kiddin' kid? I don't report til the end of August. Got a long summer down the Shore before I think about football." Publicly Gino was not known for conscientious off-season workouts. But his one hundred pushups and the same of sit-ups in secret everyday kept him close to his playing weight.

Jo-Jo loved being around his brother's teammates. While he conversed with Gino about the freshman upcoming season, Wee Willie and his friends preferred to whisper about Rosemarie Masino, now dating a guy, seven years her senior.

Gino, sincerely conveying some helpful hints on running the football in high school, could still not prevent Frank's younger brother from overhearing the gossip. Gino's lips were moving, but Jo-Jo's mind was not hearing any words. Confusion and disillusionment had taken over, images of Marty's car being his den of seduction at the Totowa Drive-in. Jo-Jo was suddenly up close and personal with the worst of the birds and the bees. For the last two years, Russell Giardella had never hesitated to unemotionally and clinically describe to Jo-Jo how his deeply Catholic parents managed to get pregnant nine times in only thirteen years. Now Jo-Jo's grammar school sweetheart was subject of more detailed discussion on the subject of human sexuality than he'd ever heard before. *Who cares what Gino's saying?* He was staring through his body, allowing his mind's eye to journey where it never had been before. An overwhelming feeling of conflict possessed Jo-Jo, and warfare within his very bosom had been declared. His conservative upbringing of celibacy before marriage had suddenly collided with his own natural development and examples set by others. That summer night, life became more complex for the thirteen year old.

In the Bonaducci kitchen, Marietta was serving coffee and left over graduation cake to her husband and Pinky and Jimmy Quinn. The young couple, who never hid their affection for Frank, had missed the previous week's party, and just dropped by to give him an envelope with some money for his graduation. Eric's record hop could be heard in the distance, easily drowning out the clickity-clack of freight trains crawling along the Lackawanna tracks in back of the neighborhood. Jimmy could not contain himself. "Rock, what's goin' on? The music and the radio with Jocko and Freed?"

As Rocky explained, Pinky and Marietta were fussing over Donna's hair, ignoring the conversation between the two men. Then, when Rocky excused himself to the bathroom, Jimmy quickly moved his very large body down the kitchen stairs into the backyard. He lit a Lucky and swallowed its smoke, seeming to refuse its exhale until he could interpret the mood coming over him. As Eric and Jocko introduced "The Closer You Are", the Channel's huge New York City hit, Jimmy quietly began harmonizing with the voices jumping out of the reel-to-reel recorder. His Public Service job may pay the bills, but his true reason for being was being snuffed out every time he climbed a telephone pole. The lump growing in his throat signaled a self-pity he could not tolerate.

Yep, Lenny's better than all of these guys, he thought. *And with his falsetto, the Four Loves are gonna be famous.*

As Quinn continued to soak up the Channel's velvet sounds, giving birth to visions of himself on stage, yearning for fulfillment of his own destiny, he was rescued from this moment of regretful intoxication by a voice he hadn't heard since the night of the motorcycle accident.

"James Quinn, I gotcha a corn beef sandwich from Stashes that's overflowin' like Mount Vesuvius. Butter and mustard drippin' all over the place, ... seepin' out of some hard Jewish rye. And the pickles are so big, ya can't get your jaws around 'em." It was Pete Frassa with his surprise package of post-pasta snacks—his regular ritual any Sunday he didn't get to eat with his sister's family.

Jimmy turned and laughed. Having just finished a piece of leftover graduation cake, he had no room left. But he knew, too, that he could not insult the jovial butcher who had not stopped smiling since not being indicted a month ago along with his Bloomfield Avenue friends. "Pete, just what I need after coffee and …"

"Ya only live once, Jimmy. If you Irishmen would eat more than you drink, ya'd live longer and be handsome like me."

Petee Five Corners had broken a spell of harmonizing spirits. Jimmy returned to the house and forgot how close he was to becoming a permanent member of Lenny Latore and the Four Loves. Little did he realize that Pinky had already pretty much sabotaged him ever substituting as one of the Four Loves that summer. She told Marietta that Frank could use her husband's sleek maroon and white '56 Chevy for any weekend down the Jersey Shore. Needing extra cash, Pinky made Jim aware they not only could not afford a weekend at the beaches, but also that she had joined Marietta and Mary on the graveyard shift at the factory. Making the car available would not only thrill her nephew, but also would represent a good excuse to give when Lenny'd call needing Jim down at one of the Loves' many shore gigs. Without a car on weekends, Jimmy's only singing would be in the shower, … just where Pinky preferred him to be.

With the clock on the card table indicating only time to play one more song before his 9 PM closing, Eric made sure he had everyone's attention. But instead of his crudely contrived poetry, he introduced his finale with: "Our good friend, Bob Hardy, leaves this week for the United States Naval Academy. He's the first from Belleville to ever get appointed there. The whole neighborhood and all of Belleville High School are proud of him. We hate to see him leave so early in the summer, or leave at all for that matter. We know he'll come back to visit, and for that we are grateful. You guys know a few friends from the neighborhood have already gone away, never to come back, … Henry, Al, Paulie. And the year started with us losing Buddy Holly, Ritchie Valens, and the Big Bopper. Well, we know Bobby will take care of himself. Thank God there are no wars in the world right now. He's gonna run track down there, and we wish him luck. He's been my friend since we were four years old. So, before anybody gets too emotional, this song is dedicated to him, and all the good times we've had over the years."

Everyone was spellbound. With only the slow moving trains and their periodic whistles now the singular sounds dancing through the soft June air, Eric placed his choice for the dedication into the record player. It was Maurice Williams and the Zodiacs who would entertain the young attendees with "Stay".

"Staaaay, just a little bit longer, … please, please, please…"

It made the crowd of kids linger a while afterwards, as Antoinette Thatcher leaned against her kitchen door, staring through the worn screen. She, too, was melancholy about Bobby, but also about the future of the hopeful young people upon whom she gazed. *With the exception of Korea, it's been a glorious fourteen years since VJ Day,* she thought. Having sacrificed her dancing and teaching career to dedicate her life to her husband and two sons, her pursuit of truth in her everyday reading of world events inched her closer to a meaningful life. However, the Southern Comfort and sweet vermouth periodically incited her to stray down paths cluttered with thoughts of what could have been. While her mind would seemingly sharpen at first as the alcohol soothed her soul, on this night she was lost somewhere between lucidity, clairvoyance, and an old fashion "buzz", ... and the cherry in the glass was red with regret and remorse. *Where would these children be with their plans and dreams in the years to come?* Antoinette marveled. *I've watched them all grow into interesting and unique individuals. But things change.* For her, the indictments, the motorcycle accident, the controversy over Paulie Puccini's death, ... all of this was too coincidental. *Change, ... a season of change is upon us.* A tear came to her eye as she retired to her bedroom to join husband Joe, who had been asleep since 7 PM. He had to be up at 3 AM to deliver milk.

Eric Thatcher and his brother, Davey; Bob Hardy and brother, Jimmy; Frank Bonaducci and Jo-Jo; ... plus Jackie Carey and neighborhood munchkins Harold Bader, Roger Bush, and Gerald Gretto; ... these made up the nine charter members in the Snatcher's Sunday show. The audience during that summer would change, but this was the loyal core that would never forget their summers of harmonizing music. It never seemed to rain on summer Sunday nights in their childhoods. But this was the last time the loyal corps would ever be together with each other for the hop, or ever again. Mrs. Thatcher's mind, fighting gloominess and the effects of liquor, had seen clouds on the horizon, ... not just over college and jobs in the future, but also of a brewing war, ... a war that would be fought by five of the nine. One would never come back.

Still gathered around Bob Hardy, the young pre-teen girls were in awe. They saw him as almost godlike, going off to the Navy, ... a great athlete, and pure in heart, ... something intangible and untouchable for them. Even Rickie Murray and Mark Brunello made the effort to wrestle free from their dates to walk over from the Shell Station to shake Bob's hand and send him off with best wishes.

A special summer night was ending. However, one more act had to follow.

CHAPTER 20

"DAS BOOT"

Bob Hardy became uncomfortable at being the center of attention. Even Jo-Jo, Gerald, Roger, and Harold were lingering in his presence. Maybe their motivation was not so much about him, but rather the pack of young teen girls still loitering. Hardy figured out a quick way to break it all up. "Hey, guys, one last game of 'Stalag 17'!" This was the summertime simulation of catching would-be German prison camp escapees, named after the recent Hollywood movie.

Eric and Frank showed sour looks of disdain. How could the imminent Navy man be so immature to suggest the Nazi version of "hide and seek"? But mention of the male-only activity made the girls vanish. Then Gino and his crowd, as well as cousin Nick, bade their farewells.

"Bob, I thought 'Stalag 17' would have died when 'impure thoughts' began to replace ideas of backyard games," said Eric.

"Don't be so crude, 'Snatcher'," reacted Frank. Then he looked at Bob and reminded him. "You may be playing your fair share of games at the Academy, Cuz. You sure you want to go one more time with our snotty little brothers and their friends?"

Both Jimmy Hardy and Davey Thatcher were now looking forward to the chance to "torture" the grammar schoolers who would surely loose the game. Then Eric busted their bubble. "OK, we play, but since Jackie's here tonight, the teams split with me, Jackie, Frank, Bob, and Jimmy on the side of the Germans. And my wonderful brother, Davey, goes with the kids to make it fair."

"Oh, crap, I don't need another 'German haircut' from you, Eric. I get one every night." Davey looked over to the younger four, doubting they had the ingenuity to win.

Bob figured he had enough agreement, so he took the role of officially restating the rules that everyone already knew by heart. "Since it was our idea, Davey's team has to hide. Remember, no houses or cars; anywhere else, but not there. Trees, garages, bushes, … use your imagination, boys. And, if we get all of you in the sixty-minute limit, you each get 'German haircutted' by us, and you have to buy sodas at the Shell Station for everybody tomorrow. Any questions, prisoners?"

"No questions, but I don't have any money, you creeps," Roger answered without taking his eyes off his bouncing basketball.

"Ask your old man," said Eric, finally getting into the militant German officer role he seemed to relish each time they played 'Stalag 17'.

"Oh, now the disc jockey is some baby-killing Nazi," taunted Davey. "Look what an animal my parents really raised."

"Gee, brotherly love," said Jackie, who really didn't want to play, but was going along with it being Bob's last weekend home.

Roger Bush was showing a touch of the rebellion and irreverence that seemed to be increasing with every inch he grew that year. The fourteen year old, who was already as tall as Frank, evoked the ire of everyone. "Can't believe you guys. First, Eric plays a love song to Bobby whose goin' away, then we're playin' a kids game with you bullies who should really be out on dates."

"You missed the whole point with the song, Roger," said Frank.

As Eric and Davey continued to noisily bicker with each other, Roger made sure his next comment only made it to the ears of Frank and Jo-Jo. "Sounded a little queer to me with that 'Stay' song. Ya know, … Eric and Bobby?"

"You sicko," said Jo-Jo, giving Bush, who was seven inches taller, a push from the side. It camouflaged his lingering embarrassment over what he'd heard about Rosemarie, earlier.

Roger ignored the physical rebuke. "Ya hear the words to that song, 'Stay'? They talk about kissin' in that song. Who's the sicko? Me or the four-eyed 'Snatcher'?" Jo-Jo and Frank still did not know how seriously to take him, when Roger relaxed. "Only kiddin', Jo-Jo. I'm not stupid. I got the sendoff thing, … but I still don't have the dough if we lose this stupid game."

Frank changed the subject and drew everyone back into the conversation. "Hey, Cuzzes, if I can't be with my girlfriend, let's have some fun. Eric, go get the flashlights. You kids have ten minutes to hide. Remember, nothing beyond the Hardy and the Profetta houses; you can come back to the Gretto's and around the Thatcher's. Can't leave the block. Make your plan and take off. We find you within the hour, … and it's torture time. If we don't, we take you to the Milk Bar this week for shakes and one dog each."

Jo-Jo was actually warming to the idea of playing "Stalag 17" because his brother seemed to be loosening up for the first time in a long time. Since the Nutley game, and then all that had gone on through the year, Frank had gotten way too serious for his little brother. Now he was as he liked him best—focusing on the moment, with almost gleeful anticipation for the future. Jo-Jo reasoned that being a senior in high school, and getting older, automatically brings on all kinds of unforeseeable situations. The rest of this night was just beginning, and Jo-Jo could not imagine just how close around the corner his turn to bid a farewell to the innocence of his youth … would be.

With Davey Thatcher taking over planning the strategy of his "escapee" group, the "German officers" were casually testing their flashlights supplied by Eric. They were loudly confident that finding their prisoners would probably be a pushover. But they misjudged Dave's competitive spirit.

Huddled between the Gretto garage and their new above-ground pool, Davey outlined his plan for the escapees. "We'll start running in five different directions during the grace period, so they see us. Then we meet where they'll never find us."

Jo-Jo cut in. "No offense, Davey, but if we played this game once, we played it a million times. How many places can we hide where we haven't already?"

"Glad you asked, little fellow," said Davey. "Here's the deal. Goofy Gary Gubitosi is always working in his garage, right? Well, besides tinkering with his television sets, the gavvone is building a boat … in the garage. Can you believe that?"

"Oh, an Amedigan calling an Italian guy a 'gavvone'", objected Jo-Jo. "Davey, only Italians call other Italians, 'gavvones'. But, you're right. He _is_ a 'gavvone'." Everyone nodded at Jo-Jo, confirming their mutual dislike for Mr. Gubitosi.

"No way we can hide in the Gubitosi garage," whispered Harold. "He's always got the door locked, and besides, Davey, how do you build a boat in such a small garage? You're nuts. It can't be a boat."

"Listen, you turds," said Davey, really pushing his assertiveness. "That's the point. When the Germans look in the garage window, they'll see the boat and how little room there is between the walls of the crappy little building. They'll figure we could never all fit, and go check some other place. Besides, … you're right, you little limey. The door's always locked, so that's another reason the guys won't bother with it."

Gerald asked the obvious. "Then, how do we get in, 'Little Snatcher'?"

It looked like Davey had a mutiny brewing even before his group was ready to head to their destination. Bigger than the other escapees (with the exception of Roger), who were two to three years younger, Davey was surprised at the obstinacy of the "Our Gang" look-alikes.

"How to get in? I was waiting for someone to ask. Ta daaaa! I can open the lock with this," said Thatcher, pulling out his pocketknife.

Jo-Jo patted him on the back as if to congratulate him for his plan, as the others showed approval with their nodding motions.

Roger, still with basketball in hand, interjected, "Nope, it doesn't work, because once we get in by opening the lock, the place is unsecured, and they could just walk in behind us. Gee, Davey, you figured it all out, I see."

"That's why you guys never win this game," answered Davey. "After we get in, Gerald locks it from the outside, and then runs around to the back of the garage, and we let him in through the broken window. He's the only one who could fit, but they'll never figure that out." Davey paused. "Yea, he might get a cut or two, but doin' it for the team and avoiding a German haircut, … plus gettin' a frankfurter with everything on it at the Milk Bar, will be worth the loss of blood." Thatcher waited for Gretto to react. He didn't. "You can do it, you tough little guinea," said Davey, whose insult drew a feeble push from the dwarfish Gerald.

"OK. Let's go before our grace period is over," concluded Jo- Jo, who now wanted to get the game over as soon as possible, because he had other things on his mind.

The five boys sprinted off in different directions after Roger threw his basketball into the Bonaducci backyard, signifying he approved of Davey's plan, and that it might actually work. The older group heard and saw their "escape", but soon lost sight of them. Giving them a few more minutes "on the run", Eric, Frank, Bob, Jimmy, and Jackie then set out to track them down.

Davey's plan, so far, went like clockwork. By 10 PM, the escapees were snuggled into the Gubitosi garage like a litter of puppies frightened about their new surroundings. Indeed, there was no room to breath. Davey had been correct; Gary Gubitosi, at forty years old, was building a boat in a garage that tilted at a greater angle than the Leaning Tower of Pisa. Even more bizarre was the fact that the boat's bow extended beyond the width of the garage doors!

Jo-Jo was first to ask, "What's big Gubitosi thinking … that he's the neighborhood Noah, and some flood is coming to destroy his building and reveal his version of the Ark?" Having listened to Nora and Queenie read the Old Testament to his mother, Jo-Jo knew more about the biblical story than his comrades.

Bader whispered, "Now I <u>know</u> Mr. Gubitosi's nuts."

"Yea, he'll just set sail when the dumpy garage tips over," laughed Gerald. "Then he won't have to worry about whether it fits through the front door or not."

"Shut up, guys. We gotta be quiet," said Davey, hardly as commanding as he had been before. The reality of the oversized boat in the narrow one car garage was becoming a mystery even to Davey.

Enshrouded in a heavy canvas, the boat partially concealed the cinder block foundation that seemed to be keeping it upright. The outboard motor opening, exposed at the back of the unfinished vessel, gave Davey an idea. He turned to the rest of the boys, whose eyes darted back and forth at each other. He whispered, "Jo-Jo, you go first. Climb into the boat and under the canvas, … rest of you guys follow. I'll go last."

Jo-Jo climbed aboard with the others behind. However, as Davey grabbed Roger's hand to shimmy himself, they all heard banging on the back garage window that Gerald had just managed to squeeze through. A gravelly voice stunned the five.

"What are you rotten kids doing in there?"

The "Stalag 17" escapees could not have been more frightened, as they each screamed their own vintage curse word. *Gary Gubitosi's about to beat us each to death with a TV antenna, and then stuff our bodies somewhere in the bowels of his Noah's Ark. We'll never see our parents again.*

An eerie stillness filled the garage. Jo-Jo had already stumbled down four stairs to the bottom level, while the others huddled behind the wooden helm, just out of sight from the back garage window. Everyone's eyes were squeezed shut. They didn't want to see their fates. They held their breaths. No further voice of Mr. Gubitosi came forth. What happened next was hardly what they expected.

"Profetta, I'll have you arrested for trespassing, … you no good, decrepit freak. Get off my property before I have your neck broken."

The "escapees" could not believe their ears.

"Gubitosi, I know what you're doing in your garage. You're a crook and a criminal. You won't get away with it, if I have anything to do with it."

The boys were petrified. Down below, Jo-Jo's hard landing on the lower deck had disturbed a throw rug that looked more like one of his mother's soiled moppeens than a floor covering. It seemed to hide a trap door that led even further below into the vessel's bow. By his fingertips, he managed to lift the wooden hatch up, revealing a dirt floor nearly five feet below. He jumped feet first. He could barely see. But before investigating further, he reached back up to the deck and positioned the trap door and rug into place the best he could. Meanwhile, outside the garage, mayhem was erupting. Now in total darkness, he burrowed himself into a corner of the mysterious cavity, surprised to feel fresh soil under his feet, now paralyzing him as much as the argument going on outside.

Outside, two adult voices traded vicious insults with threats of bodily harm. And what Jo-Jo had already figured out, gradually dawned on the other four boys; the first voice that had screamed at them was not Mr. Gubitosi, but his next-door neighbor to whom he never spoke. Apparently, Mr. Profetta, who was known to hate kids as well as all other living creatures except cats, saw their scramble through his overgrown back yard jungle to the garage. When he shouted to his common law wife that he was going to chase down the intruders, he must have gotten Gubitosi's attention, as their kitchens were only separated by less than fifteen feet of gravel and dirt driveway. Profetta got to the back of the garage just seconds before Gubitosi, and then the battle began.

No one was stranger in the neighborhood of Belmont and Smallwood Avenues than the Profettas. "Common law" marriage was the label all the area parents tagged on the old man's relationship with his female companion. With Roman Catholics dominating the local citizenry, the Profettas were a shunned couple few knew or cared for. With stringy white hair, crooked nose, darkened eyes, elongated jaw, dimpled chin, hump back, and black shawl from head to ankles, the "wife" seemed akin to a cauldron-stirring witch, whose specialty was boiled cat. Old man Profetta fared no better. His limp soiled gray fedora and black overcoat were worn twelve months a year. Plus, he had dirty farmer blue jeans and paratrooper boots that looked like the shoes of Frankenstein. "Stay away from the Profettas," was parents'command to all the neighborhood children. The only positive about the enigmatic couple were the blackberry trees which had invaded their property over the years, covering it from anyone's clear view, but providing area children with the challenge of retrieving the juicy fruit in the face of possible abduction, shooting, decapitation, … or fate of more significant bodily harm.

The confrontation raged on.

"Gubitosi, I'll see you behind bars, … you guinea grease ball."

"Oh yea, you'll never see the light of day, Profetta, and nobody's gonna miss ya. Now get off my property, or I'll get ya killed, you stinkin' excuse for humanity."

"Gubitosi, my ol' lady and me know the whole thing, you thief," countered Profetta. "You're a lie, Gubitosi. You're lower than anything I could ever be."

The four boys peered through an opening in the canvas, expecting fisticuffs any moment with the two crazed men now nose to nose. With the final insult, Gary Gubitosi shoved the old man off his property, just missing with a kick to the back of his knees. Profetta stumbled, but quickly stormed back into the overgrowth, onto his back porch, surrounded by broken screens barely hanging upright. Gubitosi offered up some final curses and insults, and then stood glaring at the Profetta house, both hands tightly clasping his hips.

Gerald was shaking as he recited the "Hail Mary". Roger was still holding his breath. Davey had his hand over Harold's mouth so he wouldn't cry. Moonlight exposed Gubitosi's image so that Davey could see him through the frayed canvas, draped only two feet from the garage window. Belleville's answer to Noah glanced back at his building. The door was still locked. He had no reason to believe anything inside had been disturbed. He felt triumphant. His property's privacy had been protected. Yet, as he began to walk back to his home, Gubitosi stopped to stare towards his nosey neighbor's. With his beer belly overlapping a frayed plastic belt, and just about to pop one more button on the gravy and ink stained tan work shirt he never seemed to wash, Gubitosi spit into the surrounding unkempt bushes.

With silence having returned, none of the boys dared make a sound. The game of "Stalag 17" was the furthest thought from their minds. It had to be after 11 PM, and not one of the "German guards" had been seen or heard. The fact of the matter was that the older boys had witnessed Gubitosi and Profetta's entire unruly encounter that convinced them to look elsewhere. The locked garage, totally darkened, could never be a sanctuary for the younger five. Gary's boat meant there never would have been enough room to hide anyway.

Deep within the damp hole he'd landed himself in, Jo-Jo sat with his knees tight against his chest, both arms grasping his legs to keep warm. The boys on the top deck had no idea he had found another "deck" on the boat.

Wet dirt on Jo-Jo's backside chilled his body, so he squirmed to get more comfortable, which triggered a sharp pain at the top of his right thigh Then he remembered the tiny battery powered flashlight his uncle had given him last summer. (Pete had dropped off a huge brown shopping bag of penknives, nail cutters, pens, and tiny lights given in barter from one of the several black families to whom he supplied chop meat.)

Jo-Jo pushed the button, and the miniature beacon lit the room up beyond his belief. What he saw would be his secret for years to come. Right before his eyes, and directly under the back of the boat, was a huge printing press like the one he'd seen at Belleville High School's print shop during his orientation last month. It was shiny and clean. There was nothing else, … just the printing press. The wooden bow of the boat could only be seen partially serving as a ceiling. There was barely enough room to stand, and as he did, Jo-Jo had a flashback to the day that Rosa Gubitosi gave his mother a counterfeit twenty. Thoughts about the indictments, Paulie's death, Al and Henry dying in the motorcycle accident, and Mr. Profetta's threats to Gubitosi sent blood rushing to Jo-Jo's head. He shuffled to the northeast corner of the hole and leaned against its dirt wall to get another look at the machine. Still not knowing what to do, he sat down again, and as he braced his butt with his left hand, his fingers slipped inexplicably through the loose moist black earth. Something was there—a slick material that moved with his touch. Jo-Jo shone down his pocket flashlight to discover a neatly wrapped package no bigger than his palm, its brown paper covering secured by scotch tape. Jo-Jo caressed it, like it was a treasure. He examined it with the curiosity of a younger child. He opened it quickly, and his spine shivered at the thought of a wad of twenty-dollar bills, as fresh as the soil in which they had been hidden.

"Allllie, alllie, in free. Gaaames over. You squirts winnn. Shaaakes and doooggs. But, ya gooottta find us this weeeeek." Frank, Eric, Bob, Jackie, and Jimmy seemed to be announcing the end of Stalag 17 from the back of the Thatcher home.

Davey was not so sure. It could be a "German officers' trick". "Shusssh, guys. No one says a word. All we have to do is win the game, and then get caught by Crazy Gubitosi." Roger, Gerald, and Harold nodded agreement. Davey continued, "Here's the plan. Gerald, you go out the back window and open the lock with my knife. I'll tell you when. I'll open the door, and each of you quietly take a couple steps, then sprint to the Gretto garage. I'll be the last out, so make it quick and quiet. If I get caught, I'll find each of you and give you my own German haircut."

After hearing the end-of-game signal, Jo-Jo pulled himself out of the dirt hole and was cleaning himself off on the deck just below where his friends were anxiously awaiting their run to freedom. His discovered treasure was secure in his back right pocket.

"Jo-Jo, did you hear the instructions?" whispered Davey. "You'll be the last just before me."

Jo-Jo just nodded.

As it turned out, all five made the close to thirty-yard run to the Gretto's safely, but breathless.

Mind racing, Jo-Jo sucked air, and said nothing.

"Davey, next time we play this game, you stay on the other team's side," panted Gerald.

"At least I don't have to steal money from my father to buy those big babies a soda," said Roger, huffing and puffing from the effects of too many cigarettes.

"Harold, what'a ya think?" asked Davey, looking for some friendly support. "At least we get a shake and dog from my cheap brother and his friends.

"Super duper," sighed Harold, usually intimidated by Davey.

"Jo-Jo?" said Davey, seeking any crumb of approval about his leadership.

Sitting on his haunches, Jo-Jo looked up at the older boy. "Well, we all learned a lot tonight."

Then each began making his way back home. The older crew had already ended the night and was at their destinations, after Jackie had been unable to coax any takers for a ride to Rutt's Hut for a late night "weller" (a well-done, grease-filled pork hot dog).

When Jo-Jo arrived in his back yard, it was nearly 11:30. Fortunately Frank had alerted Rocky about their evening's events and held off his father from calling Jo-Jo to get home ASAP.

Jo-Jo lay down in the patio hammock beneath the kitchen windows and stared momentarily at the cloudless sky. Then he closed his eyes and "saw" the image of Rosemarie Masino. The lyrics of "Oh, Rose Marie", from earlier in the evening, haunted his brain.

Rosemarie was as vivid as if she really were standing over him, … her jet-black hair bangs hanging gently above her dark eyebrows. She was definitely an adolescent version of Betty Page, the fifties pinup hanging all over the back wall at the Shell Station's mechanic's pit where the late Henry Davidson had carefully taped her pictures. While an eighth grader, Rosemarie was too mature for her own good, and Jo-Jo knew that his ex could never be right for him. But devilishly fueled by the drive-in rumors, he could not get her to disappear until he imagined Father Francis at Saint Peter's Church. *Yes,* Jo-Jo thought, *I'll think about Father Francis standing next to me.* The old priest appeared. *It worked.* Rosemarie's image finally left, only to be replaced totally by the buxom Betty Page. *Oh, God, not her! This time a "Hail Mary". That'll do it.* It didn't work. *A prayer to the Sacred Heart of Jesus?* That failed. Betty Page was about to lean over to kiss him. *Oh God, I can't get rid of her. Maybe a Baptist prayer from Queenie and Nora?* he thought. "Satan, be ye hence!" Jo-Jo blurted out. *Nope, that didn't do the job either.* Then he thought of his brother's advice to always ask for Jesus' assistance when in trouble. "Jesus, help me, … please!" Jo-Jo closed his eyes, and then slowly opened them, but only half hoping Miss Page had finally returned to the glossy picture on the gas station wall. *Whew, she's finally gone,* thought Jo-Jo. *Man, this religion thing is getting pretty confusing, too!*

Jo-Jo wondered how Martin Peltz handles these temptations. The only Jew in Jo-Jo's eighth grade class, and a weekly attendee at Hebrew School, Peltz seemed to be mature about the opposite sex, never talking about girls, let alone "impure thoughts". *Well, for now at least, it seems as long as Jesus comes to the rescue, I know who to call on. If He ever fails me though, I'll just call Peltz.*

Even though just delivered from an onslaught of visions of the birds and the bees in heat, Jo-Jo's thinking process still would not slow down. It now switched to Gubitosi, Profetta, and the dark cavity under the oversized boat that hid the machinery behind the biggest counterfeit scheme to hit Essex County in years? Just a few hours ago, it was only football and the anticipation of a great summer. Girls were becoming a bigger deal in his life, but now with all the other stuff, it was becoming too much for Jo-Jo. He wanted to have another wonderful summer, just like all those since he could remember. *Yea, no sleepover vacation again this year; we still can't afford it. But what about bicycles, baseball, softball, buck-buck, trips to Branch Brook Park with peanut and jelly sandwiches, off to the lake with Uncle Jimmy and Aunt Pinkie, hot fudge sundaes at Joe Stein's Candy Store, followed by Wise Potato Chips in front of a great Twilight Zone, or Paladin, or Gunsmoke, ... even the Ed Sullivan Show? Would that ever be the same? Why do I have a stomachache? Is it a stomachache? The feeling goes deeper. God, why do things have to change?*

On this last Sunday in June 1959, the final summer of childhood innocence in Jo-Jo's life had already ended. His eyes closed as he inhaled lilac scent gracefully passing over him, a sweet reminder of his mother's gardening diligence. A trace of purity touched his soul, ... a flower sharing its gift. The discomfort had departed. A measure of God's perfect creation was the antidote. But then, a raindrop interrupted Jo-Jo's childlike yearning to perpetuate the perfumed moment. He never remembered it raining on Sunday nights in the summer before.

Two weeks later on a Saturday, the entire neighborhood was awakened early by police cars and two ambulances surrounding the Profetta house. Its two inhabitants were found hanged. The deadly odor that week had become intolerable to passersby. Later, the final police report stated it was a double suicide.

It seemed that Jo-Jo could never capture that lilac scent in his backyard again.

CHAPTER 21

"WILDWOOD DAYS"

The summer of '59 was hot and humid in northern New Jersey. Frank was getting into the best football shape of his life, not playing summer baseball for the first time since he was nine. Shock over the double suicide at the Profetta house was still high. Its effect on Jo-Jo was profound, having witnessed the clash between the old man and Gary Gubitosi, but also finding the stack of twenties. On the other hand, the thirteen year old still had not decided what to do with his evidence that was now snugly nestled between his underwear and the 1959 edition of *Street and Smith's College Football Magazine*. To make sure his older brother did not go fishing for the college football predictions bible, Jo-Jo bought him his own copy. He had still not yet decided what to do with the stash, and had not even asked for prayerful guidance. In fact, he seemed paralyzed by the whole set of circumstances.

Surprisingly, that summer Marietta seemed to be forgetting about the counterfeit situation. Not only had Pete dodged his name being on the suspects' list, but she also could not be more grateful that Frank's education at Cornell was being covered totally by scholarship, financial aid, and a part-time job. And, if he needed extra, her brother assured her Sneaks Babula had given the OK to tap into his "gift". The pressure was off, at least for now. She seemed to seize on any bit of good news around the household, and give it life far beyond its worth. Frank and Maria's impending visit to the Giardina relatives at the Jersey Shore was an example.

On this morning of vacation planning, Rocky was already at work, Donna still sleeping, and Marietta had just arrived home from her graveyard shift. Jo-Jo joined her and his brother at the kitchen table.

"Frankie, when does Maria want to take you down to Wildwood?" asked his mother.

"Oh, Ma, I forgot to tell you. It'll be next weekend, and she said her mother and father want me to invite Jo-Jo and one of his friends to stay over, too."

"Did you tell your brother yet?" asked Marietta with a sly smile, as Jo-Jo's eyes instantly bulged with delight. Marietta felt that, too. This would give Jo-Jo his first time on vacation for more than a one-day trip, as well as take pressure off her and Rocky to supply their own version of a mini-holiday.

No longer waiting for his brother's formal announcement, Jo-Jo exclaimed, "I'll come. I'll come!"

Frank was also looking forward to his first trip to one of the state's southern most resort areas. The summer phenomenon of Wildwood was often referred to on American Bandstand. Also, the Giardinas and their relatives there were not only generous people, but with so many sisters marrying brothers from the same paese, anytime they saw a potential betrothal brewing, they would do anything to solidify it, and make the relationship grow. Inviting Frank's little brother was simply part of the process.

The idea of staying at the Jersey Shore was giving Jo-Jo a feeling in his stomach that resembled his initial reaction to his first kiss with Rosemarie Masino. Was he also fantasizing about the Bandstand girls he might meet on the Wildwood boardwalk? Maybe he was looking at another first time experience which could never match its anticipation. That would not be the case for the Bonaducci boys this time.

The plan was for Frank to drive Uncle Jimmy Quinn's '56 Chevy, leaving the last Friday in July, returning Monday morning to their summertime jobs, … Maria as a playground director at Belleville's Recreation House, and Frank with the town's Public Works Department. Jo-Jo would tag along with his guest, whomever he might choose.

After Jo-Jo revealed his choice for his traveling companion, Frank asked, "Why Russell Giardella? You could ask the guys from around here like Gerald or Roger.

276

What's up with Russell?" In Frank's mind, the near-sighted paperboy had been somewhat of a paper-tossing pest over the years.

"He's like me," answered his brother.

"Oh, he'll be just like you even more when he sets his four eyes on the Philly girls on the boardwalk."

"Frankie, forget that," said Jo-Jo. "Not Russell."

"I know, Jo-Jo. But I'm curious, and so will Maria be when I tell her. After all, she knows all your buddies. I mean this kid is going to be sleeping at one of her Aunt Maggie's places. It's important."

"Well, Russell's like me," Jo-Jo repeated.

"Yes, you said that already. Be more specific, little brother."

"Well, he never stayed anywhere overnight, … just like me."

Frank was surprised. "Really, Jo-Jo? Never once?"

"Frank, they got another kid on the way! Mr. Giardella just works his head off with Wonder Bread, comes home, ties all the kids to their chairs, except Russell, kisses Mrs. Giardella, feeds his family, goes to sleep, then goes back to work. You know what?" asked Jo-Jo, without waiting for a response. "With Russell coming, it'll be Mr. Giardella who'll be delivering *The Ledger.* They don't know what the word 'vacation' means. None of the kids complain like we always do to Mommy and Daddy." Now Jo-Jo was worried Frank might not give Russell his approval.

"I know one other thing Mr. and Mrs. Giardella do do," said Frank. "They must go to mass every day." His subtle sarcasm of Catholic commitment to no birth control caught both Jo-Jo and Marietta by surprise. "You're a good man, Joseph Bonaducci," Frank relented, kissing Jo-Jo's head and squeezing his cheeks. "You have Mommy's heart and Daddy's loyalty. Russell's got a good friend."

Jo-Jo could not sleep the night before the day of the trip. Marietta had been busy making eggs, pepper, and pepperoni sandwiches on fresh Giordano hard rolls she got Pete to buy the day before. From after dinner that night to right before Uncle Nick Durso picked her up for work at 11:45 PM in Norma Desmond, Marietta dutifully prepared the feast, artfully wrapping the sandwiches in wax paper to prevent the moist flavors of butter, olive oil, onions, green peppers, and the freshest and hottest pepperoni Charlie Buccino from Silver Lake could find, dripping inside Jimmy Quinn's car. Eighteen sandwiches in total had been created, with Marietta envisioning all of Maria's cousins and other family members tasting her very wet and tantalizing Bloomfield Avenue sandwich specialties. Burning smoke from her excessive use of oil and butter so engulfed the entire house with appetizing scents that Jo-Jo quickly devoured one of the eighteen soon after his mother left for work.

Marietta had silently enjoyed the sandwich making, because it let her mind drift back to trips to Coney Island she remembered, back in the thirties, before her father died. She also appreciated the fact that Frank was getting closer to the Giardina family, who like her Bonaducci in-laws, looked for any excuse to enjoy life and be festive. She had missed that in her own childhood. She thanked God her children were surely gravitating to a lifestyle full of more hope than the worry that had filled hers.

Wildwood would be a new world for Jo-Jo and Russell. The trip took three and a half hours. It was only noon, as Frank pulled the car into the open space in front of Aunt Maggie Corino's brick porch home on Surf Avenue in the northern part of Wildwood. While it was only noon on this last Friday in July, the four eyes, four ears, and four nostrils that belonged to Jo-Jo and Russell were working overtime already. The temperature was heading for ninety according to the Philadelphia DJs who provided the radio music on the ride down.

As Frank and Maria prepared to exit the vehicle, their two thirteen-year old guests sat, almost paralyzed in the cramped back seat by the smell of sun tan lotion coming from people strolling by, … possibly a potion of baby oil and iodine, with a sweet, tropical, and fruity trace. It was a telltale sign they must be near, for their first time, the legendary, expansive … Wildwood Beach.

Jo-Jo and Russell also got their first whiff of ocean air rolling in over the boardwalk, across the hot asphalt street, and meandering through the heavily- leafed trees dotting Surf Avenue. And it was not just any ocean air in <u>their</u> minds. This came from the spray of the mighty Atlantic Ocean that they'd only read about in schoolbooks. While its foamy waves were caressing the sandy shore just a quarter of a mile away, its invisible aroma was already beckoning Jo-Jo and Russell to head quickly to the beach to behold its majesty.

The caw of seagulls had joined in titillating the imagination of the two who had never stayed overnight. These gray-headed airborne creatures were welcoming the visitors from the sweltering neighborhoods of northern New Jersey, simultaneously soliciting some delectable handouts to be spread by human fingers.

The two boys were tattooed further into the leather seats, which had moistened the backs of their Levi dungarees. Their ears were now being provoked by a familiar sound, not unlike the endless, slow-moving freight trains behind Smallwood Avenue back in Belleville, ... a clickity-clack staccato they would be able to recall for all their lives. But this metal on metal concert was without clacks; it was only the clickities ... of roller coaster cars as they labored to the zenith of their routes, about to require human screams to complete their score, officially welcoming the boys to the Jersey Shore destination. It was clearly the dominant noise of the moment, with spinning of wheels of fortune and calls of barkers only faint in the boardwalk background.

While the aroma of Mrs. Bonaducci's peppers, pepperoni, onions, and eggs was exuding from the trunk of the '56 Chevy, totally having escorted any of Jimmy Quinn's favorite pine smell away by the Perth Amboy Bridge, even those flavorful temptations had met their true match. A final scented tidal wave of banquet table proportions overwhelmed Russell and Jo-Jo in the form of boardwalk popcorn, French fries, pizza, and sausage, now making their own bid to capture the smelling pleasure of the two teens. Indeed, while it was only twelve noon at the Jersey Shore, the sights, sounds, and smells of Wildwood at its best had already seduced both infant travelers!

Maria's Aunt Margaret was the oldest of her dad's four brothers and three sisters. Known to all from the Big Tree and Avondale sections of Nutley and Belleville as "Maggie", she had followed her husband, Armando Corino, to Wildwood after he was discharged from the Army. She and her sisters had watched their father, Ernesto Giardina, build a modest excavation company with her younger brothers. Originally when she relocated to Wildwood to buy a small ten-unit motel, many thought it would have been Maggie as the one who should have succeeded her shrewd, hardworking father as head of the family's profitable dirt moving enterprise. Her brothers would also have agreed.

As much a good businesswoman as she might be, Maggie was even more well known for her warm hospitality, twenty-four hour kitchen, and her drive to enjoy each, and everyday, as a gift from God. She had sported broad shoulders and a tiny waist as the bride of her husband from the Nutley side of King Street. Cocoa brown hair, contrasted well with olive skin, stemming from her family roots in Calabria. A tiny bump at the top of her nose that made her, her mother's daughter, only accentuated the warmth and childlike faith that projected out of her closely set brown eyes. The years in Wildwood, helping Armand lug mattresses and dressers up and down motel stairs, not only aged her, but also strained her back into a slight right tilt. Always sampling her own cooking, and never allowing leftovers to go uneaten, her short stature gave her body a sturdy look. Her perpetually worn apron reminded everyone that glamour was not her style, but rather hard work and commitment to her family. Naturally, her motel business was a success and destined to grow in the future. Two daughters and two sons worshiped the ground Maggie walked on.

"Maria, Maria, my brother's daughter. Come, come." Maggie, reached to hug her neice as she walked up the front steps. "And I finally get the football star to visit us. Frank Bonaducci!" She kissed and hugged him as if she had known Frank since childhood. "And these two must be our special guests."

With her arms opened, Maggie expected hugs from Jo-Jo and Russell. The boys did not hesitate. After all, Maria's aunt was the reason they were on their first overnight vacation.

Unloading the luggage on the porch, it was impossible for the guests not to see the ferris wheel, roller coaster, and countless food and game stands that dominated the nearby boardwalk. "Mrs. Corino, my mom asked me to give you this," said Frank, "… as a thanks for having us all down this weekend."

Ushering them all into her kitchen, Maggie's two boys took the luggage around the corner to the Wellington Apartments where their male guests would be sleeping, while her daughters set the table for coffee and cake. As Maggie sat down and slowly opened the daintily wrapped package, her eyes lit up. "Oh my, oh my, … the portrait of the 'Sacred Heart of Jesus'. So thoughtful; our blessed Jesus. Thanks to you and your mother, Frankie." Maggie hugged the framed picture and turned again to her niece's boyfriend. "Frank, your mother's Marietta, right?" He had met Maggie on several occasions at the assortment of wakes and Communion, Confirmation, Marriage and Baptism celebrations that sometimes seem to dominate the every social hour of a large Italian American family. But she had never sat down to speak with him. "You know, I know her. You know how?"

Frank shook his head. "Nope."

Jo-Jo was quiet as a church mouse. Maria also tuned in. All Russell was thinking about was devouring the beckoning crumb cake.

"You have an Aunt Bella," Maggie continued. "She and I, and a bunch of girls, used to get together to go out dancin' Saturday nights, ... down the First Ward of Newark, before the War. We were all single. Jesus, Mary, and Joseph, ... when we walked into the room, all eyes would go to Bella, ...such a beauty. And she would tell us all about her family, especially her brothers fighting overseas, and how one of them was gonna marry this beautiful girl from Bloomfield Avenue. I mean we weren't that close, because there was so many of us. But who could forget Bella, ... or your mother's name, ... 'Marietta'? I mentioned it to my brother, Ang, when he told me about Frankie. But you know your father, Maria ... always forgets. So, I do know the Bonaducci family a little bit. So, Frankie, give your mother a kiss for me, and make sure she knows to come down and visit."

"Gee, I didn't know," was all Frank could say.

As always, Maggie was in motion, not only talking with her hands in between words, but also helping her daughters set the table and cut the cake, all at the same time. She continued. "And you know what? Your Aunt Bella comes down every time Louie Prima shows up at the Riptide. She's always with her husband and a couple of other couples. Well, guess who's in Wildwood this weekend? Mr. Prima! So, maybe Bella will show up."

Small world, thought Frank.

Maggie's sons returned to tell Frank that he and the boys were all set up in the small rooming house around the corner. Over the last twelve years, Maggie and her husband had made the Sonata Suites into such a favorite motel for the goomods and goombods from Newark, Belleville, Lyndhurst, and Nutley that they had just acquired the Wellington as their second property. Every time she had vacancies, Maggie would make the call north to invite whoever could make it down. This weekend most of her nieces and nephews were coming to town to cash in on her generosity, as, of course, there would be no charge. On the other hand, all guests were required to be at Maggie's crowded home on Friday nights for fresh fish and "olyule" with the "allige"; then again on Sunday afternoon, ... after the beach, for macaronis with the red gravy, sausage, meatballs, and pork. No one would ever dishonor this commandment.

That Friday the sun could not have been hotter and the Atlantic Ocean more refreshing for the visitors from Belleville. Jo-Jo could not believe the vastness of the Wildwood Beach, compared to the eroding shorelines at Sandy Hook, Long Branch, Asbury Park, and Belmar, ... locations just within the "daytrip" limits of his father's ailing '49 Chevy. Russell's freedom from his seven other brothers and sisters seemed to be revealing a different side to the underweight and nervous thirteen year old. Finally he had time for himself, so he didn't know what to do first; just sit in the sand, stare at the blue-green ocean water, or wait for someone to say he had to return home to deliver *The Ledger* and strap all his brothers and sisters in for dinner. Frank was playing touch football on the beach with Maria's other cousins, down for the week with their parents, several of whom had played freshman ball at Belleville High last year, and were relishing tangling with the college-bound running back.

Maria, who was strolling the beach with Maggie's daughters, Judy and Barbara, stopped in amazement at seeing a statuesque woman with deeply suntanned bronze body and gigantic floppy white hat with red ribbon. Her stylish black bathing suit accentuated every natural curve the Good Lord had bestowed on her. Aunt Maggie really was prophetic. Maria announced to her cousins, "God, it's Frank's Aunt Bella. She's here, just like your mother predicted."

Standing in the middle of a circle of beach chairs, full of others her age, Bella was being her normal, expressive center of attraction. As Maria surveyed Bella's audience, there were five other ladies and two men. Uncle Emil Bruno was not there.

"Aunt Bella, it's me, Maria Giardina!"

Bella reacted, "Mother Mary, it's my handsome nephew's beautiful girlfriend! Maria, come, … come meet my friends." And noticing Maria's cousins, she added, "And who are these two Italian beauties?"

Maria made introductions, and then Bella went around the circle. "Darlings, I want you to meet my nephew's future wife, … we hope. You all know Frank, Rocky's kid. Well, this is his girlfriend, Maria, and her two cousins." Bella turned back to the three teenagers. "Now meet my friends." After announcing each woman in her entourage, she focused on the "special" guests. "And now, these handsome gentlemen, … my dashing cousin, Carmine Bonaducci from Brooklyn, and his associate, an old friend, … and 'enemy' of all of us girls, …Benny Badalamenti from New York, too."

Every one in Bella's circle laughed, except the three teens. *What did Aunt Bella's "enemy" label on Mr. Badalamenti mean?* Maria wondered. She was biting her lip, figuring out what she would say to Frank. Indeed, she knew he would love seeing his Aunt Bella, and even the chance to talk to his second cousin, Carmine. But after Frank's winter encounter with Badalamenti on the rescue mission to find

Gino, and now his being on the list of counterfeit indictees, perhaps her boyfriend would rather stay clear of him this particular weekend.

Carmine Bonaducci was just as gracious as all the male Bonaduccis that Maria had met. Slowly raising his sculptured body from the chair, his furry chest reminded her of Frank's father, although his full head of black hair was more like her boyfriend's than Rocky's receding hairline. He reached for her right hand. "My dear, you are as beautiful as your intended father-in-law describes you. And with my young cousin Frank, you make a dashing couple." He then slowly turned towards Judy and Barbara. "I am pleased also to meet your acquaintances."

By now, Badalamenti was on his feet, and in just the manner Maria expected, greeted them. "Youse kids from the Lake?"

"No, Mr. Badalamenti," answered Maria. "We are not from the Silver Lake section of Belleville. I'm from King Street on the Belleville-Nutley line, and my cousins are from here in Wildwood."

"Great," said Badalamenti, now with disinterest. Not only were the girls too young for Bad Boy, but the relationship to the Bonaduccis put them totally off limits.

Maria shared chitchat with Bella about their plans for the weekend, as well as the coincidental mentioning of her name by Aunt Maggie.

Addressing all three girls, Bella affectionately recalled her dancing days. "Ladies, those were so special," she reflected. "And your mother, Margaret, so beautiful. I remember she was engaged to your dad, so she didn't dance too much. But guys loved her. Could she talk about any thing? No wonder she and your father are so successful down here. You know, I see her once in a while at Louie Prima shows. Tell her we're going tomorrow night."

Later that afternoon, Maria told Frank about the chance meeting. His father's cousin's presence peaked his interest. But with Badalamenti in tow, Frank had a sick feeling in his stomach.

At dinner that night, Aunt Maggie only slightly helped Frank put his concerns at ease, because after raving about glamorous Aunt Bella, her daughters mentioned talking to a gentlemanly ... "Mr. Bonaducci"! After the fresh fish feast, which had been supplied by Armand from his day's fishing on Thursday, the house full of relatives and guests scattered to the front porch and eventually to the boardwalk.

Maggie insisted on a little anisette for everyone to cut the fat and oil of the meal. Even Jo-Jo and Russell had their own tiny shot glasses, which made them feel they'd died and gone to heaven. They looked at Maggie in disbelief as she poured. "You're both on vacation. I'll talk to your parents." The boys smiled at each other as if they had just gotten away with the crime of the century.

As the girls did the dishes, Maggie sat in her big rocker next to Frank on the porch. A cool sea breeze began to pick up. "So, Frank, Carmine Bonaducci is your father's cousin?"

"Yes."

"You know, I like him very much," Maggie continued. "I know him from Chamber of Commerce meetings this winter. He's quite a gentleman, and an even better businessman."

"You know him that well?"

"Well, he's a big player, and we have mostly small operators down here. He stands out. Bought a couple of motels, he tells me, after bailing out of Cuba. Had a chance to go to Vegas, but wanted to get involved in the family market down here. He's done a beautiful job with the Beachcomber, the Chandelier, and the Casa Mia. You know, he loves the music business, too. And with all of the groups and individual talent that comes down here, he's going to parlay that, too."

"Honestly, Aunt Maggie, I've met him only a couple of times. He seems a great guy, but my father worries he's mixed in with the wrong people sometimes, and could embarrass the family name if he doesn't watch out."

"I don't know anything about wrong people, but right now, he's putting money into Wildwood, and he's helping our cause. We have a great history here, and want the future to be even better." Maggie was all business. Judgments came later. Then she added, "But listen, Frank. What somebody else does should not affect your life. Just because you have the same last name doesn't mean your fortunes depend on anyone else's behavior."

Almost in disbelief of Maggie's lucid advice, Frank nodded in agreement. "I think my father gets bothered by it more than anyone."

"My brother Ang tells me what a good man your father is. Listen, you make sure he visits Aunt Maggie this summer, and we'll sit." Maggie smiled, waiting for Frank's reaction. He smiled back.

In the next half hour, the forty-four year old Maggie Corino, the grammar school graduate, educated Frank on how she and her husband came to Wildwood with little money, but lots of dreams and courage to take risk. Now the resort town was growing along with her business. When she originally arrived from Belleville, Wildwood was quiet. She fondly recalled Vaughn Monroe and Woody Herman at the Hunt family's Starlight Ballroom. Then she paused for a time that seemed interminable for Frank, given Maggie's penchant to fill every moment in life either with a generous deed or a meaningful flow of words. Continuing, she said, "But you know what, Frank? That's changed. Rock 'n' roll has become more profitable, so the acts are changing. Me and Uncle Armand don't mind, as long as the Jersey and Philly kids don't go crazy. Yea, it's changing. And the only constant in life is … change."

"But it's still amazing how all of the old big names have come through Wildwood." Frank was enjoying this time with his girlfriend's aunt, and her appreciation of music and the entertainment business.

"Yes, Frank, the big bands and the old big names still come through. Just up the street, ya know, is where the Manor Supper Club used to be. I'm going back now. Tony Bennett, The 4 Aces, Pat Boone, Peggy Lee, Rosemary Clooney, and even Ella Fitzgerald would always be showing up. They still appear from time to time, … especially Boone. And as your Aunt Bella knows, Louie Prima and Keely Smith are at the Riptide this weekend; Julie LaRosa's at the Club Avalon. Then the rock 'n' rollers, … Bill Haley and the Comets are at the Starlight, and this Chubby Checker guy, at the Hofbrau House. Tommie, my younger brother, has been bringing down this kid, Marty DeRose from Newark, to try out in the different clubs. My Lord, he sings all the Italian stuff. Yes, we know all the owners. They get us good seats. It's still a small town. I have to know which stars are here so I can tell my guests." Maggie loved the vitality of her Wildwood. It was a long way from digging foundations in Belleville and Nutley.

"Have Dion and the Belmonts been through, Aunt Maggie?"

"Don't think so, but as I said, rock 'n' roll dominates now, all because of American Bandstand. That's why your cousin is putting his money here. Even though it's a short season, there's money in real estate and music, and he sees it."

Another person's perception of Carmine Bonaducci was far from that of Frank's father. "Very interesting," was his reaction.

"Looking at it honestly though, Frank, it's all timing." Maggie's enthusiasm level was changing. "It all started quietly in the late forties and early fifties. Then the high point had to be when the American Bandstand people came in. They started record hops at the Starlight back in '56 with this DJ who later got in trouble back in Philly. Then Dick Clark shows up the following summer, … and the rest is history."

"What do you mean?"

"I'll never forget it. On August 5th that year, they somehow broadcast the record hop that had now been named American Bandstand. I mean Dick Clark stands up and says, 'Live on ABC-TV, it's American Bandstand from the Starlight Ballroom in Wildwood, New Jersey.' Wow, it made us all proud. Uncle Armand and I figured we had made it to the right place at the right time."

Maggie stared at the boardwalk, alive with music and lights as the crowds passed right in front of her house.

"Gee, Aunt Maggie, good foresight, huh?

"Well, yes, Frank, but I think it's changing again."

"Why?"

"The fifties is an era that's ending. That Buddy Holly crash? Took the heart out of this rock 'n' roll thing."

"But Aunt Maggie, as much as that affected all of us kids, you've been telling me how it's a good time in Wildwood."

"It is now, Frank, but things change. Yea, things are always changing. The real test of whether Uncle Armand and I can really run a business is if these crowds go elsewhere."

"So what about my cousin, Carmine? You said he has an eye for big business opportunities."

"He does. That's why he's interested in music," said Maggie, not backing off of her admiration for the Brooklyn Bonaducci.

"But, you said there may be a change going on. So won't he get hurt, too?"

"You get into real estate for the long haul. You need staying power, and he has it. As far as the music thing, if he gets involved, it just won't be here. Music is universal."

"Got it, Aunt Maggie."

"Frank, you've got a good head on your shoulders. Plus my sister-in-law, Santina, tells me you're a good boy. But, don't judge other men. Jesus didn't. Look for the best in them. And if you have faith in God, take some risks like your cousin, Carmine. Look at what he does. Learn something. You don't have to like it all. Just eat the meat, … and spit out the bones." Maggie looked directly at him. "Capice?" (understand)

For Frank, Maria, Jo-Jo and Russell, the weekend proceeded at breakneck speed. The weather was totally cooperative, so the grateful, younger vacationers had to deal with a sunburn problem by Saturday night. It seemed a small price to pay.

That night it seemed all of North Newark, Belleville, and Nutley was on the boardwalk. Mickey Geltrudi and a contingent of Nutley footballers were doing their strut up and down the boards, until they saw Frank. Then, as if seeing a righteous prince who had given them glory at his own expense, they slowed up and crossed over in front of the passing tram to shake his hand and talk about football and the girls from Philly. Then noticing Maria at his side, they changed the subject back to football only. Jo-Jo and Russell were impressed and proud of the respect the Maroon Raiders gave Frank.

Buying tickets on Hunt's Pier, Frank was startled by a tap on the back. Hunched over slightly to minimize the weight on his left hip was Vinnie Giampietro, Belleville's faithful bus driver and one of the surprise names amongst the counterfeit indictees.

Nonetheless, Frank was pleased. "Vinnie, long time no see, Cuz."

"Miss ya, man," said Vinnie with a hug and eyes filled with tears.

The crippled, overweight ex-Bellboy's liquored breath caught Frank by surprise, and triggered an obligation to help in some way. "Vin, what are you upset about?" Maria watched her boyfriend's compassion as his younger brother and Russell were already off to the rides. Frank continued, "It's the indictment thing, right?"

"Frankie, I'm sick about it. If my parents were alive, they'd be shattered."

Then Frank noticed a small group lingering in the shadows behind the ticket booth. Each appeared to have had too much to drink as well, being even more loud and boisterous than the emotional Vinnie. He saw "Crazy Louie" Montana who'd also been indicted. It was the worst of the Bloomfield Avenue crowd … young, brash, violent, and out of control.

Frank pulled Vinnie aside. "What are you doing with those hoods, Cuz? You're better than that."

"Frankie, they're on my annual fishin' trip. Ya know, I sponsor it, and some of the boys from the North Ward and Bloomfield Avenue show up. I can't stop 'em. I mean I also got Father Giambalvo from St. Francis wit me, too. It's a mixed crowd." Then, adding soberly, "And we caught a lot of fish today, too."

"All right, Vin. But go have one of those Philadelphia cheese steaks or something to get rid of your booze breath. You know, Cuz, get some onions going for yourself in case you meet some New Jersey State Police down here, and they start asking questions."

"Hey, Frankie. I ain't never done anything wrong. Yea, some of the guys get on my bus and hand me these big bills over the months. I cash 'em. But what was I supposed to do. How'd I know they were bad?"

Frank stared into the bus driver's sad eyes and cupped his fat face in his hands. "Listen, my mother and I have been praying for you, Craigie Francello, Two Tones, Greenie, Costello from the candy store, and the rest of the good guys. I mean Henry Davidson and Matte are already dead, Lord rest their souls. Listen to your attorneys and be honest. It'll work out."

They embraced one more time, and parted; the loud screams of amusement ride customers, the sounds of the carnival music, and the sizzling of a nearby sausage and peppers stand seemingly absorbing all the emotion of the chance encounter into the vacuum of life on Wildwood's boardwalk.

Frankie turned to Maria. "He needs big help."

She nodded agreement.

After church on Sunday morning, Aunt Maggie's house was once again overflowing with people. Judy and Barbara were frying dozens of eggs, bacon was sizzling in the frying pan, and the aroma of freshly percolated coffee was drifting out the front door and beckoning to all within range to enter into the Corino abode. Between bites of the breakfast buffet, Russell and Jo-Jo glanced at each other. Their looks reflected that there was only one day left before the ride home, early Monday morning, to avoid the weekend traffic chaos.

Aunt Maggie called out to Frank who was on the porch with her sons, Nick and Bobby. "Hey, I saw your Aunt Bella last night."

That news sent Frank into the house to find a seat at the kitchen table, overflowing with breakfast buns, Italian bread, and fruit.

"Yes, she's as glamorous as ever. And your Uncle Emil will be down tonight to spend a few days off from his pharmacy job."

"You saw her at the Louie Prima thing?" Frank asked.

"Bella was the star. Somehow, she got on stage and took over for Keely Smith. They all had a good time, … like Louie and Keely knew her. And your cousin Carmine was there with his business associates taking all kinds of pictures. Good clean fun."

"No kidding," marveled Frank.

Then, Maggie sat next to Frank, speaking in a lower tone so only he could hear. And she told him how she had spoken with Carmine Bonaducci and learned how he was putting up all of these rock 'n' roll stars with their managers and agents in his motels … for free; how this was part of his business arrangement with them.

As she spoke, Frank was figuring Badalamenti had to be present because he was probably one of Carmine's "associates". Then he flashed to the "backstage Johnnies'" night in Brooklyn, and how Bad Boy was right in the middle of the activities.

That's it, thought Frank to himself. *Cousin Carmine must be deep into the pockets of some of these stars and their managers. God knows he's in with the disc jockeys, too.* Legal or not, Frank knew his cousin was not getting involved just for the fun of it. *Could Carmine be the mastermind in this Essex County counterfeit thing as well, with Badalamenti his main man in Newark?*

Frank started to eat his eggs and said nothing. Aunt Maggie headed back to the stove where her gravy for dinner that night was already simmering. Maria stood next to her as she stirred the pot and barked directions for Judy to get some "basinigole" (basil).

"Aunt Maggie, I must ask this question," said Maria. "What is the difference between sauce and gravy?"

"Maria, I get that question all the time, especially from my Amedigan friends down here," said Maggie, taking a deep breath as if to recite the definition for the millionth time. She turned around to everyone in her crowded kitchen. "All right. The Amedigans have brown gravy, but the Italians have red sauce. The Amedigans never call it 'brown sauce', right? Now, the Italian gravy has the juices of the meats in it, … the pork necks, sausage, meatball, etc. It'll have the onions, garlic, basil, and that stuff, too, but the thing is the taste of the meat. Now, the sauce is just the tomato sauce, onions, garlic and such, and no meat, ... but we Italians call everything … gravy."

The whole room had been listening—her children, cousins from Belleville and Nutley, her husband, and some local friends who'd stopped by for coffee and … As they all waited further explanation, Maggie had already returned to her stove to test her concoction. She sensed the baffled silence, and turned around again. "That's it. We call it all gravy. We start with the sauce, but regardless, once it goes on the macaroni, it's gravy, whether it's got the meat in it, … or not."

The subject was closed. Maria smiled and hugged her aunt.

On their short walk back from the beach late that afternoon, Jo-Jo asked Russell, "What do you think, Russell?" Both were shuffling along in wet and sand-caked black sneakers, looking down at the sidewalk, just beyond the boardwalk and a short distance from Aunt Maggie's Sunday afternoon macaroni.

"Bout what?"

"Our first overnight vacation."

"Don't want to go home," said Russell, as serious as he had ever been. "I bet I could make some money down here. More than my *Ledger* route."

Jo-Jo said nothing else, but wondered what a whole week would be like in Wildwood; surely enough time to meet some Philadelphia girls. *I bet all of 'em danced on American Bandstand at least once, and they probably even met The Dell Vikings and The Belmonts.* Worst thing about the weekend was his sunburn. Running in the sand and playing touch football with some of the Nutley guys was great. *Imagine a whole summer of running in the sand. I'd get faster than Frank and Gino!*

Jo-Jo whipped his neck skyward.

"What's wrong?" asked Russell.

Jo-Jo took a deep breath. His sensitive nostrils could smell the intoxicating gravy, as it flowed out of Maggie's kitchen, past her porch, and now heading oceanward, colliding with his senses and mind. The salt sea air that had risen from the deep blue Atlantic had met its match as the two scents faced off just where the trees started on Surf Avenue. The onshore breeze was not strong enough to overcome the sausage, pork, and meatball essence of the gravy that had escaped the black pot sitting on Maggie's stove, … a huge black cauldron-like pot that had simmered its first guest of gravy back in '46 on a pot belly on Saint Mary's Place in Belleville, … right on the Nutley line. The huge industrial fan rumbling on the front porch of the Wildwood house gave the red tomato potion its unfair advantage over the slight wind off the water. The clash of the ocean and the gravy was happening deep with Jo-Jo's very bosom. Russell, nursing a runny nose, was oblivious. Jo-Jo was in a trance. The Jersey Shore and Aunt Maggie's gravy stimulated his young mind to make two conclusions: Frank had found the right family to marry into, and someday Jo-Jo would take a week's vacation in Wildwood.

On the way back to northern Jersey next morning, Jo-Jo's desires were split between his dream of a high school football career like his brother's, and at least spending more overnights in Wildwood in the future. As Frank sped his uncle's Chevy closer to Essex County, the Newark exit signs affected both brothers the same way—thoughts of the trial coming up, the deaths, and how close it all had come. Jo-Jo remembered the twenties he still had. Now he knew what to do with them.

CHAPTER 22

"MAMA"

For the next several weeks, Jo-Jo and Russell could not stop talking about Wildwood. Truth was being stretched more each day, as listeners would hear of the "friendly" high school girls from all around Philly who liked younger Jersey guys. Only when Roger Bush, Gerald Gretto, or Harold Bader showed looks of disbelief in the credibility of one story or the next, would Russell and Jo-Jo change the subject. First they would stray to how Jo-Jo and Frank were on winning teams all weekend during the hours of touch football on the beach; how Russell and Jo-Jo both attended a record hop at the Starlight Ballroom, and were "only this far away" (measured by thumbs and index fingers) from touching The Dell Vikings who had made a surprise appearance that weekend; and how Maria's Aunt Maggie fed them around the clock.

This would be the last summer in Jo-Jo's life without a summer job that would ultimately rob him and his friends of ... daily bike rides to Branch Brook Park in Newark, endless softball games at "The Knoll" by the railroad tracks, meeting up with girls of the neighborhood to tease the raging teen hormones, swinging in the backyard hammock after a late afternoon thunderstorm, breathing in steamed heat rising off of the backyard driveway, as skies cleared above. Forcing these memories into the corner of his mind was Jo-Jo's imminent challenge of matching his brother's high school football exploits, the still constant visions of Rosemarie Masino's cherub-like face, shapely little body, and adult-like attitudes, ... and the boiling pot of the counterfeit indictments, with its now mounting list of people around the case prematurely dying.

293

Then there were those twenty-dollar bills hidden between pages 27 and 28 of his college football magazine. After the Wildwood trip, Jo-Jo had decided to destroy the money. He felt dirty every time he thought of the counterfeit twenties, and then sick to his stomach envisioning his innocent, sometimes naïve, mother being questioned by authorities about briefly accepting Rosa Gubitosi's "deal" to circulate one of the illegal pieces of currency into her pure life. Jo-Jo came to two conclusions: First, he and his friends should have never been in the Gubitosi "boat house" in the first place. Second, with no one else knowing of his treasure find, the twenties should just vanish.

On the last day of July, his mother was food shopping before her mid-day nap, Rocky and Frank were at work, and Donna was in the Gretto pool. It seemed the perfect moment to set the bills ablaze with one of Marietta's pack of matches, and then quickly flush the ashes down the second floor toilet. Jo-Jo immediately felt cleansed. Cheap, illegal, and quick ways to earn income were totally against the Bonaducci ethic of hard work through ethical means to succeed in life. Besides, now his mother ought to be totally insulated from the December trials of the eighteen indicted suspects. It was not that he wanted to obstruct any justice, but being so sure of the innocence of so many of the accused, he knew something else must come up to make the whole thing go away. *Anyway, how do I know if I just burned counterfeit bills? If I did anything wrong getting rid of them, I'll ask God to forgive me, even if Father Francis and the FBI won't. And, if I really got rid of real money, that wouldn't be a sin, but a real stupid thing! ... Ah, no problem.*

Just then, the phone rang. It was Aunt Bella. "Wasn't Wildwood marvelous that weekend, Jo-Jo?" she asked. "You were with Frank's future in-laws, my old girlfriends were there, Cousin Carmine and his associates, and then Uncle Emil surprised me on Sunday night. And I even spent time with Margaret Corino. Oh, did we reminisce. Now listen hard to your Aunt Bella. Always take vacations. Work hard, yes. Love your family, yes. But darling, take time to see the world and learn from other people. I know my brother and your mommy don't have lots of money yet, but you'll be going to college and be very successful some day like the rest of us. Save your money and go. Didn't you have a great time?"

"Yep."

"Now, talking about a great time, is your mother there?"

"Sleepin'."

"Well, here's my message, Joseph. Got a pencil and paper?"

"Go ahead, Aunt Bella."

"Tell her and my brother Rocky that Grandma and us have decided to have Grandpa Joe's seventy-fifth birthday in two weeks. On Sunday, after church, everybody come here. I want your mother to know her brother Pete and Mrs. Frassa are invited, too. OK?"

"Got it, Aunt Bella. I'll have her call you for details, though."

"Oh, my smart nephew, of course I have to tell her what to bring and all that. And by the way, tell my brother that cousin Carmine and his family will be there, so no Bonaduccis will be missing, except Grandpa's sisters in Argentina."

"All set, Aunt Bella. My mother'll call you." Just how memorable this future Sunday would become was well beyond Jo-Jo's expectations.

It had been sixty years since Grandpa Joe Bonaducci arrived on Ellis Island. His family did not keep the birthday celebration planning secret, so he was able to enjoy its anticipation and collaborate on the guest list. Proudly he spoke of how the family of his late brother John would all be there; four boys, two girls, and all of their children coming from Brooklyn, in a caravan of cars. In addition to the families of his own children, there'd be some of his ex-coworkers from the Edison Plant in West Orange, smoking one DeNobli stogie after another. Then old friends, not only from the First and North Wards of Newark, but also the ones from Brooklyn who ran the borough's streets back in the early 1900's, ... and who knew how Giuseppe Bonaducci had defended his businessman father in Avellino. The back of a shovel had sent an alleged perpetrator to meet his Creator quickly and prematurely, requiring young Giuseppe's disappearance to the United States at the age of fifteen. Extortion was not limited to the Black Hand in Sicily.

Grandpa Joe had not seen John's children since their mother's death a year ago. His brother passed away the year before that. It was Carmine, the oldest Brooklyn Bonaducci son, who always appreciated his Uncle Joe's regular calls of encouragement to his family. Indeed, John had followed Joe to the States to assure his survival. With hands as big as baseball gloves and arms so hairy it was hard to see skin, Giovanni (John) Bonaducci secured Joe's safety and a meal every night. Fiercely competitive and a tireless worker, John quickly established himself as a powerhouse figure on the New York docks, before eventually leveraging his reputation into the city's building trades. However, when Joe fell in love at first sight with a beautiful young lady from Calabria while visiting friends at the Saint

Lucy Church-Saint Gerard Feast in Newark, the devoted brothers were destined to part. John went on to become a feared and respected underboss on the streets of Brooklyn, while Joe earned his money as a laborer in Newark, New Jersey. Over the years at family gatherings, neither brother spoke to the other about their chosen callings.

The backyard on Oraton Parkway was decorated with balloons and signs hanging from several fig trees and grape arbors, as well as covering Grandpa Joe's precious tomato plants. The record player was on the backyard porch, and paper-covered sheets of plywood set on shaky wooden horses. Folding chairs had been delivered that morning from Megaro-Cundari Funeral Home on Roseville Avenue in Newark, and extra tables had to be put up in the driveway beside the house, after some of the neighborhood blacks accepted Aunt Bella's late invitation to join in her father's birthday celebration. Close to one hundred guests shuffled to the back of the house, as the records began to spin. The first was "Mama", ... by Connie Ferro.

This mid-August Sunday would turn out to be unbearably humid. So the men slowly shed their garments, making their undershirts targets for the red gravy delicacies that would dominate the feast. Homemade wine, supplied by practically every invited relative, was at every table. Pete Frassa was particularly proud to have convinced his mother to part with a gallon bottle. His rare display of assertiveness made Marietta happy, as it won a bet with her husband that her sad-sack brother could deliver the red nectar of the Italian saints their mother would rather have worshipped by herself. Red macaroni, and then the white with ricotta and butter, was the first dining treat, while Rocky, his brother, and each of his brother-in-laws had the charcoal burning perfectly for multiple pounds of steak, hamburgers, and hot dogs to follow. It was so hot by grilling time that all the chefs had even removed their undershirts. Wine and ice-cold beer flowing from multiple kegs contributed to the celebration spirit. Even single Aunt Josephine, the family's resident Mother Superior, did not complain. It was a day to be savored.

By the time all the Brooklyn relatives found a seat, some of the neighborhood black children had to be relegated to the back wall of the property. Bella had reminded Pete to bring Jerome Yarborough, and he was at home with the East Orange kids. With paper plates of macaroni and meat overflowing in their laps, their eyes were bigger than their stomachs. Watching the Italian-American feast, they seemed to find it unbelievable so much food and drink could be devoured so quickly, plus that Aunt Bella had even invited them and their families in the first place. Grandpa Joe had come to respect his dark-skinned neighbors for their efforts to build a respectable refuge for their families in East Orange. He marveled at their faithfulness to church and their ever-present Bibles. In his household, he was the only one who read the Good Book, often saying that learning about God's miracles made more sense than sitting in some huge cathedral and hearing what some priests had to say.

As Rocky, his brother Anthony, and brother-in-laws Caesar, Emil, Nick, and Jimmy Quinn sweat over the burning coals, the gruff sounds of Louie Prima began to fill the air. And that's all Aunts Bella, Josephine, Millie, Pinky, Mary, and their goomods from the old neighborhoods needed. More than a dozen of the girls from Down Neck, Clifton Avenue, Garside Street, Lake Street, and Seventh Street jumped up when they heard his hit song, "Angelina". Newark's version of the Rockettes took center stage on the cramped backyard's grass and began a flurry of dancing ranging from the "dadandelle" (tarantella), to the Jitterbug, to a chorus line kick, to a Mambo, … all women! No men were allowed to get into the swing of things until Louie, Keeley, and their band had finished the twelve-song album.

Sitting with her always-somber mother, Marietta refused to join in, but was unable to stop laughing and clapping as everyone sang and danced, …even the black families. The happy frenzy was at its zenith when Uncle Caesar abandoned his fellow cooks. With his towel acting as a makeshift bra and his shorts rolled up as high as he could above his black socks and black flyweights, his Milton Berle-like attempt to dance in drag took center stage. Led by Rocky of all people, all the other perspiring chefs then followed suit. Jo-Jo, Frank, Maria, and Donna could not believe their eyes. The seventy-fifth birthday had become a great excuse for everyone to forget their troubles, … and inhibitions!

Cousin Nicholas, finding his father and mother dancing in their own flying beads of sweat, looked to Maria with a straight face. "I am so glad that I'm adopted. Maria, why don't you run off to Dayton with me, because your handsome boyfriend has some of this crazy blood in him, too, you know."

Maria punched his shoulder and then hugged his arm, saying, "Who you kidding, cousin? Any minute, you'll be up there, too."

Nicholas knew she was right.

Puffing on a Cuban cigar courtesy of nephew Carmine, Grandpa Joe was tapping his feet and pounding his knee as he sat like a wealthy Italian landowner enjoying his family and workers frolicking for one day of the year.

Carmine whispered something into his uncle's ear in Italian that caused the older Bonaducci's smiling face to turn inquisitive. He gestured with his right hand as if questioning, "Why?". Then he retorted, "No, Carmine, you should save your money for better things for your own family. So much she must have cost you."

Within moments, Carmine could see Grandma Mamie motioning from the kitchen window that he had the telephone call he was expecting. He casually walked to the porch and entered the house. The message was that Connie Ferro and her entourage were now leaving her home in Belleville.

Earlier, Carmine informed Bella about his "surprise" for Grandpa Joe, so that when he gave the signal, Bella knew to drop out of the dancing. With husband Emil, she went to the front of the house, … and waited. Two cars soon pulled up. Inside was not only the young entertainer, but she was also with her mother and father, sisters, guitar and violin players, as well as some cousins to handle the record playing.

Bella returned to the yard, waited for the last of the records to stop, and then asked everyone to quiet down. "… Dear friends and family, complements of cousin Carmine and his family, and in honor of his Uncle Joe and my father, please welcome the most popular female voice in America, our own Miss Connie Ferro!"

Then Connie's mom escorted her around to meet the stunned family members, many of whom Mrs. Ferragamo knew from years gone by. As her equipment was being set up, Connie kissed Grandpa Joe's bald forehead and wished "happy birthday". After shaking Carmine's hand, she glanced toward Frank. Her cold stare, at seeing him with Maria, meant Connie would never even talk to him that day.

Even without a professional recording studio, Connie's melodious silk-like voice amazed the crowd, singing all her hits plus the Italian standards she was beginning to sell around the world. Italian American pride filled the air, marveling at what Newark and Belleville had produced.

When she finished, cries for her "Mama" filled the yard, … just as Carmine had anticipated, setting up his second surprise for the day. He had convinced Connie to sing a duet with his cousin, Bella, who was totally oblivious to what was about to happen. Carmine was confident in his cousin's musical ability; she'd sung the classic song many times and surely had the entertainment savvy to improvise. He worried more about Connie, half Bella's age, and not accustomed to such impromptu performing.

All eyes were on Carmine. "And now, friends of my Uncle Joe, Miss Connie Ferro will be joined by our own one and only, … Bella Bonaducci Bruno!"

That afternoon, Connie Ferro was a great sport. On the kitchen porch, serving as a stage, two Italian-American beauties delivered their emotional, nostalgic tribute to mothers, Italian style. One was a household name throughout the country. The other was a women's shoe salesgirl who had dreamed for years being in the spotlight professionally as a dancer, actress, and singer.

Applause for this once-in-a-lifetime performance was modest, ... because so many in the audience were crying. "Mama" always seemed to do that to Italian immigrants and their first generation family members, ... this time even more so. As congratulations were being offered, Bella and Marietta embraced. They cried in each other's arms ... for an uncomfortably long time. Their slightly excessive emotion puzzled some in the crowd, until Rocky lovingly separated them. Then everyone surrounded Connie, seeking autographs or talking to her parents and family. Both Bella and Marietta were still quiet, overwhelmed by what had just happened.

Standing together, Rocky, Jo-Jo, Frank, Maria, and cousin Nick maintained a focus on the moment shared by the two sister-in-laws, who were seemingly as different as day and night. Only Nicholas had the courage to vocalize his assessment. "Well, I almost cried, too." Never lost for words, the college-bound Nick continued. "Sure, Aunt Bella kept her beauty all these years. But my mother stills says Aunt Marietta was the most beautiful of all. Having the three kids, losing one, and working the graveyard shift didn't help. Aunt Bella couldn't have children. Plus she worked in that plushy 'Footnotes' up there in Millburn. Slightly different than the 3 AM assembly line at Tungsol's." Nicholas had his still-confused audience's full attention, so he continued. "Here's the deal. Aunt Bella was 'Bella LaStarr' when she ran away in the early forties before the war. Wanted to sing and dance. Ended up in the burlesque in Philly, ... right, Uncle Rocky?"

"Keep going, Nicholas," said Rocky, his curiosity overflowing about where his nephew was headed with this.

"Well, Grandpa Joe and Judge Liloia finally caught up with her in some theatre just over the bridge in PA. Then he made her promise she would never go into show business. He didn't raise his hand to her, as she anticipated, so she always kept her word."

"Aaannnd?" asked Frank.

"... and her dreams were quenched. You know, she really put them on the shelf. But, any time she gets a chance, she runs up on the stage and tries to do her thing, laughing all the time, but crying inside."

"What about my mother, Nick?" asked Jo-Jo.

"Look, my mother and Aunt Marietta always talk. After all, working from midnight to 7 AM every day, you get pretty close. Ever notice how your mother comes home sometimes so happy?" All four of Nick's listeners nodded. "That's when she talks to the big boss about ideas how to motivate the assembly line girls, make the factory more productive; you know, better working conditions and everything. The guy is so impressed that he tells her in front of the other girls that she could run the plant."

"That's why Mommy's so happy some time?" Jo-Jo asked his father who quickly nodded.

"Nick, you're so perceptive," said Maria.

"In the end, Aunt Marietta and Aunt Bella have both let their dreams die for the good of other people. For Aunt Bella, to obey her father and devote herself to Uncle Emil and her parents, brothers, sisters, nieces, and nephews. For Aunt Marietta, it's Uncle Rocky and you kids. Whatever she missed out on in her own life, she'll kill herself to guarantee it for you guys in your lives."

"But, Nicholas, why crying in each other's arms?" asked Maria.

"Because of what I just said. They both know this about each other, but they'll never talk about it. I mean they've both sacrificed what may have been their destinies, and realize they've chosen to be in the same boat. They just keep giving themselves to others, not letting anyone know how much they're hurting about what they may have missed out on."

Without a word, Rocky left the young people to look for Carmine. The group scattered into the crowd, never to forget what Nicholas had said.

Almost as entertaining as all that had already happened in the Bonaducci backyard was what occurred next. Aunt Josephine called for Caesar, who by now had shed his "bra", to look like one of the chefs again. What did these two have in common? Both had just been re-elected to the highest posts within the National Catholic War Veterans organization, ... Caesar as President, and Josephine the head of the women's auxiliary. Some knew what to expect. The younger people, new friends, and guests would be in for a treat ... of sorts.

"In honor of Papa's seventy-fifth, the Saint Francis Xavier Church Chapter of the Catholic War Veterans is here to honor him and our great country," announced Josephine, while Caesar vanished into the kitchen.

"You ever been through this, Maria?" asked Nicholas.

"Been through what?"

Nick looked to Frank and Jo-Jo and addressed them, "How about you two guys?"

"What's going on, Nick?" quizzed Jo-Jo.

Frank just shook his head, thinking back to Friday, May 15, at his house.

"Well, my cousins, welcome to the march of the old wooden soldiers, featuring all the Italian American 'goomods' and 'goombods' from Bayonne to Belmont Avenue," announced Nicholas, as he sat down next to Clifton Oliver and his wife, Grandpa Joe's black next-door neighbors.

A reverential silence blanketed the partygoers, as a trumpet, tuba, and drum began be heard at the front of the driveway. Then Caesar and his Newark chapter president, Joe "Juicy" Papsaderio, led a rag tag team of fifteen World War I and II vets, with their wives, into the backyard. Wearing the powder blue sport jackets of the CWV over their t-shirts, aprons, shorts, and anything else they may have had on during the earlier festivities, the patriots marched onto the grass to a feeble rendition of "The Battle Hymn of the Republic". Those revelers who had been through this Bonaducci-Catholic War Veteran ritual before put hands to their hearts as their eyes rolled, particularly when Josephine appeared at the back of the line holding the American Flag, with Father Alphonso Giambalvo struggling with the Catholic banner. Stout and bowed-legged, the priest had a face as fleshy and chubby as a bulldog. Marching next to the lean Josephine, it seemed more like Olive Oil and Popeye had just joined the party.

Hand still on chest, Jimmy Quinn looked to Pinky, inquiring, "Is this gonna last until Labor Day, like the July 4th thing at Saint Francis' Church?"

"Jimmy, shut up, or my sister Josephine will ask you to sing, ... or maybe just kill you."

Ignoring his wife's warning, Jimmy simply added, "God, they sound like one of those Sicilian funeral marches."

The procession halted, and Juicy Papsaderio stepped forward. "We are here in force to honor the patriarch of this great Italian American family, who sent his two sons overseas to defend our freedoms." Then turning directly to Grandpa Joe, he continued, "And we assemble to remember that days like this should not be taken for granted."

Nick nudged Maria. "It's almost over."

Juicy ended his short speech by encouraging the singing of "The Star Spangled Banner".

In the meantime, Clifton Oliver, who had vanished as the procession passed him, suddenly appeared on his back porch dressed in his army formals, retrieved from a mothballed closet in his damp basement. Having served in Europe, he joined the white, Italian American Catholic War Veterans as the national anthem continued. Caesar greeted him with a hug and put his right arm around Clifton's neck, with everyone singing proudly at the top of his or her lungs. Only cynical Nicholas reminded Frank, out the corner of his mouth, that it was Uncle Caesar who had tried to discourage Grandpa Joe from moving into this black-dominated neighborhood. Frank just laughed. As always, Nick was being honest … to a fault.

When the surprise ceremony was over, cheers rang out. Rocky had stood by his father proudly, but did not participate in the procession. He looked to his cousin, Carmine, who was all smiles, having only heard of the legend of how such displays of patriotism often characterized gatherings attended by Jersey's Catholic War Veterans. Rocky walked over to him, and they filled plastic containers with cold beer from a newly tapped keg, before slowly heading up the driveway to the front of the house to find some privacy. The emotion of the day was at its peak.

Both leaned against Carmine's new Cadillac. Behind them, the young Garden State Parkway was filled with cars returning from the Jersey Shore. "You guys do this every Sunday afternoon, Rocky?" asked Carmine, trying to remain serious.

"No question about it, … if my sister Josephine had anything to do with it," answered Rocky, sipping his beer, and then changing the subject. "Carmine, that was beautiful what you did with Connie, …asking her here for Pop, and then getting Bella up there."

"Hey, I've always idolized my Uncle Joe," said Carmine, taking another gulp of refreshing beer himself. "And my glamorous cousin, Bella. Well, God made only one of her. She would have been a better 'Auntie Mame' than Rosalind Russell."

Rocky nodded. "So, how's business?"

"Getting better."

"Castro hurt you guys in Cuba?"

"Hurt ain't the word. Lost a lot. We didn't get wiped out 'cause we were just startin'. So, we got lucky."

"Hear you're in Wildwood," said Rocky, as he told Carmine what Maggie Corino had said to Frank about the "gentleman from Brooklyn" who was putting money into the seashore town.

"Yea, giving that a shot," said Carmine, not offering any further details.

Then Rocky changed the tone of their relaxed conversation by mentioning Benny "Bad Boy" Badalamenti. "Listen, Carmine, it's not my business, but we got the same last names, and our fathers were brothers. Why's this jerk always around Jersey when he's from New York, ... and why's he hanging with your guys? I mean ... he's bad. Remember how he chased Bella? He's still chasin' her after all these years. Now I hear he's always around you, which makes me seriously worried. Carmine, our fathers were different, and we're different. Now we got this counterfeit thing in Essex County, and who's involved, but Badalamenti! It gets me sick to think your group could be pullin' the strings so close to us."

"Rock, let's get something straight. First of all, we <u>are</u> different. But my old man had to make some tough decisions when he got to this country. And everything he did, he did for his family, ... his wife, his kids, and his brother, ... your father."

"Yea, I know."

"I'm not finished. Yea, much has changed since my father fought to get himself and his people some respect in New York. I mean the drugs and the prostitute thing is bad, and he hated the thought of it when that stuff showed up. But, his life gave your father the chance to decide what he wanted to do with his own. He came to Jersey when he married your mother. Fine. But, don't forget the stories are legend about Uncle Joe's temper in the old days. My father taught him how to control it. OK, your father has always been legit, God bless him. But my old man gave him the opportunity to make that choice, … with all he did for him."

"Carmine, I'm not questioning my Uncle John in the old days," Rocky retorted. "It's you. Your father did what he did because he had no choice. Yea, he gave my father a choice, and he made it; came to Jersey, married my mother, and worked more that sixty hours a week doing crap jobs. But you know what? Your father also did what he did to give you and your brothers a choice. And what do you do? You stay in this thing that's now gotten out of hand with violence, extortion, counterfeiting, drugs, women, … and it goes on and on."

"Hold it, Rocky," said Carmine, tossing his unfinished beer to the ground. He needs both hands free to talk. "Yea, I had a choice, and I still do. I want the best for my kids, and I'm gonna get it for them. Slowly, I'm putting my dough into things they all can be proud of. Those are the decisions I've made. But you know what? I don't want you to get mad or anything, but you made decisions, too."

"What'a ya mean?"

"You left school for a job in your brother-in-law's butcher shop. Not so bright! You took this laborer's thing in that perfume factory, … backbreaking, for less than a hundred dollars a week. You could've worked with me on the New York side, or even in Jersey. But no."

Rocky jumped in. "Stop. Carmine, this is nuts. Let's be honest. You and your organization are breaking laws me and some other guys fought for over in the South Pacific. Now you're trying to get me to think I made the wrong decisions by staying away from your thing by just going straight? I bloodied some noses for less than that in the old days."

"Don't get violent, Cuz, … it's against the law."

"Be serious, Carmine."

"I will be. Listen, first of all, forget the counterfeit thing. We ain't involved. But I can't say some stray New York City cats aren't. That's that. We have lots of businesses, but I got accountants and lawyers all working to keep them clean. We're not perfect yet, but we're getting there." Carmine was serious as he put his finger into Rocky's chest. "But as a Bonaducci, I do get upset about you not finishing your education, becoming a laborer when you could be an artist, teacher, coach, or something like that. I'll tell you something, cousin, only because I love you—you quit long ago. You quit when that gifted kid of yours started playing football and doing well. Then you really checked out when Jo-Jo followed. What about you? You're getting all your satisfaction from what your kids are doing, and nothing from your own thing. That's worse than some of the stuff you and the Feds accuse some of us of doin'."

"Tell ya where you're wrong, Carmine," said Rocky, his finger now in his cousin's chest. "It ain't over yet. Yea, I did, or didn't do, what I did. But now my kids are listening to me and my wife, and doing better than we ever did. When they're off and on their way with school and everything, then me and Marietta will have time to do for ourselves. The game ain't over yet. I just don't want my cousin, Carmine the Artist, to mess it all up for himself, and for us, if the law comes down hard on him. Then we all get hurt."

"You're makin your point, Rock. But don't be so self-righteous. I deal with legitimate bankers, lawyers, … business guys, you call 'Captains of Industry'; ya know, the ones who went to fancy schools like where Frankie's goin'? Don't get me wrong. I'm so proud of my cousin's kid. But let me tell you; these so called legit big wigs are worse than the Gambinos, the Bonnanos, the Boiardos, and the little guys from my neighborhood and yours. It's just that the Feds are so stupid, because they don't think educated guys do illegal things. You know what? I'll give you this; some of these business guys are just smarter than all of us. But, I'll guarantee something else; they're even greedier. Some day, some studious accountant's gonna turn them all in, and what you think is so righteous is gonna smell worse than baccala … the day after."

The two cousins stared at each other. Rocky finally reacted, "I hope you're wrong."

"Listen, my handsome cousin. I'm not wrong. But here's what you gotta remember: The Bonaduccis are … 'good leaders'. I'm not gonna hurt anybody, and neither are you. A great leader does not inflict pain, … he endures it." Then Carmine hugged his cousin. "We just gotta be careful we don't hurt ourselves."

On the front seat floor of Carmine's car, where he jumped in when he saw his father and cousin coming toward it earlier, … Jo-Jo had heard everything!

The night ended with the cutting of Grandpa Joe's birthday cake, after which he thanked everyone for coming, in slightly Italian-accented speech. He was happy to be seventy-five years old, most proud that Nicholas and Frank were destined to be the first grandchildren to get college degrees, with a note of regret that Rocky had to drop out to take care of his family. As he finished, everyone raised their glasses and yelled, "Chend don." (centi anni or 100 years, the Italian wish for a long life, spanning a century of time.)

The end of the summer of 1959 was coming fast. A now rapidly maturing Jo-Jo would be getting ready for the freshman football team at Belleville High. Frank would start practice at Cornell later that week.

CHAPTER 23

"FAR ABOVE…"

Rocky borrowed Caesar's new Bonneville to drive Frank to Cornell, knowing his tired Chevy would probably die by the Liberty Diner up on Route 17 in New York. The day before the trip north, Caesar had frankly reminded Rocky that he also ought to be concerned about the Bonaduccis creating the proper impression upon their arrival in Ithaca.

"You serious, Caesar?" asked Rocky.

"Don't feel bad, brother-in-law, but you show up in that little '49 coupe, and then another player's old man shows up in some chauffeured Caddie, or Lincoln, or something."

"Frankie don't care, Caesar. And neither do I."

"Yea, but we want to see Frankie playin' when we make the journey up there. Who's the coach gonna start, … kid from the cancer-stricken Chevy, or the one who got out of the limo? It's all money," he reminded Rocky.

"Hey, they'll start the best kid," fired back Rocky. "Besides, they're givin' money to Frank. We can't look too prosperous."

"We're talkin' about the Ivies, Rock, … not Essex County high school football. You know, … blue bloods! … old money! When Pop and Uncle John were runnin' the streets of Brooklyn fightin' to put "scoddall" (escarole) on the table, these

Amedigans were runnin' banks." A supervisor at Jergens, Caesar worked for big bosses that fit the crusty, wealthy, and conservative mold, so he knew what he was talking about.

"Well, in that case, Mr. Generosity, the Bonneville ain't no limo either," joked Rocky, adding that his sister's husband was also far from qualified to be waving a Cornell banner, while wearing a full-length fur coat and flashing a flask of vintage scotch at the Princeton game in a couple of weeks. "Don't forget, Caesar, you barely got out of Garside Street School."

Caesar smiled. He had not forgotten his past, and just flipped the keys to Rocky.

In the kitchen that late August morning, Marietta was very emotional bidding farewell to her older son. She let him know just how proud she was that he was about to fulfill a dream she and her husband once had for themselves, … Rocky playing college football, and then going on to teach art and coach.

Not giving Frank a chance to react to anything she was saying, she also revealed how Nora had "prophesied" back in winter that Marietta would be visiting her son at a school on a lake. And, Cornell overlooks legendary Cayuga Lake.

"Ma, isn't that fortune telling?" said Frank, hugging his mother as Jo-Jo and Donna completed packing Uncle Caesar's car in the backyard.

"No, Frank. God gives each of us unique gifts, and Nora claims prophesy as one of hers. And with Cornell being on a lake, well, … God picked it for you."

"Hey, Ma, don't forget Yale helped pick Cornell, too, when they rejected me!"

The phone rang and Rocky picked it up. "It's Uncle Jimmy, Frankie."

"Uncle Jimmy, thanks for calling," said Frank.

"Listen, kid, me and Aunt Pinky want to wish you all the best."

"Gee, thanks, Uncle Jimmy. And also for letting me use the Chevy this summer.

"No problem, Frankie," said Quinn. "And another thing, listen to your Uncle Jimmy: while you're having a good time up there, spend some of it figurin' what ya love to do, … then try to find somebody to pay ya for it."

"Sounds like good advice, Uncle Jimmy. Thanks."

"Go get 'em kid." Jimmy hung up.

No sooner had Frank cradled the phone, than it rang again. This time it was Uncle Pete. "Frankie, ya gotta forgive me not makin' it up to Belleville. Greenie didn't show to relieve me."

"No problem, Uncle Pete. My mother told me you couldn't leave the store."

"Yea, but ..." The phone went silent.

"Uncle Pete, you still there?" No sound. "Uncle Pete?"

"Yea, kid, I'm OK. I just wanted to be there for ya. Gonna miss ya." Pete was regaining composure. "Well, make us proud, Frankie."

"I'll do my best, Uncle Pete. And thanks for all the food you dropped off last night."

"Yea, no problem. Hey, can't wait to make it up to the Princeton game. I'll be countin' the days."

"See you then. Take care of yourself, Uncle Pete."

"God bless, Frankie."

As Jo-Jo then led everyone into the backyard, Blackie, from out of nowhere, appeared at Frank's feet. "Ma, you better wash Blackie here; he's looking a little dirty," said Frank, as he picked up the sad-eyed mutt, hugged him and whispered, "I'll miss you, Pal." He then released the dog, which raced around the car and jumped into the tattered hammock, head down, as though he couldn't face this final "goodbye".

As Frank and Rocky climbed into the car, Marietta again thought about Sneak's "scholarship fund" and how everything had turned out so well for her son's education. She silently gave all the credit to God, even the Yale denial. When it seemed that her goodbyes were finally over, a final burst of energy provoked her to say, "Frank, I'll be praying. God willing, we'll see you at the Princeton game. Uncle Pete, Aunt Bella, Uncle Caesar, and Uncle Jimmy and Pinky are coming. Remember, straight A's."

But Jo-Jo made sure he had the last word as the car began to pull away. "And be a little bit more selfish up there than you were at Belleville, big brother. I mean, take it all the way into the end zone when you get the next chance." Frank instantly understood the backhanded complement, and waved.

Six hours later, the cream-colored Pontiac braked at the steps of Schoelkoff Hall, the ancient brick edifice overlooking Cornell's trademark crescent stadium. As Frank stretched the cramps out of his lean muscular frame, his breath was taken away by the panoramic view. While it was hot and humid, the skies were clear, and you could see the western New York State countryside for miles. As the warm late summer breeze unsuccessfully attempted to lap the perspiration off Frank's neck, he began a minute long stare that created an image in his mind he would treasure forever. The many farms scattered across the landscape reminded Frank these must be the harvest fields from which those farm boys were being cultivated to play college football, ... those same strong competitors his dad always lamented as being on the other team. Now they would be on Frank's side.

The Bonaduccis had made it ... to the Ivy League. It was far from Bloomfield Avenue, counterfeit twenties, the Tungsol graveyard shift, Friday night's eggs in the gravy with peas, and Uncle Pete at the back door every Saturday morning of a Belleville game. A mother's prayers and the sacrifices she and her husband made had finally paid off. One of their children would have a better chance than they had, ... and it would be a second chance for Rocky and Marietta as well.

That night Frank began a two-week stay with the other freshman players on the top floor of Schoelkoff Hall. While not the best sleeping conditions, Cornell's newcomers would get to know each other and have little else to think about other than football.

Rocky, who was staying overnight downtown at the old Ithaca Hotel on State Street, got a knock on his door from room service. Assistant Coach Jake Hetrick, who had recruited Frank, had specially ordered a rye and ginger for his guest. Jake was fond of the ex-Marine and two-way end from Newark. On top of respecting his war record and Rocky's humble reflections on the greatness of the American game of football, the coach had lost a brother in the South Pacific.

Rocky had just showered. Relaxed, he placed the drink on a dainty doily on the tiny table next to the window. Through shear curtains he could see the sun setting over rolling hills surrounding Cayuga Lake. Even the old hotel room's musty odor could not diminish the beauty of the moment. Raising and sipping the high ball, he began to cry. He was proud of his son, but at the same time, he began to drift back to that summer after the war when he and Marietta visited St. Bonaventure University to begin his own college football career. His glance back became a stare that wouldn't go away. He did not sleep well that night.

During the short preseason workouts, Frank impressed the Cornell coaches. His high knee action style of running and rangy body made him a versatile candidate for several positions. Slated from scouting reports as a running back, they now saw potential as a receiver and defensive back. But Frank viewed it differently, like how much faster and stronger many of his teammates seemed. With the world-renown Cornell School of Agriculture just on the other side of campus from the Lower Alumni practice fields, he, indeed, had come face to face with those fabled farm boys. And they were complete football players, just like his father said.

Part of Frank's financial aid package included washing dishes at the Sigma Epsilon Fraternity on the lower part of campus, just up from downtown Ithaca. After his first day of classes and practice, he made the long walk from Schoelkoff Hall across the idyllic Cornell setting, praying on the way. After giving thanks for his family and this opportunity, he explained how he missed his girlfriend and asked God to make sure he wasn't distracted by any of the college's coeds. Chances of finding a more tempting female with better dark brown hair, a softer round face with bright brown eyes, and sleeker curves that would stop a truck driver at eighty miles an hour, actually seemed to be remote in Ithaca, New York.

What was as beautiful and pure to him as his Maria was Cornell's campus. Lively brooks crossed the grounds rushing to meet the university's popular gorges, refreshing Frank on his trek. Rolling hills tucked the fraternity and sorority houses into their own unique dells and valleys. And ancient stone edifices housing the classes, run by professors who looked like they'd been at Cornell since its founding in the 1800's, had to be the perfect prototype every college should copy.

Stray dogs began to tag along on his journey as he passed Williard Straight Hall, the student union in the center of this amazing idyllic setting. Old and tattered, they look as though they could have been around when Cornell football was in its "glory" in the late thirties, forties, and early fifties, ... the days when Ohio State and Michigan were on the schedule; and of the legendary "Fifth-down" game, when the gentlemen of Cornell forfeited their 7-3 win over Dartmouth, because the Big Red had scored on an illegal ... fifth down, destroying their national championship drive. Frank petted one of the friendly rag-tags and laughed. Not only were most of these animals not yet born during the school's gridiron heydays, but now Cornell was more interested in academic excellence than football fame.

311

The air was cooling on that early September afternoon, as the sun seemed to be diving into Cayuga Lake, sitting majestically in the midst of New York's lush Finger Lake's region. *Man, my mother could write a poem about this— how this lake's calling all us newcomers at Cornell to splash just once in its mystic waters. Yea, she'd somehow tie it into the alma mater: "Far above Cayuga's waters, with its waves of blue..." God, I can't wait for her to get here.*

Frank made his way down the hill that was known as Libe Slope, gazing up at the library tower which stretched to the sky, subject of millions of photographs depicting Cornell's beauty. He stopped to get a last look at the lake and suddenly the panorama lost its detail. Instead, he began to see his mother, preparing dinner for his brother and sister; his dad rolling into the driveway at a quarter to five with his sputtering Chevy; Uncle Pete placing some numbers with Two Tones on Bloomfield Avenue; Greenie sitting on the wooden chair, leaning against the front window of the corner butcher shop; Belleville High's football team, preparing for their opening game with East Orange; and his last experience of "Stalag 17" with his childhood friends and his brother. As a small plane sputtered above him, he again saw the snow-swept night that claimed the three rock 'n' roll stars back on February 3rd. Then there was Dion who chose the bus, ... still alive and well on Belmont Avenue in the Bronx. Immediately forcing himself to trot down the hill so he would not be late for his first day at work, Frank suddenly knew he was running away ... from severe homesickness!

Seymour Berg, the cook in charge of everything that happened in Sigma Epsilon's kitchen, including dishwashing, greeted Frank at the fraternity's back door. "You the Bonaducci kid?"

"Yes, sir."

"I like this. No kitchen's any good without a Dago in it?"

"Sir, my grandfather was born in Lioni in the Province of Avellino in Southern Italy. He and his brother came here as teens. My father fought in the South Pacific and will always be ... a Marine. Closest he's ever been to Italy is the red wine my grandmother rations out on Sundays. If he, his father, or his uncle ever heard you call me a 'Dago', or 'Guinea', or 'Wop', or anything judging their status as human beings, you just might not be able to do 'number one' again, if you know what I mean." Frank could not believe what just rolled off his lips.

"Oh yea? Well, I like you kid, 'cause you got guts," said Seymour, putting an arm around him. "I'm a 'kike', or 'Jew boy', or 'Heeb', or whatever your relatives want to call me. My old man was the biggest shylock in Brooklyn until the Black Hand made him into a shoe salesman. I was in Normandy, plus six. Killed me a few Germans, while they got rid of a few of my relatives. Those Black Hand guys made Hitler look like an altar boy, though. Hitler killed Jews; those Sicilians, … they kill their own. Your relatives ain't from where they come from, my Neapolitan prince. In the end, we're all Americans, kid, and we all got darkness somewhere in our past. You just call me Sy the Jew, and I'll call you Frankie Boy, … if that ain't too offensive?"

Frank almost fainted from the alcohol stench of Sy's breath. But his frankness started a friendship that would last all four years at Cornell. Sy's sweaty undershirt and stained-filled apron recalled Uncle Pete's butcher shop uniform. Sy's huge belly overwhelmed his leather belt, convincing Frank the alcohol-cooked cook had not seen his knees, let alone his feet, in years.

All Frank could say was, "Sy, nice to meet you."

While he began training Frank in the fine art of dishwashing at a Cornell fraternity, Sy continued his life story … of how he came to Ithaca after the war to work at the famous Ithaca Gun Factory. He also confessed that his life-long affair with Vodka began from being introduced to it by a couple of Russians he met in Berlin. He also made clear that Stalin's white lightning was a perfect antidote for endless pains in his back cause by a Nazi grenade. Sigma Epsilon was his sixth fraternity since he got fired from Ithaca Gun in '49, for "drunken lapses". His campus popularity was due to his reputation as the cook who could drink any Cornell man under the table, no matter what the concoction. However, this also guaranteed his cooking jobs at each frat house not lasting too long either.

Smells in the kitchen were unlike anything Frank had ever imagined. Dirty dishwater mixed with the residue of days' worth of rotting food could be expected, but there was also this sharp pungent odor he could not place. Only weeks later he discovered it was … a dead rat in the fat tray under Sy's ancient stove! Before Homecoming Weekend that fall, the fraternity brothers launched a "Search for the Smell" treasure hunt. The winning sleuth got a month's long open bar tab at Teddy Zinck's drinking hole on the edge of campus, funded by the Sig Ep social fund.

By the end of September, Frank was completely overwhelmed by his schedule. He'd earned a starting running back position on the freshman team, but had failed his first quiz at the School of Industrial and Labor Relations. Still missing his family and Maria, he also hated being a dishwasher. On the other hand, Sy had actually become somewhat of a mentor. He provided inspiration with stories of some of the great Cornell footballers he'd known through his multi-campus jobs; Rocco Calvo and Billy DeGraaf, two of Sy's favorite quarterbacks, were at the top of the list. Then, Bo Roberson was declared the best pure athlete. Sy mentioned Freddy Westphal and Bennie Babula, whom Rocky always talked about, … two more of the Jersey greats who played at the end of the war. Some of Cornell's more recent recruits from the Garden State like Tony Pascal and Clifton's George Telesh also made Sy's credible Cornell student-athletes list. Knowing local high school football as well, the big cook also caught Frank's attention when he mentioned a high school senior from the Cortland area. "Hey, Frankie Boy. The best one is still to come though. His name is Wood, from up the highway a bit. I think it's Gary Wood. He's a real player, … a quarterback who does everything. He comes here, and you guys all look good."

Frank just nodded.

Despite a growing fondness for Sy, Frank had one other big concern to add to his growing discontent over his schedule and the "washing dishes for meals" part of his scholarship—that was … "Mo So"! Sy never talked about this behemoth creature that answered to that name at this fraternity known for its wild parties and wild brothers. One day he simply informed Frank of the dark room at the end of the hall where a … "Mo So" lived, whatever that was. From time to time, a giant shadowy figure could be seen dashing in and out of the small room adjacent to the kitchen. Frank might never have noticed him, if it wasn't for mysterious Mo So's obsession for the music of The Kingston Trio that seemed to play endlessly from within the dark cave, where this ape-like thing resided. Even more bizarrely, young coeds would also dash in and out of this same dwelling, never glancing right or left, and never one at a time, … always pairs.

A week before the opening freshman game with visiting Princeton, Frank discussed with his parents over the phone the idea of quitting his job, getting his grades in order, and then finding some other way to pay for food. Marietta was in agreement and assured Rocky and Frank she would find additional funds somewhere for Frank's bills. But Rocky, while sympathetic for his son's concern about his academic challenges, called the pressure Frank was feeling just "adjustment problems". Of course, he knew nothing of Sneak's bank account for Frank and was concerned his wife might start calling her brother Pete to bet on the "Italian numbers" she might be seeing in one of her dreams, … a collaboration not beyond the spiritual Marietta and her "enterprising" sibling.

In the end, Sy the Jew helped make up Frank's mind. Sober, the shoddy cook was perceptive and imaginative. When under the influence, he could be nasty and rude, but still discerning. "Listen, Frankie Boy, Cornell ain't gonna be easy, and dishwashing is just a small part of it. Quit this, and it might start a bad habit. Don't forget once you get out of here with the degree, life surely ain't gonna be harder than without that sheepskin. Stick everything out. Besides, I'll miss bein' around a clean-cut kid for a change, even though he's an Italian from Jersey."

"Sy, thanks. You've been great, but this smelly kitchen, the schedule, and everything else; well, it isn't me. Now, I'm starting to worry, Cuz, and the Good Book tells me I should relax. I know you're a Jew and I'm Christian, but do you know what I mean?"

Being called, "Cuz", the perceptive chef knew his young assistant was totally serious. "Hey, don't forget Jesus was a Jew," Sy replied. "And I never told ya, but my first wife was a 'Holy Roller'. She's still prayin' for me. So, I understand, kid." Sy put both hands on the stainless steel counter also holding up his flabby belly. "What's this 'everything else' you're talkin' about, Frankie Boy?"

Frank did not hesitate. "Take this Mo So guy. He's very different from me. My girlfriend's down in Jersey, and this hunchback of Notre Dame mindlessly has all these coeds visiting everyday. His long, heavy coats, that floppy cowboy hat; man, it all gives me the creeps. Reminds me of this old guy in my neighborhood who hung himself this summer, … younger version."

"OK, I got it. Let me straighten you out, kid." Sy turned around and now leaned his back against the counter piled with chopped meat waiting to be seasoned, folding his arms. "In case you didn't make the association, Mo So is not only a senior, but the same Moses Sofranac who is Cornell's All Ivy defensive tackle. He's from Chicago where his father's a surgeon. His mother's a Cornell alumna. She had more money goin' into the marriage than her successful husband will ever earn. And, their cute little boy is … Mo So."

Frank was stunned, as Sy continued, "And Mo So is in the Hotel School up here, … and he ain't never been off the Dean's List. Those coeds goin' in? They ain't coeds, but Ithaca High School Cheerleaders. And he ain't tutorin' them in history either. The Kingston Trio is music the girls like. Mo So prefers the Everly Brothers. Have I confused you yet, Mr. Bonaducci?"

"Sy, don't make this up."

315

"I figured a kid from around Newark would be a little more savvy, but that's OK, Frank. I like your innocence. But if you ever get up nerve to talk to Mo So, you'd find him so intelligent, that you'd run away. He's a loner, except he's out of control with girls, as well as out of control on the football field. If he was a little taller, his father would get him drafted by the Chicago Bears this winter. Just as you figured, he doesn't study, … doesn't have to. He's got a photographic mind. When his parents show up, which is rare, he shaves and gets dressed up in a sport jacket. The only people who recognize him is his ol' man and ol' lady. To them, he's their darlin' Moses. To everybody at Cornell, he's Mo So. And one last thing—he's the only one since I've been on this campus who can drink more than me and not show it. Lefty James and the rest of the football staff just ignore him. He's such a great defensive tackle; they don't want to change anything about him. They say he should'a went to Illinois, or Notre Dame, or some bigger school. They figured they lucked out with him comin' to Cornell"

"Unbelievable," was all that Frank could say.

"No, Mr. Bellboy," Sy said, referencing the questionable Belleville High nickname. "It ain't unbelievable, because it ain't so rare. Here's the lesson: up here and in life you're gonna find lots of Mo So's. They're all different than you—not honest, don't believe in the baby Jesus, drink, take advantage of girls outside of marriage (excuse me), don't study, don't seem to care, break all the rules, … and still get by. In some cases, they get by on top. And you know what, Frank? There are not only Mo So's all over this campus, but throughout life. The sooner you stop judgin' 'em, stop comparin' yourself to them, and start learnin' from them, the better off you'll be."

"What do you mean?"

"They don't worry, they just … do."

"Sy, I don't understand."

"I know about this worryin', and comparin', and fearin' stuff. I'm like you. But difference is I turned to the booze, got hooked, and it's not so easy without it. You turned to the real Jew boy, Jesus. Only problem, you and your Italian family like to worry. It's part of the culture. And that's the part of the Bible you keep forgettin'. 'In the world there shall be tribulations, but be of good cheer, I have overcome the world.' Jesus didn't say worry about it, and it'll be OK. Stop worryin', kid, and just do it. Just do it like all the other Mo So's you're gonna meet at Cornell, in business, and in life. Sooner you learn this lesson, longer you'll live, … and more successful you'll be. And if Jesus is who He says He is, what are you worrying about in the first place?"

"Sy, I can see you've been doing some reading."

"Frankie, weren't you listenin'; my wife number one was a religious nutcase. Now, here's what ya gotta do. Give me that apron and get the hell out of here. Start studyin' and playin' football. You can't handle this schedule yet. But when you can, tell the coaches I'll take ya back anytime."

That day Frank left his job as dishwasher for the last time at Sigma Epsilon fraternity. But he made sense of two things; he'd follow the advice of Sy the Jew, an alcoholic cook and Purple Heart World War II veteran, whose heart was bigger than his belly; and he made sure he would visit with him in his kitchen at least once a week. Frank knew an honest man when he saw one. He also saw a hurting creature that Frank could not walk away from.

The cost of long distant telephone calls didn't take long to turn Frank, Maria, his parents, and, surprisingly enough, his cousin Nick at the University of Dayton, into prolific pen pals. Marietta's letters always had cash hidden in a card as well. She found the money for his food bills, but primarily the letters were an opportunity to rekindle her ability to write poetry and prose that should have had her published by now. Her "current events" from Bloomfield Avenue, to Belmont Avenue, to Belleville Stadium, made Frank less homesick as each letter brought his roots closer to Cornell.

Dearest Frank,

The two twenties should help with food this week. (They're real twenties; Rosa hasn't come near the house since the indictments. Ha! Ha!) By the way, the counterfeiting thing has been all over The Ledger and The News ... in the Belleville Times, too. The Italian Tribune won't talk about such things. They concentrate on the good that Italians are doing in America—boys like you, promotions at jobs, newly published works by Italian Americans, ... all nice stuff.

Here's the update, ... some good news and some bad. Daddy tells me the counterfeiting case is weak because Giantempo didn't chose Daddy's friend, Bobby Zarcone, to help prosecute the whole thing. Trying to say Paulie Puccini was murdered instead of overdosing himself is getting little news. Cops in Belleville and on Bloomfield Avenue are keeping Daddy posted. Everybody's got their attorneys. Some of Richie's boys have the same ones. A public defender is handling Craig

Francello's situation, ... Vinnie Giampietro, too. (By the way, here's the bad news: Craigie's mother told me he dropped out of Amherst College after only one month. She claims it's not the trial, but rather his interest in writing. I don't know. Did you know he could write? You know me, I don't ask questions. I just pray.)

Can you imagine this? Sneaks is planning to defend himself. Daddy says it's like back in the thirties when he used to compete with Giantempo in football at Central. I hope it turns out for Sneaks. He's always been good to me and your Uncle Pete. Another thing, Grandma Mamie's cousin, Judge Leroy Liloia, will be presiding. He helped build the old First Ward. He knows these guys and has locked up a few over the years. But, Daddy says the prosecutors better have lots of evidence.

The Gubitosis never come out of their house. Their garage collapsed, and the boat fell apart. Honestly, the neighborhood had a good laugh. I speak with Antoinette Thatcher when I walk with Blackie. She's so smart and claims Gary had the Profettas killed. I asked her the motive, but she says she hasn't formulated that yet. I like her. Says she's down to only one Southern Comfort Manhattan per day. I told her I'm praying to the Sacred Heart for her.

None of us can get over the motorcycle accident. Markie Brunello took over the business for Henry's family. Daddy says he's not the same. I sent Queenie and Nora over to the Shell Station to talk to him. He seems more peaceful now they tell me. Thank God you never forgot Daddy's rule about ... "a quarter to five".

And do you remember the church we visited over on West Street in Bloomfield, ... where Queenie and Nora go? Well, their black pastor retired, and when they told me their board elected a white guy to replace him, Daddy and I almost died!! It's Tony Votolo. Remember Barringer's great quarterback that grew up next to Daddy and everybody on Lake Street, before Grandpa and Grandma moved to Seventh Street? I have to get over there with Daddy, because I hear his brothers, 'Tweet' and 'Honeydew', help him out when they're not teaching and coaching. Imagine that—old friends from Park Avenue in a full gospel church. I know I can get Aunt Bella and Aunt Josephine to church now. They loved those boys; helped them with their five sisters and mother when the father left. Isn't it funny how God works?

Have to go. As Daddy will tell you, Jo-Jo is doing great in football and has a new girlfriend. I told him he still better get straight A's. Donna is as sweet as ever. Her brothers are her heroes. Grandma Frassa is fine; just drives Uncle Pete and me nuts. She gave me the two twenties for you. Uncle Pete misses the Saturday morning pre-game meals, but says he'll start them with Jo-Jo in a week.

We will see you at the Princeton game.

Remember:

> *A flower garden so grand to behold,*
> *Even if weeds have taken their toll.*
> *A single beauty will always stand out,*
> *But cannot conceal the few seeds of doubt.*
> *A sign of God's presence is seen by all,*
> *As long as that one forgets not its call.*

You have always been that special flower for all who have come to know you. We love and miss you.

Love forever,

Mom.

P.S. We hope we can meet Sy the Jew when we come up. He sounds like a good man.

Dear Frank,

So proud to hear you will be starting against Princeton. I saw Mrs. Babula at Chet's Candy Store, and she's very happy for you. She told me that Gino is first team fullback at Fork Union, but he's not happy. He's complaining they don't like Italian kids from Jersey down there. She told me Sneaks hasn't been able to get out of jail to go visit. I'm surprised he hasn't at least made a call down there to set the coaches straight. Chet told me a carload of the Bloomfield Avenue guys are going to be headed south to watch Gino play, and then report back to Sneaks. After those guys make that visit, Virginia won't be the same,... and they'll probably elect Gino, Captain of the team!

Chet looks bad. I think he lost fifty pounds worrying over this counterfeit thing. I think he's innocent, but don't know about some of these guys who show up there for cigarettes and cherry cokes.

Daddy, about the dishwashing job, don't worry about it. Mom and I will get the food money. That's no problem. Just study hard and keep running hard.

Did you hear about Craigie Francello leaving school? I figured they'd been pushing this kid too hard over the years anyway. What do his parents expect from a kid with cerebral palsy?

Saw Mr. Thatcher and Mr. Hardy at the Shell station last week. Eric is loving Montclair State. He's the disc jockey on their radio station. Bobby is getting ready for indoor track at the Naval Academy. Loves it down there. Says this kid Bellino is going to be great in football. He's from Boston. I saw Jackie Carey's sister at Charlie Buccino's deli; her brother's still in the police academy. Can't picture Jackie as a cop.

Your brother is doing great with the freshmen, but I think the coaches are going to switch him to quarterback. Mr. P. says it's his natural position. I agree. They gave him your #7. He's proud of that. And Gino's #22 went to the Richie Luzzi kid. They're saying that he's a combination of you and Gino. With Jo-Jo at QB and Luzzi running the ball, Belleville is going to be great in a couple of years.

Mom told me you aren't reading the Bible as much. You know I'm not too religious, but get to mass, or one of those Bible churches up there. I know how much it helps Mommy.

See you at the Princeton game.

Love,

Dad

My Darling Frank,

I miss you much, but will see you at the Princeton game. Just so glad we talk every Sunday night. It makes our separation easier. Congratulations on starting. Your parents are very proud.

Uncle Pete and Aunt Bella are coming up with us in his Cadillac. I'm looking forward to being with those two in the back seat. What a pair! ... "Marty the Butcher" and "Auntie Mame". Your father will be driving. Uncle Caesar, Aunt Pinky, and Uncle Jimmy will be in the Bonneville.

Newark State is hard, but I'm doing OK.

This counterfeit thing is all over the papers. So embarrassing. The murder claim about Paulie Puccini is terrible if it's true. And you know what? Some people are starting to wonder about Henry and Al dying in the crash, as well as the Profetta deaths. God, never thought this would happen in our neighborhood.

Some of the Nutley Cheerleaders who go to school with me say you're a real Rock Hudson type; at least that's what they heard about you—you know, quiet, handsome, and strong they say. I get jealous at first, and then I'm proud we're going together. They also say what you did at the Nutley game last year, none of their guys would have ever done. You're a hero, Frank, ... all mine.

See you before the game. Can't wait.

Love forever,

Maria

My good cousin, Frank Bonaducci:

Greetings from the University of Dayton—that wonderful Catholic institution in the Midwest, where no one ever heard of "gabootsells". Imagine their ignorance and their loss at never having eaten the head of a calf or lamb, and everything that it entails.

Hey, is Cornell living as foreign to growing up in Newark and Belleville as Dayton is? Actually, I love it here. I lost 15 pounds already from the food, or whatever it is that I've been eating. But I met this great girl from Pittsburgh. She's a misfit like me, being an only child, too. I'm having a ball. Drinking too much at parties, but I understand that the priests here like to tip a few as well.

Hey, my mother told me you quit the fraternity job. Good move, Frank. You'll be working the rest of your life. Have a good time up there, because once we graduate, it'll be back to the old neighborhood and a job.

Don't forget they'll be having the counterfeit court case when we're home for Christmas. That's going to be fun to see what happens to all of those characters. We'll have to take a couple of trips down to the courthouse and see how cousin Leroy Liloia handles this crew. Imagine when Craig Francello walks in the door. What a riot that's going to be.

Remember, don't study too hard, have a good time, and stay in touch.

Cousin Nick.

Because he was from Jersey, Frank was named one of the honorary captains for the Princeton game. He played well, and Cornell won. However, by mid October he had lost his starting position to one of those farm boys from western New York State. Late night studying had taken toll on his performance on the field.

Sitting alone at the top of Schoelkoff Field one Saturday, waiting for the beginning of the Cornell and Colgate varsity game, Frank gazed across that spectacular multicolored vista of countryside. The air was sweet with the slight trace of manure that always seemed to drift toward the crescent from the acres of farmland surrounding the majestic Cornell setting. It mixed with the smell of boiling hot dogs and mustard emanating from the bowels of the concrete stadium, awaiting hungry fans pouring in from different directions. For a moment, a peaceful calm came over Frank that he had not felt for weeks. But it only lasted until the band's pre-game show began, tackling him back to the harsh reality of what opportunity Cornell represented. The truth of its rigors coldly changed his mood. He now realized excelling in football, and in the classroom, was never going to be as easy as he thought.

A sick feeling suddenly rose up in his stomach. The orange, red, yellow, brown, maroon, and wine-colored tints to the autumn visual spectacle seemed to instantly dull to a haze. The warmth of the sun vanished. The only sense that seemed to be working was his smell. He took a deep breath. The smoke of burning leaves had wafted past his face, … that annual reminder of the game of football his father had taught him. He was homesick again, as well as intimidated. He had begun to lose self-confidence ever since classes started. His mind reacted quickly returning to safer waters. He was wandering back to Jersey again. Even with the ups and downs of his senior year, he'd rather be back in Belleville.

A new vision arrived, … of his father as a tall, statuesque teenager, boarding a train at Newark's Penn Station, waving goodbye to his family. It was 1942, and he was off to war. Then, through the hazy confusion, the broken English of his grandfather could be heard. "Frankie, whena youa looka back, … glance, don'ta stare." Self-pity continued to well up as he remembered Sy the Jew and his New Testament quote of the words of Jesus: "In the world there shall be tribulation. But be of good cheer, I have overcome the world". *What's this all about?* Frank pondered over visions of his father, Grandpa Joe, and Sy, … an unlikely trinity whom he admired. And miraculously it all came together. He recalled that kids his age had fought World War II, with their college lives either postponed, if not eliminated. *Grandpa's voice, and then Sy quoting the Bible?*

Frank decided now was the time to buy a hot dog.

After their team scored early in the first quarter, the band played Cornell's fight song, which went to the tune of "Give My Regards to Broadway". Its legendary lyrics had been sung for years every time the football team got into the end zone. Frank learned it was a drinking song the Ivy League school had chosen as its victorious cry to fight on. He pondered the strange bedfellows of alcohol and athletic excellence as represented by "Give My Regards to Davey" as it was entitled, ... the farewell request of a mythical freshman about to flunk out because he imbibed too much bubbly, and not enough books during his first semester. *Ah, the paradox of Cornell,* Frank thought. He smiled again, thinking of Mo So.

There were still four tough years of education ahead. But were it to end for Frank in this first autumn, the experience had already been priceless. Cornell might be "Far above Cayuga's waters", ... but it was also light years away from Frank's roots in Jersey.

CHAPTER 24

"HEY, MA, GREENIE'S ON THE PHONE."

By mid October, after the freshman coaches switched Jo-Jo to quarterback, he and Rich Luzzi were tearing up Belleville's opponents. As Rocky forecasted, Luzzi, who could run like a deer, was being compared to both Frank and Gino. His magnet-like hands complemented Jo-Jo's pinpoint passing. Lonnie Luongo, who had never played midget football with his teammates because of his size, was on the line. A five foot ten inch, 225 pound fifteen year old, he was a fire hydrant that had no mercy on opponents. He literally ate any ball carrier that ventured near him like a ravenous lion. With the freshmen undefeated at mid-season, varsity coach Eddie Popalinski announced all three would sit the varsity bench for the game against Irvington. The trio was fast becoming the future of Belleville football.

Marietta, Rocky, and all of the other Bonaduccis were really enjoying the 1959 season. Frank was now playing more defense than offense, but his grades were improving, and he was beginning to relax and enjoy Cornell. Late on this Saturday morning before Halloween, Frank called to announce he had scored on an interception against Manlius Prep School. Only his mother was home. "Hey, Ma, with Gino a thousand miles away in Virginia, there was nobody else to wait for to lateral to, so I took it all the way this time," Frank said, knowing his first college TD would help further erase the Mud Bowl game from his mother's mind.

Having just completed leading the freshmen to their fourth straight win, Jo-Jo was getting ready to join the varsity for the bus ride down the Garden State Parkway to Irvington. Rocky would stop home before going to the game.

The family could not have been happier on this Indian Summer-like day. In addition to the good football news, Marietta had yet to be called by the counterfeit case prosecutors, and Pete was miraculously being spared as well. The only disappointment had been Pete's inability to make it to any of Jo-Jo's pre-game meals, those early Saturday mornings he hoped to cherish as he had during Frank's high school career. He complained Greenie had taken a Saturday job down at Port Newark, thus leaving Pete to open and run the butcher store himself between 8 AM and noon.

Barringer was playing cross-city rival South Side that day at Newark City Stadium on Roseville and Bloomfield Avenues. With the City League deadlocked and both schools undefeated, it was one of the biggest games in Essex County. When Barringer was at the Stadium, Pete always had a horde of neighborhood kids hanging on his corner. Today was no different.

But that Saturday, Pete was particularly irritated. Greenie called that he could not make it back to the store. His increasing workload for Boiardo-related business was getting on Pete's nerves. The butcher had been hoping to make it up to the Irvington game to see his nephew run on the field with the varsity. Two Tones was ready to drive, and a couple of other Bloomfield Avenue crewmembers were planning to go in the car as well. Now Pete had to run the store by himself and handle the post-game crowd of Barringer loyalists.

"Pete's concerned about Greenie," Marietta had reminded Rocky for weeks. "He's not around as much, and my brother's missing watching Jo-Jo play."

"Look, Marietta, I know Pete wants to see Jo-Jo, particularly if he gets in the varsity game. But he's really upset 'cause his lazy buddy's helpin' the Boot's boys down at the Port, … and not Pete."

"Rocky, Pete would never get involved."

"I didn't say he would, but he would love to."

"So?"

"So, Pete's jealous. That's all."

Actually Greenie made it to the butcher shop by 4 PM that day as the temperature got up into the uncomfortable and unseasonable eighties. Pete was sleeping out front, his white hard-backed chair leaning against the wall. Uncharacteristically at that hour, the Five Corners of Fifth Street and Bloomfield Avenue were deserted. Two Tones, who had returned early from Irvington, was meeting with his men at the Chinese Clipper restaurant, next to Zarra's Funeral home. All of the neighborhood kids were still at City Stadium.

The game could not have been played at a more edgy time; tension had been building between the blacks of the South Ward and Barringer's mostly white Italian American and Irish Catholic students all week.

"Petee, Five Corners, Greenie Delaney at your service."

Startled, Pete almost fell off his chair in surprise.

"Oh, it's you. Yea, real friend, Greenie. You're out makin' extra money, and I'm here mindin' the store with no break to go see my nephew."

Greenie helped Pete steady his chair, and then sat down next to him. They were quiet, until they looked west on Bloomfield Avenue to get their first glimpse of a crowd of Barringer fans. Then Greenie announced, "Hey, 5 C's, they're quiet; sounds like the Big Blue musta lost."

"Now, Greenie, if they are quiet, ... and they are, ... how can they 'sound' like Barringer lost? Does that make sense, my English language grammar connoisseur?"

Greenie just shrugged, refusing to admit his proclivity at speaking Bloomfield Avenuese. Pete was now more amused than impatient with his sidekick.

When the pack of close to twenty kids made it to the corner, they updated the final score: "Tied, seven-seven."

Pete went into the store, motioning them to follow. Cold sodas were on ice, and he still had some of his famous minestrone soup that had salivated every patron over the years. "What's your pleasure, kids, ... soda, soup, or both?"

"Petee, Five Corners, can't you tell it's hot out?" One of the teens impatiently snapped at the perspiring butcher.

His buddy next to him scolded, "That's no way to speak to Mr. Frassa." Then he added, "Price is right, ... right, Five C's?" confirming the soup was complementary, since it <u>was</u> coming from the bottom of the pot.

"Of course, it's free, boys, but main thing is that some hot soup in yas now will cool yas down," answered the tired butcher, filling the cardboard cups to the brim.

"Petee Five C's, you're da best," the previously impatient teen was quick to remark.

Suddenly, Greenie called out, "Hey, Pete, we got trouble."

Pete stopped pouring soup and followed the teens out the door. About fifty yards up Bloomfield Avenue, close to thirty black boys and girls with black and gold South Side High banners were singing the Bulldogs' obscure fight song that sounded more like a rock 'n' roll tune concocted somewhere in a South Ward garage. Their strut toward the Five Corners further inflamed the brewing rage amongst the white Barringer fans since the game's frustrating end. By the time they reached the stone weather tower that served as an island between Sixth Street, Fifth Street, First Avenue, and Bloomfield Avenue, an eerie silence covered the neighborhood. The few girls in each opposing group seemed more agitated than the boys. The South Siders were out of their territory, and the North Ward crowd was about to remind them.

As both gangs began speaking heatedly amongst themselves, Pete silently prayed that cooler heads would prevail. Greenie's knees seemed to be knocking. Unbeknown to both, some Barringer boys who lived within walking distance had already sped home. And by the time the South Side faithful decided to not go to the other side of Bloomfield Avenue, but rather head right toward Pete's Butcher shop, the white crowd was armed with baseball bats and belts, as well as Pete's four wooden chairs, waiting to be broken up. The South Side-Barringer football game was about to go into sudden death overtime, right at the Five Corners.

Girls screaming and bats swinging, both crowds attacked. South Side pennants were used like spears, and the chairs were flying through the air, … with Pete and Greenie in the middle, separating kids and trying to reason with the raging whites and blacks. Heads popped out of walkup apartments, and customers ran into the street from the liquor store on First Avenue and Calandra's Bakery around the corner. Cars stopped in the middle of Bloomfield Avenue as their passengers joined the madness.

Deep inside the Chinese restaurant, Two Tones and his crew couldn't help but hear the ruckus. Once their table waiter gave them an update, Boiardo's Bloomfield Avenue boys slipped and slid into action with their black flyweight shoes providing little traction, their arms flailing to get on their shark-skinned suit jackets before joining the battle.

Two Tone's platoon totaled just seven, so he was only thinking about breaking up the fight. He stopped short of hand-to-hand combat, raising his voice to call for calm. Shortly, all his associates were pushing, shoving, punching, kicking, or pulling, as he screamed for calm and order. All of a sudden, Louis "Crazy Louie" Montana froze, and stood calm and erect, slowly extending his right arm under the left side of his shiny gray suit. Pete had retreated into his store to catch his breath, leaning against his glass meat case. He was focused on Crazy Louie, fearing the wiseguy's intentions. As a silver forty-five caliber gun came out of Crazy Louie's shoulder strap, Pete's vision blurred.

The hood even surprised himself when he pulled the trigger, ... not at a South Side black, but up at the sky. He emptied the gun with scores of combatants scattering in all directions. Within moments, no South Side fans could be found within the Five Corners, while the Barringer kids nervously calculated their injury count and damage done. Quiet gloom overtook the battleground.

Two Tones made it to Montana first and ordered, "Take off, you jerk. We didn't need that. The cops are gonna be here in seconds, so you better disappear."

Crazy Louie was smiling at him. On one hand, he was proud to think his gun had brought the war to an end. On the other, he was disturbed with himself. "Should've killed one of those chocolate bunnies. They'd would'a never come back. Why'd I shoot into the sky for?"

Two Tones interrupted. "You forget you got a trial in December, plus a record datin' back to your Confirmation Day? Get lost, ... and get lost quick."

A scream split the air. It was Greenie. "Tommy, come. Two Tones, ... Pete's havin' a heart attack."

It was 5:30 PM as Donna answered the phone at 711 Belmont Avenue. Only she and her mother were home. Rocky was picking up Jo-Jo at Clearman Field.

"Hello".

"Who's dis?"

"It's Donna, ... who's this?"

"It's Greenie, honey. Put your mother on."

Upstairs Marietta was napping, so Donna yelled, "Hey, Ma, Greenie's on the phone."

Exhausted from work and not having slept since Friday morning, she slowly walked down the center hall steps to the phone. "How are you, Greenie?"

When Greenie was upset, Marietta knew him to speak in a high-pitched voice. On this day, it could not be higher. "Madiett, listen, Pete got sick. Get Rocky to take you to Columbia Presbyterian. I'll meet you there."

"Greenie, is he dead?"

"Madiett, I think he had a heart attack. I don't know."

"Who's with my mother?"

"Oh crap. Nobody. I forgot about her."

"Listen, Greenie, have Two Tones go up to sit with her. He'll keep her calm. OK?"

"Yea."

"Now listen, Greenie Delaney. I know you since I can remember. Tell me now. Is my brother dead?"

"Madiett, I don't know."

It was the first, and last, time Greenie would ever lie to his best friend's sister.

Marietta hung up.

"Mommy, what's wrong?" asked Donna, standing next to her mother and hearing the entire conversation.

"Donna, your Uncle Pete died." Marietta fell to the floor, letting out a blood-curdling scream.

Only thirty-nine years old, Peter Alfredo "Petee Five Corners" Frassa was dead on arrival at the hospital. Almost twenty-five years before, his father had also died of a heart attack in that same butcher shop.

That night after Rocky and Caesar made all the arrangements with the Megaro-Cundari Funeral home, Jo-Jo and Donna accompanied their parents to be with Mrs. Frassa at the apartment above the shop where the family had lived since the early twenties. She had never shed her black garments since her husband's death. Her emotions went out of control, and her cries could be heard all over the neighborhood. Rocky, Marietta and their two children were silent most of the night.

Greenie tried to be calming. "Mrs. Frassa, he was a good boy. He did his best. He was a good son."

"My Pete, my Pete. He <u>was</u> a good boy. We never argued," she distraughtly screamed in broken English. She would not stop. "We never argued. We never argued!"

Marietta had yet to cry in front of her mother. Rocky was encouraged that she was so controlled and whispered, "Your mother's saying they never argued. Where was <u>she</u> all these years? That's all they did … was argue."

"Rocky, that's the way she lived. She yelled at him constantly, never giving him a chance to say a word. In her world, since he didn't respond, she thinks they never argued. All she did was rob him of his life."

Knowing her love for her brother and how she hated the way her mother treated both her and Pete, Rocky stated, "Marietta, this is no time to blame anyone. We're all gonna miss Pete. He was great to the kids and to you. I got a real kick out of him. He was OK in my book."

That made Marietta finally break down. Rocky, Jo-Jo and Donna surrounded her in love. But her grief quickly turned to anger … directed at her mother.

The next fifteen minutes would never be forgotten by Greenie Delaney, or the family. Marietta attacked her mother's demonic belief that children in an Italian family should not do better than their parents. She reminded Mrs. Frassa that she discouraged both of her children from continuing school and had forbid Pete dating Greenie's sister, Katherine, just because of her Irish name; how Pete remained a lonely butcher on the Five Corners because his mother hated the one love of his

331

life; how everything Pete did was to please his mother at the expense of his own quality of life, only to lose it to binge-eating and chain-smoking, guaranteeing his early death.

Rocky stepped in to remind his wife that her mother had been widowed at only thirty-five years old, and how her own life had been less than joyous. But it would only be the doorbell that would finally calm her down. It was Aunt Bella, and with hugging her sister-in-law, Marietta's true tears of loss for her devoted brother began to flow. Adjusting to life without him was going to challenge all the Bonaduccis.

The two days at the funeral parlor were busy. All the kids from the neighborhood paid their respects. Black families from down on Orange Street who often benefited from Pete's generosity came in large numbers. The Bloomfield Avenue boys never left the wake. While never really one of them, Pete was always around them. As it turned out, they were all also awaiting the arrival of a special mourner.

Sneaks Babula, who received permission to pay his respects, was given a prison guard and Newark Police escort to the funeral home and was accompanied by his wife, Sylvia. As they approached the casket, Rocky and Marietta along with Frank, who had traveled down from Cornell, all stood to greet his ex-running mate's father.

"Madiett, we go way back," said Sneaks. "I loved your brother, and I also loved your father. They were like family to me."

Marietta and Rocky said not a word.

As they stood there, the Boiardo boss became overwhelmed with emotion. "Rocky, I failed," said Sneaks. "I promised Frassa Sr. I'd make sure his kid stayed away from the kind of business I was headed into."

"Sneaks, go easy on yourself. He always wanted it, but he knew you'd never permit it." Rocky was being generously kind to the crime kingpin whose lifestyle the ex-Marine really loathed.

"But, Rock. I should'a got him off the Five Corners. Should'a given him the money to move the butcher shop to Belleville, or Nutley, or maybe up to Verona, … or somethin'."

"The old lady would've never gone for it, Sneaks."

"Somehow I should'a taken him away so he wasn't around all The Boot's businesses and the guys. It hurt him," concluded Sneaks.

Marietta stepped in. "Sneaks, you helped us over the years. Yea, you could have taken my brother out of Fifth Street and Bloomfield Avenue. But nobody could ever have taken Fifth Street and Bloomfield Avenue out of 'Petee Five Corners'. He wore his nickname like a badge of honor, ... because you gave it to him. Not only was that his tie to you and the old days, but it also showed everybody no matter what would happen in life, you could always find Pete Frassa at the Five Corners he grew up on. I think he saw his name as something of loyalty, ... loyalty to the guys, his mother, his father's memory. It let him be somebody. The only other name I think he cherished more was ... 'Uncle'."

As others had crowded around the casket, Silvia drifted off with Rocky to chat with friends. Now Marietta and Sneaks were alone.

"Madiett, you gonna be alright?" asked Sneaks, putting his big hands on the shoulders of an old friend to whose family he was indebted for help after he first arrived in America.

"Sneaks, thanks for the money for Frankie."

He looked around the funeral parlor, and then looked into her eyes and whispered, "What are you talkin' about?"

Surprised, she gazed back at him. His eyes were hardly those of a ruffian from the streets, but rather open windows to the soul of a powerful man who had made regrettable commitments as a young immigrant that he had to fulfill and live out for the rest of his days. Her silence spoke to him.

"Ya know, Madiett, 'Five Corners' loved the ponies. And he especially loved your Frankie!"

Marietta would mention the $10,000 only one more time in her lifetime, ... and it would not be to Sneaks.

The pallbearers for Pete Frassa's funeral were Sneaks and Rocky at the front of the casket, Greenie and Two Tones in the middle, with Jo-Jo and Frank at the back. Pete would have been proud; his two heroes, his two best friends, and his beloved sister's sons escorted him to his final rest, late in the fall of 1959.

For the next several weeks, Marietta seemed to cry every day. She only took work time off for the two-day wake and funeral. Back at the factory, Queenie and Nora would encourage her about how Jesus would fill the void of Pete's passing. However, she could not embrace that miracle. She was still mourning her brother and suffering for her lack of forgiveness of her mother. Her two black friends from Alabama wouldn't give up and finally thought they'd found the key. "Marietta, you have to come to the church," said Queenie one day at the factory.

Nora added, "You said you know Pastor Tony Votolo. He heard late about Pete, and wants to see you and Rocky. Come."

Rocky's patience with his wife's grief was wearing thin, so he agreed, telling Marietta he would drive her to a midweek service at the little full gospel church on West Street in Bloomfield. The Bonaduccis had been there earlier in the year when the black pastor was still in charge. Now Rocky was curious about his old neighbor who had become a Christian while at college in Missouri. Besides, he figured the family had nothing to lose.

On a late November Wednesday night, Rocky and Marietta pulled up at Pastor Votolo's church. It was as if the congregation was waiting for them. In the parking lot, a group of black kids, who could have passed for Central High's starting basketball team, surrounded the dying Chevy, assuring they would provide a VIP spot.

"You're not gonna steal my car, are you fellas?"

"Sir, if Jesus would allow us to steal cars, we think yours would not be one of them," said the tallest.

An amused Rocky and his pensive wife were then escorted by three of the five to the front of the church where Queenie and Nora, in their "goin' to meetin'" finest, waited. "Welcome to you both," the sisters said in unison, surrounded by a glow that Rocky couldn't ignore. Marietta, still grieving, was oblivious.

The congregation was already well into the service's praise and worship portion, singing the interdenominational favorite, "Amazing Grace". The moving words and angelic voices filling the packed church put Rocky at ease, although the absence of stain glass windows, burning candles, and statues bothered him. *Nuttin' like the Catlic Church,* he thought.

Marietta smiled at Queenie and Nora, thinking how strange it was for two rural black girls to take such interest in her spiritual and mental healing. She and her husband did not pay much attention to the other congregants. As Catholics from birth, in spite of Marietta's open-mindedness to the Gospels and her simple spirituality, they were still awkwardly uncomfortable. Their eyes just focused upon the plain, bare altar and the hanging golden cross on the wall. No image of Jesus was to be found.

As the singing ended, the door by the modest wooden altar opened, and Rocky and Marietta could not believe what they saw—Tony Votolo, handsome as ever at thirty-three years old, but entirely gray. They had not seen him in over ten years. He had been behind Rocky at Barringer. Next to him were his two younger brothers, "Tweet" and "Honeydew", as tall and wide, as Tony was short and svelte. They looked more like bodyguards, or enforcers for Richie Boiardo, than elders in their brother's church. Now, here were three Roman Catholic kids from down on Lake Street off Park Avenue that Rocky had known since he could remember. And with all his stories about them, Marietta felt she knew them forever, too.

Rocky was now inquisitive and turned his head to scan the other parishioners. Before completing a full 360-degrees, he nudged Marietta to look for herself. Mothers, wives, sisters, and girlfriends of just about every one of the Bloomfield Avenue crew under Sneaks were there. They wore everything from black smocks, signifying their own state of mourning, to high heel shoes and low cut dresses, also demonstrating their still-powerful connection to the glamorous, but temporarily satisfying lifestyle of being married, or connected, to a local crime personality. Each had a love-hate relationship with all that organized, or disorganized, crime had brought into their lives. With so many of their men no longer, remorse, depression, and confusion were mostly what they now tasted. All eyes glued on Pastor Tony as he took the pulpit.

Tony's preaching seemed to be just for Marietta. It spoke of the forgiveness of Jesus in his atoning sacrifice on the cross, much of what Rocky had heard at mass all his life. What caught Rocky's attention was this personal relationship with Christ that Pastor Tony emphasized.

After service, all the ladies in back from Bloomfield Avenue came up to greet the two guests. They spoke of old times at Garside Street School, of days at Barringer and Central Highs, and about growing up in the First Ward. They told Marietta they were praying for loved ones who were either in lives of crime or had gone away never to return. Their faith that Jesus was watching over their fathers, husbands, brothers, and boyfriends seemed genuine to both Marietta and Rocky.

As the night ended, Pastor Tony and his brothers approached and embraced the Bonaduccis. It turns out that in Missouri Pastor Tony ended up in Bible School, and later also entered the ministry there. Returning to Jersey, his two brothers and five sisters instantly saw his remarkable change, from being a conceited All County quarterback and gangster wannabe, into a true Christian believer. Mike, known as "Tweet" for his high-pitched voice, and Steve, called "Honeydew" because he was such a sweet person to all, offered to assist their brother in growing his church. Both younger than Tony, they taught and coached football as assistants in the Newark school system—"Tweet" at Barringer and "Honeydew" at West Side. Being at their brother's church had one condition, … they could still go to Sunday mass at Sacred Heart Cathedral with their mother, sisters, and wives, before Tony's full gospel services. Of course, Pastor Tony's understanding in this respect was even motivating other members of the large Votolo family to come and hear his preaching from time to time.

"Mrs. Bonaducci, ya know that my little brother and I knew Pete real well," said Tweet, reaching to hold her hand.

"Yea, he made us laugh," added Honeydew. "We hung out at Ting-a-Ling's a lot because of all of our friends up on Bloomfield Avenue, and we'd go over to his shop to pick up our mother's meat order."

Pastor Tony and Rocky smiled as the brothers' memories made Pete come alive in Marietta's heart.

"His Ralph Kramden and Ollie Hardy imitations made us laugh so much, we cried," related Tweet. "And when Greenie was there, Pete made sure he'd be Fred Norton or Stan Laurel."

Then Honeydew added, "But, I'll tell ya what. When we asked him to do Ernie Borgnine in 'Marty', he'd get quiet."

"He wouldn't do it?" asked Marietta, recognizing the recent movie hit's less than humorous theme about a lonely butcher searching for love.

"No," answered Tweet. "He'd do it. He had the script down perfectly. So good, it was scary!"

No one said anything for a few moments until Marietta broke the silence. "I can understand." She paused, biting her lip. "He was Marty, ... before Ernie Borgnine was Marty."

As the church continued to empty, Pastor Tony led Marietta and Rocky in a prayer, and then offered condolences for Pete. Listening to the conversation of his well-meaning brothers, he felt the true sadness of Pete's life. Therefore, right before closing the church, the minister told Marietta the key to filling the void in her heart was that she had to forgive her mother. "Madiett, judge not, so you won't be judged. Remember we're all sinners, but God forgives us through Jesus. He paid the price for each of us, so that we could be like Him and forgive people as well. Forgive your mother and experience God's freedom and peace." The Pastor's dark brown eyes seemed to penetrate deep into her soul.

By midnight, Marietta did begin to understand forgiveness' powerful healing process, and from that day on her life received a supernatural charge that would never leave her. Pastor Tony also convinced her that with all the times she had spoken to Pete about the Sacred Heart of Jesus, he <u>had</u> to receive the touch of God. "The word of the Lord shall not return void," Pastor Tony explained, persuading her the seed of truth of Jesus' saving divinity would surely usher her generous brother into heaven. Rocky's old friend from Lake Street seemed to lift a million pounds of hurt off Marietta's heart.

As she and Rocky left, the choir was practicing an old time favorite:

I'll fly away, oh Lord, I'll fly away.

The promise of such freedom in finally making it to heaven was so tantalizing to Marietta, it fueled a final prayer that night: "God, please take me first."

Rocky was exhausted, but now the terrible night of his brother-in-law's passing seemed far enough away for him and his wife to move on. As they drove back to 711 Belmont Avenue, Rocky could not help commenting on the sincerity of the Bloomfield Avenue girls. "Ya know, Marietta, those gals let God come into their lives and take the place of their fathers, brothers, sons, and husbands. That makes sense. No reason to cry about it for the rest of their lives." He definitely had Marietta's attention. Rocky continued, "Yep, I don't make a big deal about it, but when I was on the islands, I was missin' all you guys. And I was scared. And ya know what? I believed Jesus was with me. He calmed me down. He was in my foxhole. I asked Him to be there, and I know you and my sisters and mother were prayin', too. For some reason I got back to Newark, when so many other guys got a one-way ticket. That's the only question: Why'd He round-trip me?"

In a soft, tired voice, Marietta answered, "And some day you'll get to ask Him," adding, "My only prayer now, Rocky, is 'God take me first'. I can't imagine what my poor mother's going through with losing a son."

Rocky could not believe his ears. Forgiveness had changed his wife so quickly. His own encounter with the Creator that night was more real than anything he'd ever experienced. *Would Marietta remain at peace now? Maybe now we can look forward to Christmas,* he thought. *I love Christmas Eve.* He bowed his head. *Oh, God, there won't be as many gifts around the tree this year. Pete's gone.*

CHAPTER 25

"BUONA NATALE"

On the morning of December 10, Rosa Gubitosi had not slept a wink overnight. But her husband, Gary, had never snored louder. Since their federal offense indictments for counterfeiting, she had been depressed. Most of her friends and family had not only stopped talking to her, but her "effort" to deal with the stunning accusation had put on close to fifty pounds. She weighed more than her husband, and he never stopped reminding.

"Get up, Gary. Get up," demanded Rosa, shoving the drooling TV repairman and part-time printer to wake him. It was 5 AM.

"Relax, Rosa. Leave me alone. We got time. Tommy D's not picking us up until 7." Gary was referring to their defense attorney, Thomas DelSordo. His price was right, but if talent had anything to do with getting Rosa and Gary off, they might as well start packing bags for some federal prison in Ohio.

"Gary, I think I'm gonna trow up."

"Again, Rosa?"

"It must be my nerves."

"Maybe it's the pickled pigs feet you insist on washing your sleeping pills down wit every night, Rosa."

"Gary, how'd this all start?" Rosa asked, ignoring him. "I just took some of those twenties you gave me and went around to some friends."

"Don't worry about it," encouraged Gary. "They ain't got no proof. Wit da heavyweight Jew boy attorneys Boot's guys got, we'll all be OK."

"Yea, but they aren't <u>our</u> attorneys. And what about that printing press some of those young boys took out after the garage collapse?" asked Rosa about the midnight excavation of Gary's expensive toy.

"Just scrap, Rosa, … junk! All we did was try to have some fun with a couple of twenties I got down at The Belmont Bar one night. They ain't puttin' us away for dat." As Gary lifted himself out of bed, his voice turned cold. "You just got stupid and thought you'd sell some bills like it was Avon or somethin'. Who told you to do dat?"

"Don't get me started, Mr. Heidleberg," said Rosa, ready for a fight.

Gary vanished into the bathroom.

When Benny "Bad Boy" Badalamenti returned home from his early morning walk in Branch Brook Park, as always, his loyal wife had coffee ready. Also, there was toasted panettone bread she made sure of having around at Christmas time. Calandra's Bakery at the Five Corners started selling it right after Thanksgiving. If spoiled Benny's wife didn't smother the slightly burnt delicacy in butter, he would ignore it. Brushing by her at the kitchen table, he reached for the phone. "I gotta call Carmine the Artist."

Mrs. Badalamenti needed no explanation. Having grown up in Brooklyn, she knew Carmine Bonaducci.

"Carmine A., … what's what?" was Benny's flip early morning greeting to the Gambino crime family lieutenant.

"What's what? Benny, I'll tell ya what's what. That goofy counterfeit trial starts today in Newark, and somehow you're in the middle of it."

"I'm worried, Carmine."

"Well, you should be, you selfish punk."

Carmine's rebuke surprised Badalamenti. "It'll be OK, Carmine. Relax."

"Well, why'd ya call me? We got you a lawyer who could get you off, but here you are doing business in Jersey. Not only do we not like that, but nothing is coming back this side of the Hudson."

"Carmine, no embarrassment will come your way," assured now unsure Badalamenti.

"That's the first thing you said that's true. It better be true." Carmine paused. "But the real problem is that <u>nothing</u> did come our way, and some people are upset about that."

"Who's upset?"

"Don't get me started, Benny. Next time, don't be so eager to play the rogue. Remember, you eat too much steak by yourself too fast, and you can choke. And if nobody's there with you, you can die." Carmine hung up.

At 5:30 AM the phone rang at Craig Francello's neat home on Cuozzo Street in Belleville. It was Sean McMahon from his bar in Queens. Mrs. Francello answered and called for Craig. It was difficult enough to understand her son from the effects of cerebral palsy, but when he'd just woke, it would be impossible for anyone other than Sean.

"Hellllooo." Sometimes Craig exaggerated his disabilities to his closest friend and mentor.

"Ya all set, buddy?" asked Sean.

"Alllll set to take some notes, yoooou old Irish bartender?"

"Take notes? I'm just a frustrated writer and storyteller who happens to own a bar. I'm not getting ready to take the ... bar exam."

"I like that, Sean. IIII got it. You just gave me an idea. One of our characters is an aspiring law student who gets indicted like meeeee, and he's the one that figures how to get the guys off; taking notes and all of thaaat."

"Well, I wasn't thinking about that. What are <u>you</u> talkin' about, Craig?"

"Ahhhh, forget the law student kid, because that's been overdone. Seriously, Mr. McMahon, I'm talking about that I'm innocent, and we're gonna write a screenplay or something about this menagerie of characters indicted for printing moneyyy. We'll just tell the truth, and have them all rolllling in the aisles. It'll be hilarious by the time we get through, Sean." Craig paused. "Sooooo, since no one can read my writing, somebody better be taking the notes about this fiascoooo."

"Well, if we're gonna turn this catastrophe into a winner for you and me, here's what we gotta do; we put a character in like you. Then we win an Academy Award, Emmy, or something."

"Nowwww I know why you're my mentor, you lush, youuu. Maybe I'll play myself."

"You better. Who could play Craig Francello better? On the other hand, Mr. Francello, it's easy for you to take this whole thing lightly. But I'm the guy lovin' the ponies who's done all the financing for his watering hole with one, 'Bad Boy' Badalamenti. You remember that 'sophisticated New York City financier' who just happens to live up the street from you in Forest Hill, ... and who just seems to take time to visit me everyday at the bar."

Craig started to laugh. His sharp mind never failed to impress Sean. "Relaxxx. I can't even figure out how all of us are supposed to be connected. Soooo I'm sure that colored guy and the broad from the Fed's office will surely botch this. III think this Giantempo guy already blew this one."

"Hope you're right, Craigie."

"On the other hand, let's start making some money together, sooooo you can stop gambling and only owe Bad Boy for nothing else but protection."

"I'll be picking you up in an hour and a half. Just say a prayer this public defender of ours is on his game," concluded Sean.

When Chet Costello arrived at his candy store next to Number 10 School by 6 AM, his major patron and occasional part-time worker, Topper Series, was waiting. "Well, chubby, today's the big time for you," reminded the retired Prudential mailroom clerk, chewing on his stogie for breakfast.

"Yea, and I hope it don't mean time in the ... big house, Topper," said Chet unlocking the store front door.

They flipped on the lights to get ready for the day's first customers. No further words were exchanged until Series tossed his soaked DeNobli into the sink behind the counter. "Listen, Chet, take a cue from your famous cousin, Lou. He's had good times and bad times. Ya gotta keep your sense of humor, cause I think you lost it. With all the connected guys comin' in here over the years for coffee and cigarettes with twenties, you became their laundry service, … their buyer of vintage fake government currency. The jury will see that. You'll make headlines when you get off, and then you'll be running the most popular candy store north of Bloomfield Avenue. Relax and just smile." Then Topper launched his soft voice into song, contradicting his usual gruff demeanor and disheveled 5-foot stature:

> *Smile, when your heart is breaking,*
> *Smile, even though it's aching.*
> *Smile, even when news is gloom and doom…"*

"OK, Topper, quit it," Chet interrupted. "First of all, if you're gonna sing, get the words right. Boy, wit life-long friends like you, who needs enemies? Get the apron on. I gotta get down to the courthouse. And remember, no bills above tens today."

"A little late for that, Chet!"

Louis Montana was a "made" guy in Jersey's underworld, who scared everyone to death with his unpredictable behavior and violent temper. To this day, Tommy Anthony cannot fathom "Crazy Louie's" shots into the air during that ugly October street battle between the South Side and Barringer kids. Since his father was rumored to have drowned back in '55 during a mid-December swim in the Passaic River, Louis Montana became vintage "Crazy Louie". Having vouched for Paulie Puccini as a young thug who would be a profitable addition to Boiardo's Bloomfield Avenue crew, he was surprisingly cold and detached when Paulie's "drug induced" death was announced. He frightened everyone, … all the way up to Sneaks.

"Ma, how do I look?" Louis asked, sporting a new black suit.

His middle-age mother, haggard from her son and missing husband's lives of crime, did not look up from her rosary beads. "Louis, don't be so proud your name is in the paper again. Even your father would be disgusted with you."

"Ma, your husband, … and my ol' man, clipped guys for a livin'."

"Don't talk about your father that way. He put food on the table for us, and he worked hard to keep you away from the streets."

"Yea, right. If he did his job a little better though, maybe he wouldn't be away so long."

"He'll be back. Even Mr. Boiardo told me he'll be back when I saw him at Giordano's last month," offered Mrs. Montana, as her son donned an expensive black wool overcoat.

"Yea, Ma, … in your dreams."

Crazy Louie exited the home on Bloomfield Avenue with a smile on his face, as if he was on his way to attend a Hollywood premiere.

Thomas Anthony lived alone on Roseville Avenue. His many girlfriends helped decorate his neat two-bedroom home. From his porch he could get a clear view into City Stadium of City League football games during the season. If he weren't following Frank Bonaducci and the Bellboys with Pete, or on Boiardo business, he'd sit there with his crew on Saturdays nursing an expensive Havana. Today was too cold to be thinking about that. His phone rang. Greenie had to be attended to.

"Stop crying," Two Tones demanded. "Look, I know it's been a tough year with Pete dying, this case, and all the rest. But just relax."

"How can I, Two Tones? Our best friend dies in our arms, we're in this stupid counterfeit thing, and those Feds are tryin' to tie in a couple of deaths—the Puccini kid, those motor cycle guys. And you know what, Tommy?"

"What?"

"That old man and his wife that hung themselves behind Madiett's house…"

"Yea? Who says?"

"Well, I hear from Rocky Bonaducci that the Belleville cops are asking questions about that jerk printer, Gubitosi." Greenie sighed. "This is getting bad."

"The Feds are doin' their jobs," assured even-tempered Two Tones. "Whoever's at the heart of this counterfeit thing will get scared if they're involved with these deaths, and the case will get cracked. You and I didn't do anything other than

344

handle a lot of 'numbers' money coming through. That's where we probably got touched. I think this is a New York thing, so you know who has his slime all over it."

"Yea, Bad Boy. But who else?"

"Who cares? Just so we get off."

"Hey, ya hear this, Two Tones?"

"What?"

"Lisa and Malafatano down in Atlanta?"

"You mean those scums that The Boot exported?"

"Yea, that's right. Well, they can't find 'em. Their cars been at Atlanta Airport for a month, and they ain't around. Left their nightclubs and all."

"Man, they're off the trial, too? Aren't they lucky?"

"Yunno, Pete always did tell us those guys were no good rats, and that they got Sneaks locked up? Five Corners always said The Boot either sent them down Sout to promote, or get rid of 'em. Now I wonder if the Feds have those two bums singin' from the treetops somewhere."

"Greenie, you think too much. I'll pick you up in an hour."

Vinnie Giampietro woke up crying that morning. From next door he could smell his sister's coffee, but it gave him little consolation. He felt so alone. His parents were dead, and his sister was preoccupied with her new husband. Because of his hip problem, he never dated. At twenty-five years old, the only things he took pride in were his playing days at Belleville, surviving Korea, and still being a part of Bellboy football because Coach Eddie Popalinski always requested him to be their bus driver. Sure he would cash big bills for some patrons boarding his Trackless Transit bus in Silver Lake on its way down Sixth Street to Bloomfield Avenue. What else was he supposed to do? His gentle personality would not let him ask for lesser denominations. Besides, he liked a lot of these guys, although he knew they weren't working regular jobs like him.

He answered his ringing phone.

"Ya gonna be ready in an hour, Vinnie?" asked Wee Willie Brindisi, Belleville's ferocious two-way tackle from a year ago.

"Yea. Hey, Willie, I really appreciate this."

"Well, don't thank me. Thank Gino. He'll be home from that reformatory football school next week. But he insisted we pick you up with his Bonneville. His mother said 'OK', so I'll be down with McCabe, Pinnedella, and Riordan."

"Those guys don't have to come."

"Yea, they know that, but who's off from school, work, whatever. And Frankie Bonaducci sends his best. He'll be in town in a week and come down to the Federal Building to support you, too."

Vinnie was silent, realizing he was not alone.

Julie Manzer awoke her father. "Dad, time to get ready." She'd taken the week off from acting and dancing lessons in New York City to accompany him to the trial.

"Yea, let's get ready. Finally prove my innocence and get away from these greaseballs."

Julie ignored him. "Dad, your bath is ready, and Mom has breakfast downstairs."

"Yea, can't wait to get back on the job and lock some of these guys up. Imagine, putting me in the same category with them."

Julie had nothing to add.

When Elizabeth Carey answered her phone, her ex-fiance, Patsie Pratola, was on the line. "Hi, babe," he said.

"Don't 'hi babe' me."

"Come on. We're gonna patch this thing up, I'm gonna be found innocent, and start singing with the Four Loves again. Lots of good tings comin' up."

"And you need a ride. Well, I'm not giving it. My brother's in the police academy, and you're a two-bit street gangster." Elizabeth hung up.

Just as he had every day for thirty-five years as a teacher, coach, and administrator, Hiram Wilhelm walked into Belleville High School at 7 AM. Today, he was bitter as ever. His profound reputation as a molder of young people had been tainted by these indictments.

Ed Popalinski greeted him in the coaches' room with a hot cup of coffee. "Listen, Hiram, you've done too many good things for these kids over the years for the judge and jury to ignore it. Just don't be so cantankerous. Answer their questions without indicting every teenager who never played a sport." Coach P. put his right hand on the grumpy athletic director's shoulder. "And please don't talk like you figured the whole damn thing out. You're a victim. Be humble."

"That's what aggravates me. They got me, … that Puccini and his gremlin friends got me. They never paid over the years, and last year during football and basketball, they were always there. Then Francello and that Manzer 'tease'—always big bills, and always the crippled kid's treating these babes. What a fool I was not to see something going on."

"Just don't be another Jewish lawyer. They'll be enough of them around you and those other wiseguys."

"Other wiseguys, Eddie? Oh, thanks a lot. Some friend." The athletic director took his coffee into his office and slammed the door.

As Sneaks Babula walked out of Rahway State Prison, escorted by guards to a New Jersey State Police car, his fellow inmates cheered louder than any City League game crowd back in the thirties when he was an unstoppable tailback.

"Show 'em how to be a lawyer, Sneaks."

"Sneaks Babula wins one for the gimpy kid and his umpteen friends."

"Let Giantempo see who's still the real boss, Sneaks."

Sunglasses and a white satin scarf around his thick neck and over his broad shoulders, softly contrasted with Gino Babula Sr.'s camelhair full-length winter overcoat. He looked more like the boss of all bosses for the New York and New Jersey crime families than Carlo Gambino or Richie Boiardo ever did. He smiled, stopped, and then raised both hands to get the full attention of three floors of convicts, and yelled out, "Let justice be served!"

The roar of approval was deafening inside of the prison.

Since May, an assortment of mob attorneys, public defenders, and local low-priced lawyers had been at work prepping their clients, character witnesses, and family members in hopes of proving this loosely crafted, supposed counterfeit conspiracy was more coincidence than a premeditated crime. Indeed, everyone following the case had their own ideas as to who were the kingpins of circulating the fake money in the first place. But few could pull all the circumstances together to prove either guilt, or innocence, of this eclectic assembly of suspects.

The alleged crime being federal, Sal Giantempo's decision to drive the case from his federal prosecutor's office was expected. But distancing himself, by naming a female and a black member from his staff to try it, led many detractors from the old neighborhood to repeat what they said when he was a Central High student in the thirties, competing with Sneaks Babula to be the starting tailback. Caesar Casciano put it best after Sunday mass, before the trial. He had stopped by the Bonaducci house to see how Marietta was doing. Frank was home from Cornell. "Ah, this Giantempo's a real pineapple. Sure he's smart, but too smart for his own good. No common sense. Always wants the limelight, but never willing to pay the full price. Like with the war. He gets out with a bad back from football? But who remembers him even being on the field long enough to take a hit? So, with his education and all, he's downtown working in the Army recruiting station, and playing golf whenever the weather's OK; and your father's in the Islands killing Japs, while your Uncle Anthony and me are fightin' Nazi's outside Berlin. Now Sneaks and Sal go face to face again. Sure, Babula made some bad decisions. But, God forgive us, he's good at what he does. He's right under The Boot. Giantempo don't have the 'killer' instinct needed to be a top federal prosecutor. So he puts this girl and this colored guy in to do the dirty work, … but he looks for the headlines. Typical Sal. Can you imagine what it's gonna be like with Sneaks trying to defend himself? No Notre Dame education like Sal, but he learned a lot on the streets of Newark. This should be very, very interesting."

The whole Bonaducci family was around the kitchen table listening. Even Blackie had his own chair. When Casciano arrived, Rocky, Donna, and the boys were dipping pieces of Giordano's hard-crusted Italian bread into a small bowl of Marietta's fresh gravy. Dinner was still an hour away, but soaking bread in the gravy after church was a ritual that was as assumed as not eating meat on Fridays in an Italian-American, Roman Catholic household.

Frank was first to respond. "You really think Giantempo and his people will mess this one up, Uncle Caesar?"

"Get that Cornell education, Frankie, but listen to your Uncle Caesar. Ya gotta do things for the right reasons. This Giantempo guy is using what evidence he has to be a hero in lockin' up some of the boys. Not really a bad thing if they broke the law. But, he's also tryin' to get revenge on Sneaks. And ya know what? This chooch thinks he's on top of the world with this jury he's got. He's also figurin' that ol' Judge Liloia will be tough as usual and send all these neighborhood guys up the river. 'Manedge a diaola' (Damn the devil)."

Jo-Jo knew more about the case than anyone could imagine. "But how does that really hurt him?"

Rocky, who had been silent, jumped in. " The jury <u>is</u> from the neighborhood, and they <u>could</u> give these guys a break. And while cousin Liloia has always been tough on connected guys, ya never know. He's gettin' old."

Caesar went on, "And, over all these months, Giantempo got sloppy. Sure they were gathering evidence and preppin' witnesses, but they never came up with any murder charge over Paulie's death, or even on Al and Henry. Then he feebly attempts to pull the Profetta suicides in at the last minute."

"I don't get it, Uncle Caesar," said Frank.

Marietta surprised them all. "Well, if he was really working hard, and not so concerned about his political career or embarrassing Sneaks, he could have spent more time on the deaths. Then, maybe he would have scared some wannabe wiseguys to spill the beans on all the details of the silly twenties."

"You mean take the hit on the lesser charge of counterfeiting and get guys locked up, but no murder case?" asked Frank.

"That's it," said Caesar as he reached to dip his own piece of bread. "Thank God, nobody too close got caught up with this. I know about Pete's friends, Madiett. But at least we don't have any family involved."

She made the sign of the cross. Marietta had more to thank God for than Caesar knew. Even Rocky repeated the ritual as all their three children rolled their eyes.

The trial had been on nearly two weeks. And with only two days to go until Christmas, everyone figured Judge Leroy Liloia would call a holiday recess. Dozens of witnesses had testified on behalf of, or against the defendants. The backgrounds of the fourteen were so bizarre and diverse that the eyeballs of everyone attending seemed to be spinning by the end of each day. Most people in the courtroom, and in the state, concurred that organized crime probably orchestrated the entire scheme, if, indeed, there was one. But a lack of any definitive link between the suspects threw major doubt on the quality of the investigation.

In the first week, a patron of Sean McMahon's bar was dramatic when he stood up in the witness stand and pointed to Benny Badalamenti. "That's the guy who's always in the bar pickin' up money from McMahon."

On the stand later, Sean explained his gambling habit, as well as how Bad Boy had arranged the financing for purchase of his saloon. Badalamenti's attorney conceded his client has a record for illegal gambling operations and extortion related to shylocking, but made it clear that he was not a counterfeiter.

Craig Francello's public defender claimed his young client's abnormal amount of cash was due to his weekly pay for helping Sean McMahon write a children's television show. "If the money was bad, he got it from New York. My client has cerebral palsy. He can hardly move, let alone groove with these street guys."

No one reacted to the lawyer's remarks, until Craig started laughing uncontrollably, pounding his arms on the table in front of him. Then the rest of nearly hundred spectators and jury joined in. Visions of Craig hanging on street corners, coming in and out of restaurants after "sit-downs", or trying to rough up somebody who was late on payments just blew the minds of everyone now seeing the reality of his life's burden.

Vinnie Giampietro's young attorney unwittingly asked the judge and jury what they would do if some local hoods jumped on a bus they were driving and paid their fare with a crisp twenty. Before Judge Liloia could, the lawyer answered his own question. "If my client told them to take a hike, he'd might be driving a bus in the sky today. Besides, these guys were always nice to him in the first place."

"Nice to him in the first place?" asked the black prosecutor. "But they'd kill him if he would not let them on the bus? Which is it, counselor?"

"Well, Vinnie does have some rough people ride on his bus, but they'd probably never hurt him. You know what I mean," was the inexperienced explanation.

Laughter again erupted.

Thomas "Two Tones" Anthony had to explain why he and Greenie were seen so often at Gary Gubitosi's house in Belleville. "We got friends in that neighborhood. And Gary prints all the menus for a couple of restaurants the guys own down on Bloomfield Avenue. Me and Greenie pick them up at Gary's house. You know, as a favor to our associates. It's Gary's night job. Plus he fixes a lot of our TV's. That's his day job."

The prosecutor's office tried to portray Chet Costello's candy store as a major meeting place and distribution channel for the fake currency. When he was put on the stand, Chet managed to uncannily imitate his famous cousin, Lou. "First of all, please let me say that with all due respect, you people don't know who's on first."

The female prosecutor, oblivious to one of comedy's classic routines, or certainly unaware of Chet's family ties to one of America's most beloved comics, reacted with, "What?"

"No, lady, what's on second."

The courtroom exploded. Sal Giantempo had to get up from the sidelines where he was sitting to tell his aide what was actually going on. Naturally, Judge Liloia sustained her objection.

During his turn on the stand, Hiram Wilhelm seemed to be following Coach Popalinski's advice, acting professionally and allowing his lawyer to build a strong case for his credibility, as well as the circumstantial nature of him coming in contact with so many counterfeit bills. Under cross-examination, the black prosecutor attempted to paint a picture of an underpaid high school administrator tired of seeing ex-students out-earn him. And the frustrated career educator blew his top! By mentioning the names of the late Paulie Puccini and each of his friends, as well as making a veiled reference to Francello being "a kid who loves for you to feel sorry for him", Wilhelm practically ordered his own pair of cement shoes. It seemed every other word coming out of his mouth was an Italian-American slur, some of which even Bloomfield Avenue never heard before. "These gabootsell-sucking, fig tree-hugging, purple-footed sons of foreigners want to ruin my career," screamed Wilhelm, pointing not only to his co-defendants, but at their relatives in the audience as well. He was even staring down the jury whose names ended in more vowels than Hiram could have ever guessed.

Wilhelm's attorney rushed to the stand to try to calm him as the Essex County Sheriff's officers had to do all they could to restrain, not only some of the defendants, but their wives, girlfriends, children, and any other proud Newark citizens of Italian descent. In addition to that, if looks could kill, most of the jury would be up for murder.

Frank Bonaducci and Jackie Carey were leaning up against a huge marble column at the back of the cavernous court. Jo-Jo was next to them. Frank spoke in Jackie's ear, "I can't believe Wilhelm. If it weren't for my mother, he wouldn't even know what a gabootsell was."

"That's right, Frank," Jo-Jo agreed.

"What are youse talkin' bout, Frankie?" asked Jackie.

"In the gym last spring, Mr. Wilhelm and I were talking about Easter and Passover, and I mentioned some Italian delicacies for the holidays. I told about my mother doing the calves' heads, pizzaiola style. My Uncle Pete taught her that. When Wilhelm's mouth started to water, I promised to bring a couple in for him. He couldn't wait."

"And?" Carey asked.

"He loved it so much, Gino and I caught him sucking out one of the calf eyes from the head, right on his office desk. And now he's making fun of Italians?" Frank shook his head and smiled. "The situation does not make the man, it reveals him."

"Boy, almost makes ya wanna be anti-Semitic," offered Carey.

"Jackie, forget that kind of stuff. Hiram's just getting old," said Frank.

As Sheriff's officers restored order, Judge Liloia rebuked Wilhelm for his insensitive and ethnic remarks, and warned everyone he would empty the court at the next outburst. At that point, an uneasy silence came over the room.

Greenie, who could never sit still for any period of time, started to squirm. Then, he stood up, stretched, and cupped his hands around his mouth, yelling out, "Hey, ya Heeb, ya ever hear of Meyer Lansky? He makes us guys look like a bunch of altar boys. And I'm half Irish by the way, buddy."

Cheers rose up for Greenie, who didn't have an enemy in the world, until now. Wilhelm scowled at the chuckling Boiardo gopher.

The trial's most serious moments came with the criminal records of Bad Boy, Crazy Louie, Patsie, and Sneaks, coupled with Manzer's questionable relationships. Attorneys for the Bloomfield Avenue boys admitted to their unacceptable behavior, especially those deeds for which they'd already been convicted. But in this case, they finally pointed to the circumstantial nature of all the evidence being presented.

The big climax was when Gino Babula Sr. was allowed to speak. Judge Liloia, known for his consistently stern courtroom demeanor, had cautioned the convict to respect the judicial system with only meaningful remarks. Liloia had given tough sentencing over the years, even to the relatives of some of his old First Ward friends, but throughout this case, he seemed to have been uncharacteristically detached.

With all eyes glued on him, Sneaks finally had a chance to defend himself, ... without an attorney. And now, sort of face to face with Prosecutor Giantempo once more, he stood tall, his chest seeming to fill with emotion as he surveyed all in attendance.

The judge deflated the moment by saying, "Mr. Babula, please begin, ... before it's Christmas Day."

"Yes, your honor, and thank you for this opportunity," said Sneaks, facing the jury. "Ladies and gentlemen of the judicial system, the jury, the Honorable Judge Leroy Liloia, a towering figure in the Italian American community of Newark, I might add, distinguished members of the legal profession, and friends and relatives from the ol' neighborhood, ... and my ex-teammate, Prosecutor Sal Giantempo ..."

The judge interrupted. "What I tell you, Mr. Babula? Keep your comments poignant."

"Yea, your honor, but only problem now is that I don't know what 'poignant' means."

Smiles and laughter returned to dozens of faces.

Babula continued. "Listen folks, I live at Rahway State Prison. It's where I'll be for Christmas. Now, don't get me wrong. I don't need sympathy today, just your understanding. Ya see, I've made decisions in my life. Some I'm proud of, and some I ain't. I embarrassed my family and myself on many occasions. But know what? I knew that some day these kinds of things could happen to me, and I took the shot. Just check the record, and you'll find out why I'm doin' time. It's got nuttin' to do with counterfeitin'. I'm a lot of other things, but I ain't involved in this fake money thing. And let me tell yas; most, if not all, these guys, ain't either." Babula gestured to the co-defendants.

"Let me explain some things. Sometimes good people make bad decisions. No, I'm not sayin' I'm a good guy, but my wife and kid love me." Faint approval could be heard from some of Sneak's supporters, including Sylvia. Gino was home for the holiday, but refused to attend the trial.

"When I got off the boat back in '30, a lot of people helped me. A guy named Pete Frassa Sr. put me to work in his butcher shop, and he treated me like a son. Yea, I had other more famous benefactors, too, but decent people helped me from the ol' neighborhood. And ya know what, a lot of these decent types really had tough times during the Depression. But they stuck together and helped each other out. Some of the people who took care of me had bigger ambitions, and took things into their own hands, … not to purposely break the law, but to get by. Ya know, help others and try to get ahead. They had no education, and sometimes certain people treated them like they weren't worthy to be here in America. But they did what they had to do. I saw how some of the real good people suffered, and I made a mistake. I thought ya had to take things under your own control and get even with those who didn't treat us right. I started doing things that went against the law."

Babula knew he had everyone's attention.

"Well, when I was playin' football at Central, I loved bein' the hero." Sneaks looked at his envious ex-teammate, Giantempo. "You remember those days, Sally. Yea, and when it was over, I didn't want it to end. So I started on the streets doin' stupid stuff, and always endin' up with a wad of cash for it. I left Mr. Frassa's business after he died, vowing I wouldn't struggle like he did. But I did respect him. He was a great butcher—fair and generous. I figured I would help people, too, but in a different way. Sorta like bein' Robin Hood. Yea, I was a hood alright!" More laughter. "Well, that was a long time ago, and a lot has happened since. Did I break the law? You haven't heard me say I shouldn't be in prison. Sure I did, but I'm payin' for it in more ways than one. Most of all, I bet you people saw my son, Gino, play football at Belleville more than I saw him. It broke my heart, but I made the choices that put me there. No apologies, no sympathy. Regrets?"

Babula paused.

"Listen, I'm hearin' a lot about organized crime. Let me tell yas, if all the criminals I know were so organized, then, what are they all doin' spendin' Christmas wit me in Rahway?"

Again, smiles and soft laughter.

The prosecutors were getting impatient. But Judge Liloia slouched in his leather chair, as if reliving the lives of so many of his fellow Italian Americans who made similar choices like Sneaks. He remembered how his own father and so many other Italian American immigrants labored night and day to help build the Sacred Heart Cathedral in the heart of the First Ward. They just wanted to put food on the table. Some wavered in the faith that they could make it with a day's wage. Others became bitter, watching politicians and big business types stretch the laws for their own good. Richie Boiardo tried to help many of them. Breaking the law evolved slowly for some people whom Liloia would have never thought could become criminals. On the other hand, most stayed the course and sacrificed, like his family. Internally, he sighed. *Ah, but who can we judge? And, I am a judge.* As Sneaks continued, Liloia pictured the lively multi-colored tapestry of celebration that had been life in the First Ward. He imagined old neighbors who had gone astray, each loving Newark and their family just as much as his other more law-abiding friends. He had to remove his glasses and dry his eyes. Too many were no longer around.

Sneaks continued, "Here's what's goin' on here, folks. There's bad things out there like prostitution and drugs comin' into town. Yea, I know guys doin' that, and I tell 'em it ain't right. We gotta respect woman, and these drugs are poison. See this bunch here in court?" He pointed to the fourteen. "They ain't connected with that stuff. Don't ask me how I know, but I know. And some of these kids like little Craigie boy, Vinnie, and a couple of these others, … just wrong place wrong time. The rest? It's all a neighborhood ting. They were born into it. Almost like a curse. They should know better just like me, but sometimes it's too much in the blood. Been handed down. Doesn't make them angels, but some of these politicians out there are just as much to blame— all politicians present, excluded, of course."

More laughter.

"They make people pawns in their games to gain their own sorta power, and even corrupt the very legal and political systems they're supposed to be protectin'."

"Mr. Babula," interrupted the judge, "Please begin to finish up."

"Well, Judge, this whole thing stinks. I should be in jail, for what I'm in for. But I don't want to see innocent people's reputations ruined because some guys with big educations think they're not worthwhile human beings and can act as cannon fodder for their legal and political careers. If you're gonna lock us up, do a better job of your investigations, and do it for all the right reasons. One thing I learned from the good people in my life—do things to help people, and all good things happen to you. But ya never do things to help yourself without putting others first." Sneaks turned to Sal Giantempo one more time. "And if you want to get a job done right to help yourself, ya at least have to do it yourself. Don't send somebody else and expect to get all the credit."

Sneaks paused.

"Are you done, Mr. Babula?" asked the judge.

"One last thing," said Sneaks. "A counterfeit conspiracy takes a lot of planning and a lot of brains. I mean no offense to my old friends from Bloomfield Avenue, but there are a lot easier ways to generate revenue. Not that these guys couldn't get it done. But I know some of these guys since they were little guys, and they ain't in it that deep. They want to, but they can't, because some people won't let 'em. That's another story." He looked to the defendants. "No disrespect guys, but you ain't as smart, or as bad, as the boys down at Rahway. And ya know what, ... stay that way."

Babula then turned to the jury and concluded, "I am sorry that your time has been wasted at this sacred religious and family time of the year. May you and your families have a blessed Christmas from my home to yours; I mean from my cell to yours."

Applause broke out, and Judge Liloia let it go until Sal Giantempo rose in protest. Bringing the courtroom back to order, the judge summoned the prosecutors and all the defense attorneys. It was impossible to read anyone's lips. But it looked as if Liloia was verbally shredding the Giantempo team. The judge, without saying another word, then focused attention on the jury.

When they returned to their seats, DelSordo, the Gubitosis' lawyer, moved to have the case dismissed. Utter silence. The judge seemed to be staring at the ceiling. He stood up and started shaking his head into a nod.

"We're going to call this thing. Case dismissed!" he said. "And may I join Sneak's wish to all of you, 'Merry Christmas, everyone,' ... or should I say 'Buona Natale'?"

"And a Happy New Year to you, Judge," said one of the jury.

Pandemonium filled the ancient hall of justice. Frank quickly left Jackie and Jo-Joe to congratulate Craig, Greenie, Vinnie, and Two Tones.

As Jo-Jo gazed at the defendants' jubilation and the confusion and embarrassment on the federal prosecutors' faces, he felt stunned. *Innocent people are being set free, but those as guilty as sin are also winning out. Good things happen to good people,* Jo-Jo thought, *but good things happen to bad people as well.* The Belleville freshman was full of conflicts. *Uncle Pete would be happy for his friends, and how relieved my mother's gonna be.* But Jo-Jo remembered that humid summer night he spent in the bowels of a backyard boat, fishing for twenties in its moist dirt floor. *Would my evidence have changed the trial's outcome?* More overwhelming was his feeling of finality as the year of 1959 was coming to an end. So much had happened since his brother Frank stopped at the four-yard line on his way to a sure touchdown, just three weeks before this pivotal year commenced. It must have been an omen of things to come, ... a year when so much change entered his and his family's lives. *So much is gonna be different now,* he thought. He wanted more time to reflect alone. He would get that chance over the Christmas Holiday, ... and would also have the rest of his life to contemplate even further.

CHAPTER 26

"THANKSGIVING EVE, 1971"

The plane into Newark Airport was an hour late. A snowstorm out west had messed everything up. Besides, it was the busiest travel day of the year. In Jersey the weather was balmy for late November.

"God, Jo-Jo, I'm nervous," Donna said to her brother. "We haven't seen Frankie since last Christmas, and I can't wait to see Maria. Frank says our pregnant sister-in-law looks beautiful."

"Nothing new there," reminded Jo-Jo. "Nobody's more in love with his wife than our brother."

The National Airlines gate was packed with travelers.

"There they are, Jo-Jo," yelled Donna. "Gee, I wish Mommy were here to see Maria expecting."

It had been a year and three weeks since Marietta Bonaducci had died at forty-seven of a heart attack and stroke in the arms of her eighteen-year old daughter. Donna was home from Montclair State College at dinnertime, as her mother was getting ready again for her graveyard at the factory. Jo-Jo was living in New York City, and Frank in Lake Tahoe. Rocky was working some overtime at Jergens. She went quickly. But her last words to Donna were crystal clear: "Tell Frankie Uncle Pete left $10,000 for him at People's Bank. I never touched it, for any of you. Make sure he gives it out in scholarships to kids like you. You know, both parents having to work, and stuff. I see Jesus now. Pete's with Him." Then she was gone. Marietta's mother had died the year before at age seventy.

The four Bonaduccis embraced at the arrival gate, and Donna patted Maria's belly.

"How's Daddy," asked Frank.

"Can't wait to see you guys," answered Jo-Jo.

Donna filled them in quickly. "It's been a tough year with Mommy leaving, and then selling 711 Belmont Avenue. But he's excited you're coming back east, Frank, and telling everybody how he's going to work with you. But most of all, he talks about your new baby, ... driving us all nuts. He and Aunt Bella are counting the days to Grandpa Joe's first great grandchild. It's an Italian thing. You know her. It's going to be another child that she couldn't have, but she'll mother it anyway."

"How about the award?" asked Frank about the special recognition Rocky was receiving that night at the annual Barringer-East Orange Thanksgiving Game Dinner, celebrating the schools' long-time rivalry.

Jo-Jo answered. "He's been getting emotional because of Mommy dying. Then he's been talking about seeing some of the guys, for the first time since the East Orange game, ... who survived the war, and who didn't come back. That's why he wants you to do his acceptance, Frank. If he has to speak, he'll never get through it."

The 1940 game, before 25,000 screaming fans, was Rocky's one glorious moment in the sun at Newark's City Stadium. His game-tying extra point sensationally ended East Orange's undefeated, untied, and unscored-upon season. The game ball, inscribed with the 7-7 score, as well as the names of all his teammates, became the family's most prized possession. It turned everyday of the Bonaduccis' lives into football season and guaranteed both sons' destinies to play, while Donna contributed as a cheerleader.

Maria changed the subject. "How's the new apartment?"

"Little cramped for the two of us. But I stay up at school with my girl friends sometimes to give him a break," answered Donna. "I think he's going to start dating soon." Heading towards baggage claim, Donna's revelation of Rocky beginning to go out a year after Marietta's passing stopped the others in their tracks.

"Donna, you never told me," scolded Jo-Jo.

"I didn't want to mess you up, … with your doctorate and all. Besides, we just started talking last week."

"Jo-Jo, it's OK. He was a good husband and father," assured Frank. "He's got to get started again. Don't judge him."

"You're too perfect, Frank," said his brother.

Retrieving the bags, the group started for Jo-Jo's car. "I've got a surprise for you two," he said.

"Yea, real surprise," commented Donna, unimpressed.

"What?" queried Maria.

Frank just smiled, in quiet expectation.

Within minutes sitting before them was … Jackie Carey's 1949 customized golden Mercury. Jo-Jo had bought it, "on time", from Frank's old friend.

"I don't believe it, Cuz," said Frank.

"Looks better than when he had it," evaluated Maria.

"How'd you do it?" asked Frank.

"Well, he divorced that young chick he married and needed extra bucks to take care of his daughter and all. Said to send his love to you two."

They piled in, while Jo-Jo put the bags in the trunk, carefully releasing the continental kit in the back.

All set to go, Frank made a request. "Jo-Jo, can you take Route 21 through Branch Brook Park, all the way past the yeast factory, and then come down by the old neighborhood?"

"No problem, Frank. Sentimental journey?"

"Na, just want to get ready for tonight."

"Don't forget the lesson you've taught me for years: 'When you look back, Cuz, glance, don't stare,'" reminded Jo-Jo. Then he placed a cassette into the music system he'd just installed. "OK, just sit back and enjoy the trip back in time, 'cause I got Scott Muni at Rockefeller Center with a reunion concert."

"You're crazy, Jo-Jo," said Frank.

"Got that right, Frankie," offered Donna. "He's obsessed with this doo wop stuff or whatever they're now calling old music of the fifties."

"No comments from the peanut gallery," said Jo-Jo. "Welcome back to Jersey guys, ... and the sounds of our lives."

The New York City disc jockey's gravel voice came through the new speakers, as if Scott Muni was sitting between Jo-Jo and Frank in the vintage Merc. "Ladies and gentleman, for the first time ever on the same stage, The Penguins, The Mello-Kings, and The Five Satins ..."

Everyone enjoyed the classic harmonizing sounds of rock 'n' roll's early years, as Jo-Jo sped up Route 21. The music took them back to a time they all would have preferred had never gone away. Not a word was spoken.

Coming down Belleville Avenue from Bloomfield and approaching the Smallwood-Belmont Avenue neighborhood, Frank asked Jo-Jo to stop at Henry Davidson's Shell station, still run by Mark Brunello, who took it over after the tragic accident back in '59.

As the car pulled up, its smooth, muffled exhaust system caught the attention of the office's three inhabitants. This corner depot had been displaying the Shell Gasoline sign since World War II, and was a neighborhood landmark. Slowly riding over the rubberized bell system that signaled a new customer, Jo-Jo parked facing the unlikely trio peering through the glass—Mark, Uncle Dominick Gretto (Gerald's dad), and John Abbottelli, a local resident who made his living as a photographer.

Frank felt goose bumps all over his body. Years had passed so quickly for the oldest Bonaducci child. His Cornell days were like a flash in the night. Its highlight was playing beside now legendary quarterback, Gary Wood, currently with the New York Giants. Pete Gogolak was there at the same time in Ithaca, making Frank's less than illustrious college football career more exciting than he could have ever imagined. His business profession became resort development sales with U.S. Properties at Incline Village in Lake Tahoe, and that was skyrocketing. Then came the chance to transfer back to New Jersey and take over their eastern region. A baby on the way meant he and Maria would be able to raise their children in Essex County, where so many family members still lived.

As Frank looked at Jo-Jo, a lump in his throat replaced the pride in his heart, as he thought of all his mother would be missing in the lives of her children. In one year, his little brother would have his doctorate in psychology. Jo-Jo had followed in Frank's footsteps with All County recognition in football, going on to Boston College on a scholarship. While only playing sparingly on special teams, Jo-Jo stuck it out until the end. But, best of all, he met his future wife there. Donna had become Captain of the Belleville cheerleaders and was now majoring in special education to become a teacher after graduation. Only Rocky was suffering. He had to go on disability, with a bad back, after his wife's death. But now he was encouraged Frank was going to train him in resort real estate sales.

Frank whispered to himself, "Lord Jesus, please slow us down."

Before the four could get out, Mark, Dominick, and John surrounded the car, opening the doors, and fussing over the surprise visit by the Bonaduccis who had grown up less than fifty yards away.

"Jesus, Mary, and Joseph," exclaimed Dominick, "it's Rocky's kids."

"Yea, Dominick, but that ain't their names. It's Frank, Jo-Jo, and Donna," corrected Mark. "Welcome back home ... and Happy Thanksgiving to all."

"Ah, two of my favorite subjects," said middle-aged Abbottelli, who'd taken countless pictures of both boys during their Belleville playing days. "And the beautiful Maria Giardina with child, as well as Miss Donata, the Captain of cheerleaders."

Mark always seemed to have grease caked deeply into his fingernails and the lines of his hands. Sometimes he worked seven days a week as the "grease monkey most in demand" in the border towns of Belleville, Bloomfield, Nutley, and Newark. His Shell uniform was never cleaned, but he never wore anything else at the station. Not a day went by without him reminiscing the life and death of his mentor, Henry Davidson, and that fateful day he took his first and last ride on a motorcycle. Trying to control his drinking by attending Bible studies sponsored by Pastor Tony

Votolo's church up the street, the accident on Friday, May 15, 1959, still depressed Mark.

Uncle Dominick, as the Bonaduccis called Dominick Gretto, was a tiny mustached family man, also devoted to the Knights of Columbus at Saint Peter's Church in Belleville and to his auto supply company in Brooklyn. He provided most of Mark's inventory.

As Dominick hugged everyone, Frank reminded them about all the Sunday mornings his mother would ask Dom and his devoted wife, Tilley, to pack the three Bonaducci children into his big Buick Roadmaster so they would not miss mass.

"He never refused," said Frank. "But I must tell you, seven kids plus Aunt Tilley and Uncle Dominick? Even in the big boat he had, left me smelling Gerald's breakfast breath every Sunday." Who could help but smile?

"Follow me," Abbottelli said.

Mark's eyes rolled as Dominick grabbed Donna's hand and kissed her head. "We miss you next door," he said. Emotion prevented her from responding. With Rocky out of work and nursing the bad back, the family home was sold.

As they approached the back wall of one of the garages, Maria's eyes nearly popped out of her head in awe and embarrassment. Donna, who had seen the collage of photos before, also blushed this time, just as she had when she was only twelve years old.

"I don't believe it, Markie," said Frank. "You added to these pictures over the years. It's unbelievable … and a little risqué, I might add."

"Well, I never thought, in my wildest dreams, that I'd be surrounded by Marilyn Monroe, Jayne Mansfield, and Betty Paige," quipped Jo-Jo. "Hey, Markie, if my mother were here, she'd be upset."

"Yea, or praying for Mark and John, like I've been doing for years," said Dominick with a straight face. "But boys, ignore the sinful undressed and take a look at what John and Mark put up over here. They're cleaning up their act ever so slowly. Prayer does change things."

Indeed, the whole back wall was like a pictorial journey through the neighborhood, caught in images taken by John, as well as headlines clipped from *The Ledger, The*

Newark News, Italian Tribune, and other local papers. Everyone except Maria now realized the scantily clad bodies of three of America's most prominent pinups of the fifties were simply there in remembrance of Henry Davidson. His calendars were not only legendary amongst the local boys, but also certainly became stimulants to their early thrusts into puberty. The priests at Saint Peter's well knew the temptations with which Henry Davidson had papered his greasy station walls.

There it all was, the heart of their lives, the very bosom of rock 'n' roll and doo wop captured in pictures, … the greatest moments during the early trek of the youths who had grown up hearing the Shell station bells wake them at daybreak, and entertain them to sleep on hot summer nights; the late Paulie Puccini with Frank Bonaducci, both proudly holding trophies after the first midget football season in Belleville in '54; Eric Thatcher, triumphant in victory as he ran off the mound, having no-hit Nutley in '59; Bob Hardy in Midshipman's attire; little Gerald Gretto sitting on the hood of Jackie Carey's "Heavenly Heap"; Roger Bush, scoring the winning lay-up in a Belleville upset of South Side in the Essex County Basketball tournament in '63; the unlikely Harold Bader, as a six foot four inch senior, winning the pole vault at the Essex County Track Meet at Montclair's Woodman Field; Jo-Jo, Lonnie Luongo, and Rich Luzzi, posing in Belleville Municipal Stadium's end zone after their stunning defeat of Nutley to seal '62 as the greatest football season in school history; Davey Thatcher at a bar in DaNang; Jimmy Hardy in his Marine Corp. dress uniform; an Eric "the Snatcher" Thatcher sock hop from his back porch with nearly twenty local kids attending, captured by John's lens from the Shell station entrance nearly fifty yards away; and a candid taken of Frank and Maria, with Jo-Jo and Russell Giardella in the back seat, as Frank filled the tank of his Uncle Jimmy Quinn's car for their Wildwood adventure, … the first overnight vacation for both his younger brother and their paperboy. And then there were the headlines: "Bonaducci Play Key in Bellboy Mud Bowl Defeat"; "Top Rock 'n' Roll Stars Perish in Plane Crash"; "Two Killed in Motorcycle Accident"; "Suicides on Smallwood Avenue"; "Superman Dies"; "Seven Astronauts Picked"; "Mr. Inside and Mr. Outside make All County for Belleville"; "Roger Bush All Big Ten Basketball"; "Local Athlete Killed in Viet Nam"; "Belleville's Finest with Wood and Gogolak at Cornell"; "It's Over! Judge Liloia Wishes 'Buona Natale' to Counterfeit Accused".

The ringing bells finally interrupted their sentimental journey down memory lane. A tear came to his eyes as Frank read his mother's obituary that Mark had framed. Next to it was a headshot of Henry in Korea. Jo-Jo was frozen in time rereading *The Ledger* headline about his brother's decision against Nutley back in '58.

Dominick was first to move. He grabbed the hands of both girls and suggested a holiday drink, "…for old time sake".

"I'll pour 'cause I can't drink," said a somber and sober Mark.

Returning to the cramped station office, John asked what Frank thought of all of the pictures and paper clippings. Without looking at him he responded, "Hey, Cuz, when you look back, glance, don't stare."

"Thanks for keeping it up, John," said Jo-Jo.

"Ah, it's as much Markie and Dominick as me," admitted John.

Around a tiny table overflowing with daily papers and magazines, Mark poured everyone, but himself and Maria, a shot of anisette. They opted for soda. "Lift your glasses." Mark proposed a toast. "First of all, congratulations to Rocky for his Barringer-East Orange award tonight. And secondly, thanks to all you kids from the neighborhood for making us so proud—never a problem for your parents, … all the kids from around here. Lastly, in memory of your good mother, Marietta, we'll never forget her passion, love, and commitment to family, friends, the Lord, … and her work. May she rest in peace. And, … to each of you, 'centi anni'."

Everyone repeated, "A hundred years."

Frank added, "And may you count every one, Markie."

After farewell hugs, Jo-Jo next steered the Bonaduccis around the corner, to pass by 711 Belmont Avenue. Not a word was said. The home seemed to testify to its own demise. Without Marietta gracing its kitchen and absent her daily 7:15 AM entrance through the back door, the heart and soul of the domicile had flown away, making it unlivable to those who could not forget the priceless moments that had forged their lives. Again, Frank wiped away a tear, not for a house now occupied by another family, but for his mother, stolen by the enemy without her Creator's approval.

Their destination was Rocky's place. It was a cramped apartment that had been built on the same location of the now departed Milk Bar. Upon arrival, Maria broke the heavy silence. "Hey, my husband, got tonight's speech ready?"

"Yep," Frank responded.

"What are you going to say?" asked Jo-Jo.

"You'll hear it all, and Daddy will be pleased."

"Well, I'm glad you're doing it, Frank," offered Donna. "He's become so emotional lately, I'll be surprised if he gets through his own 'thank you' for the award."

"That's why we flew in, Donna," said Frank.

Valet parking attendants at Biase's Restaurant on Bloomfield Avenue were busy that night. Situated across from City Stadium and a short walk from Saint Francis' Church, the Italian American eatery would barely be able to hold the three hundred plus alumni and family celebrating Thanksgiving Day's classic football game between Barringer and East Orange. Rocky proudly turned the car keys over to one of the teenage parkers. His 1968 Malibu had been purchased by Frank on the West Coast, and given to his dad after Marietta died. It was the newest car Rocky ever had. So he insisted on driving all the family that night.

Although more than thirty years since Rocky's day of glory that earned him this special recognition, it would be as if time had turned back. The same people, who faithfully followed the wavy black haired two-way end in high school and during his brief college and pro career, were there once again to congratulate their hero. Traditionally, the dinner had been closed to women. But for special awards, female family members were allowed, as long as they could stand the thick cigar smoke that fogged the cramped banquet room and permeated both food and clothing with a vengeance. On the other hand, nothing would have stopped Aunt Bella getting through the door, even without permission. She had arranged the attendance of as many Bonaducci family and friends as space would allow. Nearly thirty of Rocky's biggest supporters were there, … all his sisters, their spouses and children, brother Anthony and his family, and Judge Liloia sitting with Grandpa Joe and Mamie, … even cousin Carmine from Brooklyn with his wife.

The emotional impact hit Rocky as soon as he arrived. Not having seen some old teammates since that game, it was as if they were ghosts returning from a thirty-year sojourn on the other side of eternity. Felix Ferrara, the other end whom Rocky had told his sons to emulate because of his good grades and college degree, looked like a state senator, with white hair and lean physique. But, it turned out he was now a successful Wall Street broker. Bobby Zarcone, the bombastic district attorney, who just happened to be the holder for the fateful kick, reminded Rocky as they embraced that if he'd been in charge of the counterfeit case, the boys from Bloomfield Avenue would now be the boys from Sing-Sing. Also, there were the

Kee brothers, black as the ace of spades, just as Rocky described them, but still nimble and sleek like they were as early forties running backs, who'd earned the label the "Light Fantastics" from local sports writers. But missing were DeRogatis, Naporano, Masino, Allen, Verducci, Caruso, Insua, Ventola, and Calabria. Before their high school graduations, they'd boarded troop ships, never to return to the streets of Newark.

When his "special recognition" moment arrived, Rocky walked slowly to the podium, his herniated disc still causing problems. As Donna feared, even his two words, "Thank You", were filled with obvious emotion. The master of ceremonies promptly explained that Rocky was so overwhelmed by this reunion and the recent loss of his wife, that he'd asked his son to give his acceptance speech. Applause for his humble father didn't stop until Frank took the microphone.

"Friends of Barringer-East Orange football, dignitaries, family, and the legendary members of the Big Blue of that '40 season. My name is Frank Bonaducci, and I am the oldest of Marietta Frassa and Rocky Bonaducci's three children. I cannot tell you how pleasing it is to represent my father in accepting your generous award. You see, all of the good that happened to our family over the years, and how we reacted even to the bad, … was all influenced by this high school game you are commemorating now!"

Frank took a deep breath, looked to his dad, and without any notes, continued. "We grew up in the home of a Marine. He hated war, but he loved the Marines. How he came back, he could never explain. But he's been forever grateful, and so is his entire family. My dad always compared God preserving him in the Pacific to that Thanksgiving Day his name became part of the list of other Barringer heroes who stunned the previously unbeaten Panthers of East Orange High.

"Like his immigrant parents raised him, Dad always told us the truth was important. And the truth was, if he had not dropped a pass in the end zone the previous year, Barringer would have won that game, rather than tied it, as well. That he kicked the extra point the following year, Dad said happened by God's grace.

"Most of all, my father reminded us that he was not much of a student, and we should do as he says, not as he did. Because of his brief moment in the sun that cold Thanksgiving Day, our family came to deify the great American game of football, the honesty with which our father told stories of those days, and his war experiences later.

"On the other hand, if you will permit me, I'd like to comment on talk I heard tonight from administrators of both schools about academics and football eligibility. You see, our entire family being here, to acknowledge our dad and a game long ago, is really about this subject you raise of higher standards for athletes. Here's my point: my father's fine play that day might never have happened if he'd been subject to some of the academic requirements that Barringer and East Orange administrators are urging tonight. Now, I'm no political person, but I'd warn you educators about a mistake you'll be making.

"To raise the grade point average required for football eligibility sounds great at first. However, when you take kids off the gridiron, you force them onto the streets. I know it's more important than football, but don't forget not all of us are the academics type. My father surely was not. But because educators of his day allowed him to play the game he loved as long as he kept up some minimum standards, there are some happenings I must share: <u>every day</u> in my house we talked about this great rivalry; <u>every day</u> we heard about the players who were better students than my father; <u>every day</u> we heard that there is no 'I' in the word 'team'; <u>every day</u> we were coached to not break the law, to use football to get an education, and to respect authority; <u>every day</u> we heard about the equality of the races, of those gentlemanly great black athletes from East Orange High; <u>every day</u> we were told not to judge others. All this parenting came out of the great feeling of self worth our dad got from playing at Barringer against the noblest of opponents from East Orange. We came to know the men in this room as heroes, and we wanted to be like them, … and our father.

"Modestly I mention, that because through my father's humble experience of playing for Barringer, and my late mother's commitment to getting her children a college education, I now call Cornell my alma mater and Gary Wood of the Giants my friend. I'm doing in my profession what my mom and dad had dreamed. My brother, Jo-Jo, led Belleville to its greatest season, and then went on to Boston College, now preparing for his doctoral. My sister became Captain of the Belleville cheerleaders and is now at Montclair State. None of this would have happened if my father was declared ineligible in the fall of 1940 because his grades did not meet standards some of you are proposing now.

"Yes, tonight I thank you for recognizing our dad. But I also encourage you to remember that if he did not play those years, few of our family's proudest moments would ever have come about. Let the kids play. Of course, they have to achieve minimum results, but don't make it tougher. If you do, your streets will become more dangerous. And these kids will make the kind of bad decisions that my father and his generation refused to make, ... perhaps because they were permitted to have a moment in the sun, one Thanksgiving Day, ... many years ago.

"In closing, let me assure you that no matter where I am on Thanksgiving mornings, I think of Newark's cigar smoke-cloaked City Stadium, and Martens Stadium in East Orange. I recall the ritual of my dad coming to these dinners the night before the game, my mother having bought him a new suit or sport jacket just for the occasion. I can't forget his coming home at midnight, perhaps one or two extra Seven and Sevens in him, wreaking of that heavenly cigar smoke, but glowing from the friends he had seen and the celebration of the game of which he was a small part. Let the kids play, to guarantee good citizens of the future, ... and memories for a lifetime. The Barringer-East Orange rivalry will always be at the center of the hearts of all of my family members. Keep the tradition alive, ... and thank you again for making Dad a happy guy tonight."

Biase's Restaurant erupted with a standing ovation. Frank appreciated this was not the Heisman Trophy Dinner at the Downtown Athletic Club in New York City, but rather an event held not far from Fifth Street and Bloomfield Avenue, ... not far from where God had planted his family roots. There was no other place in the world he would have rather been that night.

Frank Bonaducci took the ball all the way to the end zone that night. Those in the audience who recalled his Nutley game knew for certain why he was special, unique enough to be honest and loving of his fellow man, ... a rare product of the neighborhood, one whose humility that evening demonstrated maturing leadership qualities. School administrators had something to seriously consider for the weeks to come.

Frank, Maria, Jo-Jo, and Donna piled into Rocky's car. They were all staying in his cramped two-bedroom apartment on Joralemon Street and Franklin Avenue. It was too late for Jo-Jo to return to his place in New York City by Columbia University. Rocky and Frank were in the front seat, with Jo-Jo leaning forward from between the girls in back. After only a few minutes, Maria fell asleep. Donna was listening to her transistor radio.

"God, that was some night, guys," said Jo-Jo.

"Yea, thanks, Frank," said Rocky. "The speech was great."

"Ah, it was all true, Dad. Thank you."

Driving slowly, even though it was approaching midnight, Rocky seemed as if he didn't want the night to end. Jo-Jo seized the moment to take the conversation into another direction. "Listen, guys. I've been thinking. You know, there's this song by this Don McLean guy, called 'American Pie'. Heard it on an album, and now it's a single."

"So?" said Frank without much interest.

"Well, it's really true," added Jo-Jo.

"True about what?"

"It's about us."

"Explain, Jo-Jo."

Frank was tired. Rocky wasn't saying a word. Donna seemed preoccupied with <u>her</u> music. Maria was already in slumber land.

"The guy's right. It all changed when those three singers went down in that plane; ya know, Holly, Valens, and the Big Bopper. I mean our lives changed drastically that year. And you know what?" Jo-Jo said, turning to Frank. "Your Nutley game foreshadowed the changes."

"Oh, thanks, little brother. Blame me."

"No, I don't mean it negatively. But from your game decision on, our family went through a lot. And when those guys died, change happened almost every day. McLean says 'the music died'. He's right. Doo wop changed slowly. There weren't any big names like Holly and Valens any more. I mean the heart was torn out of rock 'n' roll! When the Beatles showed up in '64, it was a funeral for the music we loved back in the late fifties."

"The music didn't die, Jo-Jo," blurted Rocky. "Those kids did. That music will be even more famous now, 'cause those kids became legends."

"What do you mean, 'legends', Dad?" asked Frank.

"When the young die, they become heroes, … legends, … all because it was before their time. They were innocent. It was a tragedy. They were good kids, too. Damn it. All heroes die young."

"Dad, didn't think you were paying attention," quipped Frank.

"See, Daddy has it," said Jo-Jo. "Frank becomes a hero of sorts, sacrificing himself in that Mud Bowl; then these guys go down in a snow storm in some corn field; Frankie gets spared with the motorcycle in May; all the people around us get charged with counterfeiting, and people start dying or getting killed; I get dumped by my girlfriend; the facts of life turn out to be more unbelievable than I could imagine; Mommy's going through this religious thing with Queenie and Nora; Frankie gets hooked on Jesus, too; McLean talks about the Bible; our cousins turn out to be Mafia; Uncle Pete drops dead of a heart attack; I have this grapefruit taken out of my neck; I go on my first vacation; Frank leaves us for Cornell; I get switched to quarterback. I mean, … what a year! And it sorta starts with the Mud Bowl in '58, then the plane crash. McLean's right; 'the music died', and then our lives really started to change. I mean this guy kills me with this song."

"You talking about the rest of the song?" asked Frank.

"Well, yea, Frank, … that too. But, more than that, it's as if he was at 711 Belmont Avenue with us—like he knew us. And the damn song just doesn't want to end. It's long. He's singing about our lives, and guess who's in the middle of it all?"

"Both of you guys," said Rocky.

"Right, Dad," said Jo-Jo. "I mean how about Frankie always going into that James Dean funk before his games; me being at Woodstock with my new girlfriend; Frank's out there by the Manson murders; can't believe my brother even buys Stones' records, which, by the way, McLean makes reference to as Satanic when talking about those crazy English dudes; prayer goes out of schools in '63 and this song talks about the Father, Son, and Holy Ghost taking off to the coast. God, that's all Mommy talked about, … the Trinity and all; the Beatles become royalty; and we <u>did</u> start to like them; the Viet Nam War; the song goes on and on how we changed with that one plane crash, and God knows how our family changed starting in '59, too."

"Jo-Jo, if you're writing your thesis on this, you'll never get a doctorate," chuckled Frank.

"Frank, seriously, 1959 was some year! I even remember that the morning of the crash you even said, 'Things were changing'. My feet froze in the snow the next day reading those headlines about Holly and Valens. Mommy cried and started to pray. Donna thought we'd never be able to play 'Donna' again. Remember dancing 'cheek to cheek' at those sock hops 'in the gym', Thatcher's reel-to-reel songs on Sunday nights in the summer, and then those make-out parties? It was all so innocent. That song goes right through me like no other I've ever heard. I mean I like the group sounds and stuff from about '55-'63, ... that stuff sends me back. But this one has deep meaning." Jo-Jo was getting frustrated. "And, Dion, your favorite, could have died in that crash, too, but now he's singing folk stuff. Soooo much started to change with your Nutley game, Frank, and that plane crash. And then you and I came so close to the junk of the sixties. Man, as McLean sings, we started to die, too."

"I guess the Father, Son, and the Holy Ghost did take off to the coast," said Frank.

"What do you mean?" asked Jo-Jo.

"The sixties did get tough," said Frank, "But at least they didn't leave us."

"Who didn't leave us?" was Jo-Jo's question.

"The Father, Son, and the Holy Ghost. Might have seemed far away, but they never left us."

With Frank's comment, silence returned to the car. They were now nearing the apartment, and Rocky offered insight. "Jo-Jo, those were the important times of your life when things were good, but changin'. We all go through it. The music of the pre-war years affects me like that, ... then the sounds after the war."

"Got a favorite, Dad?" asked Jo-Jo.

Without hesitation, Rocky said, "Yes."

"No kidding, Daddy. What is it?" asked Donna, whom the boys thought was uninterested.

"...Under My Skin' by Sinatra in '55, arranged by Nelson Riddle and written by Cole Porter." Rocky stunned his children with detail.

"Holy cow, can you believe that?" marveled Jo-Jo.

"Hey, Dad, maybe you become a disc jockey or something," laughed Frank.

Rocky was serious, ignoring the commotion he had created. "Yea, Sinatra's a wiseguy and hangs out with the wrong people, but that record is tops with me."

"Why Dad?" asked Donna, who'd taken her radio from her ear and shut it off.

"Well, the song's bigger than Sinatra. He starts out slow and easy as if he knows the big band sound's comin' center stage, … like he's almost reluctant, lookin' forward to it. Then it comes. I mean Riddle steals the show with that arrangement. Trumpets and trombones seem to be competin' at first. Then they come together like no other sound I ever heard. Talk about climax and stuff—the best of the big band sounds. I just wish they could've gone longer. Then Ol' Blue Eyes returns, soft and gentle, out of character for him, … still smaller than the song itself, almost modest, if you can believe that for Sinatra. But now, he's doin' his part to bring it to an end, fading out like it started. Just right. Smooth as a glass of the best scotch. In between, the beat's great, and the arrangement's the best in history."

Silence was speaking to everyone. Then Maria stirred. Rocky was about to pull into the driveway of his apartment.

"What about the words, Dad?" asked Jo-Jo.

"The lyrics?" pondered Rocky. "His lover is so important to him that she's under his skin, … a part of him. The two become one."

"What else, Dad?" asked Frank.

Rocky did not answer. Donna saw his shoulders tighten, and head nod forward, with a labored swallow. Emotion was overcoming him. She knew her father's every thought and emotion. While she was only nineteen years old, last year had required her caring for him to such an extent that she had come to now know the complexities in her father's psyche better than her brothers who had been around him more years.

"It's about Mommy," Donna advised Frank and Jo-Jo.

Rocky continued, "Our lives were like that song. She was beautiful. She made me become a better person, because she became a part of me. Our lives after the war started nice and slow like the song. Raising you kids, work, and all we went through with her having to work the graveyard shift were like that big band climax—so many good things happening, but a lot of others we didn't plan. Then, after takin' care of you kids, we're supposed to enjoy the quiet time together at the end. But she went away."

Jo-Jo raised his left hand to massage his father's neck as he parked the car.

"You OK, Dad?" asked Frank.

Rocky regained composure. "So, Jo-Jo, that's my favorite for lots of reasons. And now with your song, I've heard it, too. And you know what? That guy tells a great story. It's like poetry, too. That song will never die, and the songs of those other guys, well, ya hear them always on these new oldies stations." He swallowed hard. "Not for nuttin', ... but, those <u>were</u> the good ol' days."

Frank directed himself to his father, but looked back to Jo-Jo. "OK, Dad, but we must correct my little brother about a few things. The guy drives his Chevy to some levy, gets disappointed or something and says, 'This will be the day that I die'. Right, Jo-Jo?" Frank doesn't wait for a response. "Here's the deal. It <u>is</u> a great song, and does tell a story about a special time that does seem to begin with 1959. No doubt that year in our lives was bizarre, and I remember saying, 'Things were changing'. But, don't let it depress you, Cuz. Here's the point: Yea, we went from good to tough times, through which it seems we haven't come out of yet. So, we've run into a couple of tough chapters since then, but it'll get better. Look at tonight, ... great for dad and all of us. Have faith in God. He didn't save us to have us suffer. Sure, we all miss Mommy, Uncle Pete, and those great days, but you have to believe that we're being prepared for better times, bigger things. That's the only way to live, Jo-Jo. God's guiding our steps, but His ways and thoughts are not like ours. We make plans, and God laughs. But don't let the song depress your spirit. It's time to live, not die." Frank then lightened up. "Besides, you're going to be an uncle soon, ... and maybe someday as good as Uncle Pete. "

"Amen," said Maria, surprising everyone she was even awake.

Rocky dropped his hands from the wheel. Jo-Jo looked to the roof of the car as if easing tension in his own neck. Donna put her head in her hands. Maria waited for someone to speak. She had a lump in her throat. Sitting in the back of a '68 Malibu in front of her father-in-law's rented apartment <u>was</u> a long way from 1959, ... even further from 711 Belmont Avenue.

Donna rubbed her temples and looked at Jo-Jo staring through the front windshield at the apartment house's barren brick wall. Frank squinted as though contemplating the total honesty and sincerity of all he'd said. Rocky had closed his eyes. Donna thought how scared her sister-in-law must now be—baby coming, and Frank relocating back home, where there are no resorts. Marietta was dead at forty-seven, and Rocky in tough shape. Their lives really had taken an unpredictable turn. Yet, Donna recognized Marietta's prayers being answered with all her children getting degrees, Frank doing well in business so far, and Jo-Jo soon to be addressed as ... Dr. Jo-Jo. *God had been faithful to my mother. But He also answered her other prayer as well, "God take me first". Yea, we've had some laughs, but, gee, we cried a lot, too. Life's not always so good, but it'll get better again.* She released her head from her hands.

Frank placed his left arm around Jo-Jo's shoulder, pulling him forward so he could kiss his temple, and then whispered in his ear, "Just remember, Cuz. When you look back, glance, don't stare."

CHAPTER 27

"THE REST OF THE STORY"

I can still see him at the backyard door. His arms were always full of gifts or bags of food, ... his look of anticipation at seeing us. And oh, ... his beard on my cheeks, ... I can feel it now. Peter A. Frassa's death in the fall of 1959 left a void in many lives. Marietta's heart mended because of her growing walk with the Lord through the counsel of Queenie, Nora, and Pastor Tony. Grandma Frassa grieved until the day she died ten years later. But her relationship with her daughter bloomed once Marietta totally forgave her about Pete. Her mother's years of controlling influence over her son were simply her own hard-headed way of trying to prevent losing him, as she had lost her husband at a young age. Of course, the life style Pete resorted to ushered in his own sudden heart attack.

When he died, Pete's only asset was the 1955 powder blue Cadillac he made known should go to his sister and Rocky. But the Bonaduccis quickly decided Greenie Delaney would be the recipient. Rocky figured with Greenie having been Pete's "driver" over the years, he'd be lost without the car. He never could afford an automobile of his own. Modestly, Greenie accepted his inheritance. Today at eighty-one years old, Greenie still keeps the Coupe De Ville in the garage he rents at the Five Corners, within walking distance from his sister's home, where he lives.

To his own children even now, Jo-Jo often talks of his chubby uncle, ... also to his nieces and nephews. Pete's example of selfless love to his sister's family will never fade in their minds and those of his two closest friends, Greenie and Thomas "Two Tones" Anthony. When Jo-Jo visits Donna, or Frank's family, he always walks in with "dirty water hot dogs", or donuts, … or just about anything that's edible. Maria and Donna just smile as their children marvel at their uncle's consistency in arriving with food to be enjoyed by all.

"You kids never met Uncle Pete," Maria would remind her two boys and two girls. "Uncle Jo-Jo, your father, and Aunt Donna had an uncle who would never drop by Grandma Marietta's house empty-handed. They'll never forget him. He set a good example that way."

Every Christmas Eve a ritual begins at 8 AM at the Five Corners. Greenie retrieves his Cadillac, Two Tones shows up, and then they proceed to Nutley where Jo-Jo is waiting. Two Tones supplies the grave blankets, and Jo-Jo buys breakfast at Schuyler Diner in Lyndhurst, … the twenty four-hour, smoke-filled truckers' paradise that was Pete's favorite, when he just wanted to get out of the neighborhood with Greenie in the old days. After breakfast, Greenie fires up the Caddie, and it's down the New Jersey Turnpike to Route 280. Final destination is the Gate of Heaven Cemetery in East Hanover, where Pete's buried with his mother. Across the field is the Bonaducci plot. The three visitors say a few prayers. Two Tones always points out the Boiardo stones, and makes the sign of the cross as they pass. Final stop is J.R.'s cigar parlor on Route 10. Stogies in hand, the three reminisce, laugh, and cry about stories featuring Petee Five Corners.

"He made a lot of mistakes, but we'd always get glimpses of who he could have been," reflects Two Tones.

"Your grandmother hurt him, Jo-Jo," adds Greenie. "He'd be alive today if he'd married my sister. God, she <u>still</u> has a broken heart."

Jo-Jo just listens. He can hardly reflect on his late uncle without getting emotional. "Every time I visit Donna and my brother's kids, I think of him."

Today there is no trace of the butcher shop, or the Frassa's walkup apartment on the Five Corners. But on warm Sunday afternoons when Greenie drives around the neighborhood in Pete's Caddie, he'll swear he gets a glimpse every once in a while of a five foot seven inch overweight butcher, with a dirty apron, ducking around the corner at Fifth Street and Bloomfield Avenue.

She took so much with her to the grave, … her poems, her books, her recipes, her advice, … the businesses she could have run. She was enlightened, but the light wasn't bright enough to sweep away the darkness. And, she missed so much. Marietta's sudden passing on a cold, windy day in November of 1970 has so many who knew her still speechless. Her daughter was the only one with her that evening. Until she gave birth to her own children in her early thirties, Donna's memories of her childhood vanished into a black hole of grief that day, excavated by her mother's first and final heart attack and stroke.

On the first night of Marietta's wake, practically the entire graveyard shift from her factory showed up to pay their respects. Dalla, her childhood friend from Sixth Street, never left Rocky's side. Strangely, after the funeral, none of the Bonaduccis ever heard from her again.

Frank would often say about his mother, "Two most passionate prayers dominated her life, … 'God take me first' and 'Let me give the down payment on a house to each of my three kids'." Only the first plea came to pass, perhaps because God knew full well she could never survive the death of Rocky or one of her children.

Back in the late thirties, after skipping two years in the Newark School System, Marietta flourished at Drake's Business School, to become an executive secretary in New York City during World War II. She wrote poems and long letters—revealing amazing and penetrating wisdom—to Rocky in the Marines, and to all her children, as well as some nieces and nephews during their college years. Her written thoughts would make their way to paper, freeing her from years of blue-collar living, like a Phoenix bird breaking hold of its subterranean bondage. The only shame of it was that she never fulfilled her dreams to enroll in college, or have any of her thoughts published.

In death, Marietta Bonaducci was the essential ingredient in the worldly and spiritual success of many. Her insistence on advanced education for her children, and the requirement that they make a daily trek toward their passions and chosen callings have reaped a harvest. Frank's meteoric climb to the top of his vocation in resort development might not have happened without his Ivy League education and memories of his mother's sacrifices; his daily Bible studies in his home in Verona, New Jersey became legendary. Jo-Jo gives her credit for his doctorate degree that propelled him into the study of leadership development where he became a noted authority, … his first book about to be published. Donna will also acknowledge that she is able to juggle managing her household with her role as Director of Special Education in a large, prosperous town in Bergen County, due to what her mother taught her. All of Marietta's grandchildren, none of whom she ever met, either have college degrees, or are in the process. Frankie's first son, Frank, Jr., is head of the Department of Journalism at one of America's finest universities; Jo-Jo's daughter is an aspiring sports journalist, who freelances for New York City's most popular sports radio station; and Donna's oldest daughter followed her Uncle

Frank to Cornell, in the fall of 2003, entering the School of Arts and Sciences where she's majoring in English Literature, and has already won writing awards.

But the shock of Marietta's death was most compelling to the bohemian, avant-garde, and cerebral Antoinette Thatcher. The news got to the well read, yet alcohol dependent mother of Eric and Davey after she'd just enjoyed her last Southern Comfort Manhattan for the day. Uncharacteristically for her, she laid down her day old *New York Times* and wept for the loss of her neighbor. It was her knowledge of decimated personal dreams in both their lives that was unbearable. So she made a very rare departure from her cluttered home to pay her respects. Her only comment at Marietta's casket was: "She gave all she had to her kids. She was a real mother."

From the day of Marietta's death, Antoinette Thatcher never had another drink to her own passing in 1995. In fact, her recollection of Marietta's counsel, often received during daily walks with Blackie, had prompted Mrs. Thatcher to rekindle her life-long passion for dancing and teaching. When she informed her boys of her desire to open a dancing school on Union Avenue in the heart of Belleville, overjoyed at her sobriety and renewed focus upon her destiny to teach the expression of art she loved, they put enough money together for her to start ... "Marietta Antoinette's Dance Academy, ... where your dreams can come true!" Each year she held recitals at Belleville High where the show's highlight was her personal award to a deserving student: "Commitment, sacrifice, and overcoming all odds to fulfill one's destiny." She called it, "The Marietta Bonaducci Award", in honor of her neighbor.

Five granddaughters, who never met their grandmother, each have the same middle name, ... Marietta!

He'll always be my hero. I smile every time I think of him, ... even some of his mistakes. Thank God Frankie got him into the resort business. There he became himself, ... a leader. Somehow, Rocky Bonaducci's back injury healed without surgery. Maybe not having to lift fifty-pound bags of powder for the compounding process of Jergens perfumed products was enough to ease his discomfort. With Frank returning to Jersey, Rocky began a new career in in-home recreational land, second home, and condominium sales. It took him seven times to pass the New Jersey Real Estate Examination. His sisters prayed to Saint Jude for doing ... "the impossible". Frank made sure his father received special tutoring from his Jersey sales managers. But when he amazingly passed, the aunts gave the credit to Saint Jude, ... and so did the sales managers!

The professional blessing to Rocky's life came when Frank's company introduced time-share vacations into their inventory. Priced lower than other forms of ownership, it allowed Rocky to prospect back to his old North Ward friends, Barringer graduates, and others who had come to like and respect him over the years. His sales success became legendary in the Northeast. No one could be Rocky Bonaducci better than Rocky Bonaducci: "…and da two bedrooms got two badtrooms, too!"

Rocky's natural talent and desire to train young salesmen earned him promotion into selling sales management positions. And his dating of younger women became so prolific that the less experienced and younger sales associates always flocked to him for social advice. Frank was sometimes embarrassed about his single dad's youthful enthusiasm for his new career. But all of Rocky's protégés would say how much he helped them, not only with their sales challenges, but also with issues in their personal lives. Their stories about "The Rock" had a common fiber. "Frank, relax," they would remind his righteous son. "All he really talks about is … how proud he is of you, your brother, and your sister, … and how his wife was the best! Hey, boss, the reason he's never remarried is because no one could ever replace your mother. His advice to us is … always find the love of your life, and surrender to her. He says that made for twenty-eight years of a great marriage to your mother."

Rocky would go on to management positions in such resort destinations as Hilton Head, South Carolina and Daytona Beach, Florida, and Frank had nothing to do with his progress. In fact, Dr. Martin Feldman, a strategic coach assigned to shadow executives in Frank's company, mentioned Rocky as its most natural of all leaders; that despite the lack of a significant formal education, his compassion for people, ability to listen, humility, and steel will to succeed distinguished him above others. That explains why in 1980 he received the "Whatever It Takes" award, which was given annually to the company's outstanding manager. Rocky had not only fulfilled his call as a father, but also as a coach, while not in football, in the game of life with assertive young sales people.

A brain aneurysm in 1981 halted Rocky's impressive career. After emergency surgery in Florida, he went on a long, hard road to recovery. His premature brush with death transformed the former high-powered fifty-seven year old executive overnight. No longer was he the last to leave a nightspot frequented by his staff, and then be first at the office next morning. Now he struggled to put sentences together rather than be able to impress a young female admirer with his life experiences. On the other hand, according to his children, it extended his life, by bringing him back to Belleville where he would fulfill his role as an aging grandfather, ... who had come full circle.

"We hated to see him come off the field," said Frank at his father's surprise sixty-fifth birthday, several years later. "But had the good Lord left him in the game, he might have killed himself."

Everyone, including Rocky, smiled as he gave his then patented victory wave. His acceptance speech was short, thanking God for his wife, children, and for the profound sacrifices made by his father when he arrived in America from Avellino in Italy.

Down, but not out, Rocky struggled for a couple of years as a security guard, before officially retiring to a senior citizens building in East Orange, just across the Newark line. His anxiety had built up over the years since having to prematurely end his triumphant resort real estate run. So Frank made sure Pastor Tony Votolo sat with Rocky. The hardened combat veteran, now seventy, shed a tear as the dynamic preacher assured him the Lord wasn't finished with him yet. That night, Rocky finally made peace with his Creator.

In his last days, Rocky busied himself following his grandchildren. The boys were excelling in football and wrestling, and the girls as cheerleaders and dancers. In fact, his small one-bed apartment was now brimming with over sixty years of family memorabilia, in which his grandchildren's awards received front and center attention. When Frank's second son, Mark, surprised Rocky with a special game ball he received at Verona High, the proud grandfather knew just what to do. Up until the last day of his life, Rocky displayed it next to his two other most proud possessions, ... his own game ball from 1940, and a black and white photo of Frank, waiting for Gino on the four-yard line, in the Mud Bowl in '58.

On December 21, 2000, Jo-Jo visited his father after stopping to pay his respects at the graves of his mother and Uncle Pete. Rocky had come off successful shoulder surgery following a fall at Donna's house. Fully recovered, after some pneumonia complications, he was as lucid and enthusiastic as Jo-Jo could remember since the brain aneurysm. Rocky insisted on making coffee. Jo-Jo finished his father's Snoopy-like Christmas tree only the two would behold that year.

A Giants' game was on television when Jo-Jo dropped a bombshell. "Dad, Frankie's in the hospital, and he might not make it." Frank had been doctoring for years, but the family decided to keep his downturn from Rocky until he was strong enough to hear the facts himself.

Startled, he asked, "What've you guys been keepin' from me?"

"Dad, he's had some blood problems over the years. But you know Frank, … keeps the tough things to himself and God. Figured they'd solve it between them."

"How bad?"

"I'll pick you up tomorrow after church. Dad, I hope he's not in a coma by then."

"Coma?"

Jo-Jo nodded.

"Listen, my Frankie's not goin' 'home to the Lord' before me. I gotta be there with Mommy to greet him."

"OK, Dad. Now just don't get yourself sick. I'll pick you up tomorrow."

They embraced.

That night, as Jo-Jo and his wife Megan dined at a Chinese restaurant on Route 46 in Montville, his daughter Tina called his cell phone. She told him Aunt Donna could not contact Rocky, and she'd ordered the security people at the senior complex to enter his apartment. A first heart attack sent the Marine to his eternal reward.

Rocky was buried on his favorite holiday, Christmas Eve. At the same time, Frank was fighting for his own life, in a coma caused by aggressive leukemia. At Nutley's Holy Family Church, the Catholic priests allowed Pastor Tony Votolo to eulogize his old hero from Lake and Seventh Streets in the heart of Newark: "When his weary heart began to give way on Saturday, Rocky went to one knee. He didn't fall. A rangy right end like him would never get knocked on his back. Don't forget, it wasn't long after leaving the streets of Newark in '42 that he was storming the beaches at Eniwetok, Tarawa, and the other atolls, … first and second waves. He wasn't going to go down easy. He braced himself, and the Lord gave him a glimpse of the other side. At that point, Rocky put his hand in the hand of the Man from Galilee. As he surrendered, he gently entered into the presence of the Almighty, and I'm sure Marietta was there to greet him. Now in total joy with Jesus, he awaits his son Frank, just as he told Jo-Jo he would."

No, I still can't get over this one. He was so good, too good, ... the best. Frank Bonaducci, who passed away exactly seven days after his father, was laid him to rest on <u>his</u> favorite holiday, ... New Years Eve. He was fifty-eight years old. The funeral was held at Pastor Tony 's full gospel church in Bloomfield, where Frank and his family had attended services since moving back east. Ninety-two cars were in the procession.

Frank's success in the resort development industry on the West Coast was actually slowed by a blood problem he developed right after Cornell, of which only he and his doctor were aware. Concern for his condition inspired his return to Jersey. While he continued to prosper as a corporate sales and marketing executive, the brand names in the mid eighties were inducing their most demanded talents to head to Sunbelt headquarter locations. But Frank decided to stay in Verona, choosing to leave the mainstream of his business so as to allow him to be close to his and Maria's families, and to give his two girls and two boys all the time they needed as student-athletes. In addition, knowing his health would be best served in the Northeast, he formed his own company, as his peers and protégés flocked to South Carolina, Florida, and Arkansas.

One by one he reconnected with his high school teammates, as well as renewing his relationships with his Cornell friends in the New York area. Becoming active in evangelical Christianity, he helped Pastor Votolo build his church, opening his house to whoever wanted to attend his weekly Bible studies.

While Frank privately battled his blood condition, his family flourished. Maria became heavily involved in the children's school activities. Their oldest son, Frank Jr., completed an outstanding basketball career at Verona High. But, it would be Mark who would truly run in his father's footsteps.

For the Hilltoppers, Mark became known, just like his dad before him, as "Mr. Outside". In the fall of 1993, Mark entered the season's eleventh and final game, tied for the Essex County Scoring lead. In Verona's Group II playoff encounter with Newark's West Side High, the scoring title would be decided. Mark was dueling with Montclair High junior sensation, Bobby McCullum. Montclair was gunning for its own state championship against Philipsburg High that day.

For Frank Bonaducci, the presence of God's Spirit all week had him weak-kneed. All his remaining family members were going to be at the game in Verona. Uncle Caesar would drive the aunts up from Toms River, with Aunt Bella leading the charge in her fur coat flowing to her ankles, just barely camouflaging the aluminum walker that she claimed she only used to keep her doctor happy. Uncle Jimmy and

Aunt Pinky would be there. Angelo and Sally Giardina were bringing up a crowd from the Big Tree section on the Belleville-Nutley line. Donny Riordan, the backup center from Belleville's Mud Bowl team, was Director of Fields and Structures for the Verona Board of Education and had been keeping all his ex-teammates abreast of young Mark's talents. On a cold and cloudy December afternoon they came from all over: ... D'Angelo, Barra, Brindisi, Bartel, McCabe, Vitella, Schoener, Long, Galioto, Szep, Augenbaugh, Pinadella, ... and Gino Babula. Belleville's incredible Bellboys were back for another December game. This time the field was not as muddy, as it hadn't snowed yet in Jersey that season.

With a car phone that Donny supplied, Wee Willie Brindisi's assignment was to travel to Phillipsburg to give play-by-play updates, so the Bellboys could keep their own Mr. Outside, ... Frank, abreast of his son's chances. Embarrassed by his teammates' attention, Frank still relished in the grace of his Creator on that game day. Tension was huge, but he discerned the providential coincidence; thirty- five years ago, it was he trying to guarantee Gino's scoring championship. Now, so many of his teammates had come together to help celebrate a similar opportunity, only this time for Frank's own son.

Mark scored on an eleven-yard burst off tackle on Verona's first drive, but was otherwise held in check most of the day. Up at Philipsburg, McCullum returned the opening kickoff for a stunning score. According to Wee Willie by phone, the mud at Philipsburg was hampering everyone. There was little passing. At Verona both teams were throwing the ball. Mark's team was still driving with four minutes left, when Brindisi called. "Games over! Montclair wins, but McCullum scored only once. Tell Frankie, his kid needs just one more to get the title."

Word traveled throughout Verona Field, and anticipation began to brew. Frank stood with Maria, Frank Jr., Rocky, Jo-Jo, and both his girls. The old-time Bellboys, now all in their fifties, were down in the end zone breaking the tops of Donnie Riordan's wooden snow fences. The tension was huge. It was payback time in Essex County, and a couple of guys from Belleville were not thinking 1993, ... but that it was windy, snowy, rainy, ... and it was 1958 at the Oval in Nutley. They were all praying that God had a good memory, and would finally reward old number 7 for his sacrifice thirty-five years ago.

Verona called a timeout. The buzz in the stands increased with each second. All the family members and Verona fans that knew the Bonaduccis were glancing up to Frank, standing stoically next to Rocky. He was smiling, but not at anyone in particular. For Frank, it was as if God was winking, a gesture that assured him he had not been forgotten. Taking a deep breath of the pure December air to calm himself, Frank detected the sweet aroma of a cigar, ... a single stogie that had mysteriously made its way into the crowd to beckon Frank back in time. It was no longer the '93 state playoffs in Verona, but rather City Stadium in Newark. The Big Blue of Barringer was battling the Panthers of East Orange in a standing room only stadium of 25,000. Frank was wearing the fur-collared overcoat Uncle Pete had especially bought for the 1950 Thanksgiving Game. He was nine years old. Next to him was his handsome dad, an ex-Marine who had returned to the scene of his own 1940 Barringer heroics. It was a brisk clear day, with the sun generously gracing everyone's faces. And Frank could not ignore this sweet cloud that hung lazily over the crowd, a cigar smoker's heaven, ...Thanksgiving Day at City Stadium, ... Barringer and East Orange, ... a family dinner waiting after the game, and thousands of cigars to punctuate the festivities. How perfect life was back then, standing beside his hero, at a high school football game.

As he cleared his glistening eyes, Frank's mind returned to suburban Verona, some eight miles west of City Stadium, and some forty-three years later. He smiled and winked back at God, anticipating His imminent unmerited favor.

At the thirty-five yard line, the Verona quarterback reverse pivoted, faked to the fullback, and gently lofted the pigskin into Mark's hands. Built low to the ground, more like his Uncle Jo-Jo than his dad, but with his father's quick feet and graceful stride, Mark hit the hole on a mission. He broke the West Side linebacker's tackle, and then dipped his inside shoulder, taking off for the sidelines. With only the safety to beat, Mark stiff-armed him to the ground, and sprinted into the end zone, ... a twisting off tackle slant that bought him the Essex County Scoring championship!

The guys from Belleville were like kids in the end zone, mobbing their friend's son as if it was <u>their</u> day in the sun. Frank, Rocky, and Jo-Jo remained motionless in the stands, soaking in the wonder of the moment. Not only would Verona win, but Mark achieved his goal, just like his father had hoped would be the case for Gino Babula back in '58.

It was Frank's proudest moment. The officials stopped the game, giving the ball to Mark, who ran over to Gino in the end zone, and placed the ball in his hands. Gino heard Mark's instructions loud and clear, and delivered the pigskin to Frank in the stands. They embraced. The ball now in his clutches, Frank waved to his son, and they nodded at each other in agreement of what to do. Like it was slow motion, Frank gently presented his gift to Rocky Bonaducci, ... the aging right end, who had made it all the way back from the South Pacific.

"Thanks, Dad," said Frank.

Rocky was choking with emotion as Frank hugged him; one of their own had made it to the end zone more than anyone else in Essex County that year.

At Frank's wake, family and friends surrounded Maria. The line at Megaro's Funeral Home on Union Avenue in Belleville went around the corner. She looked for Donna's husband, Joe Zinicola, Nutley High School's principal, who had practically grown up in the Bonaducci home before Marietta died. Finding him, she requested that he give Frank's eulogy. Everyone knew Jo-Jo would not be able to handle it emotionally. On the other hand, Maria was not settled in her mind that it should only be Joe Zinicola. She had to find Gino.

Oh, how we respected him, ... so quiet, yet so strong. You could see the depth of character in his eyes. Belleville's All State running back in 1958 had experienced as broken field a run in life, as he had on the gridiron. After one year at Fork Union Military Prep School in Virginia, Gino discovered his less-than-average abilities as a student would preclude him ever playing big time college football. Sneaks made calls all over the country, but only tiny Upsala College on the Newark-East Orange border would finally accept his son. After two mediocre seasons at fullback, Gino hung up his cleats for the last time. A sore right knee had stolen the thunder from his piston-like legs that once made enemy tacklers regret ever facing Gino Babula from Belleville, New Jersey. He never earned his college degree.

Refusing all job opportunities from his father and his high revenue producing crew, Gino spent most of the seventies and eighties at the Jersey Shore. A fixture as head bartender at the Surf Club in Ortley Beach, Gino attracted hundreds of Newark, Belleville, and Nutley faithful every summer with his stories about the old neighborhoods. After all, they all knew his famous father, but would never bring up his name.

Gino was able to save enough money to buy a small motel in Wildwood. Then, during his first summer, early morning robbers left him fully disabled with a smashed face and broken kneecaps. No one was ever arrested. It seemed as if the perpetrators vanished off the face of the earth. Gino, who hadn't asked his father for help, received it anyway. The money stolen was returned in a brown paper bag, plus another $5,000, which Gino donated to Santa Lucia of the Sea, Roman Catholic Church in Wildwood Crest.

After a failed marriage, Gino started to attend bible studies at Frank's house whenever he visited his mother and father in Essex County. Gino's encounter with the Lord in that musty motel in College Park, Maryland back in '59 was finally harvesting results.

"I'm still a Catlic," he'd remind his old running mate. "But, I know Jesus like a friend, now."

Frank would always say, "Cuz, it's about time. I've been praying for you since we were kids."

At Megaro's, when Gino finally made it to Maria to offer his profound condolences, she asked him about saying the other eulogy. He was never a public speaker, but without thinking, Gino accepted, and then immediately broke out in a cold sweat of confusion. What would he say? He stood at the back of the funeral parlor alone. Then he heard, …"Gino Babula, Belleville's Mister Inside! Eric 'The Snatcher' Thatcher says 'hello'." Still lanky and black-haired, Eric was wearing his same "Buddy Holly" black rimmed glasses as they hugged.

"Not enough cash to buy a new set of eyes?" Gino queried.

"Ah, sending six kids to college will do it to you every time."

They talked about Frank, and then as if hit by a bolt of lightning, Eric slapped himself on the temple and quickly retrieved a CD from his inside suit pocket. "Gino, listen. I flew in from North Carolina. But I had a lot of time on my hands, and I bought this oldies CD. You remember me with rock 'n' roll. I could never forget how much Frank loved Dion and the Belmonts and doo wop. Anyway, I've listened to this thing dozens of times on this trip, and each time I thought of you and Frankie. Here, it's yours."

On their way back down the Garden State Parkway, Gino and his wife listened to the songs, … and he cried. But now he was inspired as to what to say about Frank at the funeral service.

Pastor Anthony Votolo's church was overflowing with people that New Year's Eve Day. Donnie Riordan had made sure his maintenance workers from Verona had wired the small building so the hundreds outside could hear.

Joe Zinicola eloquently related the Christ-likeness of his wife's brother, and how Frank had always been like a father to him with his saintly advice over the years. He credited Frank for much of his success in teaching, coaching, and administrative leadership

When Pastor Tony introduced Gino, the many in the audience who knew him were hoping he could get through his eulogy. His awkwardness at public speaking, and the emotion of the moment, seemed insurmountable, but he began: "So that I can get through this, folks, I won't be speakin' to you. Nope, I'll be talkin' to my friend, Frank. You can eavesdrop if you like. I won't mind, and I think Frank will have no problem with it either." Nervous smiles appeared throughout the church. Taking a deep breath, Gino continued. "Frank, you know I could only do this with the help of God and your OK. I know it's approved by you because Maria asked me to speak. And I know how you and your partner for life agreed on everything. By the way, I know God will be helpin' me, because he chose Eric Thatcher to give me some ideas. Nobody else other than a forgiving God would chose Eric to do <u>anything</u>. You know, God will use a donkey to speak, if he has to." Light laughter. Eric took the backhanded complement well.

Continuing, Gino said, "Frank, we had a dream one wintry night. Remember that Friday before the Nutley game how we talked about runnin' all over the field; how we'd rip through their defense and set the scoreboard on fire? Me inside, and you outside. That night we had a dream, Frank. But you always said how you were gonna get that TD for me, ... make me a champion, ... make me a star, ... make me All State. You got me so mad, because you were supposed to be the scoring champ, not me. You were the one who did everything the coaches, teachers, and your parents asked. Not me. I had some problems. But, you insisted God made '58 my year, and He was gonna use you to get that TD for me.

"Well, you waited at the goal line for me, Frank, but I couldn't get there for you. You waited and waited. I tried, but it didn't work. We lost on the scoreboard, and you took the grief for me, just like you taught me about Jesus. I never understood that, Frank, until some kids almost killed me. Then I finally figured it out, and now I know you and me will be together again ... someday. I know I've fallen behind a few times and lost my way. So, I'm askin' you to wait for me one more time, Mr. Outside. Wait for me at the goal line, one more time. I know the Lord has been patient with me, and so have you. So just wait some more. This time I'll make it to you, and our dream that wintry night will finally come true. We'll light up God's scoreboard when I join you, and the angels will be cheerin' forever. And thanks, Frank, for explaining all this to me, because without it, I'd be lost.

"Before I let you go, Frank, a couple of other things. You know about me and my father. I thank God how you and <u>your</u> father always taught me to be patient with Sneaks and his thing, ... to pray for him and all. Well, he's here at Pastor Tony's today. He'll never forget what you tried to do for me at the Oval in Nutley. And guess what, Frank; he's coming to Pastor Tony's church 'til the day he dies he says, ... all because of you. And you know what? All the guys are here from the Mud Bowl, too. They're thankin' God for your life, just like me. Yea, we lost that snowy Saturday to a great bunch of kids from Nutley, but we'll win the big one because we saw God in you so many times. It took us a long time to figure it all out, Frankie boy, but we did. So tell the Lord about us all, cause one day we'll be joining you. Just wait again there for me, ... one more time.

"In closing, folks, I just want to say to you that I've thought of what my friend did for me every day of my life. And every time I think of him I know I'm ... I'm just a little south of Heaven."

He was the thief on the cross. His huge hands still scare me, until I see his Silvia, ... and then when I hear his voice. Gino "Sneaks" Babula Sr. walked out of prison for the last time in November 1970. He was headed home at last to his beloved Silvia. But he also had to make a stop on the way, ... at the funeral of Marietta Bonaducci. Renewing old acquaintances that day, he privately made a commitment to himself to get out of his "lifestyle". It was time.

After meeting with Richie "The Boot" and representatives of New York's five families, a deal was cut. The Mafia "tradition" of it being impossible to leave would be waived in Sneak's case for a price, ... $1,000,000! When Sneaks heard the verdict, it was as if a band of rabid bats came catapulting out of his bosom, leaving him empty, but purified. Sitting in the furnished basement of Benny Badalamenti's home in Newark's Forest Hill section where the heads had convened, Sneaks almost collapsed with relief. It was the easiest check he ever wrote.

Sneaks and Silvia never moved from their Belleville home on Carpenter Street. Over the years, he still received young wannabe visitors seeking advice on how to generate the kind of earnings he had running the Bloomfield Avenue crew. He would chose his words carefully, and simply share the business principles he'd learned from his prolific reading as a retired "entrepreneur".

After trading heartfelt apologies to each other, ... the son for having judged his father so harshly over the years, and the father for having put his lifestyle before his wife and son, Sneak's relationship with Gino flourished. The changes Sneaks now saw in Gino made him curious. He began an exhaustive search for the Higher Power. The day he was informed of Frank Bonaducci's terminal illness, Sneaks found Him. At that moment, thoughts of racketeering, witness intimidation, gambling, money laundering, and violence totally vacated his spirit.

Now, Sneaks splits time between Belleville and Wildwood Crest where he owns a condominium. Most of his hours are spent following Gino's children's business careers, or helping his son manage his two motels there. Every so often he calls a friend at People's Bank in Belleville to check on "Petee Five Corners'" account for Frank's college education. Thirty-three needy Belleville kids have received scholarships out of that fund since Marietta's deathbed revelation to Donna. It brings a smile to Sneaks' face every time he thinks of his old friends, Marietta and Peter Frassa, ... and then a tear always follows.

There'll never be another like her. She had so much to give, and she gave it all to her family. The sin is the rest of the world never met her. Bella Bonaducci Bruno was eighty-six when she died in the spring of 2002. Her strength and zest for life began draining after her beloved Emil's sudden death in 1964 at the Fontainebleau Hotel in Miami. They were on their first extended vacation since their honeymoon in 1940. While many thought the glamorous widow would surely reinvent her adventurous spirit as an unattached woman, instead, she and her younger, righteous, unmarried, and devoted sister Josephine became inseparable. Visits to their growing brood of nieces and nephews, Catholic War Veteran activities, and Frank's bible studies in Verona kept Bella busy. With her hips beginning to give out, and blood pressure problems haunting the sexy lifetime smoker, she settled in a Toms River seniors' community. Next stop was a rest home quickly thereafter. When she learned of the deaths of her brother and her nephew, she stopped talking. She took her own last breath two years later.

Nick Durso, oldest of the thirty-one Bonaducci nieces and nephews, gave her eulogy at St. Francis Xavier Church on Bloomfield Avenue across from City Stadium. Now a distinguished fifty-nine year old Columbus, Ohio executive who had three sons, who all played football at Ohio State, he didn't need notes.

"If I could entitle this eulogy, it would be 'Beautiful Bella', ... or 'Glamorous Bella', or 'Sexy Bella', or 'Devoted Bella'. There is no way you could use one adjective to describe our Aunt Bella. The sparse crowd's light chatter confirmed Nick's description.

"She was the second of seven children who survived birth and the Depression in the household of Joe and Mamie Bonaducci. A brother and a sister died in infancy. Bella was her mother's daughter, with she and Grandma traveling the world together, without their husbands, and always seeming to end up in Cuba. I always thought the State Department should employ her looks, charm, and ability to communicate to get us together with Cuba again. At eighty years old she actually went back there; how, I don't know. But her reaction was classic: 'It was like visiting an old friend of mine, …a glamorous, aging actress.' Indeed, was she not that glamorous, aging actress?

"The stories of Aunt Bella are legendary. But I remember that anytime she announced a forthcoming visit, my father and mother would act as if some celebrity was about to grace our doorstep. How about when she commandeered that TV set for my cousin Jo-Jo, when he had that neck operation? Did she not treat each of us like we were her favorite? Stories of her dancing in every nightclub from Newark to New York City, from Miami to Havana, charming saints and sinners with her glamour, were also true. But she was always waiting for her prince charming to show up, … and that was Uncle Emil Bruno. And yes, guys with big cars and expensive suits would send flowers and such every week, hoping to lure her into becoming the wife of one of New York's most wanted. Of course, Grandpa Joe discarded everything before she could see it.

"She loved her name, Bella Bonaducci, Bella Bruno. But her stage name, 'Bella La Starr', was the one she adored most of all, because Bella meant 'beautiful' and, … and because she wanted to be … a 'star'.

"Grandpa Joe and Judge Leroy Liloia <u>did</u> make that trip down to South Philly to pull her off a burlesque stage before the war. But the story is also true when he demanded she never dance or sing on stage; that she obeyed him until the day she died. Instead, she received her enjoyment from her nieces and nephews, her service to the veterans of war, and her love for family. Her stage was Footnotes Shoe Store in Millburn. It was there where she performed for the wealthy and wise. They never forgot her. 'Bella,' they'd say. 'It was <u>you</u> who should have done 'Auntie Mame', … not Rosalind Russell.'

"She would reply, 'Wasn't Rosalind marvelous,' as if the two beauties were the closest of friends.

"One more important story is also true: on Grandpa's death bed, at Soho Hospital in Belleville, he apologized in front of Aunt Josephine for having stopped Bella from pursuing her show business destiny. 'Pa, forget about it. We've had a great life,' she reacted.

"His last words in Italian were about how he prevented God from doing what He had planned for her life. At that moment he died. Aunt Josephine and Aunt Bella cried, knowing that Grandpa finally got it right.

"In the end, Aunt Bella Bonaducci Bruno led an adventurous life, ... but I don't think it was as adventurous as she hoped it would be. I do know right now, the good Lord and she are talking all about that, ... and He's getting such a kick out of the glamorous creation He manifested back at the foundations of the earth. And He's probably agreeing Grandpa Joe made a mistake. But, we know God and Aunt Bella have surely forgiven him for that by now."

He fooled us, but we all had this awe and respect for him. He could have been President Bonaducci. Carmine Leonardo "Carmine the Artist" Bonaducci retired to Key West when he was only sixty-five. A power play in New York's gangland forced him to abandon what he privately dreamed, ...the opportunity to lead what he always called, "the tradition from our roots".

No one in the five boroughs and northern Jersey was as articulate, or respectful, as the well-dressed Bonaducci. While he never took his business interests totally legitimate, Carmine did manage to prevent all four sons from sliding into illegal activities. Each of them finally earned college degrees after stints working in jobs sponsored by their father's lieutenants. Not one of the boys ever served a jail term. For that, Carmine said he was indebted to his cousin, Rocky, who had always reminded him a college education was essential for all the Bonaducci grandchildren on both sides of the Hudson. Then they could be totally independent from the sometimes-questionable decisions of some of their ancestors. Carmine made sure his four boys left their high paying "internships", and enrolled in schools across the country.

When Rocky's star was rising in the resort development business during his stint in Daytona Beach, he attended a surprise birthday for Carmine in the Keys. His cousin's oldest son sat with Rocky and asked, "Cousin Rocky, what do you think of my father?"

Alone with the young man on the estate patio overlooking a tranquil, aqua blue lagoon, Rocky took a long drag on his Lucky Strike. He knew how his answer would not only define him with his cousin's family, but could also imprint on the young man's mind an opinion of his father he might not be able to process without embarrassment and confusion. What Rocky said made it word for word to the ears of "Carmine the Artist" by the end of the night.

"My cousin has never been a violent man," began Rocky. "The intensity of his business interests could've often forced him into such behavior. But Carmine never went that way. He's been an entrepreneur of precision judgment, when he never had the benefit of a formal education. While he got into some investments

I would'a stayed away from, he was always discreet. Your ol' man knew when to keep his mout shut." Rocky hesitated, wanting to be honest without being overly patronizing, because at thirty years old, the oldest son was mature enough to be as much aware of "Carmine the Artist", as he was.

Rocky himself looked like a retired mobster in his white linen suit and black silk shirt. His body relaxed as he surrendered to the truth. "Ya know, your father straightened me out once. Yea, he reminded me while it's great to be a good father, you can't forget you have your own life and your own talents, and you have a responsibility to yourself and your kids to be who you really are. After my wife died, I decided to follow your father's advice. Now, for the first time in my life I know I'm doin' what I love to do and what I'm good at, too. It's also what I'm supposed to be doin'. Yep, your dad straightened me out."

The young Bonaducci reacted with only four words, "Thank you, cousin Rocky."

On the morning of Rocky's funeral, Jo-Jo was informed a Marine Corp Honor Guard would enter the parlor to act as honorary pallbearers. Then they would perform a twenty one-gun salute in his honor at the gravesite. Full of emotion, Jo-Jo said, "But my dad was just a PFC."

"He still qualifies," responded funeral director, Sal Megaro, who knew Rocky from his playing days at Barringer. "We won't forget he stormed the beaches for us in the South Pacific."

"Who organized this?" asked Jo-Jo.

"Your father's cousins from Brooklyn, ... Carmine and his boys." Then Sal added, " And, Jo-Jo, don't worry about seeing us afterwards about the funeral, or with the limos, or when Frankie goes. It's all been taken care of, ... even the repass at Tommy Apicella's restaurant for both of 'em."

Jo-Jo looked across the room where cousin Carmine, his four boys, and all of their wives were standing. "Carmine the Artist" had a white silk handkerchief to his eyes.

Frankie respected him more than anyone in the world, ... even before what happened in his life. When word got out that Craig Francello had left college before the end of the first semester, few were surprised.

In 1974 Frank was relaxing in his new home in Verona, enjoying the annual Emmy Awards Show, and trying to stay awake to hear the announcement of the "Variety Show of the Year". He called Maria down from the kitchen.

When the winner was revealed, its comedy writing team took center stage. A handful of handsome male writers, each sporting custom tuxedos, filed up to the stage. Their female peers, one younger and more beautiful than the next, followed. Then, holding their golden statues, they waited patiently in silence with the master of ceremony until a roar came from the theater audience that announced the late arrival of the leader of this award-winning team. As he shuffled up the stairs to the podium, Frank and Maria leaned forward in their lounge chairs, their eyes bugging in disbelief. And then a gentle smile appeared on their faces. There was Craigie Francello, ... or Craig Francis, as Hollywood had come to know him.

It was the same young man with cerebral palsy who each day back in the late fifties would step onto an exhaust-filled, broken down number 32 De Camp bus heading into New York City and Sean McMahon's bar. There he and the wisecracking Irish pub owner would collaborate on a children's show that would eventually make Sean a legitimate force in New York comedy. In those days when few others would slow down their thinking to listen to Craig, Sean had the compassion to strain to hear the sharp wit within the twisted young Belleville High student. Their collaboration, "The Sean McMahon Hour", won a local Emmy in the sixties. Craig eventually became one of the lead writers on a New York City high school-based sit-com where his hilarious characters would go on to Hollywood greatness as comedians and legitimate dramatic actors. He helped produce the first full-length comedy film for the fledgling HBO cable station. Craig wrote and produced a romantic comedy for the big screen about a female Army recruit that eventually became another award-winning TV show. Then he was named lead writer at Disney Studios, ... Craig Francis, ... Craig Francello from the Silver Lake section of Belleville.

By the way, Sean McMahon not only still writes comedy today, but has also become a highly demanded voice-over talent. Back in the late sixties, he even landed a role as a dumb mute in a successful Hollywood film. His Academy Award "Best-Supporting Actor" nomination surprised everyone in the industry, but Craig Francello. "Deallllling with me all these years, heeeee had to have the patience of a saint," commented Craig during the award festivities. "Annnnnd, if there's a God in Heaven, Heeeee knew this old Irishman had to be paid back somehow."

When he flew home for Frank's funeral, Craig's wife and three healthy children came, too. A stretch limousine transported him and his twelve-member entourage from Newark Airport to visit his mother, still on Cuozzo Street in Silver Lake. Then everyone piled back into the limo to go to Megaro's Funeral Home.

When Maria greeted Craig at the wake, he leaned over to her, and slowly and deliberately said, "Yourrr Frank was the first person at Belleville High School that actually forced himself to hear what I had to saaayy. He listened to meee. I made him laugh, and in return, he gave me hope. IIIIII … will never forget him."

A couple of people really became famous from the neighborhood. Some you expected. I could never have predicted the others. And then there were the near famous. Connie Ferro is now retired in Palm Springs, where her two daughters live nearby. At the plush desert retreat's airport, the grounds crew has affectionately dubbed her regular Jersey visitors as the "Goomod Squad". Connie has not forgotten her girlfriends from her old neighborhood that helped with the global singing career that she enjoyed from the mid fifties to even her periodic appearances today.

While several rocky marriages were low points, Concetta Ferragamo enjoyed a majestic reign as the Queen of the heart of rock 'n' roll. American Bandstand, her number one hits, several beach blanket films, success in Europe, and her classic Italian beauty have forever etched her into the history of American music.

In spring 2004, Connie will be inducted into Belleville High's Hall of Greatness as one of the charter members of an elite list of graduates who impacted the world after leaving their hometown. A street is also to be named in her honor.

Reviewing her career, closest friends say her only disappointments came with … men. There is disagreement, however, as to who really was the love of her life. Most say it was the bandleader with the Amedigan name that her mother detested. But, her two sisters say it was a handsome Belleville High football player with black hair, soft lips, a big heart, and a Christ-like spirit. They remember his name as … Frank!

Joe Pelli continued to cut hair at the Pentagon Barber Shop, until he got into some trouble on Bloomfield Avenue by again running numbers for extra money. His mother insisted that he move to Little Italy in New York City to live with her sister. It would keep him away from the temptation to supplement his income as a barber and part-time comic. His comedy partner, Ralph Benedetto, was always at Joe's side, even in New York, … whether waiting tables, or opening for cheap nightclub acts.

Joe and Ralph never gave up hope. Given a supporting role in a fight film directed by one of his best patrons at the restaurant where he was working, Pelli experienced instant success. Within ten years he received an Academy Award for his role in a New Jersey-based gangster movie. Critically acclaimed for his portrayal of a crazed "made guy", Joe just shrugged and said he was imitating about a half a dozen "fellas" he knew from Newark.

Ralph, with his classic head of thick black hair that seemed to start just above his eyebrows, has never wanted for work. When Joe got his shot, he took Ralph with him everywhere. While their comedy act has been on hold for over twenty years, when alone with each other, they can't stop laughing.

Joe will also be honored in the same Hall of Greatness as Connie Ferro. However, on the morning of induction, Belleville's Board of Education will hold a special ceremony for him to receive a high school equivalency diploma to make him eligible. His eighty-seven year old mother, partner Ralph, and a few of the boys from Bloomfield Avenue will be there to celebrate his honor. Some say DeNiro and Scorcese are also going to show up.

Lenny Latore and his falsetto voice made it all the way from Stephen Crane Village in North Newark, to the Rock 'N' Roll Hall of Fame in Cleveland. The Four Loves changed over the years, and every time he had an opening, Lenny called Jimmy Quinn. But his wife, Pinky, always made sure her husband politely refused the now world-renowned singer.

During the sixties, Lenny and his group, along with the Beach Boys and Motown, were credited with being the homeland forces that prevented total victory for the British invasion of American music started by the Beatles. Today while his voice is failing at sixty-five, Lenny still sings at doo wop revivals and often returns to Atlantic City and the Poconos to help bring back the memories for his nostalgic fans. When he calls to invite Pinky and Jimmy Quinn to attend and hang out with their old friend, they accept, … as long as he promises Pinky he won't ask Jimmy to join the group. Lenny reminds her, "Pinky, … it's all over now."

Walking down Fairway Avenue in Belleville on warm summer nights when it seems sound travels well beyond its acceptable bounds, you might hear a faint voice harmonizing with some of the classic singing groups from '55-'63. If Pinky is baby-sitting for one of her grandchildren on the other side of town, you can be sure it's Jimmy Quinn joining in with whoever is on WCBS FM radio in New York City. His Irish tenor voice still blends smoothly into any song made famous many years ago. The oldies but goodies bring Jimmy back, all the way to a place where he only spent a short time. Sometimes he can't finish the song.

Dion DiMucci has become an American music icon. His professional, personal, and spiritual journeys have cultivated millions of fans worldwide.

A month before he passed away, Frank was dining in Boca Raton at the Cucina D'Angelo Restaurant. His host, Jake Maloney, was one his many protégés, and he wanted Frank to begin a special consulting assignment with his resort development company that had just gone public. As they sat in the open-air eatery, Frank caught a glimpse of a thin, middle-age man walking quickly through the chic mall surroundings. The dark glasses and beret compelled Frank to ask Jake, "Isn't that Dion from the Belmonts?"

"Didn't see," said Jake. "But wouldn't be surprised. Dion's got a place down here. Wanna meet him, Frank?"

"All my life, Jake."

"Take the consulting assignment, come back after the holidays, and I'll arrange it."

"You can arrange it?"

"Take the job, and consider it's done."

"Let's do it," said Frank.

Frank Bonaducci died before he could return to Boca. He never met Dion. Certain questions in life never get answered. Perhaps, we just have to wait until we get to the other side.

Don McLean's "American Pie" may be the most interpreted song in rock 'n' roll history. It's anthem qualities have immortalized its words and the events it seemingly depicts. Since the day Frank died, Jo-Jo cannot listen to it.

The counterfeiting thing just drove everybody crazy. I still can't believe it happened in our backyard. There were saints and sinners in the group of counterfeit indictees that December 1959. A collective sigh of relief could be heard all the way to Nutley when Judge Leroy Liloia threw the whole case out.

At eighty-one years old, Greenie Delaney, now widowed, still is a huge help in attending to his sister's needs and providing a "father" image for her boys and their families. Katherine, who waited for Pete to his dying day, finally married an elderly gentleman, who helped her adopt two sons from the streets of Dublin, before he passed away.

Greenie doesn't have a pension, and his social security is minimal. On the other hand, he always has cash in his pocket. Every day he makes a pilgrimage to the "social club" that still stands next to where the Chinese Clipper Restaurant used to be on the Five Corners.

On the Christmas Eve visits to the cemetery, Greenie finds it hard not to get emotional. On the other hand, Thomas Anthony keeps him smiling. Having been one of the first connected guys to enter the witness protection program in the early seventies, Two Tones' smooth talking ways and expensive clothes still have not changed, in spite of his new identity. Greenie has yet to guess where his old friend now lives. He does know that Bloomfield Avenue's once "most eligible bachelor" has been married for twenty-five years and fathered three children. Greenie also remembers the day Tommy vanished, … right after an order to "hit" some big-talking lieutenant came down. Two Tones thought of his old friend Pete, and knew immediately he could never end someone's life. From a chubby butcher he had learned the love of his fellow man. After the cemetery trips, Greenie and Jo-Jo drop Two Tones off at Newark Airport, … destination unknown.

Benny "Bad Boy" Badalamenti was killed at a restaurant in Queens during a "civil" war between Joe Bananno's crime family and rivals supported by the rest of the mob's New York City Commission. On either side of the Hudson, no one cried for the Newark resident, … not even his wife.

Louis "Crazy Louie" Montana is serving a life sentence for his hand in the murders of fellow indictees, John Malafatano and Larry Lisa. It took ten years for Georgia, Jersey, and federal authorities to get him convicted. Montana behind bars put a lot of nerves at ease on Bloomfield Avenue.

Patsie Pratola never sang again for the Four Loves after the 1959 case. Then he was in and out of jail all the time before dying of lung cancer at age forty-five.

Vinnie Giampietro continued to drive a Trackless Transit bus for ten years after the indictments. In 1969, Frank, Gino, and a couple other members of the '58 football team put together some money so that, combined with his limited work benefits,

Vinnie could get his bad hip replaced. Able to walk upright and exercise for the first time since his days in Korea, he lost one hundred pounds, got married, and continued bus-driving until reaching retirement at sixty-five. Now a grandfather, Vinnie can be found high atop Belleville Municipal Stadium at every home football game. He's always telling his grandkids about two running backs he'll never forget, … Frank and Gino.

Chet Costello died of a heart attack making a cherry coke for a young customer at his candy store in the late sixties. When his friend Topper Series bought the business and the building from Chet's wife, the former Prudential clerk paid cash. He turned it into "Topper's Pizza, …our Pies are Tops". While the food was acceptable, most notable about his operation were the big, flashy cars that always seemed to be parked in its front lot. The pay phone at the back of the store was in constant use. He sold out in 1979.

In the early sixties, Rosa and Gary Gubitosi moved to Florida, where he reportedly opened a TV repair business just like he had in Belleville. After Gary died in 1983, Rosa quickly purchased a home on the intercoastal waterway in Boca Raton. Two years later, at age sixty-five, she married her thirty-five year old chauffeur. He takes her out on her boat, every afternoon. Her daughters, who no longer speak to her, can't understand how she buys everything, … cash! When Jo-Jo was told by his father about Rosa and her young handyman, he laughed, "But has she explained to the kid yet … what a 'moppeen' is?"

Hiram Wilhelm spent the spring semester of 1960 apologizing to all his Italian American students for his bigoted comments at the trial. They forgave him, so he thought. On the day before Easter break that year, Hiram arrived at school to find two-dozen rancid gabootsells waiting for him on his office desk. He was inducted into Belleville High's Athletic Hall of Fame in 1979, the year he died.

Reinstated as a Newark police officer immediately after the trial, Mike Manzer was convicted five years later of receiving stolen goods. After a short jail term, he entered the security business as a part-time supervisor.

But where would we be without the Lord and His ambassadors in our lives? The morning after Marietta's death, Queenie phoned the Bonaducci household. Donna answered, "Hello."

"Is this Donna?"

"Yes, who's this?"

"It's Queenie, darling. Is your mother OK? Nora and me heard she got sick."

"Oh, Queenie, … she died."

The phone clicked.

The Bonaducci family did not see Queenie and Nora until the morning of the funeral. They quietly entered the parlor before the family and other mourners would pay their last respects. Both were dressed in their blue work uniforms, with identical cream-colored overcoats. A torrential downpour outside had soaked their worn black sneakers. They meekly walked up to Rocky, and the children rose out of respect. Queenie had a black Bible tucked under her right arm.

"Folks, Marietta is in glory now," said Queenie, as Nora remained silent. "We knew her since 1958. Her constant prayer dat God take her first got answered, but she went home too soon. Here's the Bible we read her da day she accepted da Lord. Please keep it. I am sure we'll all be seein' her again, … on da other side."

Everyone embraced. No tears were shed.

In the weeks after Marietta's funeral, her sister-in-law Mary mentioned in passing that she heard Queenie and Nora quit the factory. Some said they headed back to Alabama. Frank said they took a vacation; the Lord had given them a little time off until their next assignment. He was always convinced they were angels on a rescue mission.

Caesar Casciano is now eighty-eight, and proudly holds the title of National Commander Emeritus of the Catholic War Veterans. Once a month he makes the ninety-mile trip from his Jersey Shore home to Newark where the vets still meet at St. Francis Church. He never takes off his CWV cap with his many designations. His half Samoan, half Japanese son-in-law, Kim Tasuiopo, rides with him in case Caesar gets too tired to drive back. Kim says his father-in-law tells war stories all the way. Some he's heard several times over. But he never corrects Caesar, because his own father fought in World War II as well, … on the side of the Americans. Kim knows full well that if his dad had been on the other side, he'd never be married to Caesar's daughter, let alone traveling with him to Catholic War Veterans meetings.

Josephine Bonaducci never married, spending all her senior years standing side by side her sister, Bella.

"You don't know half the stories," she says, every time Bella's name comes up.

Josephine, too, still serves the veterans as a past National Commander of the Catholic War Veterans Auxiliary. Since VJ Day, she has never missed a Christmas Eve at the Veterans Hospital in East Orange. She was eighty-three in 2003.

Now sixty-eight, Pastor Tony Votolo has virtually retired from leading his church on a daily basis. His son, Pastor Tony Boy, now does most of the weekly services. His father will step up to the pulpit when he has a special message for his congregation. Most of the time, Pastor Tony is traveling, and is at Newark Airport every Monday. Only he and God know where the spry and still energetic teacher of the Word is heading. His ministry now focuses on preaching in prisons and visiting the multitude of men he knows are scattered around the country in the witness protection program.

The Pastor's first book, chronicling his work with former organized crime figures, will be published shortly. In it he highlights, as well, the good people on the perimeter of that lifestyle. He says any doubts he may have had in the past, about the reality of Christ's saving grace, were quickly eradicated by the miracles he saw in gangster's amazing conversions.

Whenever Pastor Tony's missionary trips are nearing their end, he always longs for Newark. It was at Sacred Heart Cathedral, as a cocky Barringer High School quarterback, when he first encountered his Savior. His return up Bloomfield Avenue to his home near his church always causes him to recall the countless people along that route that came to know the Lord … at the last moment. He says, "… I know, that I know, … that I know, … that I know, …that I will see each of them again."

They were so small to us, but so significant. Jerome Yarborough cried for days after being told by his mother that Mr. Pete from Bloomfield Avenue had gone home to be with his daddy and the Lord. Rocky heard about the grieving boy through Greenie, and he encouraged Frank and Gino to visit him at Christmas time at the family's apartment on Orange Street. Presenting the tiny youngster with one of the game balls Mr. Inside had won the previous season stunned Jerome and his mother. Gino's idea brought a smile to Jerome's beautiful black face, … the first since he last saw Pete Frassa.

On his breaks from college, Frank continued to visit Jerome and his family, and during his early selling career, he'd also send small checks to help the Yarboroughs out. Jerome never became an athlete, but rather an honor roll student who was also the class valedictorian at Newark's prestigious St. Gerard's Prep on High Street. He graduated from Harvard four years later.

Today, Jerome is one of the finest orthopedic surgeons in New Jersey. Pictures of his wife and children dominate his orderly and provincial office. However, when asked about his most prized possessions, he points to a small table displaying two items, …a dry, withered old football from the fifties, and a photo of a chubby white man, with a stained butcher's apron, hugging a tiny black boy on his counter top.

Blackie the dog was sleeping under the hammock on the day Greenie called to tell Marietta of Pete's heart attack. Her piercing single shriek sent the startled Blackie running off towards the Gubitosis' backyard. The Bonaduccis never saw their beloved dog again.

Jo-Jo's buddies were cute, sometimes obnoxious, and very different. Russell Giardella stopped delivering papers after graduating Belleville in 1963. His part-time job prevented him playing sports, or engaging in any extracurricular activity in high school. Devoted to his parents and the eventual total of ten brothers and sisters, his teen years were dominated by his newspaper route, helping the family, and studying. His only date during those four years was a cousin he invited to the Junior Prom. He received financial aid to attend Newark Rutgers. After graduation, he was drafted and saw combat in Vietnam. Returning to New Jersey, he earned a Masters Degree in Business Administration at New York University. Afterwards, he only had one job, … a computer programming position with ATT. Retiring at age forty to move his aging parents to Naples, Florida, he never married. He also never worked professionally again, and now devotes daytimes to online trading, as well as caring for Mr. and Mrs. Giardella. His net worth is now larger than some third world countries. None of his brothers or sisters tries to take advantage of his wealth, but they each know they can call on him for anything.

Russell sends Jo-Jo a birthday card every year, followed by a phone call. And he always reminds him that their short stay in Wildwood in the summer '59 was not only his best, but last, vacation. One moment of their youth he claims he'll also never forget is placing *The Newark Star Ledger* on the icy doorstep at 711 Belmont Avenue, with its headlines announcing the plane crash that killed Holly, Valens, and the Big Bopper. That day, death became real to him, and as he peered through the Bonaduccis' window-paneled front door, he said a prayer for his friend and his family. He would never want to lose them. And during his once-a-year call, Russell reminds Jo-Jo that he still prays for the Bonaduccis every morning, not just those that are still here, but also those that are gone.

Gerald Gretto was part of the first graduating class at Essex Catholic High School on Broadway in Newark. He and Jo-Jo spoke little during their college years, with Gerald hustling several jobs and earning his degree at nights from St. John's. One night before leaving his Belmont Avenue home for college, he stopped for gas at Mark Brunello's Shell Station, and ran into the still tempting Rosemarie Masino, who was now an executive secretary at Prudential in downtown Newark. They exchanged phone numbers, but never expected to call each other with Gerald still attending mass every day, and Rosemarie having just ended her second engagement. Besides, with her grammar and high school reputations, Dominick and Tillie Gretto would never permit their son to date the sexy little neighbor from around the corner.

Today, Gerald and Rosemarie are happily married and proud parents of four sons who each graduated from Catholic universities, ... Notre Dame, Boston College, Seton Hall, and St. Joseph's in Philadelphia. She is active in their local church in Tinton Falls, Monmouth County. Gerald owns his own insurance agency. Before her sons start to date anyone of interest, they each know to get their mother's approval. Rosemarie assures her husband and her boys that she knows how to judge young girls, having done, or thought of doing, many wrong things as a teenager in Belleville.

Jo-Jo was never invited to his next-door neighbor's wedding. If he were, Frank always insisted his brother would have declined.

Harold Bader grew to six feet, four inches tall in high school. Still gawky and clumsy by his senior year, and never losing his heavy English accent, he found fortune in track and field. Growing up on Belmont Avenue next to his cousins, Jimmy and Bobby Hardy, he had idolized their every move. While they expected him to go out for track, they could not believe it when the humble beanpole from Bermuda broke all of Bobby's scoring and pole vault records, and won the Essex County Pole Vault Championship in 1964, his senior year.

Without good grades, Harold enlisted in the Navy, and got to Vietnam. But he saw little action, before returning to Jersey to marry twice, and father four children. He followed his cousins when they moved to New England, and now lives just south of Boston, running one of Bob Hardy's five real estate offices in the area.

Roger Bush broke Belleville High's freshman basketball scoring record in 1960, and actually got into a couple of varsity games that year. However, again because of poor grades, he was ineligible to play the next two seasons. In fact, Red Bush got help from some of his priest friends at Montclair Immaculate High School to convince Coach Wilhelm to fight to get his son on the squad for his senior year. "Miraculously", Roger's grades became acceptable.

Roger was the spark needed in the winter of '63 for Belleville to have its first winning record in ten years, as well as upset perennial Newark power, South Side, in the quarterfinals of the Essex County Tournament. Roger made the All Big Ten Team that year, and Red Bush was humbled by his son's success. His years of coaching him about school and basketball had finally paid off.

After his senior year, Roger began drinking excessively, so Red convinced him to enlist in the Army. That ended his drinking almost immediately. He loved the Army and its discipline. He planned to attend college on his return to the States, as well as continue his basketball career.

In October 1967, Roger Bush was killed in the Vietnam Province of Quang Tri, when the VC overran the tank he commanded. He had no chance.

Today, the Belleville and Nutley Veterans of Foreign Wars make their home together on Washington Avenue in Nutley, just north of the Belleville border. There just isn't enough support for each town's veterans to have separate meeting halls. Entering the building and turning right, you'll see the high school graduation picture of Roger Bush over the entrance to the bar. The room was named in his honor. Inside, and behind the bar, are all his basketball trophies and military memorabilia. There is also a picture of his dad embracing Roger after '63's South Side game. Red reportedly died of a broken heart several years after his son.

On every New Year's Eve, Jo-Jo stops by the VFW to buy its patrons a drink in memory of his old friend. Jo-Jo sips a Coke. Of all the Belleville and Nutley stories they tell, the most popular is when Jo-Jo recounts how he and Roger walked into the Bonaducci kitchen one day with the legendary Aubrey Lewis' Notre Dame helmet.

Frankie's friends teased me to no end. I love that they still do it today. Jackie Carey spent thirty years in Belleville's Police Department, retiring into the home security alarm business. He didn't marry until his late thirties. But that tough relationship with a girl, fifteen years his junior, lasted only long enough to give him a healthy, beautiful daughter. His sister, who's never married, helps him raise her. The three of them still live in their old family home on Mill Street in Belleville.

Wounded by marriage, Jackie is quiet today. Having worked hard to clean up his vintage Jerseyese, he chooses his words carefully. Since Frank's passing, Jackie looks forward to the neighborhood's reunion every Labor Day at Jo-Jo's summer home in Newport, Rhode Island. He always drives there in the pickup truck he uses for business. On its back panel are the scripted words, "Heavenly Heap II". The truck is gold.

But Jackie jokes there will be only one "Heavenly Heap", which Jo-Jo "stole" from him in 1971. Every year he declares his frustration: "Dose Jesuits up in Boston College surely taught Jo-Jo to bargain like a Manhattan Jew jewelry merchant. Only reason I come up here every year is to sleep in da back seat of my golden Mercury. Now Jo-Jo wants $55,000 for it. If he knew all of da stories about dat heap, he'd ask for $100,000. Hey, Jo-Jo, ya don't know half about dat trip to Brooklyn to get your brother to see the Belmonts. What a night!"

Jimmy Hardy was two years behind Frank, but the closeness of the Belmont and Smallwood Avenue neighborhood made them pen pals for years. Jimmy went on to Oregon State on a track scholarship, and then stunned his family by enlisting in the Marines. He saw serious action in Vietnam, but came back whole, both mentally and physically. Today, he, too, works in his brother's New England real estate development business. Jim lives in New Hampshire, but commutes to the company headquarters in Boston.

At 2001's reunion at Jo-Jo's, Jimmy presented him with a copy of the best selling book, *Flag of our Fathers.* On the inside cover, Jimmy included a dedication letter: "Dear Jo-Jo, I am alive today, the father of two children and happily married, because of your father, PFC Rocco A. Bonaducci, USMC. One hot, humid summer day in '59, your mother and father insisted all the guys stay for one of your dad's great barbeques. As we ate, I asked him about the Marines and what it was like to fight the enemy hand-to-hand. He said it was hell, and prayed all us guys would never go to war. Well, many of us did, and I became a Marine because of your father. He was a stud. But he told me if I was ever in combat, I should do one thing, whether taking a beach or running into enemy territory under fire, ... 'Hit the dirt, Jimmy. Then roll as fast as you can, as far as you can'. I had to do that once, and I was the only one of my assault team to survive. When I hit the dirt, I thought of your father, and then I rolled for my life. His advice saved me. Once last thing, ... in my home in New Hampshire, I have a room for my heroes, ... black and white shots of the men who poured wisdom into my life. Do you have a picture of your dad in uniform? Semper Fi, Jimmy Hardy."

Davey Thatcher was the same age as Jimmy. Brazen and self-assured as a basketball and baseball star at Belleville, he also promptly enlisted after graduation and headed to Vietnam. He returned quiet and serene, spending the next thirty years working as a meter reader at Public Service Gas and Electric. His career there ended because of a recurring back injury from the war. Now into his second marriage, he helps his wife manage his late mother's dance studio.

Since returning from Vietnam, Davey never drove a car. His bicycle rides around Belleville, where he still lives, give him the peace he seeks every day. War took its toll. His favorite day of the year is Labor Day. His brother flies in from North Carolina to pick him up to drive to Jo-Jo's reunion, where they all look forward to Davey's recollection of that summer night hiding in Gary Gubitosi's boat during that last game of "Stalag 17". He doesn't say much for the rest of the day. He just listens, smiles, and sips a couple beers.

Eric Thatcher, still called "The Snatcher" at reunion time, is now a professor of psychology at a small private college in the Appalachians of North Carolina. He still possesses the reel-to-reel tapes that hide the treasured words of those legendary disc jockeys, and the music that has become known as doo wop, during the era now lionized as the "heart of rock 'n' roll". Most recently, he insured his collection for $1,000,000.

After graduating from Montclair State with honors, his potential professional baseball career sabotaged by a torn knee ligament, Eric ventured into the world of psychology, motivated by his mother's daily mystical interest in discovering "truth". Stories of her have helped to fill his lecture halls in the small liberal arts college. His podium has become his pulpit as he encourages freethinking and original thought to his students. When he uncannily weaves current events into his talks, visitors who knew his mother can just about taste the Southern Comfort Manhattans and smell the smoke of a Pall Mall in the lecture hall. After Frank's death, it was Eric who conceived of the neighborhood reunions.

Late on Saturday nights at the quiet campus in the South, far from New Jersey, "The Snatcher" can be heard on his three-hour "oldies" show that is produced at the local college radio station. Students from the Bible Belt get a chance to hear the fifties sounds of The Paragons, The Jesters, The Moonglows, The Students, The Five Satins, Buddy Holly, Ritchie Valens, The Mello-Kings, Dion and the Belmonts, Connie Ferro, and even some early recordings of Lenny Latore and the Four Loves. They learn about Bloomfield Avenue in Newark, Silver Lake in Belleville, the Milk Bar, the Park Oval in Nutley, and Rutt's Hutt in Clifton. Requests are welcome, but The Snatcher rule is that no songs recorded after President Kennedy's assassination will be played. His reasoning is not quite clear to his listeners, ... something to do with a football game in the mud in '58 that started a change, accelerated by a plane crash on February 3, 1959, and then punctuated by Oswald's bullet, and a war in

Vietnam. He says he researched the times with an old friend whose name is Jo-Jo. He ends his weekly show the same way every Saturday night: "You've listened to the heavenly music that bridged the gap between rhythm and blues and rock 'n' roll. We now call it 'doo wop'. If any one of my listeners this night grew up in the fifties, I can only give you one piece of advice: Cuz, when you look back, glance, ... don't stare." Then he adds, "And ... good night, Frankie boy, where ever you may be."

Bobby Hardy fulfilled his obligation as a Midshipman at Annapolis by spending the next four years commanding an aircraft carrier off the coast of Vietnam. At one point, Roger Bush, Davey Thatcher, Jimmy Hardy, Russell Giardella, and Bob Hardy were all in the war zone at the same time. Now semi-retired in Jamestown, Rhode Island, after a short stint teaching for the Navy in Newport, Bob has become a successful real estate broker, developer, and investor. And many of his family members work for him in New England.

Because his father had been a jukebox vendor in Essex County all his life, Bob began collecting classic music boxes after his death and has his garage full of them. He and Eric battle every year about whose collection is more valuable, ... Eric's on tape with the original DJ segues, or Bob's 45's. On Labor Day 2002, Bob was waiting for the boys to arrive from Jersey. He needed help to load a special gift for Jo-Jo onto Jackie Carey's pickup.

I'm trying to help Jo-Jo, and he's trying to help me. Joseph Bonaducci met his future wife, Megan Murphy, at Boston College. Her mother's maiden name was Mangiapane, and Marietta was thrilled her second son had found an Irish beauty with Italian blood. She always said that if her brother, Pete, had been permitted to marry Katherine Delaney, he might have lived a fuller life. Marietta made it clear to all that with a name on her mother's side like "Mangiapane", which means, "eat bread", Megan must have come from strong stock. "Not to change that surname took much pride and courage!" commented the Bonaducci matriarch.

The most curious of the three Bonaducci children, Jo-Jo continued with his education after college. It wasn't until he was awarded his doctorate in organizational behavior in 1973 that he and Megan finally married. He started writing articles about sales, management, leadership development, and strategic planning as a doctoral student, encouraged by what he learned as a part-time salesman in Frank's national recreational real estate development company. However, Jo-Jo chose teaching at the masters level as his profession. With his business experience, he heads up a leadership department at a major east coast business school. On the other hand, most of his income comes from his writing and busy national speaking schedule.

Although Megan was raised in Newport, during the early years of their marriage Jo-Jo would make sure his family spent at least a few summer days in Wildwood, New Jersey. Their two boys and one girl would hear the story of their father's first vacation at the Jersey Shore resort, over and over again. Jo-Jo would go into every detail, … from the sounds of the rides to the cawing seagulls, to that enticing aroma of Aunt Maggie Corino's gravy clashing with the scent of sizzling sausage and peppers and the salt air rolling in from the direction of the boardwalk.

"Can you smell it kids? Did it make it to your nostrils yet?" Jo-Jo would ask his children at a young age, as the family walked off the beach on a hot summer day.

Megan would smile. Their oldest boy, William, would question, "Gee, Dad, first of all, Aunt Maggie lives down by Wildwood Crest now. How can we be smelling her gravy?"

Rocco, his younger son, was once quoted as coming back at his brother, "Oh, William, Daddy's right. Just stop for a minute, picture Aunt Maggie, and you can smell the gravy mixed with the salt air."

"What can we expect from a kid with a name like … Rocco?" was William's response.

Before Jo-Jo could react, his younger son retaliated, "Oh yea? You should talk with that Amedigan name. So, not too many kids are named Rocco, but it's Grandpa Rocky's name, and he stormed the beaches at Eniwetoc! I don't care what you say, William, I can smell the gravy!"

This past summer, Jo-Jo took Megan and Frank's widow, Maria, down to see Aunt Maggie at the nursing home that now takes care of her. At eighty-seven, she is healthy, except for Alzheimer's disease. She welcomes them to her "hotel" and insists they stay for macaroni.

Maria spoke first. "How are you, Aunt Maggie? It's Maria."

In spite of her condition, her aunt's answer was as much like the practical businesswoman she always was. "It seems I'm lost, and I can't find my way back to my home. We work all these years, then we lose our minds." This was Maggie's last lucid comment for the day.

Judy, her oldest, kept the conversations going. Everyone laughed a lot and cried a bit as well, as they talked to Maggie. She asked for Bella, Marietta, Rocky, and Frank when she's reminded who her guests are. Then she got quiet when told they are all gone now.

As her visitors prepared to leave this last time, Maggie finally understood they could not stay for her macaroni and gravy. "OK, be careful everyone," she said. "Now, I'll have some time to spend with Bella, Marietta, Rocky, and Frank. You know they visit me every Sunday. Marietta brings her andibast."

Jo-Jo is still dealing with Frank's sudden passing. His personal heartbreak has created many doorways in the corridors of his mind. From his leadership development work, he knows some of those passages lead to personal growth, while others, to frustration and sentimentality. He still is avoiding opening most of those doors. While he attends mass every Sunday, when asked about God, he says, "We're still talking over a few things."

Today, Jo-Jo and Megan live with their family in Nutley, just two miles from 711 Belmont Avenue. They don't get down to Wildwood as much because they built a second home in 1998 on a piece of property Megan's dad gave the couple on their wedding day. While Buddy Murphy's income as a Newport florist was modest over the years, the stock tips he received from Vanderbilt, Auchincloss, and Kennedy helped him slowly build an enormous real estate portfolio in that fabled seaport town. Jo-Jo, Megan, and their children spend most of their summers there. Their French provincial home made them a financially independent family. Their next-door neighbors are Salve Regina College and the Vanderbilt Estate.

Since 1984 when Belleville and Nutley switched their game to Thanksgiving Day, Jo-Jo has been intimately involved in the annual Gridiron Classic Reunion Dinner commemorating the rivalry. It's held every Thanksgiving Eve, just like the Barringer-East Orange banquet was before those schools stopped their holiday encounter. Jo-Jo gives out a scholarship in Frank's name to the outstanding Belleville player of the game. He just stands there and hands over the check. His brother-in-law, Joe Zinicola, does the talking. Even now, it's still too emotional for Jo-Jo. Over the years, consensus amongst the thousands of Belleville and Nutley alumni who've attended is that the greatest game in their rivalry that began back in the twenties is the Mud Bowl. Frank and Gino are always mentioned.

This past Labor Day, Jo-Jo and Megan once again hosted the annual Belmont-Smallwood Avenues Reunion in Newport. Jackie Carey drove Eric and Davey Thatcher up from Belleville in his gold pickup truck. Jimmy and Harold came down from New Hampshire and Boston, respectively. The first rendezvous location was Bob Hardy's home right across the water from Newport. The boys had to load a classic Wurlitzer jukebox onto Jackie's truck. It was a gift for the Bonaducci family from Bob, but to be delivered to Jo-Jo in Newport for keepsake purposes.

When they rolled up Jo-Jo's driveway, he could not believe what he saw. "But this has to be worth a fortune," he said.

"Well, don't get too excited about the machinery," cautioned Bob, "It's the 45's that have some value."

Jo-Jo was speechless. Before they could roll it into the house, Megan read a gold-plated inscription that was on the glass face:
"In remembrance of Marietta, Rocky, and Frank Bonaducci.
Thanks for the memories.
With love, your friends from the old neighborhood.
'...And, Cuz, when you look back, glance, don't stare.'"

Needless to say, it was nostalgic and emotional last Labor Day in Newport. It was midnight before everyone would be leaving.

As the group readied to drive away to stay at Bob's for the night, the last words spoken by Eric Thatcher gently danced across the warm summer air, touching a place in Jo-Jo's heart that was still sore from loss. "Hey, Cuz," Eric called out. "Today we had a little taste of yesterday, and it was delectable."

Looking back at Jo-Jo waving, Davey whispered, "If yesterdays could only be tomorrows."

Only Eric heard his brother.

Jo-Jo and Megan were the only ones in the house. Their children were still visiting their Murphy and Mangiapane cousins in the area. Jo-Jo, who had drunk soda all day, decided to take a glass of port wine and a cigar out to the back patio. The night was warm with a soothing breeze flowing in off the ocean. Salve Regina College next door seemed to be in silence out of respect for Jo-Jo's contemplative mood.

Megan was still cleaning up the kitchen, but watching Jo-Jo through the corner of her eye. Sentimentality at times seemed to overtake him that summer, and she was a little concerned. Then she heard what she feared. With cigar in his right hand, and wine glass in his left, Jo-Jo began to whistle The Dell Viking's "Come Go

With Me". In slow tempo, he hit every note to the song that his wife knew was his favorite from childhood. She held her breath. There was another tune, which, if Jo-Jo's lips would form its sound, would signal he wasn't glancing back to olden times any more, … but rather, … now staring!

A puff on his cigar, a sip of his wine, and then it began, … Sinatra's "… Under My Skin". Now center stage belonged to Rocky's favorite. Slowly did the haunting sounds roll out from Jo-Jo's heart and through his lips, and quickly did his initial glance back turn into a melancholy stare.

Knowing she had to break his deepening mood, Megan called to him, "Hey, Dr. Jo-Jo, let's practice our dancing with this old music box."

Jo-Jo was startled, but composed himself and quickly agreed. Slowly, he put his cigar out, laid his glass down, and hoping his wife was not looking, wiped his eyes before walking back into the kitchen. "OK, Miss Mangiapane-Murphy-Bonaducci, let's dance. Who's gonna pick?"

"You kidding? It's my turn," said Megan, not known for her familiarity with pop music, but aware enough of her husband's emotions to avoid any song from the mid to late fifties.

Hardy and Thatcher had spent hours organizing the classics in the jukebox by decades, naturally starting with the fifties and ending with the nineties. Therefore, when Megan flipped to the eighties greats, she figured she was in safe, less than sentimental waters for Jo-Jo's sensitive reflections. Little did she realize as she randomly selected an '86 production of the Capris, that this song was more reminiscent of the essence of doo wop than most of the legendary creations between '55 and '63. "Morse Code of Love" leaped out of the plastic time machine and immediately a sympathizing smile came over Jo-Jo. His Labor Day addiction to memories would now only be heightened by the contemporary singing group's tribute to the "bop shoe bop, oopa ditti, dum di dum" language that would once again enslave Jo-Jo like some tribal ritual chant. The fifties funk would linger for a couple of more minutes in Jo-Jo's psyche.

As they danced, Jo-Jo looked into his wife's eyes, more to convince her that he was back to reality, and not in 1959. She could not camouflage her doubt.

"OK," he admitted. "I wasn't glancing, … I was staring. I'm OK now, though."

However, as the music played on, it was no longer Jo-Jo and his wife in the kitchen of their new home after a Labor Day party in 2002. Rather it was Rocky in his Marine Corp dress uniform, and Marietta in a sheer white dress and high heels. Blinded by the emotional image, now Jo-Jo was a spectator in the caverns of his mind. It was the summer of 1946. The evening had started at Jack Dempsey's Restaurant in mid-town Manhattan, and was now ending in the ballroom of the Waldorf. The song was Glenn Miller's "Moonlight Serenade". Marietta's beautiful eyes were focused upon her handsome hero husband. Their second honeymoon had been financed, and arranged, by Bella, who took care of little Frank and baby Jo-Jo for four days.

"Oh, Rocky, tomorrow will be so exciting. We'll take the train to Olean and meet the coaches at St. Bonaventure. Between the GI Loan and the scholarship, you'll get a great education and make All-American. I'll take that job as secretary to the president of the university. Then I'll take some courses, too. We'll get babysitting help for the boys. It will be just fine. You get your degree in commercial art, and I'll get one in creative writing. You start teaching and coaching and have an arts studio at home. I'll have a writing studio. We'll own a home wherever you're coaching. Then we have two more children. We'll give them the down payments for their homes. Oh, Rocky, God will help us. I can't believe you came home alive. God has been so good to us."

I can't believe I just turned fifty. The years have just come and gone. Jo-Jo and I have got to shake this oppression. Dad's passing was a shocker because he looked so good, and had come from so far back. But he had a good life. We're still trying to get over my mother's sudden departure. It can't be thirty-three years. But, losing Frankie? I search the scriptures and pray, but just don't get settled with it. Then I see my brother's family. Maria, Frank Jr., Mark, Corrine, and Christina are so full of hope and anticipation for every day, as if that will be the one when they'll see Frank again. Oh, they have so much faith. I have to speak to my brother, Jo-Jo. Frank would be so mad at us for not snapping out of this. I can just hear him, "Listen Jo-Jo and Donna, when you look back, glance, don't stare."

"Mom, when are Daddy and Erica coming home?" asks Donna's eighth grader, Jessica. "It's so cold out there. They must have frozen to death. I'm glad we didn't go."

Thanksgiving's my favorite holiday. Oh God, I'll have Frankie's seven with the wives, Jo-Jo's five plus little Rocky's girlfriend, my Joe and the girls. That's seventeen plus some of my husband's wrestlers who always show up. Then Jo-Jo says Gino's up from the shore, and he's going to stop in. So much food, and so much work, but it's Thanksgiving.

The dinner last night was standing room only at Tommy Apicella's restaurant. My husband was MC again. They honored the Mud Bowl teams. Jo-Jo's daughter, Tina, brought in these cameras from her cable TV sports show. She says she thinks there's a story there about the years of dinners commemorating the rivalry, and about the Mud Bowl; Frankie and Gino and all; how close the Belleville and Nutley players have become over the years.

Tina's Uncle Frank was her favorite, like all of us.

God, my husband came home smelling of the sweetest cigars, and he doesn't even smoke. He said the place was packed, and Apicella had to bring out more tripe for the crowd. Jo-Jo hardly said a word all night, with all of the guys coming up to him about Frank's attempted lateral to Gino, and that whole story. One after another they told my brother how Frank's life was such an example for them. My husband said it was the best of nights for Jo-Jo, ... and the worst.

Oh, how I remember my father coming home from those Barringer-East Orange dinners, same aromatic cigar scent and that smile on his face as he'd keep my mother up telling her about the guys he'd seen.

I can't even go to these Thanksgiving Games. Bring back too many memories, ... mostly good, but I get so melancholy, particularly since Nutley and Belleville moved their game to the holiday. So I get lost for two days preparing for the Thanksgiving dinner.

"Mom, you OK?" asked Jessica. "You're daydreaming."

"Just exhausted, honey. Waiting for everybody to start showing up."

Jessica snuggled next to her mother on the sofa as they both gazed out the front window, the leaf-less trees waving at them as if teasing Donna to embark on one last journey back in time.

"Mom, before they come, tell me a story when you were a little girl."

Oh, God, she would ask that. This kid is so much like my mother. She looks just like her, and always wants to listen to stories, ... really interested in her roots and the reasons why.

"Please, Ma."

I can't swallow. She should see the hundreds of pages of my journals. My mother always told me to keep a journal. How could I not, ... the stories about 711 Belmont Avenue, the Five Corners on Bloomfield Avenue, and everybody? I would just sit, watch, listen, and write. I can't talk now. I'll start to cry. I can't forget.

"Maaaa, they'll be getting home. Please. Just one little story when you were a little girl."

Lord, don't make me get emotional. I need to take a deep breath. Oh, ... OK. That helped.

"Jessica, ...OK. Here we go: 'In the late fifties, some people did not know what a day off was like, let alone a week's vacation ...'"

THE END

About The Author

Joseph Rocco Cervasio has spent over thirty years in the resort industry as a corporate executive, strategic coach, leadership development expert, and entrepreneur. A demanded public speaker, he has tested the stories that have evolved into the tales of this fiction on audiences around the country. And you'll react the same way: "You must be kidding!" Based upon these responses, he decided to write *Bad News on the Doorstep*.

"It seems Jersey gets their attention, and when the characters appear with all their color and charm, the listener is ready to learn. They laugh and cry, and sometimes I get emotional, too. But most of the time, we achieve our objective: We make some history in our business and change a few lives."

In his first novel, Joe escorts us through New Jersey's fabled Essex County in a way that will make *Bad News on the Doorstep*...the good news you're seeking.

Except for his years at Cornell, Cervasio has never moved from New Jersey where he lives with his wife, Maria.

Printed in the United States
18849LVS00001B/37-168